THE
LIGHTNING
KEEPER

THE LIGHTNING KEEPER

A NOVEL

STARLING LAWRENCE

HARPER ⬤ PERENNIAL

NEW YORK • LONDON • TORONTO • SYDNEY

HARPER ● PERENNIAL

A hardcover edition of this book was published in 2006 by HarperCollins Publishers.

P.S.™ is a trademark of HarperCollins Publishers.

HarperCollins books may be purchased for educational, business, or sales promotional use. For information please write: Special Markets Department, HarperCollins Publishers, 10 East 53rd Street, New York, NY 10022.

FIRST HARPER PERENNIAL EDITION PUBLISHED 2007.

Designed by Joseph Rutt

Library of Congress Cataloging-in-Publication Data
is available upon request.

ISBN: 978-0-06-082524-9
ISBN-10: 0-06-082524-3

ISBN: 978-0-06-082525-6 (pbk.)
ISBN-10: 0-06-082525-1 (pbk.)

07 08 09 10 11 ❖/RRD 10 9 8 7 6 5 4 3 2 1

for Jenny Preston and Earl Shorris

in memory of Linda Corrente

THE
LIGHTNING
KEEPER

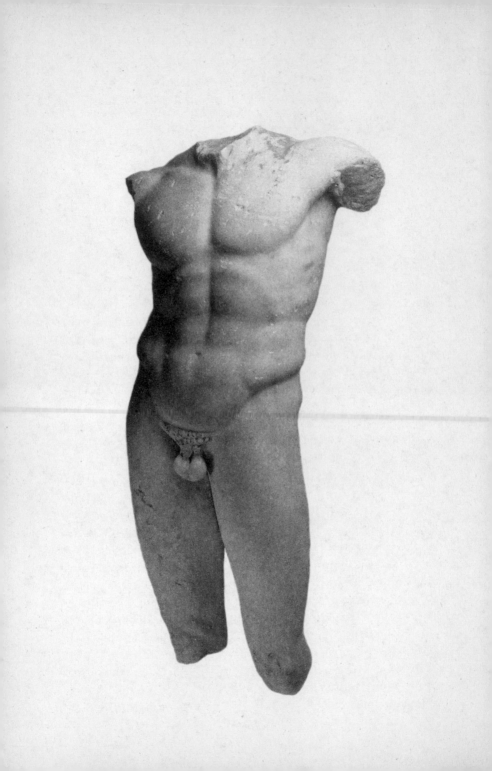

PROLOGUE

I have always hated my name, though perhaps I did not even know that until I told him what it was—Harriet, I said in a loud, clear voice because he was foreign and I thought he might not understand unless I spoke very distinctly, even though he had addressed the question to me in what seemed to be unusually good English—and he simply looked at me for a moment, and I began to think he really *hadn't* understood me. It was quite odd . . . he was looking at me but not really looking at me, or at least not seeing me, and for all I knew he was an idiot or a madman as well as a foreigner, though I'm sure I didn't feel afraid. I felt so strange, as if I weighed nothing, as if he could lift me up by the very power of his eyes alone, do anything at all with me, and yet I was not afraid. I was a child, or barely more than a child, and what does one know of such things at the age of fourteen? And yet I did know. What he said when he finally found his voice was simply this: It doesn't sound like you. I hadn't the faintest idea what he was talking about. I wanted to hear him speak again, and so I said, in a more conversational tone this time: If you do not understand I shall spell it for you. I was trying to provoke him, to show him that I was something more than a child to be trifled with. And he laughed, meaning no harm, and his laughter was the most beautiful sound I had ever heard. When I had spelled it out, he said: "H" is enough: that is what I shall call you, until we find something better. And when will that be? He just smiled and shook his head. And how will you find me, I asked, if I do not even live in your country? (How was I to know, then, that he was anything other than an Italian boy, like all the rest of them there on the docks of Naples, trying to earn a few pennies by carrying baggage?) Said he, I am bound for the New World; you may count on seeing me there.

I very nearly neglected to learn his name in all this discussion of mine, and I forgot to worry about Mama, who had such a coughing spell right there in the customs shed, and was taken away by Father in search of the port physician. He was half carrying her, and something dropped from her hand. When I went to see what it was, I was horrified to find my initial, H, embroidered there in the linen, which was filled with blood. I had forgotten that I had given it to her, and I had never seen the blood before, as she was careful about hiding all trace of her illness from me. And perhaps I took this as an omen: there was my name, H, on that ruined handkerchief, and I wouldn't touch it at all.

We sat there for well over three hours. Father glared wildly over his shoulder at me as he was leading Mama away and he said: Don't you move from this place. And the boy and I—perhaps he thought Father meant him too—stayed with the luggage through the afternoon, finally taking seats on two upended cases. And some of the other boys who had crowded around the ship came by out of curiosity, and one of them made a sign, rubbing two fingers and his thumb together to mean money or perhaps something vile, and Toma, as I had now learned his name, stood and fixed his eye on them and they all ran away.

An officer of some sort came after a while and asked some questions in really dreadful English, and then he came back with a cup of tea for me. I asked him would he bring one for my friend, and the man looked very put out, but he did as I asked. So we had a tea party and we talked, though there were long periods of silence between us that were not unpleasant at all. And I wondered, What is happening to me?

Father came back at last, and Toma supervised the transfer of the baggage to the hotel. He wouldn't take anything from Father, nothing at all, even though he must have expected to be paid when he first caught our eye coming off the ship. It filled me with pride that even now makes me blush: He did this for me, I said to myself. I'm sure I wasn't wrong about that. What other reason could there be? And I was as proud as if he had laid his cloak in the gutter for me. I had read that in a book.

Mama recovered in a week's time, and every day when I went out walking with Father, there was the boy, sitting against the wall, waiting for us. He impressed Father with his English and with his whispered caution about walking unaccompanied in such a place as Naples. Father must have wrung some confirmation of this lurking danger from the hotel management, for he did not object to having Toma follow a couple of paces behind us. He was only sixteen at that time, but you would never have thought it to look at him, and you certainly would have thought better of offering him any provocation.

Poor Father was no traveler, and certainly no linguist, and he was very much caught up in nursing Mama back to health. If he needed something he was likely to send Toma to the chemist or the lace maker for a dozen handkerchiefs rather than bother the staff at the hotel, as they tended to get things wrong. He was ever impatient in the matter of details, and had a difficulty in conveying, in any language, precisely what he meant.

Well, there are other ways of conveying a thought, a meaning, an emotion too teeming and urgent for words. And as we walked, sometimes to the esplanade by the bay, sometimes to the museum to see the charming mosaics and those disturbing great torsos of the naked gods, he would walk behind us, never speaking unless Father asked him a question, but with his eyes boring into the back of me, consuming me. Every so often I would contrive to turn in order to catch this gaze, to reassure myself that I was not imagining things. He did not try to hide his interest or avert his eyes, except of course when Father turned as well. Sometimes he was smiling, an expression I imagine he wore before I turned to look back at him; but more often there was a thoughtful, even a sad aspect to his features, which I could not understand because looking at him made me happier than I had ever been. So happy, and so confused: it was a week before I dared to write in my journal that I was in love.

A love unconsummated and unspoken, but there was fuel enough for the fire, fuel to keep it burning, banked and all but forgotten, for those six years when I saw nothing of him, heard nothing, did not even know if he had arrived safely in this country or perished in the hold of some pestilential steamship, as so many of those immigrants were said to have done.

My mother did recover her strength, almost miraculously, and I think it was as much an effort of will as anything else, for she so wanted to see the murals of Pompeii and even more the excavations of Hercu-

laneum, that city buried for centuries in the volcanic mud. My father
did not care at all about such things, and consoled himself in the absence of work by scanning the papers for quotations on the price of
steel and pig iron. But he did care very much about Mama—her health
being the whole reason for this trip—and was ready to humor her least
whim. So he arranged for a motorcar—I sometimes think this was the
only device of the present century that interested him at all—and we
made a holiday outing of it, with a picnic hamper and bottles of chilled
wine. With the driver, all the seats in the car were taken, and so Toma
rode on the wheel well, lying wedged between the fender and the
motor. And by feigning great interest in the passing countryside and
the road unfurling ahead, it was now I who had the luxury of devouring
him to the last detail: the clean line of his neck descending into the ballooning collar, the angle of his wrist and corded arm as he held fast to
the chrome bar supporting the lamp, that torso—more like a god than
anything I had seen in the museum—limned in the fluttering material
of his shirt. Mother put her hand on my shoulder and drew me back
into the protection of the car, saying that the wind was making my face
quite red.

We first visited Pompeii, with Mt. Vesuvius as a backdrop sending
an innocuous plume of vapor up into a clear blue sky. The brightness of
the day made the interiors correspondingly dark, and in one such turning, with my parents lingering for a moment in the previous chamber,
admiring the burnt marigold of those walls, I tripped on a piece of
fallen masonry, and Toma reached out and caught me. I needed only
the slightest touch to regain my balance, and had I put my hand to a
wall it would have sufficed. But there was his bare forearm, and mine
suddenly lying lengthwise upon it. I experienced a shock, as if from
electricity, or as if I had been touched by lightning, and my hand closed
in reflex upon that warm unyielding flesh. I must have gasped, for my
mother called out to me, and I replied, still holding fast to Toma, that
it was nothing, I had merely stumbled.

How much darker and more mysterious the labyrinths of Herculaneum, a city entirely buried in the same eruption as Pompeii, and just
now being excavated inch by inch from the thirty-foot layer of hardened mud. Everything there must be seen by torchlight, and Father
grumbled at the extravagance of having so many lit in our honor. And

it was in a far chamber where the gorgeous marble of the pavement swam and shimmered in so many colors that Toma kissed me. I was standing on the step to a bath so that our faces were very close when I turned and the embrace seemed the most natural thing in the world. Then he folded me into his arms and put his face into my hair, where he whispered a sound, or a foreign word, or even a name, though I know it was not mine. And just as I was puzzling over this, with my heart likely to burst within me, I heard my mother's footsteps on the marble, and she called out: Do be careful, dear, one never knows in such places. And Toma moved silently to the far side of the room.

My mother was no fool, and I have the impression that she watched me more carefully after Herculaneum. At any rate I had no more chances to be alone with him, and that was the thing that I wanted above all else. He had drawn me to him, and I seemed to have no will toward anything or anyone else. I did not know exactly how long my parents planned to stay in Naples, nor Toma either, and a feeling of desperation closed over me. I dreamt about Herculaneum and Toma, and slept badly. My mother thought it might be my time of the month, and framed a careful question. No, I said, it is not that. From the way she looked at me I knew it would have been better if I could have spoken that lie.

My mother slept very lightly, perhaps on account of her illness. One night I was having an astonishingly vivid dream about Toma, a dream full of incidents and images of which I had no experience, not even an inkling. We were in a river together, and he had taken away my clothes, and I was not ashamed. I was calling his name, calling him to come and touch me, touch me, for I had literally no idea of what men and women actually do in such situations. And he was touching me, and the river was flowing around and through us with the most exquisite sensations, when I heard a harsh voice in my ear and felt a harsher hand on my shoulder, shaking me awake.

I had indeed been calling to Toma, and this had roused my mother in the adjoining chamber. But it was I who had taken away those clothes, or fought free of the bedding, and I who touched myself.

Get up, hissed my mother, and she dragged me to the bath, gasping for air herself. She placed me on one of those indecent porcelain fixtures that the Europeans use for washing themselves instead of bathing properly, and she hitched my nightdress up above my breasts and told me not to move. I closed my eyes for shame so that I would not have to look at my own body. She went into the sitting room, where there was a bowl of melting ice that had chilled the sherbet for our dinner, and this freezing mixture she threw upon my belly and thighs, quite taking the breath from me. My humiliation was almost complete. Then my mother, who had always been so gentle with me, seized me by the hair and told me that I must never again touch myself. Did I understand? I nodded, although I had no comprehension of what I had done to offend her. She kissed me then on the forehead and told me to dry myself and go to bed. This was the first and only discussion of love that I ever had with my mother. Perhaps we would have had them, but she was dead within a year of our return from Europe. And what do I now know of love, except for this one moment? I have been married, and am now a widow, and I have never found the way back to that beautiful place in my dreams.

I do not believe that my father's sleep was disturbed by this drama. The next morning my mother managed to put in front of him an English newspaper full of speculation about the crisis in the Balkans provoked by Austria's annexation of Bosnia and Herzegovina. In my wretchedness I took satisfaction in the mere recitation of those names, for I knew that Toma's country, Montenegro, was the neighbor to these, and the Austrians his sworn enemies. It was the opinion of this newspaper that war was imminent, and so my father found us passage on a liner leaving for New York the following day. We barely had time to pack, and I did not see Toma before our departure. I thought I would never see him again, and so I took a terrible risk and gave all my pocket money to a porter, who barely comprehended a word I said. Somehow I made him understand that he was to take my note of farewell and deliver it into the hands of the beautiful boy.

—from the diary of Harriet Bigelow Truscott,
on the eve of her marriage, September 12, 1919

PART ONE

1914

CHAPTER

ONE

It had begun to snow, and she had been sitting in the car for so long that the snowflakes, such extravagantly grand and varied snowflakes, fixed themselves to the dark green cowling, like butterflies pinned to a board, for the motor was now as cold as she was. Her watch had stopped—it was a pretty, unreliable thing, no more than a piece of jewelry against the dark silk of her dress—and she did not know quite what time it was, only that the meeting between her father and Mr. Stephenson had been fixed for half past two in the afternoon, and they had driven at an immoderate speed down from Beecher's Bridge that morning, with her father wedged in the back by the great half-moon of iron, urging the driver to hurry.

MacEwan, a dour man in any circumstances, shrank into the collar of his coat and muttered to himself.

"What's that you say, MacEwan?" Her father must have seen rather than heard the remark, for his hearing was now reduced to the point where the only sounds that animated his reflections, other than conversation directed at him in very emphatic tones, were the thump and wheeze of the tub bellows at the Bigelow Iron Company or the clear ringing of the trip-hammer as it fell to the anvil, pounding, shaping, and purifying the glowing metal into bars. It was not much of the universe, Harriet thought, when compared to her own appreciation of music, quiet conversation, even the sound of a brook, and she knew, because her father had told her, that he once recognized and took pleasure in the songs of many birds, particularly the black-throated green warbler in the spring, and the cry of the loon in autumn, far away on the lakes of Great Mountain. It was fortunate, she thought, that the sounds remaining to him, the bellows and the hammer, were so deeply reassuring.

"I said, sir, it's no use asking me to go faster than the Packard wants to go, without it'll come to some harm. And that's a terrible weight of iron you've got on that seat with you, sir." Which indeed it was, and MacEwan had the grace or sense of self-preservation not to reiterate his point when the Packard experienced a puncture of the rear left tire, the one directly under the iron wheel, or piece of a wheel, that had been loaded into the car just before they left the Bigelow works.

Looking at the light now, and allowing for the snow, which made the day both darker and brighter, she guessed that it was sometime after four o'clock, an hour etched in her mind by virtue of the whistle blast marking the end of the shift in the furnace and forge. The eye knew that hour in all seasons, and the stomach too. What would she not give now for a cup of tea? She had not eaten since breakfast, and so it was not just the bracing warmth that she imagined but the odor and texture of iced seed cake, a fat slice of it, or a sandwich of any description, even a crust of unbuttered bread. Father had promised her a fine dinner at Delmonico's as soon as he had finished, had talked Stephenson around to his proposal, and he didn't imagine that would take very long at all. So if you'll just sit here like a good girl?

She had felt a burning in her cheeks when he said that, and had almost made an answer. At any rate she had turned sharply in the direction of this remark and found herself staring into the face of the fellow trying to shift the iron wheel off the seat and out of the car, a well-fleshed, confident, and not unattractive face, which, by dint of exertion against such a weight, matched or exceeded the rising color of her own. There were two of them struggling with the wheel in that awkward space, joking under their breath about how the old fellow could only make half a wheel at a time, and when the man caught her misdirected glance he grinned and even—was she imagining this impertinence?— winked at her before taking the entire burden of the iron onto his flexed knees, turning, and heaving it clear of the car with an explosive grunt.

Like a good girl . . . she could make herself blush simply by repeating the words. Her father often spoke to her thus, out of distracted affection, and she did not mind it. There's a good girl, he would say, perhaps in acknowledgement of a piece of toast. But today she minded very much indeed, particularly as the automobile trip from Beecher's Bridge to New York City, with the urgency of time and the anxious interruptions of the blown tire, was hardly an opportunity to discuss what would be said, what must be said, to Mr. Stephenson. She had hoped her father would remember that she wanted, and out of no mere vanity, to be included in this discussion on which the fate of the Bigelow works very likely hung. Perhaps she had not spoken loud enough, or been sufficiently assertive? Or perhaps her father simply had not wished to hear.

It was Harriet who had brought to her father's attention the item in a trade journal—*Iron and Steel News*—about the John Stephenson Company's contract to supply two hundred and eighty-five new subway cars to the IRT.

"Isn't that the same Mr. Stephenson who once took us to the baseball game?" she asked, putting the magazine by his plate. Yes, he thought that very likely, and a few solemn forkfuls later he wondered how old Stephenson might be getting on.

"Getting on very well indeed, by the sound of it," Harriet replied, wondering how many wheels each of those many new cars was to have. "You don't suppose . . ."

"Suppose what, my dear?" Amos Bigelow was very little inclined toward supposition or abstraction of any kind.

"I was wondering where Mr. Stephenson would get all the wheels he will require. Have you not done business with him before? Was that not why we went to see the baseball?" Of the game she remembered nothing but the fierce roar of the crowd, the pitchers of beer consumed by her father and the jovial Stephenson, and an enormous concoction of spun sugar that had later made her ill. The next day her hands were swollen from clapping so hard and so long in her effort to please.

"Well, I don't remember exactly whose idea that was, but yes, certainly, I've known Stephenson for thirty years, and I should think he knows me. Let me read this now."

Her father warmed to the idea of those wheels, then appropriated it as his own, and soon it grew to the proportions of a mania. He would not willingly entertain other topics of discussion, nor could Harriet qualify his enthusiasm for the project by any normal business consideration such as costs, scheduling, specifications, and possible modifications to the plant. The Bigelow Iron Company would manufacture the wheels as subcontractor to the John Stephenson Company; he and his old friend would see to that. There was no arguing with this proposition that bloomed so suddenly in his mind with no encouragement, correspondence, or information from Stephenson, who could not have known how things were progressing in Beecher's Bridge. The contract, and its successful conclusion, became a fixed star in Amos Bigelow's firmament, and to express reservation or even to ask too many questions would have been as offensive to him as standing on the broad porch of the Congregational Church after the service and entertaining doubts about the existence of God or the certainty of eternal salvation. Her father was fifty-nine years old, but sometimes he seemed much older than that, and she wondered whether he had always been so . . . mercurial, and whether his judgement now was perfectly sound.

Amos Bigelow became obsessed with catalogues, and where he might once have spent the better part of his day prowling the furnace building or engaging Horatio Washington in discussion about repair or modification of the breast wheel—the waterwheel was a source of endless concern—he now spent his time perusing and annotating Hitchcock's Machine Tool List, or the Patterson, Gottfried & Hunter catalogue of power transmission devices.

Harriet, who attended to the ledgers at the works, noted the changed composition of the mail pouch and formed in her mind grim auguries of the future. Her office, no more than a cubbyhole, adjoined that of the ironmaster, and sometimes he would call out to her to come look at this splendid object, a double-arm split pulley on the Reeves patent model, or this Walcott & Wood turret lathe. Harriet looked, and was as enthusiastic as she could be, but what always caught her eye on the page was the price of these devices. She asked, as if she did not know, what use the Bigelow Iron Company would make of such things. But her father's enthusiasm for the Stephenson project knew no bounds or measure, and even today, when they had been so anxious about the time, he had made MacEwan stop the car at Park Avenue and 142nd Street so that they might admire the Patterson, Gottfried billboard and the model, looming out of the muddy expanse of pasture, of what was proclaimed the largest wood pulley on earth.

Harriet had undertaken the actual correspondence with Stephenson, though her father seemed to believe that he had already broached the business and received a reply. She showed her father draft after draft to reflect the refinements and reservations suggested by Horatio Washington and Mr. Brown, the foreman of the furnace, both of whom expressed doubt that so many wheels—her estimate—could be produced on any tight schedule. It was Horatio who pointed out that there hadn't been much snow this winter, and the holding ponds up the river on Great Mountain were already low. Come August, who knew what they'd be using for water.

Stephenson's response—to Amos Bigelow, of course, rather than Harriet—was cordial but not very encouraging. Yes, he would be subcontracting the wheel assemblies along with many other items in the undercarriage and couplings, air-brakes, upholstery, and of course the electrical systems. The John Stephenson Company's long experience in the construction of public conveyances—from New York horse cars in the old days to railroad carriages in Hong Kong and New Delhi—had given him the advantage in this competition, and while he could certainly manufacture the entire subway car, it was not practical given the constraints of time. Certainly he remembered the pleasant association with Bigelow over these many years, and he had never heard the slightest complaint about any of Bigelow's products. Come to think of it, he had received a letter not long ago from the maintenance department of the Boston & Maine Railroad inquiring into the availability of certain items of renovation—brass fittings and upholstery—and commenting, parenthetically, on the durability and excellence of the wheels, even after so many years of service. Rolling stock, after all, was no better than its wheels, however fancy the hat racks and the paint job might be.

"What an excellent fellow," exclaimed Bigelow, relishing this paragraph of the letter. "I couldn't have put it better myself."

That compliment delivered, Stephenson went on to say that he had already been in discussion with several foundries on the subject of

wheels, and so it would come down to the matters of price and specifications: it was not yet clear whether iron wheels—granting the excellence of the Bigelow product—would do, or whether he must turn to
the steel available from the open-hearth operations in Pittsburgh. It
was a complex decision, and he would be in touch when he had further
information. There were, of course, other subcontracts to let: had the
Bigelow works any experience in the manufacture of springs?

Finally, all of this was on hold for now, as the commissioners—following a fatal derailment in the Steinway Tunnel and acrimonious debate in the city council—had announced that an entirely new list of
specifications would be forthcoming to assure the safety of workers
and passengers, to restore public confidence in the most extensive and
modern metropolitan subway system in the world, embracing not only
the island of Manhattan, but . . . etc. When they finally got down to
brass tacks and issued the new specifications, the guessing would be
over and the race would be on.

The correspondence had been the occasion for Harriet's sudden
education, her real education, in the ways and workings of the Bigelow
Iron Company, from the blast furnace itself and the foundry, where the
metal would be cast, through to the forge and hammer shop, where the
collars and bolts would be fashioned, and finally to the grinding and
finishing operation. She knew things well beyond the payroll and expense ledgers that had been her original responsibility, knew things
that her father certainly knew well enough in his bones from all those
years of experience, but not well enough to express in writing, much
less in discussion with so careful and expert a man as Stephenson. She
knew the quantities of ore, charcoal, and limestone flux necessary to
produce a ton of pig iron; she knew the temperature of the furnace and
had studied the results of the chemical assay of its product; she knew
how many revolutions per minute Horatio's great waterwheel was capable of, and the cost of each abrasive grinder and lathe chuck in the
finishing shop. And she knew that she could tell Mr. Stephenson, in the
fewest possible words, what the Bigelow Iron Company could and
could not deliver.

She had been educated in unexpected ways as well, for the workmen were not accustomed to having a woman anywhere in the vicinity
of the furnace or shops. Sometimes they didn't know she was there; at

other times, by force of habit, they let slip indecencies that they would never have uttered at home, but which must be, she thought, the common currency of that workplace. Horatio, whom she dealt with almost every day, had expressed his violent scorn upon reading Stephenson's letter.

"Springs!" he said, followed by an epithet linking the place of eternal damnation to an adjective of the most appalling coarseness. She had heard that word once or twice before, and she knew exactly what it meant. Horatio, as shocked as she was, spat to cover his embarrassment, then turned away. She had spoken to her father about it, hoping to introduce the idea of some morally uplifting influence on the workers, particularly Horatio.

"Well, what did he say to you?"

She made no reply but set her shoulders in annoyance at the stupidity of men. Nothing in the world could force her to repeat those words.

"Harriet, never mind. I'm sure he meant no harm by it. I'll try to speak to him, but it's an ironworks, you'll remember, not a Sunday school, and it wouldn't do to upset him or any of them with all the work ahead of us now. He lives down there, you know, down below, Horatio and that woman of his. I don't even know that they are married. Black people have their own ways, but I'm told she goes to church, the other church."

Harriet knew where Horatio lived, down in the shabby ruins of the silk mill below the Great Falls, and knew that he was not married to Olivia Toussaint. She had even spoken to Olivia, across the great chasm of her color, her religion, her situation as Horatio Washington's kept woman, and found her charming and well-spoken, in spite of everything. And very beautiful too, she had to admit. A soul worth saving.

A RAP ON THE WINDOW brought Harriet back to the present, and as the isinglass was completely fogged with her breath, she opened her door in response. She had no idea who it might be other than her father or MacEwan, who had disappeared ages ago down an alleyway with a muttered excuse. There was the man, the man who had winked at her, and he was alone now. In the instant before she pulled the door closed she noted that the dangerous color of his face was very much as it had been before. He rapped again on the window, more insistently now, and her first thought was to ignore the summons, ignore the fellow altogether, as he was undoubtedly drunk. She would have let MacEwan deal with this situation if only he had been there, in which case this never would have happened in the first place. The thought formed in her mind that MacEwan, wherever he might be, was very likely drunk as well. She thought she had smelled liquor on him before, even in the petroleum reek of the carriage house, which had been given over to the Packard.

The third rap was accompanied by the sound of laughter, which, however genuine its mirth, had the effect of infuriating Harriet. Here she was, told to wait in the car like a good girl, and now this lout had come to make free with her, as if she were . . . what? She lowered the window and glared at the man, who stood at his ease, one arm resting possessively on the roof of the Packard, and an incongruous little crown of snow upon his hat.

"What do you take me for?" she hissed at him, surprised by her own tone of voice.

"Take you for, miss? Why, I ain't taken you at all. Just I was wondering how you was getting along out here in the cold, since I seen that other fellow going off a while back. Would you be wanting something hot at all?"

"Thank you, no," Harriet replied, trying to be civil. Her real annoyance was with her father and MacEwan for putting her in such a situation. "I'm sure my father is just finishing his business now. He said it wouldn't be very long."

"Well, you can suit yourself," he said, with his face perceptibly closer to hers than before, "but it's been going on two hours now, and them still jawing away in there. An excitable chap, the old boy, I mean your father, and I think the boss broke out the bottle to calm him down." These words struck her like a slap. She thought she had an understanding with her father, who had very nearly ruined himself with drink in the months after her mother's death.

"And I suppose you were drinking with them, saw this with your own eyes?"

"Oh, I know what goes on in there, even if I ain't invited to drink with them. No, when I need a nip myself, I know where to turn." He tapped the sagging pocket of his coat, which returned a hollow clinking. "Would you take a drop yourself? It would fight off the cold, you see, just as I've done."

The expression on her face cut short his laughter, and for a moment they simply stared at each other. When he spoke again it was in a harder tone of voice, and what kindliness she had seen in his eyes was gone.

"Well, then, if my liquor's not good enough for you . . ." and he pulled the corkless bottle from his pocket, took a swallow, then rested it on the window frame. "Sure? No offense, but this is a very bad part of town you're in here, miss, a bad place for a young woman like you, so high and mighty, to be sitting by herself. Do you see over there?"

He gestured with his bottle, and a woman, bundled in shawls, who had been pacing in front of a low building on the far side of the street, stopped, then lifted her hand to him. Harriet could not make out her face.

"You see what I mean? There's Flora Hanratty waiting for the boys to come off the shift, and her thinking I'm waving at her, as if I'd . . ." Here he drank again, and wiped his mouth on his sleeve. Alcohol fumes overcame the smell of the axle grease that had coated the sample wheel. She would have to air these clothes for a week, at least. "Not on your life, Flora, d'ye hear me?" he called out violently, giving Harriet a start. "Not if you was the last woman left on the Bowery, and not if it was free!" And in a softer tone, almost to himself: "Who the Hell does she think I am?"

Harriet could find no words at all, but suddenly the outrage she felt at everything that had happened today boiled up within her, burning her throat like bile, and when the ginger-haired lout turned to her again, closer than ever, the cat advancing on its prey, and began to speak, she astonished herself by spitting full in his face.

"That's a nice thank-you for my trouble," he said, wiping his face carelessly with the back of his hand. And holding her gaze effortlessly in his, he licked the back of his hand, then kissed it.

"There now," he mocked her, "I've had my kiss after all without even asking for it, and I know how you taste. What if I was to offer you the real thing?"

Out of the corner of her eye she saw a figure trudging diagonally across the road in front of the car, heading for the entrance to the Stephenson works. The light was failing now, and the snow falling in veils of finer particles, and she could not trust her eyes. But the young man was lightly dressed, seemed oblivious to the snow and the cold, and there was something about him that triggered a memory and a rush of feeling. When she spoke the word No to the ginger-haired man, it was in a distracted, wondering tone, quite lacking the emphasis she had intended.

"There's No that means No, lass, and there's No that means Yes. So I'm thinking . . ." and here he put his hand on her shoulder.

"No!" she bellowed, with a vehemence that drove him back a pace.

The young man, at the edge of her vision, stopped and let fall from his shoulder the coiled length of cable so that it lay like a black snake in the snow. He turned and walked toward them around the car, resting his hand for a moment on the fender and then smoothing the snow away. And at that instant Harriet had a vision of a dusty road, and of this man clinging to the fender, the scented wind making a sail of his shirt.

"I know you," she said.

He looked at her for a long moment, not in confusion, but in awe. He said nothing, and after he had reassured himself, comparing the physical presence to the image held so long in his mind, he dropped his eyes to the task of recoiling the cable, which he did very deliberately.

"Well now, lad, I'm sure Mr. Stephenson ain't paying you to stand out here talking to strangers. Better be off with you."

"It is Mr. Stephenson who pays me, Mr. Boylan, and not yourself, and I must answer to him. Miss Bigelow, Miss Harriet Bigelow, is not a stranger, she is my friend. Please to move away from the automobile. I think she does not like you."

"And what's it to you, puppy, what she likes and dislikes? Run off now, or I'll give you something to remember me by. You foreign lads got to be taught your place, and not just the once, because you're so fuckin' thick, but again, and—"

The young man had about six feet of the cable free in his right hand when he was finished with the coil. He gave it a little shake and made an explosion in the powdery snow between him and Boylan. When he raised and twisted his hand suddenly, the cable whined once around his head and darted forward, shattering Boylan's hat but not touching him otherwise.

"Fuckin' Jesus but I'll have your hide," Boylan growled, planting himself like a boxer, but making no advance on his antagonist. "Fight me fair and I'll kill you."

The cable sang in reply and attached itself to the boxer's ankle, was jerked violently back again, and Boylan sprawled in the snow, making a caterwaul that masked the sound of breaking glass. As he struggled to his knees he drew the broken neck of the bottle from his pocket and tried to conceal it down by his hip.

"Our fight is finished, Mr. Boylan. Or, if you want, I can kill you with this thing." The cable flailed the snow a few inches from the kneeling man and lay still. Boylan let the bottle neck drop from his hand and rose unsteadily to his feet.

"All right, Peacock, my lad, I'll leave this little spitfire to you, since you're such friends, and I'll settle up with you another day. You'll be watching your back, I'm thinking."

THEN THEY WERE ALONE, and the young man fell to coiling his cable again with a concentration that was almost comic.

"Toma," said Harriet. "You have found me after all. Will you not look at me?"

He did as she asked, but with an unsmiling intensity, as if he were still locked in some combat. "You are safe now. I am happy to see you."

"Well, you certainly don't look happy. How can I thank you?"

He shrugged his shoulders and gave her what was at least half a smile. She removed her glove and held out her hand to him. He made a little sound of protest and showed her how filthy his own was, the grime diagonally shadowed with darker markings of the cable. He wiped his hand on his trousers and gave a rueful laugh at the result.

"I do not mind at all, I'm sure," she said. "But where is your coat? Surely you are cold?"

"The coat was stolen when I was working down below, but I was a fool to take it off. Anything can happen down there."

"Yes, the subway," said Harriet, feeling the warmth in the hand that enclosed her own. "You must tell me about it." But just as he began to answer, for it seemed that her touch dissolved his reticence, she broke in, as her own mind veered in many directions at once: "And why did that man call you 'Peacock'?"

"My name . . ." began Toma, and now a burst of conversation from the far side of the car distracted her. She gave his hand a reassuring squeeze.

"It's Father, coming out at last, and he will be so pleased to see you again."

Toma opened the door for Harriet and glanced over the roof of the Packard at the familiar, portly figure of his employer and the gaunter, stooped version of the man he remembered from Naples, Amos Bigelow. The snow on the steps of the building made for treacherous footing, and Toma saw that the energetic Stephenson had his guest firmly by the elbow, supporting him.

"Take care, my friend, these steps are cruel unless you know 'em as I do, and there's your daughter waiting for you, I believe. Has she been in that car all this while, for the love of God?"

"What? Oh, Harriet, yes, yes, she must have been. But is there nothing more you need from me? I'd be more than glad to—"

"No, no, Mr. Bigelow, thank you. We have your wheel, and we've had a good long discussion about . . . oh, I'd say we've covered everything. And I'm sure I never heard a more entertaining tale than your father standing up to the minister on the matter of that railroad right-of-way."

"Well, you see, without that railroad, the Bigelow works were done for, and—"

"And here's Miss Harriet, all grown up into . . . into, well, I'm sure I never saw a lovelier young woman. I'm very sorry you've been here all this time. I had no idea."

"Thank you, Mr. Stephenson, I think Father forgot about me, as he was so excited to show you his wheel. And, Father, do you remember the young man in Naples who helped us when Mama was taken ill? This is he, Toma, the very same boy. Can you believe it?"

Amos Bigelow had been smiling absently at his daughter, but his mind still pursued that train of thought that had been his preoccupation for weeks: the making of iron wheels in such quantity as to assure the continued operation and good fortune of the Bigelow Iron Company. He was making a mental calculation of the existing and potential stores of hardwood charcoal, the fuel without which he could not make even a hat pin, and he did not study the young man's face, did not see the proffered hand.

"Oh, I'm sure you're right, my dear. How d'ye do, young man?" And turning back to his host, he picked up the thread of the conversation that Mr. Stephenson had made every effort to conclude. "On the matter of that sample casting I was suggesting, would not the commissioners, or board of the IRT—"

"Mr. Bigelow, let me introduce you properly to this young fellow, my assistant, who spends most of his time down in the subway and knows the track and the electrical system down there better than the IRT itself does. Thomas Peacock, Mr. Bigelow."

Amos Bigelow now shook Toma's hand and gazed with some interest at his features, giving an occasional sidelong glance to the beaming countenance of his daughter. "Yes, perhaps we have met before. Naples, you say? I'm sure it will all come back to me. That's not an Italian name, now, is it?"

"No, sir, indeed not. It is the name given to me on Ellis Island when I came here, as a joke, I think. My true name is Pekočević, and I come from Montenegro. It is very pleasing to me that we meet again."

"Montenegro? Montenegro?" Bigelow repeated the word, which was evidently neither familiar nor quite respectable. "Well, I suppose everyone must come from some place or other, but I never heard that one before. Hi, where's MacEwan gone off to?"

"He hasn't been here for two hours and more, Father, and I'm afraid he may have been drinking all this while," said Harriet, with a certain artificial cheerfulness in her voice. And as if on cue, to break the embarrassed silence following this remark, a figure emerged from the alley and made its way slowly and unsoberly across the snowy cobbles of the street. It was MacEwan, and he was humming "Danny Boy" to himself, oblivious to the judgement awaiting him.

"MacEwan! Are you drunk, man?" roared Amos Bigelow.

"No sir! No sir! Not drunk at all, sir."

"And have you not been drinking, then, Mr. MacEwan?" asked Harriet.

"Drinking? Well . . . well I cannot deny that, miss, but drunk? Never."

"You are drunk, I say," said Bigelow, in the same tone as before, "and you have left my daughter alone in the car. You are drunk and you are fired!"

"Dismissed, sir?"

"Fired, I say!"

"And who is to drive the Packard back to Connecticut? Or is the Packard dismissed as well?" MacEwan, with little left to lose, seemed to find a grim humor in the situation.

"I'll drive it myself if it comes to that. I'll not have you driving us off the road in a snow like this. Be off with you now."

Harriet laid a hand on his arm. "You cannot possibly drive the car, Father. Do you not remember when you—"

"Oh, that was just practicing, my dear. MacEwan, before you go, show me the pedals again and the spark."

Harriet reflected that she would rather walk the hundred miles to Beecher's Bridge in the snow than be driven by her father, and yet MacEwan, in his condition, was equally useless. She turned to Mr. Stephenson.

"I do not know what to do, Mr. Stephenson. It is impossible that my father should drive us. Perhaps there is a hotel nearby?"

"I shouldn't think so, Miss Harriet, not one that you could approve." He jingled the coins in his pocket. "But just give me a minute with young Peacock here, if you will."

At this moment the streetlamps blazed suddenly, unexpectedly, and to Harriet's eye, as if by magic. She was familiar with the gentle glow of the gas lamps around the green in Beecher's Bridge, but how astonishing now was this hissing electric glare that tinged the snowy twilight rose and spat brilliant sparks of carbon, like shooting stars, to the street below.

"Thomas, my boy, you must get this gentleman out of New York, or he will drive me mad. Have you ever worked one of them automobile things?"

"Never, sir," replied Toma in the same half whisper.

"Well, now's your chance. You'll be doing me and them a favor, and there's an extra week's wages in it for you."

"But the cable, sir? Coughlin says the whole wiring system of the cars is defective, or inadequate to the third-rail voltage. We had a fire down there today, testing it, and I brought it back here so—"

"I'll worry about the cable, and you worry about the Bigelows."
And in a louder voice now, "Mr. Bigelow, my friend, and Miss Harriet,
I'm pleased to say that young Peacock here has agreed to drive your car.
And I tell you what, Mr. Bigelow: Peacock's as handy a lad with any bit
of machinery as ever I saw, and he can look at the works up there and
see can we smooth out our differences. He knows the operations here
as well as I do."

"But can he drive?" asked Harriet.

"Of course he can drive, Miss Harriet. It's only a machine, and I
think you'll find there's nothing he can't do in that line. MacEwan
there can show him the particulars. Well then, a very good evening to
you all."

HIPPODROME POLKA.

COMPOSED FOR THE

PIANO FORTE,

BY

P. H. VAN DER WEYDE.

50 Cts Nett

TWO

It was, as Stephenson had said, only a machine, and after a few attempts at engaging the motor—attempts that provoked encouragement from Bigelow and Stephenson, and mirthless deprecation from MacEwan— Toma perceived the reciprocity between clutch and throttle, and the car lurched off through the snow to the delight of Flora Hanratty, who stood on the curb and clapped her hands. It is not unlike a horse, Toma thought, depressing the throttle and producing an impressive backfire. Very like a horse.

Although he had no experience in driving an automobile, he knew well how one should sound, and the Packard, making erratic progress on the slippery cobbles, sounded anemic. He dared not take his eyes from the street, for there was a heavy pedestrian traffic of workers bound for home or for the saloon, and their footing, too, was unsure. He put his hand out like a blind man, grazing the knobs and levers with chill fingers, careful to disturb nothing, trusting that the desired one would announce itself to him. It was then that he felt the touch of her hand guiding him to the lever that would advance the spark, for she had a keen memory of the sequence of MacEwan's ritual. The car leapt forward with a full-throated roar, causing a horse-drawn dray to veer off, and its driver hurled his oath after them.

Amos Bigelow, in the back seat, seemed so thoroughly absorbed in his reflections on the afternoon's business that he took no notice of the Packard's slewing and lurching, and his only advice was that the young man should turn north on Fifth Avenue when they reached it, that being the surest route to Delmonico's and dinner. He settled back then, the collar of his coat turned high, and counted his wheels.

Toma was scarcely aware of the knots of pedestrians and the challenge of other vehicles. The cold stench of axle grease gave way, by degrees, to the perfume of the young woman, crouching, who fumbled with the control of the heater hanging beneath the dash on the passenger's side, and he was reminded, suddenly, of how she had smelled in that one moment of intimacy in the echoing baths of Herculaneum.

"What is this street, boy? Are we lost already?" Having bent forward to deliver this question to Toma, Amos Bigelow sat back again, knowing he could not hear any answer over the din of the motor.

"Tell him, please, that I must not leave my things. I cannot travel to . . ."

"To Beecher's Bridge."

". . . to Beecher's Bridge," he said very slowly, "with these clothes only. We are almost at the place."

They had now entered the tangle of streets west of Seventh Avenue, following the route that Toma took every evening from the Stephenson works on the East River across the tip of Manhattan to the place where he slept, a long narrow room heated only, in winter as in summer, by the bodies of other men sleeping in serried ranks.

Toma brought the car to the curb and Harriet's head was outlined by the glow of a lantern in the saloon window. Had her face changed? Or was it the light? The planes and angles were more defined, but the eyes, large and expressive, were still the dominant feature, and the unbroken line of her eyebrows reminded him, as it always had, of the look of his own people.

"This is your home?" she asked, looking at the buildings and briefly at the slack faces pressed to the glass of the saloon front. He smiled but did not answer.

"Please to wait. I have not many things, but I must speak with the landlady about the money. I would not have paid for the month if I had known."

"I'll speak to Papa. Toma, why do those men stare at me so? I can feel their eyes, even though my back is turned to them. Have they never seen a woman before?"

He smiled again at the naïveté of her question. "They have seen many women. It is the automobile that confounds them. What is it doing in West Eleventh Street, they are asking themselves. Perhaps they are thinking this is some man of influence from Tammany Hall. You will wait here, please."

He took his hands from the wheel, eased his feet from the pedals, was interested to note that the motor ran on imperturbably. He would leave it so: she would need the heat and if he did not have to restart this machine in the dark, so much the better. Already he was beginning to imagine how this thing worked, the gathering of fuel, air, electrical impulse; the sudden compression of volatile gas in the cylinder was like the clenching of muscle in his belly, and the explosion, over and over.

The hallway seemed narrower, the staircase more forbidding, and he nearly fell across the outstretched legs of the man who had been bedded down on the first landing for days, waiting for his place in one of the dormitories. You're a lucky man tonight, Toma said under his breath.

Toma knew that Mrs. Pringle, the warden of this place, would be in her kitchen, the door open a crack so that she could hear anything from the dormitories above and below that required her attention. There's only the one o' me, she was fond of saying when some problem was brought to her attention, and when the sun went down, after a long day of lugging her pails of disinfectant from one twilit room to another, the time for complaints, suggestions, and even conversation was over. Mr. Pringle, in Toma's experience, never left the apartment, but perhaps it was he who added the drop from the bottle to Mrs. Pringle's tea, and who closed the door by degrees upon her immobile seated bulk until by eight o'clock the door was shut fast, and the Italians and the Poles could murder one another in their beds for all she cared.

"Mrs. Pringle," said Toma, directing his voice through the sliver of light between door and frame, "may I come in?"

It was Mr. Pringle who came to the door, spoke without opening it. "Mrs. Pringle is resting."

"Sir, it is for my money. I must leave tonight, and I do not know when I can be coming back. My deposit is—"

"Mrs. Pringle is resting. Ye'll have to come back in the morning if it's a question of money." Before Toma could reply or move his foot, the door closed in his face.

Sounds from the stairwell: the rustling of silk, a sharp in-drawn breath, a murmured exclamation. "Sweet Mary mother of Jesus." And now hurried footsteps on the stairs.

"Did I not tell you to stay? Women do not come here. Not even the others."

"I wanted to see the place where you live, that is all. The man on the stairs surprised me, and I was not paying attention to where I stepped. You are not angry with me, I hope?"

He was not angry but ashamed, and so he said nothing.

"You are angry, then. You will not even look at me."

"There is nothing to see here. It is simply the place where I sleep, that is all."

Her eyes roamed the ochre walls and the cobwebbed recesses of the ceiling. "I wish I had seen your real home. It is not very clean here." So saying, she gathered her skirt an inch higher and then added as an afterthought, "Will I be disturbing anyone else if I see where you sleep?"

He took her wrist and led her like a prisoner up the stairs and down another corridor, where two doors faced one another under a smoking lamp. He put his finger to his lips and opened the right-hand door.

The room stretched away left and right, so shallow that Harriet's skirt grazed the foot of the bed opposite the door once she had stepped inside. By the light from the hall she could see how many beds there were, and how closely set, and her imagination multiplied that number. In the far corner of the room in the deep shadows she could make out what appeared to be wide shelving, or platforms, each level punctuated by its row of boots. One of the boots moved. The door closed behind her and she was sightless, enveloped by the stale smell of the sleepers and their sounds: snoring, an unhealthy shallow cough, and an indistinct, disturbingly wet noise from that far corner of this human warehouse.

Toma found her hand and led her toward the front of the room, toward that odd bright shape, which turned out to be a tear in the hanging cloth. He pulled the curtain to one side and the eddying snow reflected light onto the bed below the window. He knelt now to reach under the bed and spoke to the sleeper in a harsh whisper of unfamiliar sounds.

The sleeper opened his eyes without stirring, nodded once in agreement to whatever Toma had said, and demonstrated no curiosity about his guest. Turning to the window, he pulled the blanket over his head while Toma foraged under the bed. When he had his suitcase and an irregular bundle of his belongings ready at the foot of the bed, he removed from the wall a painting there, whose dark colors, shot with gold, had held Harriet's attention in the meantime. She put out her hand so that he would not have to carry three things at once. She did not look at the picture, but the image resonated in her eye, investing the darkness with its colors. She tucked it under her arm, leaving her hands free to hold her skirt tight to her body. A likeness to what? she wondered. Something not of this world.

When they had reached the door, when the sharp air of the street allowed her at last to take a proper breath, she asked: "Wasn't that your bed?"

He smiled without humor, startling her with the whiteness of his teeth: "It is my bed, and it is his bed also. In two hours my friend will go to his work, which is making steam. Tomorrow he will have to share it with him you met on the stairs. It is not so bad as you think. There are other lodgings where you pay for eight hours only. I have slept there too."

She could think of no word or gesture, everything she had said or done having served only to further his humiliation, and so he finished the conversation for her. "You were wanting to know if this was my home. Now you see that it is not."

THE SIMPLE FACT OF turning north onto Fifth Avenue ignited in Amos Bigelow a slow fuse of conversation that flared up occasionally into loquacious monologue. Perhaps his good humor had to do with being pointed generally in the direction of home and the ironworks, perhaps it had to do with the anticipation of his dinner. An ordinary lamp-lit street corner might prick his memory; he had a clear recollection of each landmark, even of some now vanished. The strangeness of the scene itself—silence, whiteness, and the thinning of all traffic—heightened his powers of observation and association, for the ordinary boundaries of this world were dissolving in the snow, each building or monument was released from obligation to its visible surroundings and submitted now to the influence of time or history as perceived by Amos Bigelow.

At the corner of Twenty-third Street and Fifth Avenue, with the gaudy illumination of Madison Square Garden to the east lending a lurid tint to the snowfall, Amos Bigelow tapped Toma's shoulder and said: "Stop just here if you will."

He gave the side window a swipe with his coat sleeve and pointed at the vast construction site on the northwest corner. Harriet leaned closer to Toma so that she could see better, put her hand carelessly, confidently, on his to balance herself. "What is that, Papa?"

"It is not much to look at now, and I've no idea what they've a mind to do, but there was a fine hotel, Mr. Astor's, standing there only a couple of years ago, and I remember it well because it was my father's favorite, and more than once I stayed there with him. Think of that, your grandfather and your father, when he wasn't even as old as you are now. And do you know, it's not even that I miss the hotel so much, though it seems a shame to be tearing down a perfectly good one. No, what I miss is what was here before that, Franconi's Hippodrome, which they tore down to make the hotel. I don't think there was ever a place like it, not that I heard anyway. Part circus you'd say, and a pleasure dome besides. Covered in canvas, it was, but painted too, and in the ring—a whole city block, it seemed, or most of it—the horses and riders would perform, sometimes just the one and sometimes dozens, or hundreds, performing in formations, almost like dancing, or a parade. And the costumes. Well, I never saw anything to beat it, and I've lived long enough to see a lot of strange and wonderful things. I don't know, maybe it's for the best that it's gone. And the music—why, they had two or three bands playing at the same time—and people, some of 'em very grand, and some just ordinary folk, walking around the gallery upstairs, eating oysters and drinking champagne, or beer if they wanted it. It wasn't a bad place, d'you mind, but you could spend hours there just looking and not have anything to show for it at the end, and your money all spent. Ah well, I was young then and had all the time in the world. I'd like to see it again, though, and I can't say otherwise." He drew a deep breath here and expelled a sigh that sealed the windows again in mist.

"And the painting, Papa?" she asked in a very loud voice over the noise of the motor. "What was the painting on the canvas, the roof of that place?"

"The painting? Oh, I don't remember rightly, just colors I think, but colors as you don't see every day. Well, I tell you what it was, it was like that place we saw with your mother, in Italy. What do you call it? Hercules?"

"Herculaneum. The baths at Herculaneum," said Toma.

"That's the very place. Stones, they were, but the same colors as I think now. She loved that, your mother, though I'm sure she never saw the Hippodrome here, more's the pity. You, young man, is that where you come from?"

"No, sir, not from Herculaneum. But I was there with you."

"So you were, so you were."

Harriet, at the mention of Herculaneum, sat back in her own seat, her eyes fixed straight ahead at the trackless white of the avenue. She relinquished Toma's hand. They wondered, separately, at this sudden turn in the conversation.

"Well then, young man, I think we'd best drive on."

The Packard moved away from the curb, and the snow had now reached a depth and consistency that caused the driving wheels to spin until they found the grit on the cobbles. Toma, sensitive to the limits of any machine, knew that their journey was nearly at an end. Bigelow felt it as well.

"A pity we haven't that weight of iron back here still. We might get all the way home and we did."

"How far is that, sir?"

"Only a hundred miles or so, and there's gasoline aplenty in the jerry can behind. What do you think, young man?"

"I think we must stop. There is great danger in this."

As if to confirm this judgement, a trolley car rumbled past them, headed south at a crawl, causing snow and an explosion of sparks to cascade from the overhead wires like a fireworks display.

"Turn the car, then, if you can. You'll go around the square and come by that big hotel on the south end. We'll see about some dinner and a good bed."

TOMA'S BED THAT NIGHT was the backseat of the Packard. Coatless and shivering in spite of the sleeveless pullover of heavy boiled wool, he buried himself in a loose pile of his other garments, where his breath, trapped in haphazard layers of fustian, twill, and linsey-woolsey, warmed him, made him drowsy, released the odors trapped there. The sharpest smell was that of charred insulation from the cable that had failed in Stephenson's new prototype subway car. The white smoke tasted like fear. It had been an awful job today heaving the remains of that car, parts of it still warm, off onto a side track where they could pick it apart and see where the junction box had failed, the connections looking more like popped corn than bits of metal. It was those pieces he had been carrying back to show Stephenson, and a half length of the worthless cable too, when he had found Boylan at the window of the Packard, smiling at her, kissing the back of his hand.

There was another scent, heavier and older, less insistent than that of the burnt insulation but more troubling to Toma's empty stomach. Three days ago he had been taken to dinner by Mr. Stephenson, who knew something of his life and had done him other kindnesses in the past. He had no proper jacket or coat and so he and the old man ended up in the back of the alehouse, right by the kitchen, with the companionable fog of frying mutton chops rolling over them where they sat.

They lingered over their pitcher of ale, neither of them in any hurry to go out into the raw drizzle. The waiter asked if they needed anything else; Stephenson waved him away with the genial air of a man seated by his own hearth. There was some small talk of a circumspect nature about the shop. Stephenson, a strapping fellow in his youth and a match for any man on the floor, now spent most of his days in his office with the frosted half-glass walls, but Toma was his eyes and ears, in the tunnels and elsewhere. When Toma made a reference to the work in the tunnels being stopped for half a day by an inspection team from the MTA, Stephenson sighed in sympathy and allowed as how it was, now, all paperwork. Not like the good old days, God bless 'em, when the emperor of China sends a letter asking would the John T. Stephenson Company please make him twelve trolley cars. A price was quoted. Several weeks later a check arrived—had to hold off a while to see if there was a real bank in Macau behind that fancy letterhead—and that was the last they heard from the Chinaman until the cars were delivered, and a letter—some kind of scroll, you'd say—arrived to express the emperor's appreciation. But there was something else, come to think of it, a package with a piece of cloth to show what was wanted in the way of upholstery. Well, you never saw such a thing: cloth of gold, it seemed, with a few red or green threads thrown in more or less to give the eye a rest. And you should have seen the cushions that we answered with. Old Fogarty snuck out to the urinals with one of them under his coat and broke his tooth testing the buttons, thinking they were gold.

But the truth of it was, and here Stephenson set his elbows on the table and dropped his voice to a more confidential tone, the truth of it was that there was more money to be made in this subway business than there ever was in trolley cars and fancy cushions for the Chinaman, even with all the paperwork, and even though it didn't look so fat, car by car. Look at your map of Manhattan, boy, and you'll see what I mean: this tunnel to Brooklyn's not the end of it, not by a long shot. Before long they'll be building another line, and they'll be wanting more cars, and new cars, and if we play the cards right, and you keep an eye on the tunnels, and I keep everything square with Tammany Hall, why, there's contracts that will come our way. Never seen a lad with such a head for details as you, unless I go back to when I was your age. And here Stephenson winked at him.

Now Stephenson's thought turned from such pleasing vistas of past and future, landscapes ennobled by monuments to remunerative folly, and entered a forest of rich, obfuscatory praise for the capabilities, mental, moral, and physical, of his valued assistant, praise punctuated here and there by shafts of dazzling light, intimations of success, if only . . . Toma perceived that their discourse had a destination.

"If only what, sir?"

"Well, I'm just thinking, boy, that I raised you five dollars more than two months ago, and I'll raise you again if I have to, but . . ."

"Yes, sir?"

Stephenson took a long pull of his ale and wiped his mouth on a vast checkerboard of a handkerchief. Then he signaled to the waiter, calling out for a whiskey, a double whiskey.

"You don't look like a man who's on his way somewhere, somewhere as matters. You come off a boat, what, five, six years ago? Well, in this country we've all come off a boat, and you look far enough back. But the point is not where you come from, it's what you do when you get here, see? Now, it's almost three years since I come across you in that tunnel, digging after some poor bastards as got crushed in the cave-in, and it looks to me as if you're wearing the same clothes as the day I first laid eyes on you."

"I always remember your kindness to me, Mr. Stephenson. As for the clothes, my job still takes me to the tunnels."

"Oh, it's not just the clothes I mean, it's everything. How long have you been living in that place over there, Eleventh Street, isn't it?"

"Yes, four years . . . I do not remember. But there are worse places."

"Sure, you could find a worse place if you tried, but it might take a while. The point is that you can do better. What in God's name do you do with the money I pay you?"

Toma folded his hands around his glass. "I send it home to my people. There has been fighting. The Serbs will be free, free of Turkey, and of Austria."

Stephenson put two small broken bits of sugar in his whiskey and stirred it with his knife. "Family is family, as well I know, but you'll remember what I said about getting off the boat. You're here now, and you're an American. You can't always be thinking of the past."

"I think of the future, of my own future, so the present is not important, except I must study. Every Tuesday and every Thursday . . ."

"Oh, I know all about the studying, and your Franklin Institute, and I've nothing to say against it, except that you know more than enough about electricity to get ahead in this world, even to make a fortune for yourself."

"A fortune, you say. I am not sure of your meaning. Is this the same as rich?"

"Rich? Yes, of course I mean rich, boy, and what else would I mean? Would you rather be poor? I guess you can have your choice."

"I am not poor, Mr. Stephenson. I have never been poor, not even when I came from the boat. But I have not been thinking how to be rich."

"And what else is there, unless you mean to be a priest of some kind? You don't seem cut out for that, though I mean no disrespect."

"In my country, sir, the priests may marry, if that's what you mean. But no, I am no priest."

"What then? Not rich, not poor, not a man of God. What?"

Toma drank and set down the empty glass. "I keep nothing from you, Mr. Stephenson. When I know what my fortune is, what I must do, I will go toward that thing, and I will not keep the answer from you."

"You must have some idea what it is?"

"I know only that I am close to it, as the iron filing knows the magnet, and then not so close. At times I have felt it, the strength of the hidden thing, when I am on the shop floor fixing the motors, or down in the tunnel helping in that work. The closest of all was when I went to hear the great Nikola Tesla lecture at the Cooper Union. I could not understand the words he was using, not all of them, but when he touched the high-frequency coil, the Tesla coil they call it now, and made it glow, I felt that he touched me. Later, like a wizard, he made sparks fly from his fingertips. The others who heard him—some of them great, important men—gasped at these things, then clapped their hands. When the lights came on afterward, the professors and the engineers are going up to Tesla to shake his hand. Tesla bows to each but will shake no man's hand. He sees me sitting there, not able to move because my mind is so full of questions I have no words for, and no courage to ask, and he smiles at me. He knows."

"This Tesla fellow, you know, he may be cracked. . . ."

"It may be as you say. I know others say it. He is a Serb, as I am, and perhaps you will say the same thing about me. But that is how I want to be: my mind will be filled with some one thing, and I will do whatever I must."

Stephenson raised his glass to Toma and then drank it off. "I'm thinking you'd make a pretty good priest after all."

HE AWOKE BEFORE DAYBREAK in spite of the sweetness of his dream. The whisper of snow had ceased and a warm wet wind cleared the stale air of his bed.

His dream was an embroidery on that wind. She came to him bearing a basket that yielded the scent of food and the music of bottles. They put it down on the grass beside the car and sat on the running board with the lap robe beneath them and the sun-warmed metal at their backs, and he told her about his country, about his family, about himself. She was chiefly interested in the dead girl.

"What was her name?" she asked, offering him wine.

"Aliye."

"What a beautiful name. I am sorry for her. What did she look like?"

And now she was twining flowers in her hands, such flowers as he knew in the meadows of the Sandžak, where Aliye had woven them into her hair. His mind was full but he could say nothing. He held up a mirror, where she would find her question answered.

THE SNOW HAD TURNED to melting slush in the street, and behind the racing gray clouds there was the promise of an even warmer day. He had stored his clothes and books in the boot and was wiping down the fenders and radiator with an old shirt when he saw her at the door of the hotel. She had a basket on her arm, and he nearly called out to her using the other name. He waited, grinning broadly, as she picked her way through the puddles of filth and snowmelt.

"Did you receive what we sent out from the dining room last night?"

"Yes, thank you."

"And did you have enough to eat?"

"Yes," he lied.

"Well, to make sure, I ordered breakfast for myself, a very generous breakfast, and as soon as they brought it I told them to wrap it up as fast as ever they could. And here I am. Look," she said, pulling back the cloth to reveal a cup, a thermos, some silverware, and several items wrapped in table linens. "I am sorry the plates wouldn't fit, so this will be a bit untidy: I made sandwiches out of everything."

She poured him a cup of strong black coffee; standing upon the running board out of the slush, she was able to look down on him and his feast spread out on the hood of the motor. He ate steadily, offering her half of everything. She declined all but a roll and one piece of bacon, taking off her glove to eat it.

"My mother loved picnics more than any other meals. She said they brought out the pioneer spirit, and that they were a relief from good manners. Did your mother like picnics?"

"I do not know this word, but I know how to eat with my hands. This is how we ate in my home. I think you do not call it good manners." He held up his hand to show her how the yolk of the boiled egg had leaked onto his fingers, and they both laughed.

"Do you know, I worried about you last night. I thought you must be hungry and cold, and I almost came to see how you were. I even made a list, lying in bed, of the things you should have: a blanket, a pillow, a bottle of soup. But it wouldn't have been right."

"Ah," he said, looking up at her and no longer smiling, "but you did come to me. I had a dream and it kept me until the morning, and here you are."

She did not know what to say. The dream was dangerous ground, and she felt the smile on her face turn brittle. Surely he could see past it to the confusion of her thoughts. She did not know what was happening, but she did not want it to stop: How could she tell him such a thing or explain it to herself?

JUST AS THE SNOWSTORM had been unlooked for, a freak of nature, so this day revealed itself, by the time they were ready to set out, as an intimation not merely of spring but of the summer beyond. Toma headed west on Twenty-third Street, then turned north on Fifth Avenue through a new lake that covered the road axle-deep from curb to curb, and the only disturbance to the blinding expanse of water was the wide, slow vortex of an overburdened drain.

Amos Bigelow sat in the back, well pleased by the air from the open window and by the contemplation of this quantity of water, even though it was, strictly speaking, useless to him being so many miles from his waterwheel, not to mention hundreds of feet downhill.

He had talked himself out yesterday, first to Stephenson, then in the car, and at dinner too, when he had questioned Harriet closely about this young man. Today he had only one question to put to Toma, which was whether he understood the principle of the waterwheel. When he had received this assurance he fell back into a comfortable silence, punctuated every now and again by a muttered phrase like a line from a play, for the sight of the two young people there in the front, both of them looking straight ahead and never at one another, put him in mind of his own courtship, of which that trip to Italy had been a last sad reprise, and he was in fact now conversing with his wife, whose answers he heard with such blessed clarity.

When they heard snoring from the back, the young people might have relaxed their poses of rigid vigilance, might have commented on the weather—now hot, now cold, would it be winter or summer tomorrow?—might have found some other topic of conversation, perhaps suggested by the city, now vanished, or by some geographical feature of the rich, wet valleys of southern Connecticut unfurling before them. Those possibilities of comparison and contrast—the city and the country, his home and hers—were present to Harriet's mind, and she further imagined how a slight rearrangement—a yawn combined with a perfectly natural stretching—would allow her to view Toma's profile and whatever scenery presented itself on his side of the Packard. And when some precipice above the river or some stately mansion came into view she would describe it to him, with the slight emphasis of her hand on his, for he really could not take his eyes from the road for more than a second.

She imagined these possibilities because she remembered so well the ease of conversation they had known in Naples, and could recall, if she allowed herself to do so, the exact sensation produced by his skin touching hers. It had happened in Naples, of course, and last night in the car, and even this morning when she was so clumsy with the napkin and he caught both the falling bread and her hand in his. She wondered if such things leave a mark, a phosphorescence visible only to her. When the ship had left Naples, in the evening, she had escaped from her cabin and spent half the night watching the endless wake whose faint glow, could she but follow it, would always lead her back to Toma.

She had told him the truth this morning when she said how near she had come to visiting him in the car. She had imagined it all at once, an instant whose intensity brought blood to her face: he would be cold and hungry and alone . . . it was like a scene on the stage. Her part was to bring him food and warming drink. Her dramatic imagination stopped short with her showing him, by the light of a candle end, that the back of the driver's seat opened just so, and there inside was the fur-trimmed lap robe.

The porter had shown them to their rooms and had humiliated her with a murmured question: No luggage then, miss? Her father, flushed with his two glasses of wine, had kissed her on the forehead and said, either to her or to the porter, Well, I guess we'll make do for the one night. He had tipped the man too generously, and when the porter put his hand to the gilt-trimmed door joining the two chambers, had said, No, no, we'll leave that be.

She removed her dress, shook it vigorously, and hung it on the door of the armoire, hoping that all traces of the journey might vanish overnight. Her face, in the mirror of the washstand, and in the harsh electric light overhead, seemed different to her, tired and perhaps older. She washed as best she could, but even soap could not erase the memory of the dormitory where her thoughts now carried her. She looked at her shoulders, at the line of her neck, and tried to remember Toma in the baths at Herculaneum, his breath in her hair. Did he still smell like that?

The room, soundless and unfamiliar, encouraged a bleak train of thought. Did not men meet women in such places, women unaccompanied by luggage? If she had thought to visit him in the car, might he have thought recklessly of coming to her here?

Harriet switched off the light, then found her way to the bed, where the linens chilled her to the bone. She said her prayers feeling very far from God and slept at last, but not without dreaming, and those dreams, and her waking thoughts, and, most of all, the ruined arc of her imagined connection to this man beside her now made her mute.

As they made their way north from New York and the hotel, the familiar landmarks of the journey tempered her despair, and she began to feel more like herself. In spite of the bright sun it was colder now as they began to climb, and the road grew less certain, alternating between open water and piles of slush sculpted by the last wheel or hoof to pass this way. They came to the foot of Great Mountain, and Toma, in response to the pressure of her hand, slowed the Packard to look up at its ice-bound heights, where stunted oaks bowed under their burden.

"It often happens thus," she said, breaking the hour of silence since they had stopped to refill the gas tank. "They call Beecher's Bridge the Icebox of Connecticut, and when the towns around us have rain we are likely to have snow, especially in the spring. But this is unusual, even for us. Look at the little birches bent right to the ground. If it does not thaw by tomorrow they may never stand upright again. Papa will be upset when he sees this: he will be worried about the ice on his wheel, about having to shut down the works."

Toma did not respond other than to nod his head, but he glanced from the road to the outcrops of ragged, glistening rock, and to those refractions of light from every limb and twig that bathed the car in a nimbus.

"This is truly a land of wonders," he said at last.

Now the road was frozen solid, and strewn with a windfall of ice shards from the tall elms. The wheels lost their purchase, and Toma slowed almost to a walking pace, keeping the left wheels on the rutted crown. When they came to a slight incline he let the Packard roll to a halt without touching the brake.

"Are we there already?" boomed Amos Bigelow, suddenly and cheerfully awake. "Well, what's this? Ice, for all love, ice. You should have woken me sooner. Shall I give us a push?"

"No, Papa, we'll wait. It's more than two miles to town, and it's uphill, as you know."

"Someone may come along, as you say, but he'd better be quick about it or I'll have to take shank's mare. Horatio will have stopped the wheel, in spite of what Mr. Brown says. Another day lost for sure."

Someone did come along: Walter Hubbard with his oxcart and just a light load of hay on it. Bigelow offered him a dollar to pull the Packard the rest of the way.

"It's no trouble to me, Mr. Bigelow. I'm going anyway, and the boys won't mind the weight. It's a slow way, but a sure one."

Slow it was, and although Bigelow's impatience was palpable, Toma seemed to be in an unaccountably good mood.

"What pleases you so, Toma? Why do you smile like that?"

"It is the beasts, only that. I am six years in your country and I have never seen an ox until now. I am thinking of my home."

The wall of the Power City canal

CHAPTER

THREE

No account of the so-called North West Corner, and certainly of Beecher's Bridge in particular, can stray far from that distinctive topography that has been our blessing and challenge ever since those hardy colonists, our forefathers, first pushed into "the Greenwoods," to bring honest industry into what had been the haunt of wild animals and aboriginal Indians. Time, patience, and a great deal of earnest labor have been necessary to channel the Bounty of Nature toward the Progress of Mankind in these parts. These steep and unforgiving hills, which for so long impeded the ebb and flow of commerce, were also, from earliest times, the source of mineral treasures not yet fully exploited, and have at last yielded themselves to the harness of the rails. The forest is now the preserve of the charcoal maker, whose exertions provide the fuel for our principal industry, iron making. The narrow river bottoms have provided for the farmer's needs if not his luxury, and many a watercourse has been dammed to power the mills and workshops where mechanicians put flesh on the dreams of inventors, so that the very name "Connecticut" is now a resonant synonym for ingenuity and progress.

But the principal feature of this landscape, to the inquiring eye of an historian such as myself and in the sober calculations of the entrepreneur, is the dramatic and dominating bulk of Great Mountain itself. Let us imagine ourselves borne aloft in the gondola of a swelling balloon—we are not so rash nor so ignorant of mythology as to aspire to such a vantage by means of the Wrights' ingenious creation—where we may view without hindrance or apprehension this noble landmark that has attracted so much admiration and indeed shaped the aspirations and fortunes of those townsmen, farmers, and mechanicians who live in its shadow.

It is a day in early spring, and the shelving rock of the broad plateau—for here is no Andean cone, no Pyrenean tooth—is softened by a gauze of faintest green, the crescent bud and leaf of the forest, dotted now and again by the glory of our shadbush, which so resembles a puff of smoke and is as soon vanished. The season is not so far advanced that maple, oak, and cherry will obscure the contours of the land, though a deeper, unfailing green marks those descents where hemlocks guard the mystery of their watercourses.

The severity of the original forest is tempered, for we see that certain stands of hardwood have been felled by the raggies for charcoal, and the more accessible hemlocks by the tanner for their bark. Those stumps, some ancient and of heroic girth, gaze up at us through the branches of more recent growth. There are pasturelands as well, though the season is too early for the farmer to trust his livestock to the conditions that prevail here. And there, practically at the western extremity of the mountain, not far from the crenellated walls that loom above the town of Beecher's Bridge, another mystery of Great Mountain is revealed to our aerial gaze: a lake ringed with acres of impenetrable alder like any mud pond on lower ground, but its color is the most brilliant sapphire blue, denoting a depth that, to our knowledge, has yet to be plumbed. For the lake has its legends, and we will not attempt here to credit or disprove them; but in the history of Beecher's Bridge it has had only one name: Dead Man's Lake.

The breeze has carried us west over the lake, over the brow of the mountain, and below us now we see the town laid out in miniature, as if for the delight of children. The disadvantage of our height is that all is flattened out to the dimensions of length and breadth, as on any map, and those works of man that have so engaged the energies and passions of generations are mere toys, and less than toys when compared to the mountain and the river.

To look on the gleaming strands of the railway track you would think that it has just been taken from its box on Christmas Day and laid down with no more trouble than croquet hoops on a lawn. You would never imagine that just beyond those benign hills to the north lies a wild tumble of rock, a gorge by the name of the Stony Lonesome, and that the construction there claimed the lives of nine men, or ten if we include the engineer of the first train to cross the trestle, who died of a heart attack.

Rails and river converge a half mile from the town where the Long Bridge, parallel to the older, eponymous structure of Beecher's Bridge—an architectural marvel in its day—conveys goods and passengers to our eastern bank of the Buttermilk. As the town was laid out before the railroad came here, and as there is not such a distance between the river and the foot of the mountain, the townsmen, both the rich and the poor, have had to make their peace with this energetic and sometimes inconvenient neighbor. And not only the townsmen, but their wives, who must wash their curtains twice weekly to banish the soot, and whose gossip must yield each day to the clamorous interruption of four passenger and six freight trains.

Once past the town, the river begins to drop and to gather speed on its way due south. It is checked briefly by the old upper dam that has diverted some water to the Bigelow Iron Company for well over a century, and again only a few rods downstream by that more ambitious concrete barrier erected by a Bigelow scion, Aaron Bigelow of Civil War fame, father to the present ironmaster. And then the water frees itself from the hand of man to plunge recklessly a hundred and sixty feet in those thunderous cataracts of the Great Falls of the Buttermilk, whose din and mists rise even to the height of our balloon.

Now rails and river diverge, for such an acrobatic display would be fatal to any machinery, and many miles of gentle gradient intervene before they are reunited at Perrysville, near the junction of the Buttermilk and the broad Housatonic. In the triangle of land between these two paths we may glimpse the traces of an even grander ambition belonging to that same Aaron Bigelow.

From the eastern edge of his new dam—which, unlike the older one, harnessed the entire flow of the Buttermilk—the ironmaster projected a canal, an earthwork faced in massive stone that descends in a slow serpentine, the better part of a mile from bend to bend, until it rejoins the river below the falls. Along the canal, at irregular intervals on the various tiers, stand foundation works and sometimes entire buildings now fallen to ruin, and this is all that remains of the dream of Aaron Bigelow, the dream he called Power City.

On the ground there is not much to see, and few to see it anyway, for there are superstitions attached to this place that distilled so much pride and ill luck and animosity. The history of Beecher's Bridge, according to the Congregational minister who preached here for almost fifty years, is by and large the history of failed enterprise; and if that be true, then here in these damp thickets entwined with the great weed-choked serpent of the canal, here is failure writ in stone, and the intrepid local historian, or perhaps the errant tourist, considers one of these canal walls, twenty feet high and vanishing right and left into the forest, with the same awe and pity as one who encounters the remains of Nebuchadnezzar's palace or the fallen statue of Ozymandias.

It was not a bad or a foolish plan, this Power City, or, if it was, then at least many people shared it, and sought to tie their own fortunes to Bigelow's vaulting ambition. He was, physically, a big man and had already achieved a great fortune by dint of his daring. In 1860, Aaron Bigelow, having recently taken control of the ironworks from his own father, set about tinkering with a new process whereby iron was cast into rings and the rings then fused together to make a tube of superior properties. Bigelow thought he was improving the performance and durability of the cast pipe of those days, and he imagined burgeoning new markets in the metropolises of Hartford and Springfield, even Boston and New York: aqueducts or sewers, depending on which way the water was running.

Then history intervened in the form of the Civil War, and Aaron Bigelow's cast ring pipe was reincarnated as a cannon barrel that could withstand greater pressure, and hence achieve greater range, than conventional cannon of equivalent weight. Patents were taken, and this efficient engine of destruction, the Bigelow Rifle as it was called, made a great fortune for its inventor, and gave him pride of place among the capitalists and industrialists of the North West Corner.

The war came to an end, and life returned to its old ways in Beecher's Bridge and at the Bigelow works. Some of the men had to be laid off, of course, for although the Bible speaks of beating swords into ploughshares, in practice the Bigelow Rifle would not be changed back into pipe. The orders never materialized: the ring-casting process was deliberate and costly, and the product was of an awkward bulk and heft for a manufactory serviced by no railroad or canal link. During the war, each cannon barrel was ferried or floated across the Buttermilk, then carted eight miles to the nearest railroad depot. Aaron Bigelow understood that he had been defeated as much by the difficulty of transportation as by the unwillingness of municipal officials to invest in plumbing of the highest grade.

Bigelow was still a young man, not yet forty, and he was very, very rich. But he did not think that it was time to rest on those laurels; he must do something, else Beecher's Bridge would be forever cut off from the outside world, or at least handicapped in its pursuit of progress. He still came to the works every day, and on his way past the cannon would rub the decorative brass B for good luck. This cannon, a Bigelow eighteen-pounder, squatted in the dust at the entry to the ironmaster's office, chained off from the general chaos and drayage of the works by huge iron links cast by Bigelow's great-grandfather and salvaged from the chain that had once prevented British warships from navigating the Hudson. The cannon was the first fruit of Bigelow's process and patent, and in order to encourage visiting generals and politicians, Aaron Bigelow would sit astride the charged cannon and light the fuse with his own cigar. When the smoke cleared, there was the ironmaster, grinning and puffing his cheroot as if nothing had happened, and his audience, mouths agape and ears still ringing, would applaud. Young Amos Bigelow, much taken with the spectacle, asked each time if he might join his father in this adventure, and was told by Aaron that this was a man's business, and no game.

The cannon and the chain were potent reminders of what Bigelows could do when they turned their minds to something, and they gave Aaron Bigelow no peace: surely some greater work awaited him than merely filling orders for iron wheels. The story, perhaps true, is that the idea for the canal that would harness the Great Falls came to him in the middle of the night, and that he rose from his bed and began the labor himself with a pick and shovel, young Amos holding the lantern. When the sun rose he stalked into the woods in his night-shirt with an axe and several yards of bright ribbon from Mrs. Bigelow's sewing basket to map the course of his dream. Saplings were cut and trimmed, then hammered into the ground with the flat of the axe, a scrap of ribbon as the final touch. Three great loops were laid out—some say the plan was determined by the amount of ribbon in his pocket—to return the water taken above the falls to the river below, and Bigelow calculated that there was room enough for eighty-five mills, each receiving water from its section of the canal and spilling it back into the level below.

Eighty-five mills representing any and every conceivable enterprise requiring power: weaving, wood turning, tool manufacture, gunsmiths, box makers, tanneries, breweries, silk spinning . . . on and on went the list. Nothing seemed impossible to Aaron Bigelow, and, as he was fond of pointing out, after the canal was built, it was all free, for so long as the Buttermilk River should flow. Yes, the canal would be expensive, as every great work from the pyramids on must have been, but Bigelow was able to paint such a picture of Power City with all those wheels turning day and night that he found many willing investors, some of whom built their factories while the canal was being dug.

To the town fathers, and to the men of substance throughout the North West Corner, the plan, and its larger ramifications, had a compelling, dizzying logic. Even before the capital had been raised, the railroad commission made a recommendation to the legislature that the main line of the railroad be rerouted through Beecher's Bridge. And this was not all: a bank note printed in 1875 by the Iron Bank of Beecher's Bridge shows a foreshortened perspective of the town and the ironworks against a background of tall masts and swelling canvas. Not only would the railway come to the magnet of Power City, but a series of locks and canals on the Housatonic and the Buttermilk would bring oceangoing cargo vessels to the new metropolis at the foot of Great Mountain.

Aaron Bigelow was an iron maker, not an engineer, and therein lay the fatal flaw of his scheme. In order to move the water of the Buttermilk past the hundred waterwheels of Power City, he needed a dam and a canal. Bigelows had built dams before: the old dam on the Buttermilk itself that diverted water through the ironworks, and several smaller dams along tributary streams to create holding ponds or reservoirs against those droughts that could shut down the works for weeks in the dog days of summer. This new dam did not daunt him, though it must be built to span the entire watercourse and would divert much, and sometimes all, of its flow. The dam was built, and it stands to this day: see how the water, still pale and turbid from snowmelt, falls like a veil over its top.

Perhaps he gave less consideration to the construction of the canal after he had laid it out; perhaps he was distracted by the great work of promoting his idea and raising the capital for it; perhaps he thought that a canal is no more than a ditch: you dug it out, and it worked. Except that this canal, because of the slope of the land, was more aqueduct than ditch, as those impressive stones in the undergrowth below us will attest. The work seemed to be done carefully enough. Every two hundred feet or so there is a section of the wall where the stones do not lap each other, and straight vertical cracks, six feet apart, run down from the parapet. These are the blanks, so-called, where the stones could be knocked out without damage to the structure and a wooden flume inserted, thus diverting water to the wheel of that particular enterprise. So proud of their work were the masons that now and again they signed it, leaving initials and dates, sometimes an inscription in Latin, like so many tombstones set in the wall.

Any child knows the difficulty of taking a handful of water and holding it aloft: the water will find its way out through the cracks. This, in essence, was the fate of Aaron Bigelow's canal, for it was—quite inexplicably—improperly lined, or the force of water underestimated. Over the stones that formed the bottom of the canal was laid a thick blanket of clay, carted in from some distance, our own soil being thin and sandy. On top of the clay a mosaic of flat stones was set down, as one would do to finish a terrace or courtyard. No cement whatever was used. Perhaps it was considered and rejected as a pointless extravagance.

Aaron Bigelow was in all respects and in all matters a forceful, persuasive man, but the water would not do his bidding. When the great day arrived—there were already eight factories built, and another seventeen at some stage of completion—the spillways of the main dam were rammed home and the sluice gate to the canal cranked open. The water rushed down the topmost straightaway, and when the cheering of the crowd abated, each witness wondered privately what that ominous noise might be that so resembled the rattling of giant dice. It was the paving stones, plucked out of their bed of clay by the onrushing water, smashing against the walls and each other, raking and rending the clay beneath.

At the bottom of the slope, where the new silk mill occupied the last site before the canal debouched into the riverbed, a smaller crowd, including the proud proprietor of that establishment, awaited the rush of water that would start the wheel turning. The mill was already stocked and fitted, the shafting, pulleys, and looms awaiting only the motive power of the Buttermilk to begin their business. Eben Cartwright, envisioning his future requirement of raw materials, had even purchased fifty acres of prime bottomland in the next township and set out ten thousand mulberry seedlings to feed his silkworms. The building, according to the diary of Cartwright's nephew, who recorded the incident, was suffused with the subtle aroma of the brand-new leather belting that connected the driver and all subsidiary shafts, gears, and pulleys.

The hoarse cheering, punctuated by a few firecrackers, rolled down from above, the signal that the sluice gate had been opened, and they waited. Seconds passed, seeming like minutes or hours, and eventually Cartwright consulted his watch: Surely it couldn't take water this long to flow downhill? When the water arrived it came from an unexpected direction . . . not by the canal, but flowing straight down the slope through the underbrush, a muddy trickle at first, and eventually a torrent that scoured the hill of leaves, deadwood, and some impressive boulders, all of which fell into the canal, plugging it and overwhelming the new wheel in its flume. A short while afterward a little water made its way down the canal bed and came to rest in a spreading pool behind this landslide.

The explanation for this debacle is already clear to the perspicacious reader, as it was clear enough to the onlookers once the sluice gate had been wrung down: those flat, heavy stones, though they might serve to keep a stone wall fixed and dressed for one hundred years in spite of the urgent thrust of the frost, had yielded in an instant to the rush of the Buttermilk, exposing the clay below, which was only a temporary defense, and in the blinking of an eye muddy water began to pour through every crevice in the rock wall on the downhill side of the canal.

The ensuing silence comprised the shock, mortification, and embarrassment of the spectators and the principals, and there may have been those gray heads in the throng who had heard and paid heed to the minister's words years ago: the history of failed enterprise had reasserted itself with a vengeance. At the top of the canal, Aaron Bigelow faced the situation, and the crowd, with a forthright, almost defiant air. The construction was defective, he proclaimed, but not the idea: purer clay and a more reliable subcontractor would be found, and the stones allowed to set in the clay until it was as firm as cement. And if that didn't work, a concrete lining would be installed, in spite of the expense. At the bottom of the hill, Eben Cartwright was heard by his nephew to mutter: Someone will have to pay for this.

The subsequent history of the canal was no more encouraging or profitable than this beginning, and far from being a source of revenue to the town, it must be seen as a rankling, debilitating thing, a succubus that fed on dreams, fortunes, even lives.

The purer clay was tried and found wanting. There was brief hope that a reduced flow of water might stabilize the canal bed, but it soon became apparent that such a stream would never support the full complement of factories, and Bigelow was not of a mind to tailor his ambition. Two years later, one of the principal backers of the canal died of natural causes, and the heirs sold his portion to Increase Lyman, a local iron maker of note, and long a rival of Aaron Bigelow's. One wonders, inevitably, at the motivation of the purchaser in this transaction: it was an odd time to be buying into the project, and perhaps he regarded the few thousand dollars—less than half of what had been paid in originally—as the acceptable price of being a thorn in Bigelow's side. This would not be out of character, for the house where Increase Lyman lived, near Salisbury, was called Spite House, and was known to have been built in order to block his neighbor's view of a pretty bend in the stream.

With the advent of Lyman, the affairs of the Power City Canal Company entered a new phase of acrimony and self-strangulation. Bigelow was no longer the only spokesman and anointed champion of the project, for Lyman was always there to commiserate with the frustration or anger of smaller investors, to play devil's advocate by suggesting that this or that thing had been done badly by the founder, and

perhaps even knowingly so. All of Bigelow's plans for repairing or al-
tering the work met with scornful opposition from Lyman, and these
rebuffs were repaid in kind whenever the latter had a proposal to make.
The opposing parties exhausted themselves in spirit and in purse. A
stalemate ensued, and for ten years no work was done on the canal.
Weeds began to reclaim the mill sites, and in 1878, Eben Cartwright,
his hopes and mulberry bushes reduced to dead stalks, his silk worms
long since rotted in their cocoons, slit his throat with a straight razor.
His nephew continued the pursuit of legal redress.

The toll on Aaron Bigelow was inexorable. He had to defend himself in court; he had to rally his supporters—not simply the investors
who still listened to him, but those persons of local and regional importance who stood to gain by the long-term success of the canal project, and whose influence must be the foundation of that success; he
had to worry about the energetic machinations of Increase Lyman; and
he had also the affairs of his own business to attend to, when he found
time. The Bigelow ironworks still turned out railroad car wheels of ex-
ceptional quality and durability, thanks to the seemingly magical properties of the Salisbury ore, which proved, when the process of chemical
analysis was developed, to consist simply of low impurities and a high
natural manganese content. But the cost of Bigelow's ambition, and its
complications, eventually outran the productive capacity of the works
and began to feast on his fortune.

Bigelow had never known poverty, and would never taste its bit-
terest fruits. But he certainly knew what it was to suffer a reversal of
fortune that encompassed his entire life, and perhaps it was disappointment that killed him in the end. The vast, sudden wealth of the
Bigelow Rifle was dribbling away—like the water through the canal
walls—and along with it the slower, surer wealth of the Bigelow wheel.
But instead of cutting his losses and repairing at least his own personal
affairs, Aaron Bigelow—riding his cannon to the end—risked all on a
dramatic gesture that was based more on the need to salvage reputation and self-respect than on any clear-eyed business plan.

He offered to redeem any shares in the Power City Canal Company for sixty cents on the dollar, and in order to do so he secured from
the Iron Bank, run by his old friend Oren Truscott, a mortgage not
only on the Power City site but on the ironworks, and even on the vast

acreage he held on Great Mountain, comprising tributaries of the Buttermilk, numerous holding ponds, and the charcoal-cutting reserve of the ironworks. This property on the mountain was known by its old name, the Bigelow Plantation.

The smaller investors, to a man, accepted the offer, not without grumbling, but with inward gratitude for Bigelow's unaccountable foolishness. Increase Lyman accepted the buyout as well. Perhaps he had tired of his sport; in any case, he had made a decent profit on his investment.

Bigelow celebrated the event by having a photograph taken. He stood directly behind his cannon with some workers ranged alongside the barrel. At the head of the file stands Amos Bigelow, the present ironmaster, who, like his father, deigns not to face the camera. The elder Bigelow presents a curious figure, still of impressive bulk — just as the vast barrel reduces him, so does he dwarf all other figures in the photograph—but slumped in the shoulders and, if one looks closely, drawn in the face, as if all flesh had begun its decline into the dust.

Three years later, in 1888, the banker Truscott, whose son is, of course, none other than Fowler Truscott, the senior United States senator from Connecticut, declined, with all heartfelt apologies, to extend the loan to the Canal Company. After reviewing the situation, he concluded that all of Bigelow's assets were fully valued in the mortgage, and not even the friendliest eye could discern any successful outcome to the canal scheme. (That the canal had descended to this equivocal or even pejorative labeling in popular parlance tells us much, in one word, about its history.) Negotiations proved fruitless, as did Bigelow's reluctant appeals to the ties of friendship. Both parties retreated into acrimonious silence, and at a reception for the railroad commissioners, who had a stake of sorts in the fortunes of Power City, Bigelow pointedly refused to shake Truscott's hand.

A week later, the ironmaster, much disheveled, arrived at the works and had his men reposition the rusting Bigelow Rifle with crowbars. They raised the barrel by means of freshly cast iron pigs so that it pointed at the Iron Bank, just visible through the elms at a range of some eight hundred yards. With his own hands Bigelow triple charged the barrel and rammed home the wadded ball, and with his own cigar, as of old, he lit the fuse. In the truly tremendous explosion that followed, the barrel failed in its final duty and burst asunder, sending Aaron Bigelow to his Maker virtually in one piece, for no trace of him was found other than his left boot and a bit of the shinbone. No one else was injured, and the ball came to rest embedded in the trunk of a sugar maple that stood just next to the post office. It is lodged there still, an object of bittersweet curiosity.

Well, that is the sad history of the peaceful town below, or at least the principal narrative, which has served as the cloth of much subsequent embroidery. But life in Beecher's Bridge did not come to a halt in that great explosion, any more than the bank was destroyed by the ironmaster's ball. There were cows to milk, children to feed, and iron wheels that must be cast, for the fire in that furnace must never be allowed to die out, else the belly becomes fatally plugged with ore and flux and the cold iron.

Amos Bigelow took over the works from his father, and with the help of the insurance money, grudgingly paid, he staved off the financial crisis, at least for a time. He was ever a careful man, and had grown up in the large shadow of his incautious parent. He made two vows and has kept them to this day: he would be a maker of bar, plate, iron wheels and such modest implements as the townsmen required for their daily business; and he would never again set foot in Power City, or what was left of it.

There is his house, the home of the ironmasters for well over one hundred years, and you may see what sacrifice was necessary to bring the railroad through our town, for the grade cuts off the bottom part of his garden. And over there, around the corner of the mountain marked by the odd outcropping of Lightning Knob, the manse of the Truscott family lies on a green sward sloping down to the lake where the senator takes his morning exercise a-rowing in his sleek scull with his bulldog, Sousa, perched on the bow. The senator will shake any man's hand, but there is a particular tone in the cordiality he extends to the ironmaster: so much difficult history comprised in that clasp, to say nothing of the outstanding mortgages, and for the most part our Montague and our Capulet maintain a polite, wary distance. I will say this, however, and trust it will not be received as any vulgar tale-carrying but rather as a thread in the warp of our history: the senator, although he is a lifelong bachelor and a man not so distant in years from the ironmaster himself, has a particular care for the daughter, Miss Harriet Bigelow, a graceful and accomplished young woman who, in addition to her discreet competence in the accounting and disbursements of the Bigelow Iron Company, is a musician of note and a principal in the affairs of the local chapter of the Temperance Union.

In a very correct and unobtrusive way, the senator has become her patron in the matters of nearest concern to her: he has hosted a fundraising gala in the Manor, as his house is called, for the Temperance Union, and has forbidden any alcoholic beverage to be served at his political gatherings; his pew in the Congregational Church, which affords a convenient, oblique view of the Bigelows', is in regular use when the senator is not attending to affairs in Washington, and he has requested of her the favor of a needlepoint cover for that little stool whereon he kneels; he has organized more than one musical soirée at the Manor, where Miss Bigelow charms the audience with her voice and her mastery of the piano, and where afterward the senator exerts himself in a vigorous reel with that young woman as his partner, to the applause of all present; and, of course, there are those private audiences in his office in the bank, when the mortgage papers are withdrawn from their iron box to be shuffled, discussed, and put away again with smiles on both sides.

The ironmaster cannot be altogether ignorant of Fowler Truscott's attentions to his daughter, but as the senator has not announced himself as her suitor, he need not acknowledge them in any way. Truscott does not call upon Miss Bigelow at home, but it is public knowledge that in order to further her amateur musical interests he had delivered to her a console harmonium, which sits in the front parlor of the house. The ironmaster, owing to his impairment, cannot actually hear much save for the deepest tones of the Bach, but he smiles at her when she plays, for her mother, too, was fond of music. And the mahogany cabinet of the instrument bears a curious mark that no amount of turpentine or beeswax can altogether disguise. To humor his daughter, the ironmaster will kneel to the harmonium and lay his teeth just there upon the corner of the case, receiving in this way the vibrations and some intimation of those now vanished higher registers. Miss Bigelow has read an article in the *Chautauqua Journal* about Mr. Edison, that man of electrical genius and keen musical interests who suffers from the

same defect of hearing, but who nonetheless has given the world his astonishing device, the phonograph, and who monitors the quality of
those recordings, even judges the relative merits of vocal artists according to the impression received thus, through his teeth. "Can you
hear it, Papa?" she will say to him. In truth, he cannot, but he would
not dream of disappointing her in this matter. It is one definition of
human kindliness that a man must suffer such things in silence for the
sake of another rather than speak his mind frankly, and the ironmaster,
of course, has every reason to perceive virtue in silence.

Our balloon, buoyed these moments by the giddying thermals of
Great Mountain, now descends, and where but a while ago we held
that lofty and foreshortening view of the town and its sad history, now
we come near the particular, the individual who sees not over the line
of trees or beyond the hill, knows not what his own destiny may be,
and has all too limited an understanding of how he came to this place,
this moment.

Look to the left, over the spire of the church rising to meet us, and
you will see the ironmaster's house and truncated garden. In the driveway stands his forest-green Packard touring car, whose fenders are
being buffed by a tall young man, and coming down the steps is Miss
Harriet herself, wearing a dress that seems quite new and an expression that betrays some uncertainty.

And there to the right, in the distance, under the slope of Lightning Knob, you may see the senator hitting golf balls on his lawn: a very
strong shot will land them in the lake, and the others will be retrieved,
several at one time, by his faithful bulldog. We cannot see the expression on his face, but he looks at his watch with some impatience, and
the exercise with the golf club seems just a way to pass these minutes of
anxious waiting. Miss Harriet lays her gloved hand on the gleaming
handle to the door on the driver's side of the Packard.

"GOOD MORNING, TOMA," said Harriet with bright emphasis as the
door swung soundlessly on its hinges. That annoying squeak that her
father could not hear had been attended to.

"Good morning . . ." He would not call her Miss Harriet, as he was careful to do in the presence of Bigelow, and something now made him stumble over the familiar diminutive of H. "Where shall we go this morning?"

The awkwardness of this moment weighed on Harriet. She had taken the keenest pleasure in these driving lessons: partly because the mastery of the machine came naturally to her after absorbing Mac-Ewan's example; partly because the modest speed and consciousness of danger were intoxicating, like taking her horse over a gate or stone wall; and partly because this was time spent alone with Toma. If she had sensed anything odd in Fowler Truscott's note she chose to ignore it. Why the urgency? Why a Saturday? Why at his home rather than at the bank? In the flush of her new competence she had answered before giving herself time to reflect. "I shall be there at eleven." She had planned to drive herself to the Manor.

"I want to try it myself today, Toma. You have taught me so well. I shall be quite safe." Her father, who observed no day of rest except the Lord's, need never know. He had been brought grudgingly to the idea of these lessons. She had insisted on the grounds of economy: Mac-Ewan's salary would be saved.

"Your father will not have it so."

"I am quite sure he will not mind. He trusts me, you see. In fact he depends on me." She made the mistake of consulting her watch, again forgetting its uselessness.

"You have an appointment? It would be better, then, if we leave the lesson for tomorrow. I shall drive."

"Toma, please. I shall be quite all right if you will only start the motor for me."

"It cannot be. This is not for me to decide."

"Who then?"

He ignored the sharpness of her tone. "Your father has told me plainly that you are not to be taking the car by yourself. He worries for your safety. And I must take him to lunch with Mr. Truscott at one o'clock."

"Very well." She made certain to smile at him here. "I am, I think, late for my own appointment." She said to herself that it would have been much more convenient to have taken her horse. This outing, which had once possessed an appearance of simplicity and innocence, was now surrounded with unbecoming nuance. How would she explain Toma's presence to Truscott? How would she explain anything to Toma? Well, she thought, setting her mouth, she would explain nothing.

It was probably her imagination, but Toma seemed to have a sure sense of her destination. "Yes, left," she said when they came to the fork, but hadn't he already started to turn the Packard? There were not many other houses on this road running between the mountain and the river, and the mist from the falls enveloped the budding elms. She had been told, or had read, that those trees were dying, though they seemed now as perfect as the day. She tried to think of that perfection, of the things that had seemed so pleasant just a short while ago.

She glanced down at her dress, which was too light and summery for April, and was certainly not new. One more season, and she would have to do something more than put new ribbons on it. But the ribbons were prettily done, with a little twist in them that she had seen in *Godey's Magazine*. It had taken her no more than an hour after supper last night and her father, who smoked his pipe on the far side of the kitchen out of courtesy, had neither commented nor noticed. Sewing was a common enough task for her, now that Mrs. Evans's sight was no longer what it had been for fine work. Dear Mrs. Evans—Evie, she had called her as a child—who had made all her dresses for her after Mama died. What would become of Mrs. Evans? What would become of Papa? How would she manage? Well, she *would* manage, that was all there was to be said. There were things she could give up, surely, and the price of iron might turn a corner. She did, of course, put her faith in the Creator of all things, and who could deny the power of prayer? But the thing that had turned up, the Stephenson contract, was no source of comfort to her; if anything, it terrified her, and more than once she had woken in the night, dreaming or at least fretting about it, and had lain awake for what seemed like hours. She would do her best there, controlling Papa's enthusiasm and asking careful questions of Horatio and Mr. Brown. And Toma was her friend. He would help her make things right with Mr. Stephenson. She could fall asleep, sometimes, by thinking of all the wheels made by the Bigelow Iron Company, that name cast in bold letters, carrying people and all sorts of freight to Albany, Boston, Philadelphia, some, perhaps, even as far as

Atlanta or the cities of California. Anything was possible in that vast mystery of tracks crisscrossing the continent, and she imagined that the Bigelow wheels were taking her to those far-off places.

Toma, she was quite sure, had noticed the dress, not just now but last night as well, when he came to the kitchen to take a jug of the spring water from the tap at the sink. He ate his evening meal with them, gratefully demolishing everything that Mrs. Evans put on his plate, and then withdrawing to his room—MacEwan's room—over the horses and the Packard in the stables by the side of the house. She did not know what he did there, perhaps read those difficult books and the *Scientific American*s that he had asked her permission, and the use of her card, to bring from the library. The light of his lamp was always burning when she put out her own. She could see it there on the ceiling, a ghostly geometry whose shape she could not name. She was somehow reassured by it, and missed it when she awoke in the hours after midnight.

He had seen her sewing the bows on her old dress because the water in the well was off: some animal—a squirrel, perhaps—had made its way in there and drowned. The horses would still drink it, but she had told Toma he should come to the kitchen when he wanted water. She had thought nothing of it then, but now she regretted the coincidence.

Fowler Truscott was so pleased to see the Packard turn into his driveway that he hit one mighty shot with his persimmon cleek and it sailed straight and true a good twenty yards beyond the edge of the lake. If he was surprised to see Toma at the wheel, he certainly did not show it, and put his hand out to him after he had greeted Harriet by kissing hers. He asked how Toma was getting on at the ironworks. Toma received the question stiffly and made a polite reply quite empty of content.

"Good," said Truscott, "I'm very glad to hear that things are coming along well. We all take an interest, you know."

One of Fowler Truscott's attractive qualities, compared to other men of Harriet's acquaintance, was his ability to converse with ease on any subject whatsoever, an ability that must be distinguished from the ordinary affability of the politician by the element of unfeigned interest as well as by the breadth of his reading, his knowledge of the world.

Whom else could she talk to about the novels of George Eliot, or the writings of Emanuel Swedenborg, or the latest issue of the *Chautauqua Journal*? And real conversations too, in which her own opinion was sought and even prized.

This quality was notable, today, by its absence. He did notice her dress and complimented her on it, though she was quite certain he had seen it before and might recognize its evolution. But once they passed through the door and into the lofty, dim interior of the Manor, his gift deserted him, as if he had left it with his golf clubs on the lawn.

They sat in the great room—it was too grand to be called a parlor—and the staring heads of all those animals on the wall made her feel cold. Truscott made a ceremony of handing her a musty shawl of soft wool from the arm of the settee, and guided her to the front window, where there was light and a little warmth. She declined the offer of coffee, and so they sat with two glasses of water on the tea table, and Fowler Truscott stared at his as if he didn't know what he should do with it.

"It was very kind of you to come, Miss Harriet, and on quite short notice too. I hope I am not keeping you from something more interesting?" His face flushed at this perfectly banal pleasantry, and Harriet realized suddenly that he was going to make love to her: that could be the only explanation of this awkwardness. Why else would he be worrying the crease of his trousers between thumb and forefinger?

Harriet was neither alarmed nor delighted by the prospect of Fowler Truscott confessing that his long-standing regard for her had, over time, been transformed into . . . or whatever the words he might use to frame his suit. But she was disappointed that it was all, now, so transparent to her, that she had such perfect anticipation of what was to follow and there could be no surprise in any profession of affection. She reflected on this for a moment, even while he was talking of something else, and decided that the element of surprise was not necessary: if one were truly to be surprised by such a declaration, then it would be unwelcome news, an unacceptable revelation. What was lacking now, even when she made the most generous allowance for the chilliness of the room and for Fowler Truscott's embarrassment, was a sense or even an intimation of joy.

He was not an unattractive man: large, squarish features—echoed in the front hall by portraits of ancestral bankers and a large, squarish frame to match. She had seen a photograph of him making a speech to the citizens of Panama at the ceremony inaugurating the canal, and another where he and Theodore Roosevelt, on safari, celebrated the day's sport, each posed with a foot upon the neck of his lion. He looked equally at home in both settings, at peace with the sure knowledge that money, a white skin, and a willingness to listen would open any door to him. This was not arrogance, or if so it was at least tempered by a humorous recognition of the accidents that had delivered him to such a pinnacle rather than to some mine shaft or clearing in the jungle. His superiority, however defined, real or imagined, was lightly worn.

Harriet Bigelow thought of herself as a sensible and practical young woman: she had no choice but to be so. And although she tried not to dwell on such things, there was no point in pretending that Fowler Truscott was not rich, or that such a consideration was irrelevant. No one had spoken directly of such things to her—when she might marry, and why—but Mrs. Evans, in response to Harriet's concern over the household accounts, had said that everything would come right when she married some fine great man. And who was that to be? asked Harriet. Oh, that's just me talking, dear, and you should pay it no mind, some gentleman as deserves you and would make your mother proud. Here Mrs. Evans began to weep foolish tears of joy mixed with sadness, and she embraced Harriet as if the matter were somehow settled, the nameless suitor accepted, happiness and family assured.

He put his hand on hers now, giving emphasis to his remark about the ironworks and how he appreciated her stabilizing influence, her quiet wisdom. Harriet, who had been lost in her ruminations on the state of matrimony as an abstract proposition, was recalled to the chilly room and the bright-eyed company of the oryx and the wildebeest. Why were they discussing the affairs of the ironworks? Why was his hand unpleasantly moist to the touch, so mottled when she dropped her eyes from his earnest gaze? Why, above all, was she sitting just here, or the Packard parked just there, so that she could see Toma's shoulders and neck as he sat stiffly behind the wheel of the car?

The journey home was a misery to them both. She had never seen Toma in such a cold, imperious mood: not only was he silent, he would not look at her. If only he knew what warm, if hopeless, feelings toward him lay shrouded in her silence. Conversation was too difficult in these circumstances, and might take an awkward turn. Instead she reflected on the puzzle of her meeting with Truscott, with two pieces in particular that, could she turn them around or over, must fit together. Although he had expressed himself warmly and almost intimately—his hand on hers was certainly an intimacy—there was no explicit mention of marriage. Was she to infer such a thing? Did not the man go down on his knee and produce a ring from his pocket to take her breath away? She stole a look at the perfectly impassive Toma, wondering how such matters were governed in his country, what looks, words, or touches would pass between a man and a woman there. And the other thing prickling her mind was that if Truscott had intentions toward her, and if, as would be proper, he intended to take the matter up with her father, was it not odd that he made no mention of the fact that they were about to dine together?

Harriet shrugged her shoulders: nothing made any sense on this day. (And here Toma did steal a glance at her out of the corner of his eye.) This afternoon, after her dinner, she would plant her peas, the onion sets, and her lettuces, with the beets and turnips in reserve if she had the strength. The seeds would sprout, bear leaf and root, be harvested. There could be few surprises or disappointments in that.

It happened otherwise: there was one more surprise in store for her that day. Instead of stopping the Packard at the steps to the porch, Toma drove into the open bay of the carriage house and let the car come to rest in that pleasant must of hay and horse punctuated by the sharper fumes of the automobile. It was chilly in this shadow, and the only sound was the ticking of the engine block surrendering its heat. This silence was pleasant to Harriet after the torrent of Truscott's earnest professions. Although she looked straight ahead, she could see that Toma had turned to her. She felt the weight of his eyes. Words would spoil the moment, but she spoke them anyway.

"Well, I suppose I should go in."

Toma came around behind the car to open her door, but stood directly in front of her, so that she had no way to step down from the running board. Instead of making way for her he stepped closer, took her hands in his and drew them gently behind her back so that their faces were nearly touching. And after a measurable pause that seemed to express confidence rather than uncertainty, he kissed her.

This was what she wanted from a man, she thought, and knew in the same instant that she would never have it from Fowler Truscott. Was she being mocked? She turned her face away to catch her breath but did not try to withdraw from his embrace, which now seemed somehow more intimate than when his mouth was upon hers. She spoke into the collar of his coat, her cheek grazing his.

"That must never happen again." When he made no sign or word, she continued, "Do you understand?"

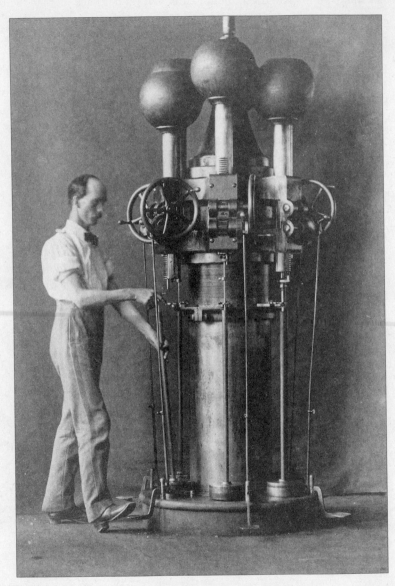

Boring rifle barrels at the Springfield Armory

CHAPTER

FOUR

He was shocked by the temperature of the water. Beyond the flimsy wall of the wheel pit, out in the bright sun, the temperature had soared into the nineties. A violent rain during the night had brought no relief but rather this pall of humidity, and peonies that had opened only days ago drooped on their stout stems. The draft horses at the rail of the depot seemed to have gone to sleep for the summer.

The wheel was down and the forge silent. The rhythmic plink of hammers, so close to his head, had slowed to the point where they might almost be the chimes of the church. The wheel was down—Horatio's precious wheel—and as a result a holiday had been declared by Amos Bigelow. The men streamed out of the gate shortly after the shift began at eight, one joking loudly that he'd soon know what the missus was up to with the postman, another commenting, to general assent, that Bigelow was as decent an employer as a working fellow could wish for. It had been announced that they would all be paid full wages for this day.

Harriet would not approve of this expense, would have frowned upon it silently as wasteful, an inefficiency whose toll would be added to others in those ledgers of which she was the sole mistress. He tried to imagine such an expression on her face. Had he ever seen it? The memory of her smiling face seemed to banish all other possibilities until he remembered Boylan and their first meeting in the New World. In the moment before she was aware of his presence, and well before she recognized him, he had seen such fury written there, a look that would have stayed the hand or frozen the heart of any man with an ounce of imagination. And if not the heart, then the reproductive impulse, as surely as such freezing water as this would shrivel a man's stones. But Boylan was different, or perhaps he himself was different, for in the time since he had left New York, he had not met a single man who seemed familiar, whose features or gestures or tone of voice reminded him of who he was or where he had come from. There was only Harriet, who was both part of the past and of the present, and whose regard, smiling or frowning, made him most painfully aware that he was different.

The sluice gate had been closed after last night's heavy runoff yielded a vile yellow water in the race and a turbidity near the chute that Horatio Washington knew immediately to be the result of some submerged peril to his precious wheel, the heart of the works. Toma had arrived at the usual time to an unsettling silence. Mr. Bigelow knew immediately what it meant: "Oh, for the love of God, what is it this time?"

Horatio had gotten there first, drawn from his bed, so one man said, by the distant reverberation of that stump entering the millrace. Ah, said his friend in a whisper that could be heard by many, if I was in bed with that colored gal I'd be making so much noise you could blow that cannon to Kingdom Come all over again and I wouldn't hear it. There was a murmur of laughter in response, but the fact was that shutting down the wheel was seen as bad luck, paid holiday or no. They would rather work than entertain the possibility that the wheel might never start again: other furnaces and forges, as they well knew, had shut down for good, and for no better reason than a stump caught in the race. They could only guess at the big picture in Bigelow's—or, more accurately, Harriet's—mind, whatever the talk might be of the new contract for cast car wheels in such quantities that a man might walk on them like stepping-stones all the way from Beecher's Bridge to New York City.

The decision to shut down the wheel was Horatio's: he was the only man in the works who could give such an order aside from Mr. Bigelow, but even Bigelow would not challenge him, nor ask a question about what was done. Horatio, any way you looked at him, was not a man who invited questions or small talk, for you knew that you could expect nothing in reply. The back of him was forbidding enough: not so tall, but wide, like a boulder, with the head set down on his shoulders like a man who expected to be struck from behind at any moment. And the face, although he smiled as often as any other man, inspired a kind of uneasiness even in those who had known him for years. He knew things about you, or about the world itself, that were best left unspoken.

Toma had kept his distance from Horatio during his weeks at the mill, for he was respectful of any man's privacy just as he guarded his own, and besides, there was the plain fact that Toma's presence was a challenge to the man who kept the wheel.

Owing to this caution, Toma, who had inspected every dusty corner of the furnace and the forge, and spent hours at Harriet's side in her tiny office inspecting the ledgers, had never until this moment seen the inside of the wheel pit, much less the wheel itself. He had tested the tension and wear of each link in the power train, from the yard-wide leather belting of the journal or central axle—three ox hides he guessed—that took the strength of the river from the wheel, on and up through the rickety housing of the furnace as those slow, irresistible revolutions were retailed through complex gearings and ancillary belts, faster and faster but with ever-diminishing force, to serve the various functions of the ironworks: bellows; trip-hammer; conveyers of fuel, ore, and flux; lathes and grinders. It was like a tree, he thought, dedicated to motion rather than growth, or like a river moving in reverse. At the farthest tributary—he puzzled over this, thinking there must be a word for its opposite—a gloved hand could act as a clutch or brake on the driving belt of a grindstone; touch the main belt and those three oxen would take your arm and maybe your life.

And yet he had never seen the engine itself, this vast idle thing whose farthest edges were lost to sight. He had a candle end in the pocket of his shirt and matches that were still dry, but he waited for his eyes, trusting the darkness.

The surface of the wood under his hands, though nearly dry, had an odd, slippery resistance, as if both wax and oil had been applied to an articulated wooden sculpture. The wheel moved soundlessly in response to his touch and each bucket, stretching away from him farther than his hand could reach, moved through a small range of motion against the resistance of a spring he could not find. He puzzled over this detail, made the wheel revolve in his mind, felt the water cocking that hidden spring, which would, near the bottom of the arc, act in concert with gravity to cast the water away. And was the speed of the wheel increased by this articulated tension? Or was the device simply to cushion the architecture of the wheel against the assault of the water? He was impatient with his inability to resolve this question in his mind: any fool could do it with a pencil, and he was not any fool.

His impatience blossomed into a deeper discontent that touched on many things but centered inevitably on himself. What had he expected to find in this sanctuary other than a carefully tended antique? And how could he justify the time he had spent elsewhere in the works, putting off the discovery of what he already knew? What would Mr. Stephenson think if he knew that the real reason for this delay was that he could spend an indefinite amount of time with her in the claustrophobic intimacy of that antechamber where the ledgers were kept, so airless on these close days that they seemed at times to be inhaling each other?

He had seen how the dark hair trembled when she shook her head in annoyance over the total of new purchases; had noted that the exertion of shifting the ledgers brought a flush to her face and even a beading of perspiration to her upper lip, which she dismissed with a brusque, mannish gesture; had felt desire as an emptiness, a void into which he might disappear at the suggestion of her breasts against the gray fabric when she reached to take an old account book down from the shelf; had taunted her with the impassivity of his eyes as he made her explain, not for the first time, how the price of Bigelow bar was determined, or the provision of charcoal balanced against the projected requirements. The walls pressed in upon them; the open door admitted air like a draft to their furnace; her father, a deaf sentry behind the turning of that post, coughed and muttered to himself, punctuating their silences.

In the two weeks since he had driven her to Truscott's house, Toma had watched her for some sign. Away from her office, he had no advantage at all, could compel nothing except polite inquiries or responses, seemed almost to vanish from her horizon. She had kissed him in the carriage house, where the shadows reminded them both of the baths at Herculaneum. But in the light he was a different person: he saw it in her eyes, felt the distance between them like a garment, as shabby as his own, that could not be cast off.

Fowler Truscott's clothes had made an impression upon him. Mr. Stephenson had worn the same black frock coat to work every day, and while it was a clear sign of precedence and authority, he cared not if his sleeve brushed the idle gearing, and would take a sample or a piece of broken machinery upon his striped knee to have a better look at it. The ironmaster of Beecher's Bridge wore a suit of shapeless black rusted with age and mended many times over. But Truscott's flannels were the color of fresh butter, his open blue shirt set off the mottled carmine of silk around his neck, and the linen jacket, elegantly belted, hung as weightlessly from his shoulders as if it had been painted there. He himself had worn such finery once, and though his silken vest with its brilliant piping in no way resembled what Truscott wore, its gaudy uselessness, too, had been a kind of advertisement. When he had come around the rear of the car to open the door for Harriet, she did not seem aware of his presence, although she thanked him. She was looking at Truscott, who had thrown down his golf club and was crunching across the gravel to greet them, and in her expression he saw no pleasure or anticipation, but a kind of measuring calculation, as if she had just looked up from her ledger in a moment of abstraction.

He estimated the wheel to be over ten meters in diameter, the sort of behemoth that he had read about in the old *Scientific American*s but thought to be as extinct as those great reptiles buried in the deserts of the west. And at least a meter and a half wide, with tons of water in those buckets or troughs. He smiled at the thought of the little mills in his own country, buildings on stilts with the wheels flat in the water beneath and a simple vertical pole driving up into the belly of the mill to turn the stones. The wheels turned lazily in the river's current, the flow catching the angled vanes on one side and overcoming the drag of the returning vanes on the other. Such a simple thing: a child could make one for his own amusement, and it was called a butterfly.

But there was a man, Toma remembered, a kinsman of his father's who lived half a day's journey away on the road to the monastery nearest their home, where the snow fed a river that ran for four kilometers before vanishing into a chasm in the ground. The mill in this place looked like all the others from a distance: the same pitch to the roof, the same arthritic poles holding the precious machinery up out of the current. But the wheel itself was not the same, for his cousin, a man with bright eyes and a lurching gait, had sited it differently. He had placed two great rocks so that the water must bypass the wheel, except for an angry jet that issued from between the rocks, caught one side of the wheel, and was hurled down and away by those whirling blades. Because there was no water to drag on the blades as they turned to meet the jet again, his cousin's wheel spun on into the early months of summer, when the flow in the streams had dried to a trickle and the men were grinding the grain by hand. His wife, a woman who always found fault, complained that the stones ran too fast, and the flour had a singed taste.

With his hand on the behemoth, Toma wondered about his cousin, about what was in his mind when he placed those stones. Where do such ideas begin? and where do they stop? Perhaps the old wheel had simply broken, and the man, partly out of frustration, had rebuilt it in a different way. Perhaps those rocks had been there all along, or nearly in the position that produced the jet. Perhaps also the man had other things in his mind, and only the necessity of gathering and grinding the barley prevented him from experimenting further with his design, positioning the wheel vertically, which would have required belting or gears to drive the machinery. Tesla, in his lecture, dressed like a wizard, his eyes burning with unseen things, had declared to his audience that what he would show them—he gestured here in the direction of the glowing tubes and the friction generator at his back—would find no practical application for years to come. They are now without use, he said, challenging his listeners to follow his mind, taunting them, perhaps, but this is the future, make no doubt on that. Tesla, too, was a Serb, and perhaps as much his kinsman as the man with the bad leg.

And why was this wheel now not more than it was? Why not a gleaming steel turbine a fraction of this size? He imagined Tesla, in his place, contemplating the wheel: Burn it, he said . . . there is enough wood here to keep a house warm for a month in the winter.

Toma slapped the wheel with the heel of his hand, and the report filled the shed.

"What was that, d'you suppose?" The mason's voice surprised him: he had forgotten how close they were.

"Maybe it's just Horatio's wheel falling down by itself, in which case we needn't be fussing with these God-damned rocks. Maybe we'll be having the whole week off after all."

"You wouldn't know what to do with a week off, Flaherty, and I don't think the wheel is falling down. I think there's somebody in there."

"Well, it's all the same to me if it keeps that black bugger busy and off our backs. I says to him, 'Why me? Can't I go home like everybody else?' And the man just looks at me, like I'm not worth the breath it would take to answer. The man has no respect."

Soft laughter greeted this pronouncement. "Well, Flaherty, you're a good enough fellow and all, but I'm not sure I respect you, exactly."

"And maybe you're as ignorant as he is, then, and you being bog Irish. But you don't turn your back on me when I speak my mind to you, or say good morning. And besides, you're white, which makes a difference as I see it."

"No denying the man is black, but who's to say what the difference is."

"Ahh. . . ."

"Come now, bucko, do you think there's another man, black, white, or green, who knows what Horatio Washington does, and could keep that thing cranking three hundred days out of the year? Have you never been down there to the place he keeps below the falls, that workshop of his? Sure he's rebuilt this thing piece by piece without anybody's help, and old Mr. Crawford—d'you remember him? or was he dead before your time?—old Mr. Crawford, who kept the wheel before, and was a fair hand at it, even he'd tip his hat to Horatio."

Silence, punctuated by several savage hammer blows, answered this remark, and the other voice continued, "And as for white, who's to say about that? The woman down there . . . wouldn't she pass for white with you?"

Flaherty groaned. "Sweet Jesus, what an ass on that woman, though I'm thinking you're too old to notice such details. An ass like some statue, I tell you, and a face. Well, now you've put the thought in my head, there's the answer to my week off: while Horatio is up here tinkering with his wheel, I'll be down there doing a bit of tinkering on my own, putting the pole to her every hour like the chimes in the church. I guess I'd have to say she's white enough for me."

"Your pole, Flaherty, your pole . . . and you wanting respect. If you're asking me, the closest you'll get to her is having her face or some other part of her in your mind as you're putting that pole of yours to your own wife, meaning no disrespect. And as for the church bells, maybe you can tell the father next Sunday what goes through your mind when you're lying in your own bed at home."

The door to the shed of the wheel pit opened abruptly, dazzling Toma, and a voice, neither loud nor hushed, demanded: "Who are you?"

"Good morning, Mr. Washington. It is Toma Pekočević."

"Who?"

"Peacock. Thomas Peacock, and I am here . . ."

"Oh, I know what you're here for. What I don't know is why you didn't ask me. Nobody touches that wheel but Horatio Washington. There is even a sign on the door."

"I saw the sign. Mr. Bigelow said that I may go every place in the works, see everything, ask any question."

"I don't remember you asking me any questions."

"I thought I should see the wheel for myself."

"Yes, a man of science. Well, now that you have been looking at it with the lights out for a while, what questions do you have?"

"I have not yet found my questions. I have been thinking."

"Mr. Peacock, why don't you get your sorry wet ass out of that water and do your thinking on dry land? I don't want to be picking pieces of you out of my wheel when we start her up again. Jesus Christ, first it's a stump knocking my head race all to pieces, and now it's some damn Polack with his hands all over my wheel, trying to find his questions. Get out, I said."

"I am not from Poland, Mr. Washington. I am from Montenegro."

"What?"

"Montenegro. *Crna Gora* in my language, Montenegro in yours."

Horatio Washington snorted at this information, and more than any of his words, the laughter grated on Toma.

"Monty Negro. Monty . . ." and here Horatio's voice broke again to a giggle. "So you're not a Polack after all. I apologize for that. You come from Monty Negro, so I guess that makes you a monty nigger. What do you think: is a Polack dumber than a monty nigger?"

Horatio bent so that his face was just inches from Toma's. He did not flinch when Toma's hand came slowly out of the water, not clenched but open, and understood that Toma wanted to be helped out of the wheel pit. Their hands clasped, clasped but were not released once Toma stood dripping on the stones. The younger man now thrust his face close to Horatio's and exerted a grip that might crush or cripple.

"In my country, in the Kingdom of Montenegro, a man who uses such words is prepared to die for them."

Horatio was caught unprepared. He was himself a strong man, but he could not shift his hand to take purchase on the other.

Toma released his grip and turned his back to Horatio, offering any revenge the other might care to take. "Here is my question: why is this thing, your wheel, made of wood at all? Steel would be lighter, faster, stronger."

"Sounds like you have the answer to your own question."

"And why this design? This is what they have in the old books, when America belonged to the English: it is called a breast wheel, yes? A maximum efficiency of sixty percent, yes? But that was more than one hundred years ago. No one builds such a thing today. You build a turbine, even the very simplest on the Fourneyron model, and you have seventy-five percent efficiency. And the high-pressure turbine, a Leffel, with double draught pipes and runners, even higher." In the grip of his enthusiasm Toma now turned back to Horatio, to that expressionless face that was the color of the shadows in this place. "I have a book with pictures of these engines, if you wish to look at them."

"Pictures. That's nice, somebody paying you to look at pictures. You won't get your face broke or your hands dirty that way, won't even raise a sweat. You have anything else that needs saying?" Although Horatio's words had an edge, he sounded tired rather than angry.

"Nothing more. That was my question, if you would please to answer it."

"If a man knows the answer, then he isn't asking a question. Or if he is, then he's going to use the answer on the other fellow, hurt him with it. I don't want any part of your questions."

"You will not answer?" asked Toma, registering shock.

"Tell you what, Mr. Engineer, why don't we move this discussion up to the office, where you can ask the man himself why this place is what it is, why we've been doing the same old things pretty much the same way—without your fine ideas, of course—since before you were born, or your daddy neither. And what do I know? Maybe you're so smart you'll look under his desk and find a sack with a million dollars that he just plumb forgot, and then you can build your toys and we'll all live happy 'til the angel blows his horn."

"You mock me."

"You could say that. And maybe when you get finished changing everything to your liking, then I'll have more time to do the job right . . . sit there all day and make jokes about Mr. Engineer. But in the meantime, you get out of this house. After you, boy."

IN SPITE OF THE HEAT, in spite of the piles of dusty account books on her table and the brimming tray of correspondence, Harriet Bigelow sat in a cocoon of pleasurable reflection occasioned by her father's absence, by the enveloping silence of the works, and by the catalogue of plumbing fixtures open upon her lap. She felt as if she had slipped through a crack in her world, like a child in the attic who lifts the lid on a trunk or finds a curiously carved malacca cane and lives a lifetime in the span of a forgotten hour.

It was a guilty pleasure to which she surrendered, comprising vanity, a measure of avarice, and, as she was most uncomfortably aware, hypocrisy with respect to her father. Had she not spoken somewhat sharply to him about the lure of those catalogues, of the wasteful and fantastic ideas that proceeded from such reading matter? She loved him with all her heart—a phrase she sometimes repeated aloud to herself—but cherished him most in the abstract. Today she was grateful for the overlapping accident of the stoppage of the works and her father's toothache.

She had arrived at ten, glowing from her walk and from the gentle stimulation of her breathing and posture class at the Hooker Gymnasium. At eight-thirty the heat had already been too oppressive for exercise with the Indian clubs or quoits, and even the more energetic elements of posture were, by tacit agreement, deferred until the following Tuesday. So intent was she on the task of drawing every iota of goodness from each deep breath, on keeping the shoulders square, the spine centered, and the abdomen taut, that she did not notice the silence of the works until she had her hand on the latch of the office door.

She was curious but not alarmed. There had been no siren, as there would have been to summon help in case of a serious accident. She heard now the clanging of hammers and saw below her Flaherty and Jessup among the torn stones in the empty headrace. She had a practiced eye, and calculated that they would not finish in time to start the wheel again before the end of this shift. A day lost, she thought. Inside, on the corner of her table, she found a note from her father, detailing the accident to the headrace and the good humor of the boys when he sent them home. He was off to the dentist to see to that tooth. A day lost, but a day paid for.

Harriet's duties at the Bigelow Iron Company were unsanctified by any title or compensation. She had come to help out in the wake of Mr. Burdick's sudden demise three years since, and the tidying of papers soon gave way to a reading of same, then to tracking certain invoices to entries in the ledgers in the passageway off the ironmaster's office. She was impressed by the precision of Mr. Burdick's mind—so at odds with the chaos next door—and by the fact that his copperplate hand so closely resembled her own.

Through gradual mastery of the accounting functions of the works, and through her ever-expanding practical knowledge of its production, Harriet's role came to be acknowledged by every workman in the Bigelow hierarchy whose understanding extended beyond the hammer or shovel in hand. It was not acknowledged by the ironmaster himself, who took an uncomplicated delight in her presence here each day but remained ignorant of what she actually did in her little space. His deafness served as a convenient barrier between him and the many consultations that took place just out of sight around that corner, for there was a second, interior door to what she referred to, with subtle emphasis, as my office rather than the office.

Her father's absence meant that Harriet found herself, now, without anything that absolutely required her attention until tomorrow. Her ledgers were current as of yesterday, and the payroll was a cloud three days distant. There was the correspondence, of course, but that could wait; on the very top of the pile was a letter that she was particularly disinclined to open, as it would ruin her day to receive the monthly advisory from the Iron Bank. Inside that cream envelope there would be a sheet of figures recording the deposits, withdrawals, loan and mortgage balances, and interest charged. In addition, there would be, quite probably, a note from Fowler Truscott himself apologizing for such exigencies of the business world, and dismissing them as well, or nearly so. She wasn't to worry: he, Fowler Truscott, had a special concern for the financial situation of the Bigelow Iron Company.

Her annoyance at the unread letter from Truscott was brought to bear upon the catalogues at the bottom of the pile. She consigned all but one of them to the wastebasket beneath her table. Her father would, in a week or so, inquire about this one or that one, and she would have to tell him a little fib. But the last catalogue of all was not discarded. At first she wondered what this display of plumbing fixtures could be doing here. A mistake, she concluded, given the primitive facilities available at the works. She had used the little shed only once, making all possible haste, and on the way out had encountered that poor hulking fellow with his flies already unbuttoned. He covered himself with his hands and mumbled apologies in a language she could not identify. Never again, she vowed, and ever since had used a chamber pot tucked in a corner of the supply closet upstairs.

Durock. The very name on the commode in the Madison Square Garden Hotel. And here it was with an oak water tank above and solid brass piping connecting the two items. She laughed, as if to dismiss the idea, for the ironmaster's house, with the exception of some primitive piping and drains in the kitchen, was unplumbed, and her father had expressed disapproval at a neighbor's remodeling to include a bath and an indoor water closet. God did not intend such things to happen in a

Christian house, he said. Harriet had said nothing at the time, but in the most recent issue of *McClure's Magazine* there had been an article on the Comforts of Home that had struck a chord: Might not her own home include such elegance? A warm tiled chamber with tub and shower enclosed in a curtain, a porcelain pedestal sink before the mirror, and, yes, a flush commode set discreetly in its own closet, windowed for proper ventilation. Her experience of such things was limited: a couple of hotels and, most recently, the little wallpapered chamber in Fowler Truscott's house that he referred to as the powder room.

Harriet nudged the door with her foot so that she would have time to put the catalogue away in case her father returned. A quarter of an hour later the door to the outer office did open, but she knew at once that it was not her father's step. Two men, at least, with much shuffling of feet and a constricting silence. She did not rise or move. A shadow squeezed through the crack in her door.

"Where do you suppose that man went to?" demanded Horatio in a tone of hollow anger. "The one time I want him he isn't here, God damn it."'

"I did not see him go," answered Toma, "and the car is still here. Perhaps he is . . . you know. . . ."

"Well, I guess we can wait for him to do his business down there. Will you look at this stuff on the table? Amazing. What does he need this shit for . . . build another factory?"

"Another factory would be a good idea," said Toma, almost to himself.

"Don't get me started, boy. The reason we are here and not down in my wheelhouse is so you can tell him what's wrong with his setup. I haven't the time to explain why water runs down the hill instead of up."

"You do not understand me. I did not give you any insult."

"Not directly, maybe. . . ."

"You were too angry to hear my words."

"But you think it's all crap, don't you? Just tear it down and build something else. And with what? You don't know enough to ask the right questions. Where is that man anyway?"

Horatio stomped across the office. "Look here at this picture. Learn something while you're waiting." Toma followed him to the far wall, next to the ironmaster's desk, and Harriet rose to stand just behind her door. Again she admired the particular set of Toma's shoulders and neck, wondering as she did so if it was possible to conclude from such a glimpse that he came from a foreign place.

"What is this?"

"That would be the Bigelow Rifle that used to sit in the yard here, and the big fella standing right behind it is Aaron Bigelow, the old man's daddy. Everybody in this picture is dead now, except that boy standing out in front; he's the man here now. And down below is the wheel, where you can't see it, same as I found it when I came here, and no house on it or nothing. They were worthless, those paddles. Worthless."

"So that much you have changed."

"I did what I could, but by the time I got here it was all rundown . . . wasn't much that could be done. The time this picture was taken, you could have built your factory or bought yourself any turbine you wanted, if they'd had such a thing. But the old man had different ideas on how to spend his money, and now it's all gone."

"I see."

"Do you? Maybe. What else do you see in the picture?"

"Well, the workmen. . . ."

"Look at the ironmaster. See how big he is? Not just the gut on him? Makes all of his men look like boys? That's ambition you're looking at, and pride, and dreams of something so big it broke him. His son didn't have that, or if he had it once it's long gone."

Horatio seemed to have talked himself out of his bad temper, and Toma was looking not at the photograph itself but at the glass in the frame, where the half-closed door behind him was reflected, and where something had moved.

"Tell you what else I see," continued Horatio, in a tone that was almost friendly. "I see a man so big and so sure of himself, why he's master of the world and not just some damn factory. And you know what he's thinking standing behind the cannon, or what he wants everyone else to think? That thing's his dick, never mind it's the wrong color: a big black dick aimed at the world. In his dreams," Horatio mocked. "In his dreams."

To Harriet's relief, Toma made no reply at all.

in care of Bigelow
Beecher's Bridge, Connecticut
May 13, 1914

Mr. John Stephenson
The John Stephenson Company
121 Worth Street
New York, New York

Dear Mr. Stephenson:

Thank you for the letter and for the cheque. Mr. Bigelow and his daughter have been most kind to me, and so the money has not been a difficulty. I am sorry that I have not written to you before now, but my time has been taken up with studies on iron making.

In this place my thoughts are like the blizzard that came upon us in our journey. I have lived in New York for six years almost, and before that, I was in the beautiful mountains of my own land. Between these two there is not a bridge: I am like the man who is sent to the moon by magic.

I understand now that the city, as strange as the moon, is my home. I was learning, every day, how to live in the New World, and in the evenings after my work, I went to the Cooper Union or the Franklin Institute and there I learned what the New World will become. What do I care for my clothes or for my bed? Edison, Tesla, Hammond, Marconi, Pupin . . . these are only a few who have given public addresses in New York. I have heard them, and someday I believe that I will be counted in their number, one of those who have made yet another New World.

But this place you have sent me to is as untouched by those ideas as my own land was. In all of Beecher's Bridge there is not a single lightbulb or motor, and the only power of steam is that of the railroad locomotives. (I have heard that there is a farmer, down the valley, who has a steam tractor, but I have not seen it.) Everything is done the way it was done fifty years ago, or even one hundred, mostly with the hands or with the help of draught animals. To be fair, I will say that the workers take great pride in what they do, and they know their work. I have asked questions about this of Mr. Bigelow and of the men who work for him. They say there is no coal, only the charcoal; or they say there is no money to change things. But there is another reason. Many years ago there was a man,

Mr. Bigelow's father, who would have changed things; you probably know the story. When his plan for the great canal came to nothing, and many were ruined, the son decided that there was safety only in the old ways. I do not blame him, but his clock has stopped.

I enclose my notes and diagrams of the furnace, the forge, the casting and rolling operations. My information on the waterwheel is incomplete, as the man in charge has taken offense at my questions, though I intended none. He is a man of great skill, judging from the ingenuity of the gearings, clutches, and couplings in the power transmission, which is also his province, and I regret the barrier between us.

If the question is whether the Bigelow Iron Company can fabricate the wheels necessary to the pending IRT contract, the answer is yes, but at a cost that may be too great to them. If the wheel fails, or the water, all will be lost. In any case, you must protect yourself against the unforeseen: Mr. Bigelow will do everything in his power, but he cannot control the flow of the river, and his ability to fulfill the contract depends on everything going right. He has made no allowance for the things that can go wrong.

It is my hope to see you before long, and that you do not doubt me.

> *Yours most truly,*
> *Thomas Peacock*

HE HEARD VOICES WITHIN, a thin, querulous demand and a grudging monotone in response. He knocked tentatively at first, then more forcefully. The echo spoke of a generous space, perhaps the whole of the old mill, one hundred feet by forty. Stone piers punctuated the vertical wooden siding, and a sagging monitor ran the length of the roof, many of its windows patched with board or roofing paper. It looked to Toma as if the roof would go in a good snowstorm.

He waited, hearing no footsteps. Now the clank of a skillet followed by an expletive. Not a good time to call, it seemed. He sighed and wondered if he should go. But there would not be another chance, so he called out, "Mr. Washington, are you there?"

The door opened violently and Horatio Washington stood there in his trousers and bare feet, the suspenders caught between his legs. He looked at Toma as if he did not know him and blinked in the bright sun. The eyes did not look good.

"Who is that?" A woman's voice.

"What do you want?" Horatio's voice was thick with sleep, or drink, or both.

"I thought we could talk. But I can come back . . ."

"I have one day off a week, and this is it."

"I will wait until you eat your breakfast."

The woman came to the door, staying in the shadow. Toma nodded to her and took off his cap. He had seen her before, in town at Wright's store, but had not connected her to Horatio.

"Who are you?" The voice, in spite of its tone, had a strange music in it. Toma squinted to see her face, but could make out only the shape of it in a shock of dark hair.

"My name is Thomas."

"That isn't your real name. Tell her the other."

"Toma. Toma Pekočević."

"Tell her where you're from."

"I am from Montenegro." Toma watched Horatio's face as he said the words. Horatio smiled at him.

"Just wanted to hear it said the right way."

The woman stepped around Horatio and into the light. "My name is Olivia." She offered her hand and Toma took it, admiring the fine bones and the chapped cleanliness of her almond skin.

"Olivia is my wife."

Toma nodded respectfully. The word surprised him. Daughter, his eyes told him, in spite of her color.

"I ain't his wife," said Olivia, looking still at Toma, and only now releasing his hand. "Not 'less he marries me."

"There isn't another word, Olivia, not one I'd care to use."

Olivia sighed and glanced at Horatio, at his drooping suspenders. "You eaten, Mr . . .?"

"Toma."

"Did you eat, Toma?"

"No, but I came to talk to Mr. Washington."

"Mr. Washington is going to eat now, so you might as well. Horatio, we need more eggs, and then you'll want to put some clothes on."

HE GUESSED THAT NOBODY, guest or stranger, ever came here. Her hands were busy, but her eyes followed him as he made his way like a visitor in a museum from one exhibit to another, trying to grasp the ordering principle in the piles of salvaged material, some in shadow, some lit by shafts of light from those high windows.

"All that is Horatio's stuff, and I don't touch it. I keep my kitchen clean, that's all. How do you like your eggs?"

"The way you will make them for him." He walked back to the table, uncertain of the forms of civility here, remembering how she had held his hand for longer than was necessary.

"In the country where I was born this building would be very grand indeed." She looked around her as if she too were a stranger: the vault of dusty air, the far wall covered in spools and bobbins of fading silk, the figured cloth that curtained off the corner behind her.

"It's big, maybe, but it don't seem like a house. I'd sleep better if Horatio would put me up a wall. Always wanted a real bedroom. It don't matter to him 'cause he hardly sleeps anyway . . . up all night doin' this, doin' that."

"He works very hard," said Toma, steering the conversation away from the personal. "Everyone at the ironworks says so, even . . ."

"Even the ones who hate him?"

"Even the ones who are not friendly to him."

"There must be plenty of them. Horatio never had no trouble making enemies. Being black is all it takes." She looked up from her work and caught Toma's eyes. "Oh yes, I am that. Almost white, you're thinking. Almost white, and ain't it a pity?"

"No man, I think, would want you different." It was a foolish thing to say, and he knew it.

"Is that so? Sometimes I wish I was something else. I'm what Horatio wants, nothing more. Maybe that should be enough."

She tried to blow some hair from her face, then raised her floured hands to him.

"Will you please? Should have tied it up." She closed her eyes as he took the strands of hair and tucked them back into the dark tangle. Just above the right temple was a patch of pure white hair.

"How did that happen?"

"What? Oh. In Cuba, when my mother died."

"You are from Cuba?"

"No, Louisiana. My mother followed Horatio there when the war broke out. She worked in the laundry. Seems that was the only thing them Spanish soldiers could hit with their cannon. Like to blow us both up. I hate to think about it."

"So he is your father?"

"No. It ain't so bad as that."

A heavy clumping of boots was followed by the door opening. She lifted her hands out of the bowl. "See? That's what I'd be if I was white."

"I'm clean," announced Horatio. "Where's my shirt?" He put seven eggs on the table.

"Wait." She wiped her hands and disappeared behind the curtain. "Here is a clean one. For company. For Sunday."

HORATIO HELD UP HIS MUG, wrapping his hand around it to show Toma the handle in profile.

"How thick is it? The handle."

"A quarter of an inch, perhaps."

"That's five-sixteenths, just shy. How do I know?"

"Yes. How do you know?"

Horatio drank from the mug, set it down, and put his thumb and index finger to the dimension. "I can feel it or I can see it, either way. But you put a caliper to that and you'll see I'm right." Toma said nothing, drank his own coffee, waited for Horatio to speak again.

"There was a man I swept for over at the brass factory in Torrington when I was just starting out. Ran away from home and all those fucking tobacco plants and I was living under a bridge. A tube threader, he was, and he never let me touch that machine of his, just looking was all he let me do between fetching the raw pipe and taking away the sweepings back to the foundry. And he had his calipers and gauges on his belt, and this old rule there too, older than he was and beat to hell. He'd hit me with it a couple of times, and I thought to tell him: You want to get my attention you got to use something bigger than that. I laughed at him, not letting him see, but thinking of the broken shaft or harness straps my daddy had used on me. One day he shows me the rule, and you can just barely see that it's marked out in tenths. And when he was a boy like me, see, he'd worked in a shop, an apprentice, he said, and they made boilers and steam engines and such, and this rule was what they used to measure, making machines like that with a tenth of an inch of slop. A wonder they weren't all killed. And he kept that old rule on his belt 'til the day he died."

Toma registered polite interest with a noise in his throat. "You were an apprentice, then?"

"Sweeper, I said. Never had a nigger apprentice in that shop."

Horatio took Olivia's arm from the table as if it were a piece of pipe or a tool. "Hold that thing up there, girl. See that?" He jiggled his hand so that Toma could see how the wrist rattled in the loose circle of his fingers. "Imagine your cylinder like this, and that's your piston, with a tenth of an inch of slop all around, or maybe, if the man's got a steady hand and good eye, only a sixteenth or a thirty-second difference in the bore of your cylinder and the diameter of the piston. Me, I can see it right down to a sixty-fourth. Well, you can pack that piston with leather rings or something so it fits better, and all your steam won't blow out, but in the long run your rods and gearing and cranks are bound to wobble and break down because they are a little shy some-where, and in a couple of hours you will have to fix that fucker, and in a couple of weeks or months you might as well build a new one from the ground up." Horatio shook Olivia's wrist again. "Doesn't matter if it's a coupling, tie-rods, or a cylinder, what you want is tight."

He jammed his fist down. Olivia's elbow hit the table with a crack, and the blunt fingers were now locked on the forearm several inches above the wrist. Toma saw how pink those fingernails were, bright pink and bled white at the tips by the pressure of the grip. Olivia had made a sound like a cough, just one, but her face was a blank mask.

"Don't mind her," said Horatio, "she's used to me." He put her arm back on the table where he had found it. He fell silent and seemed so lost in reflection that Toma thought the conversation was over. He gathered himself to rise.

"What's your hurry?" Horatio looked up at him with an expression that Toma had not seen before, almost like a child. "If you ask me a question, you have to be willing to listen to the answer, the answer I want to make." Toma could not remember having asked a question.

"You excuse me now for a couple of minutes. I've got to do my business. But you be sitting there when I come back."

When Horatio had left by the back door, Olivia rubbed her elbow, looking at Toma as if she expected him to speak. He sighed, could think of nothing to say.

"You see how it is."

"Was it always like this?"

"No. He was good to me after my mother died. Kept me because he promised her he would if anything happened. Keep me safe. Maybe he did. Anyway, it changed after he . . ."

"What?"

"You know, took me"

"And that was when?"

"I was twelve, that's when. Didn't know any better. 'I need this' was all he said. Not like it was love."

He stared at her without seeing, heard the blood ringing in his ears, felt the pull of his own need. He was by the pool under the pillar of rock, and Aliye was next to him, covered with fine dust and a filigree of his sweat and seed. Was that love?

"And does it shame you? First your mother, then you."

"Maybe. I'm just glad she don't know."

They heard Horatio whistling on the path.

"I oughtn't to tell all that," she said low and quick, getting up and going to the stove. Then, louder, for Horatio's benefit, "There's more coffee if you want it."

"Give it to him, he'll need it. I got a lot to say."

AND INDEED HE DID, a torrent of words from some broken dam, by turns a jeremiad, a local history, an autobiography, a comment on technology, an analysis of natural resources, a lesson on the virtues of self-reliance . . . and all of this barely punctuated by a word or question from Toma.

In the light of Horatio's reasoning, the history of American enterprise was the history of tolerances. Toma misunderstood the word at first, could not connect it to the tale of the measuring stick and the brass factory until Horatio put on the table before him another measuring device, a precious thing in a velvet-lined case, like a jeweler's, that had calibrations down to one ten-thousandth of an inch. From a tenth to a ten-thousandth, and all in one century, said Horatio, two lifetimes if you put me and that son of a bitch in the brass factory together.

The study of cylinders was near to his heart, because the last job Horatio had before coming to Beecher's Bridge was shop foreman in the motor division of the Hartford Accelerator Automobile works, and it was there that the beautiful micrometer had been applied to engine parts milled to such a strict tolerance. Toma held the gauge in his hands. Now he understood the word, and he was beginning to understand his host.

Before Hartford Accelerator, Horatio had seen active service in Cuba with the Fourth Regiment of the Connecticut State Militia, the only black man among the noncommissioned officers. He had seen those poor boys—the Cuban conscripts, men of color, like us—cut down by the weapons he himself had helped make, for Horatio's job had been that of lathe operator in the Springfield Armory, where some of the first experiments in mass production were carried out, with the goal of creating interchangeable parts for all the rifles used by the United States Army. An interchangeable part, boy, being the truest test of your tolerances, your milling accuracy. You set that standard, and then you hit it every time. Every time, not seven out of eight, not nineteen out of twenty, otherwise you're going to get a bayonet up your ass while you try to jam the bolt home in a breech that's a hair shy. You follow?

Horatio himself, though skilled and experienced in metalworking, had ended up at the armory in the shop where the Blanchard lathe was turning out tens of thousands of identical wooden stocks for the 1893 model of the Springfield rifle. It was here that he learned about wood, about its various properties, the tricks it played on you, the memory held in its grain and forks that you could put to use only if you knew your job. Wasn't like iron or any other metal at all, more complicated for having been alive, and although Horatio was, by his own account, a man who never forgot anything, he could spend the rest of his life studying on wood and still not know all there was to know.

After Cuba—and now, although he did not mention it, with a nearly white child in tow—Horatio had found a position with Hartford Accelerator, and had worked his way up using his head and the skill in his hands until management had no choice but to make him foreman in the motor division. And even then he'd had to fight for it, even with that piece of paper in his pocket. You ever seen men fight with pipe wrenches? No? And here Horatio rolled back his sleeve to show the furrowed flesh of his forearm, long since healed, and canted his head so that the light fell on the broken cheekbone covered by a long, smooth scar. That other fellow looked a lot worse by the time we finished. I never had trouble with any man there after that time.

And how did he succeed, in spite of his color? By using his hands, and his head, and by never forgetting or throwing anything away. You, boy, that's a lesson you could learn: you must know a thing inside and out before you try to change it, and even then you don't throw it away. It didn't do any good, said Horatio, to be asking why the Bigelow Iron Company didn't look like some picture out of an encyclopedia, or why they didn't put a hot blast to that fuel and ore, then send it through some fancy puddling or shingling furnace. Why not make steel in one of those Bessemer contraptions instead of plugging along with the warm-blast cast iron for wheels, and the hammered iron, the wrought, for tools and bolts and whatnot? The right question, the useful question, was why things *are* as they are.

There's a logic here, you follow? You have charcoal, not coke, for fuel: can't change that. For the ore you have the finest, purest stuff this side of Sweden, the Salisbury hematite, and you wouldn't *want* to change that. You don't want to go adding crap to it with a hot blast, you want to cook it long and slow, then cast it the same way, so the rim on that wheel is tough and the core of it hard, and no open hearth in the state of Pennsylvania can touch the Bigelow wheel for quality, even though they can make them as fast as doughnuts.

Did Toma know what it took to be an inventor? He did not. Well, according to Mr. Thomas Edison, it took imagination and an ample supply of junk. Here Horatio made a gesture with his hand to embrace the entire contents of the silk mill, to indicate his mastery of all that lay in view. Know what's in all those piles? Toma shook his head. Ideas. Toma did not agree, and ventured the word "solutions." No, said Horatio, ideas, or parts of them, trapped, you might say, in the wood or the metal and waiting for me to come along and get it right: complete the idea, free it. Toma didn't have to take Horatio's word for this, but it would be hard to argue against Mr. Edison if he said that's how it's done.

Horatio Washington seemed to have talked himself to a standstill, and they were both silent now. But Toma was thinking about Edison on the one hand, and Tesla on the other; Tesla, who did not look strong enough to pick up one of Edison's pieces of junk, and whose tools of creation, as Toma imagined them, were a spare white room, a piece of paper, a pencil. Or Rudolf Diesel, who imagined the engine that bore his name, deduced parts of the process from the laws of physics, inferred others, and never even bothered to construct a working model of his machine.

Horatio blinked and seemed surprised to see Toma still sitting at the table. He rapped twice on his mug with a spoon to show that it was empty, and Olivia came with the coffeepot. "No more questions?"

"Some other time, perhaps. You have given me much to think on."

"Well, here's a question for you: what are you doing living up there with those folks? Learning to be a white man?"

"I am a white man." Having said this, Toma blushed because he could feel Olivia's eyes on him.

Horatio laughed. "That's what you hope to be, just like Olivia there."

"I know what I am. What's got into you today, Horatio?"

"She says that, but maybe she sees a pretty boy like you, no offense, who looks white, and maybe then she thinks she can be white too. And maybe when you're up there to the ironmaster's house, and using the right fork at the right time, then maybe you're thinking you can be one of them."

"No. I think . . ."

"Speak up, boy."

"It cannot happen."

"See? We agree on something after all. You are as much a nigger as I am, or Olivia, and the sooner you understand that, learn to live with it, the better off you'll be. Won't go getting your feelings hurt, or hoping for things you can't have."

HE HAD LOST TRACK of the time, but now the letter was finished and
sealed. His clothes lay on the bed, folded and ready for the canvas
satchel, beside them the painting that would have to be wrapped in his
cleanest shirt, then wrapped again in further layers to preserve it on
the train ride back to New York. One corner of it had been bent during
the car journey as a result of his haste. He must not let that happen
again. He wished he had a piece of cardboard, but he did not want to
ask for such a thing because she would know what it was for, and he did
not know how to say good-bye. The train would leave before dawn.
The letter would explain everything. It would be easier that way.

He took off his shirt and took from around his neck the woven silk
cross, laid it beside the painting. He would leave the room clean for its
next occupant, whoever that might be.

He was on his hands and knees in the corner behind the bed, mar-
veling at the accumulation of dust and mouse droppings, when he
heard her tread on the stairs, a rapping on the door. He did not respond. Perhaps she would go away.

"I brought your dinner. I thought you were not feeling well." She
tried to cover her embarrassment by arranging the plate and the setting
on his table, and there was the envelope with her initial on it. And
there on the bed were his belongings.

"You are leaving."

"Yes, tomorrow morning, very early."

"I see. I would have wished to discuss Mr. Stephenson's letter with
you, and the particulars of the contract." He could not read the tone in
her voice. Sadness disguised as reproof?

"I know the terms; he has written to me, as you know. It seems fair.
If all goes well, Mr. Stephenson will have his wheels and the Bigelow
Company will make a good profit."

"If all goes well."

"Yes."

"And is that what you wrote in this letter?"

"No, there is more. I was asking you to return to the library those
books, and thanking you for having me in your house. Also, I wished
for your happiness. I do not know if the words in my letter are the
right ones."

"And we would not see each other again?"

"I did not think you would want that. Your life will be different soon."

"If I marry Mr. Truscott?"

"Yes. It was easier for me to write that."

Harriet sighed. "Everyone has decided that I will marry Mr. Truscott, although he has yet to ask me."

"And if he asks? Will you not do this?"

"I don't know."

"I am thinking you will do it."

The effort to feign interest in the objects on the desk was unbearable, and so she faced him, the bed and his belongings between them. The light was failing, the color of his eyes already lost. Soon those fine chiselings of flesh would dissolve, leaving only his luminous outline, and by morning he would have vanished altogether. The shaft of the broom might have been a spear, the pan his shield. "I do not think I can love him."

"Perhaps it is the thing you must do. Perhaps love will come later." How much better to have left without seeing her, without this humiliation. He dropped the implements to the floor and moved around the bed to stand facing her, an arm's length away.

"What do you want from me?"

She could not miss the anger in his voice, or the sharp smell of him. It would be better for her, too, to order her thoughts in a letter, but by then he would be gone, and that was the fact that no pretty phrase would change. In this moment of bewilderment, she fastened on his imminent departure as the only certain thing, the beacon on the rocks.

"I want you to stay."

"And do what?"

"Make certain that all goes well. You know we are ruined if this thing fails."

"You could choose a safer course: let someone else manufacture those wheels."

"My father has fixed his mind on this contract. It is an obsession with him. And you have seen my ledgers. There does not seem to be much safety there."

"Mr. Stephenson . . ."

"I will make it a condition of the contract. He will not refuse, and if you are here he will be more forgiving."

"I cannot betray him. You cannot ask that."

"If you leave, you betray me. Would you do that?"

"Never." He could no longer see her face distinctly, and this moment between them had lost its boundaries. "Never." He spoke the word softly this time. It was, as she saw it, the seal of her triumph.

Making charcoal on Great Mountain

CHAPTER
FIVE

In the weeks following the arrival of Stephenson's letter, the Bigelow works came to life in a way that gave Amos Bigelow a sharp and peculiar pleasure, mixed with sadness. He remembered those glorious months, punctuated by ceremonial firings of the Bigelow Rifle, when triple shifts of workmen kept the furnaces going full blast night and day to manufacture the cannon barrels that were to be the salvation of the Union. His father, in that prime of his life, seemed not to sleep at all, and the furnaces were pillars of smoke by day and pillars of fire by night whose soaring sparks illuminated every corner of Beecher's Bridge like an endless Fourth of July.

The biblical allusion to those pillars was fixed in young Amos's mind by the sermon of the Congregational minister, delivered on the town green to all who would come, wherein he yielded to patriotic sentiment and announced that it would be more pleasing to God for this work to continue through all seasons of the year until His victory was won, through fire and flood if need be, and even on the day of rest. The priest of the other church could not be seen to be less patriotic than a Protestant, and he too found divine sanction for breaking the Sabbath. It is a curious fact, and testimony to Aaron Bigelow's powers of persuasion, that the monument on the green, erected on the very spot where this divine dispensation was announced, mentions but three casualties of the Civil War, and after 1862 not a single man from Beecher's Bridge was conscripted into the Union Army.

Harriet Bigelow knew that such a mood of celebration was premature, for the contract had not been signed. And yet she too had a stake in this new enterprise that gripped the ironworks and the town and every soul in it. How could she not respond to the happiness, the almost childlike happiness, of her father? He seemed suddenly a much younger man, not lost in his catalogues and daydreams now, but engrossed in the daily requirements and crises of the preparations: 2,280 spoked wheels for the 285 carriages at three and a quarter hundredweight of iron each—at least they were lighter than the solid wheels needed for a railroad car. Here was a task that even the cannon maker would have relished, the grandfather she had never known, and on one occasion she saw her father pause in front of that now odious photograph and square his shoulders.

From early morning until evening she was tethered to her desk, the comfortable rhythm of her life as distant as a dream. Her mornings at the gymnasium, the Tuesday evening Temperance gatherings and the Thursday afternoon reading and discussion group of the Chautauqua Circle were counted among her sacrifices; in her garden the lettuces struggled against rampant chickweed and crabgrass, coming to the table as thin and pale as if they had been grown under pots, like French asparagus. The boy she had hired to help Mrs. Evans had no talent or understanding beyond the chore of turning the compost heap. She thought of the evening in May when Toma had helped her thin the young beets and turnips, and at his suggestion she had made a dinner of the thinnings, blanched briefly and mixed with maccheroni, butter, parsley, spring onions, and hard Italian cheese. It was as if they were again in Naples, and even her father had approved of the feast, a celebration of spring. On another occasion, when the frost was gone for good, they had set out the tomato plants together, he burying the roots and laying the first few inches of stem in a horizontal trench, she tying the tops to strong stakes with the strips of old linen that she saved from one year to the next for this purpose. She remembered the perfume of bruised tomato leaves and the dew of golden oil on her hands. They told the names of every plant in the garden, she in her language and he in his, and laughed when they came to one that neither of them knew.

She missed his help now that he was gone. Where had he spent that night, and all the ones after that? When he did not appear at breakfast the next morning she went again to the carriage house and found the room swept bare except for the envelope on the table.

She saw more of Toma now than she had when he was living under her roof. He was polite, prompt, attentive, and, she thought, incredibly well informed on the arcana of iron production and metallurgy. But something about him was different. Together they sorted through the inventories and potential availability of ore, pig iron, acceptable scrap, charcoal, and limestone. In the brutal heat of early July she drew a crude map on the back of an envelope and sent him up onto the mountain to make an accurate count of the cords of seasoning hardwood to be stacked, covered with dirt, and fired. It would be a dangerous undertaking because of the heat and drought of the season, and difficult because the wood itself was not fully dry. But it would be cheaper than buying the charcoal from a supplier.

Together they made calculations of the output of the Bigelow Iron Company, under optimum conditions and under the assumption that the entire production would be directed to the cast wheels, at the expense of all wrought-iron articles and, in all likelihood, to the aggravation of some customers of long standing. Harriet had charge of the column of figures that yielded the number of tons of cast iron the plant could make in a twenty-four-hour period. This number was reduced somewhat to allow for spillage, defective castings, and the weight of metal lost in the grinding and finishing process. Then she divided by the weight of the finished wheel and multiplied, prudently and piously, by six in order to get the weekly production figure.

Toma had the easier task: he knew the number of wheels required, and the date given by Stephenson as the cut-off, and he had simply to divide the wheels by the number of weeks from start-up—a few days hence—to cut-off, and hope that the number at the bottom of his paper matched the number at the bottom of Harriet's.

A mood of playfulness overtook them, a counterweight to the solemnity of their reckoning. "I want to see your number," he said, holding the paper to his chest.

"You must show me yours."

"In your country, unlike mine, the lady must always be first, is that not so?"

"In the drawing room, yes, and at the table, or getting into a carriage.

But where there is danger, or where strength and clear thinking is required, the man must show the way. Do you not agree?" She leaned close to him, as if she were debating an impulse to kiss him, and at the last moment drew back, laughing, having snatched the paper from his hand.

Her triumph was momentary: he could see from the sag in her shoulders that the game was over. She put the two papers side by side so that he could see how many wheels or weeks had to be made up, accommodated by new calculations.

"Perhaps we have been too scrupulous in the allowances for casting. Mr. Brown is so very conservative, an old woman, I sometimes think, though it shames my sex to say so."

"Mr. Brown knows his job, and it is the precise cooling that makes the Bigelow wheel the equal of any steel from Pennsylvania. The subway cars are in service almost without stopping."

Harriet laid her nib on the part of her sheet where several calculations yielded a daily tonnage of molten iron, then made an arc and an arrow point to another corner to escape those conclusions.

"Increase this amount by twenty percent and it is done."

"Yes."

"Did you not mention, or rather read to me from a book, the almost magical effects of heating the blast of air before it enters the furnace? You showed me a picture of how it is done . . . in Pittsburgh, I think. There is our twenty percent, and more."

Toma took his pen and crossed out her figures. "That is what I thought, but both Horatio and Mr. Brown told me otherwise. You will make more iron, but the higher temperature puts impurities into the metal, and further . . . further processes are necessary to remove them again. For that, you would need new machines, a whole new plant. The quality of the product is what interests Mr. Stephenson."

"And the price," Harriet added sharply. "And the delivery schedule. I wish I had never mentioned this to my father."

Toma seemed not to notice this petulance, for he was drawing a little map in the last white space left on her sheet of paper. She recognized the river from his rendering of the falls in a few energetic strokes, then the ironworks and the canal, and finally a shape, almost a rectangle, that was endowed with lines suggesting radiance, and the number 3

"And what is that?"

"That . . ." he drew fine lines to suggest stones in his sketch, "that is furnace number 3."

"Number 3 has been plugged for forty years."

"I know, I have seen it."

"There is no wheel there, not even a flume or a race now."

"I know this also."

"Then why do you bother . . . ?"

"It is your twenty percent."

"You believe that?"

"I know it."

A WEEK LATER, on a Tuesday morning, Harriet put the finally revised Stephenson contract on her father's desk, having first cleared away some piles of paper and a few catalogues, all of which had acquired a gritty film of dust, aggressive dust that left smudges. Gathering in the necessary charcoal had been a very dirty business, involving such a traffic of wagons, and the blackened raggies made a small mountain of their product above the furnace where once the single storage shed had sufficed. Harriet's hands had not been spared: her cuticles were gray and the same tint traced the slight wrinkles at her knuckles and the creases in her palms. She had been anxious about the quality of each charcoal pit's production, and had helped Mr. Brown with his inspection as the long lines of carts arrived, usually after noon, in the cruelest heat.

She pushed the pot of ink and a pen closer to Amos Bigelow, but her mind was plowing another furrow, and her attention focused on the distraction of those gray lines. Necessary creases, she reasoned with herself, for otherwise the flesh could not bend. Still, she was displeased with what she saw, for it was an advertisement, an exaggeration of a fact that no young person can accept or even believe, except in the most abstract sense. Her hand did not lack grace, but it was large and long, lacking the delicacy of her mother's, those hands that seemed to grow more beautiful as the disease advanced on her. On her deathbed they had seemed like doves settled on the sunken chest.

No, her own hands were much more like her father's. Now he took the pen and looked into the faces of those gathered there—Horatio, Mr. Brown, and Toma—to see if they understood the significance of this moment. She looked intently at his right hand as he made his mark, at those deep crevices lined with the same soot, at the scars of old burns of his trade—her trade—and at those other brown marks that were the truest sign of age, and realized with sad astonishment that it was simply a matter of time. She determined to scrub her hands tonight, and every night, no matter how much it hurt, until they were absolutely clean.

"There," said the ironmaster, "it's done, and may God give us all the strength to carry it through to the finish. What do you say, gentlemen?"

"Amen," said Mr. Brown, in that odd squeak, as he removed his hat. Horatio nodded silently, as did Toma, who did not think it was his place to speak.

"He drives a hard bargain, my old friend Stephenson. But I guess it's fair enough. Otherwise Harriet wouldn't let me do it, would you, my dear? And you, Mr. Peacock, wouldn't still be here, working night and day as if the devil himself was standing behind you with a pitchfork. Well, boy?"

Toma caught Harriet's eye and allowed himself a brief smile.

"He's a fair man, as you say. And I know that the specifications for the cars have been made more broad because he went in person to the city council to tell them of the quality of the Bigelow wheels. He wrote this to me."

"Good, good. I'm very glad to know it." Amos Bigelow seemed pleased but in no way surprised by this mark of confidence. "And when will number 3 be up and running, Mr. Brown?"

Mr. Brown looked at Toma, and Toma in turn looked at Horatio. Brown spoke first: "Thomas—Mr. Peacock here—and the boys have her pretty well cleaned out. That was a terrible mess of iron left in there and we must have broke half a dozen drills just chipping the pieces off it. But it's coming, it's coming. We'll have the new hide on them old bellows tomorrow. The rest is up to Horatio."

Horatio's long pause may have had something to do with his not

being addressed as Mr. Washington on this occasion. But it had more
to do with his mental calculation, or recalculation, of the shafting and
gearing necessary to take the power of his wheel several hundred feet
to the refurbished furnace, of the slippages in the belting, the compro
mise in efficiency of the machinery supplying the main furnace with its
blast. "Three, maybe four days. The rest depends on the water."

Everyone in the room knew that since the night of the downpour
when the stump had been driven into the headrace, not a drop of rain
had fallen on Great Mountain.

HARRIET DID NOT THINK of herself as a deceitful person. Perhaps it
is not in human nature to entertain such thoughts; perhaps the most
practiced fabulist finds extenuations to explain each exaggeration or
violation of the truth, and even the true felon, insofar as he reflects
upon his crime, finds that the act was not representative of his nature.
Harriet was no criminal; there were several influences in her life—the
Church, the Temperance Union, the Chautauqua Circle—which encouraged reflections on one's actions, the measurement of one's
progress toward a goal of perfection or at least improvement, and these
she had embraced with her whole being. That list might also include
the admonitory presence—ghost, if you will—of her mother, for in any
situation where Harriet struggled to find the path to her own happiness, her fullest flowering, she had to contend with an all-too-lively
conception of what her mother would have wanted for her, or would
have objected to, and those arguments had a terrible power over Harriet's mind. How can one argue with a ghost?

Or two ghosts? In some ways Harriet was an orphan in this world,
her father hardly more alive than her mother, owing to his deafness,
and certainly no easier to argue with or cajole. She would always be a
child to him, even if they lived together another thirty years; time had
stopped for him at the moment of his wife's death.

Some women would have been more accepting of such a situation,
or would have thrown off the shackles and made a brutal divide between the past and some new life. Harriet did neither. she had too
great a sense of obligation to her father, too strong a yearning toward
that ruined happiness, to make any such break. And yet she was a

woman, not a child, and she had an aptitude for the workings of the world, as she had discovered to her surprise in that elbow of the iron-master's office.

As a result of negotiation with the true ghost of her mother and the living ghost of her father, Harriet had developed a system of coping with the practicalities of life. There were things that had to be done, feelings she could not deny, and to look too closely into motive, or to measure the actions against the ideal, could only lead to confusion and perhaps to a kind of paralysis.

As soon as her father had signed Mr. Stephenson's document, she placed it in the waiting envelope, and when the discussion of furnace number 3 had run its course, she made her excuses and put on her hat and gloves, leaving the men to their lunch. From the decrepit saloon that Martin McCreedy had kept for twenty-five years just across Mill Street from the entrance to the works, she had ordered hot sandwiches and a bucket of sarsparilla, but she knew, or guessed, that the sweating pail by her father's desk contained something else entirely.

Fowler Truscott, freshly shaved and smelling of the best that the barbershop had to offer, ushered her into his office in the cool stone recesses of the Iron Bank, where the necessary papers were already laid out in neat order on his desk. The room had an unused, ceremonial aspect, for with the exception of the Bigelow Company affairs, Senator Truscott's time was devoted to his political career, and the day-to-day operations were handled by the able and deferential vice president, Mr. Smyth. Harriet nodded to Mr. Smyth on her way, conquering her aversion. He knew everything there was to know—nearly everything—about the Bigelow Iron Company, and she read a menace in his pale accountant's eye that was ineffectually cloaked in servility.

"This matter is between us. That is my condition."

"Condition? Well, this is a serious sum of money."

"I should not have put it that way. What I mean is that I would like this transaction to be confidential. I place my trust in you."

"Of course you do, my dear Miss Bigelow, dear Harriet, and that is why I am here. And when the affairs of the Senate require me to be in Washington, Mr. Smyth will—"

"It would relieve my mind greatly to deal only with you, as you have responded to my trust. I do not think that Mr. Smyth can have the same attitude or delicacy, which is what prompted me to speak rashly of a condition. Of course it is you who are acting so generously toward my father, and it is your right, not mine, to speak of conditions."

"Mr. Smyth has many other matters to attend to," said Fowler Truscott, with a broad smile that embraced every nuance of this conversation. "This matter, unusual as it may be, will be our concern alone, our secret, though surely an honorable one."

This honorable secret, touched on in the contract and explicated more fully in the papers on Truscott's desk, might be summed up as Stephenson's prepaid insurance policy against the failure or inability of the Bigelow Iron Company to deliver all the wheels on the agreed date. Stephenson, who faced penalties and considerable inconvenience should he fail to complete the cars on time, had required an escrow deposit of ten thousand dollars, which, steeply prorated for the number of wheels in default, would be available to compensate him for breach of the contract. This sum of money must come from some other source than the ready cash reserves of the Bigelow Iron Company, and Fowler Truscott seemed ready, even eager, to put the bank's money at risk.

"Now then, my dear, to business." Senator Truscott drew a visitor's chair to sit by Harriet's side, an informality that spared them having to confront one another across that expanse of red leather, tooled and gilded around the border. He was a large man, particularly so when seated, and he towered above her as he leaned close to place the papers where she could read and then sign them.

"I must ask, first, if you have considered all the terms laid out by Mr. Stephenson. These documents are very thorough indeed, and quite out of the ordinary for business in Beecher's Bridge. Your father has read them all?"

"Yes, of course. We have spent a great deal of time going over all this, and Mr. Stephenson, on his part, has gone to some lengths in order to direct this business to the Bigelow Iron Company. He has shown great confidence in us."

"And you can do it? This is a great number of wheels." He laid his hand on hers to emphasize the gravity of the negotiation.

She turned to look up into his face, hanging there like an expectant moon.

"We can do it, Senator Truscott, and we will do it." The grip on her hand tightened in reassurance, and Senator Truscott leaned closer, as if this important moment might be sealed by something more than a handshake. "And as you are aware, we have taken the precaution of re-opening the old furnace, number 3, which will yield more than the required additional capacity. The answer was right there under our noses, but it was Toma—"

"Who?"

"Thomas Peacock, the young man who drove me to your house."

"Indeed. Your chauffeur?" The features of Truscott's face registered both tolerance and amusement.

"Yes, he was, for a period, our driver, but he is in fact Mr. Stephenson's trusted employee, and he has done most of the work, the physical labor of freeing number 3 from the forest and from the bloom of old iron that had blocked it for all these years."

"A foreign fellow, as I remember." Truscott sat back in his chair.

"Yes, foreign. We met under the most unlikely circumstances years ago in Italy, and then again in New York, quite recently."

"I would not have guessed Italian, such a tall, well-set young man, quite fierce in his appearance."

"A Montenegrin," said Harriet, rolling the word in her mouth the way Toma had taught her to do so long ago. "He is very ambitious, and very scholarly too."

"The point, I take it, is that he has the quick perception and the broad back that are the necessary foundations of so many great American enterprises, or, in this case, the rebirth of an old and honorable one." Senator Truscott perceived the raw material of a speech here, or at least a new ingredient to flavor his usual offering. He would mull it over this afternoon on the train ride to New Haven, where he was to meet with the Elk's Club and the Manufacturer's Association before dining with his old friend and classmate, the president of Yale. The creak of her chair brought him back to the business at hand.

"This must all be enormously gratifying to your father, to whom you will please remember me."

"I will."

"And you have discussed all of this with him?"

"Of course," said Harriet, coloring slightly. "He would have come himself but for all the pressing arrangements at the works."

"I cannot regret his absence. Here then," and he put a document in front of her, which she signed as Harriet Bigelow, Vice President of the Bigelow Iron Company.

"It is our secret," he said, and in spite of her reservations, she allowed him to kiss her.

WHEN HE HAD FIRST seen furnace number 3 Toma had not recognized it for what it was. It had been his habit, during those weeks when he was studying the ironworks by day and reading his texts on metallurgy and hydromechanics far into the night, to clear his head by walking the old canal when the noon whistle sounded. It was a vigorous walk, for there was no clear path; the waterway, now dry, was choked with the mint green of new brambles and saplings of maple and beech as big around as his forearm. On one occasion, his mind entranced by the complexities of imaginary gearings and waterwheels, he reached the very end of the canal, where the great stones were lapped by the spring runoff of the river, and he saw a face like a ghost staring at him from the window of the last building, where the canal had become a midden of old bottles and bobbins of thread. This was the silk mill, and the face in the window, he now knew, was Olivia's.

It was a sedentary life he had led in this place, compared to the brutalities of tunnel work or shop labor in New York. His job consisted of reading books and inspecting things, a daily ebb and flow of the theoretical and the practical. He was always ready to lend a hand, whether in the Bigelows' garden or when castings or pieces of equipment had to be moved at the works, but though his willing strength may have impressed the stokers and teamsters, he felt himself going slack from inactivity. Hence the regimen of this energetic walk, and hence, when the limb of a tree presented itself at a convenient height, the exercise of pulling himself up so that his chin touched the bark. Thirty, fifty, even a hundred times during the course of his ramble. There was no shortage of trees here, and the pleasure of physical exhaustion was an antidote to the circularities of thought that infected his mind.

It was at the end of one such walk that Toma stopped by a maple at the top of the canal, and he was determined to push himself beyond the limit he had achieved previously. On the thirty-fourth instance, which would bring his total to one hundred and fourteen, Toma hung for a long moment with his chin on the branch, wondering if he could pull himself up once more. His eyes had been focused only on the branch, willing it toward him, but now through a gap in the leaves directly ahead he saw the massive stones and tapering profile, a tower of some description that reminded him in that instant of the ruin at the edge of the Sandžak where he and Harwell, the English, as he had called him, had taken refuge from the pursuing hussars. He let himself down from the branch; the strength was gone from his arms, his mind was full of wonder.

When he stood at the foot of this tower it was still difficult to make out exactly what it was. He guessed it to be about the height of the canal's retaining walls, but sumac saplings had rooted so freely in the crevices of rock that he could not get a good view of the top. When he worked his way to the downhill side and saw the casting arch he knew it for a furnace, an older, dwarfed version of the main furnace in the works just a few hundred feet off through the thick undergrowth. He could hear the voices of the workers against the clang of the trip-hammer and the deep rhythm of the compressors.

He made a circuit of the furnace, saw that the rough fieldstone was held in place by rusted iron plates and tie-rods from corner to corner. Stepping back to get a fuller view of the construction, he staggered and lost his footing, falling backward into the old race, now a choked ditch, and was saved from a serious injury by catching a sapling in his left hand. A few yards farther into the brush he found the remains of the old waterwheel collapsed into planks and struts, and the ruin of the bellows, where the shreds of blackened leather clung to the frame, nailed there like the rotting pelts of so many small animals. There were other foundations here as well, whose timbers and boards, he guessed, had been scavenged for use in the newer outbuildings of the forge. Under a thick matting of bindweed, just beginning to bloom, he found the slag heaps, one comprising some broken pigs of cast iron and forge scrap, the other, much larger, a muted rainbow of glasslike lumps and shards, the most arresting of which were a green the color of sea foam, or cobalt shot with marblings of pure white. In such beauty were the impurities of silica, phosphorus, and sulphur drawn from the ore by the fire and the limestone.

He made his way back to the works a little dazed by what he had found, by those relics that reminded him of the primitive furnaces and forges of his own land, where iron had been extracted and shaped, first into spear points and swords, later into crude firearms, to do battle against the advancing might of the Ottoman Empire. But he did notice one other curiosity on this day of discovery: at the top of the failed canal, a stone's throw away from the works, a pool of water had collected behind a plug of stones, trash, and brush. Knowing the sorry history of the canal, he was puzzled by this little body of water that seemed permanent enough to have its own modest growth of weeds. Just above the water level on the wall opposite, he noted the dark line of what looked like tar. He gave it no more thought. The fate of the old furnace seemed to him a more compelling mystery.

On a Sunday, Toma borrowed an axe from the tool shed at the works and, laboring alone, to no clear purpose, he cleared the ruin from the clutch of the forest. When he was finished, it stood in the sunlight of the clearing like a bizarre planter, for the sumac saplings still flourished in its cracks and made a wreath of green at its brow.

By making inquiries among the older workmen, he learned the identity of the furnace and the circumstances of its demise. Business had been down in the recession of '74, and furnace number 3, already some fifty years old, needed to be relined and fitted with a new wheel. Since the new furnace could meet the demand for iron in those hard times, number 3 was abandoned. Could it be used? he asked Horatio. Nothing much wrong with it, was the reply, but clearing the race and building a new wheel and power train was a labor of months. Horatio looked at him impassively: he was used to Toma asking questions whose point escaped him. And suppose the power train from your wheel could be extended to number 3: would it drive the bellows? Horatio was silent for a moment. It might do, he said at last, but you'd be pushing it, losing power all the way with the belts or gearing, whatever way you did it. Think about it, Mr. Washington, if you would be kind enough, and we will talk about this matter again.

Toma collected his information in small pieces and made his calculations of what would be needed to put number 3 back into production. The foundation of the casting shed was still intact, and only a roof of light construction would be needed there: the Stephenson job would be finished, one way or another, long before the true cold set in. An old roadway between the old furnace and the works would have to be cleared, and the trestle from the top of the charging wall rebuilt so that the ore, limestone, and charcoal could be fed into the top of the stack. Above the charging wall the old spur from the railway line seemed serviceable: the rusted iron rails ran straight and true through the brush on a shaped bed of the same slag he had found in the heap below.

The greatest challenge would be to remove the salamander of iron and slag that had hardened within the furnace the day it had shut down. Several tons of material must be removed by drilling and fracturing, or the whole hearth and base of the furnace would have to be dismantled and rebuilt, a job that would require weeks to accomplish.

Once he had Harriet's approval, Toma attacked the salamander. While his recruits cleared access to the furnace and began construction on the trestle, he worked with a twelve-pound sledge and the long drills from morning to evening for two days, every so often changing places with the boy who held the drill and turned it a few degrees on each stroke. For the first two days the job seemed an impossibility, and a few chunks of the salamander were all he had to show for such backbreaking work. The men on the trestle and at the edge of the clearing would pause from time to time to marvel at the fury of those blows: work like that could kill a man, no matter how young or how strong.

But time and the slow drip of water from the open top of the furnace had done their work on the salamander too, and at noon on the third day Toma's drill found a deep flaw. The ring of the drill was muted, and with two more strokes the mass inside the furnace cracked roughly in half and settled several inches, exposing further veins and avenues of attack. By four o'clock the furnace was entirely cleared of the debris, and Mr. Brown took a candle inside through the casting arch and pronounced the firebrick sound enough; only a patch of a half dozen bricks would be necessary before firing the furnace. Horatio Washington offered Toma his congratulations and invited him to come home to the silk mill for dinner and some whiskey. But Toma declined, saying his arms were too tired to lift a fork or a glass. He thanked Horatio and hoped he might accept on another occasion, perhaps when the first iron flowed in a red river from number 3 to the molds in the casting shed. He made his way to the drummers' hotel, where he slept for sixteen hours.

THE ARRIVAL OF Amos Bigelow's niece, Lucy, was an inconvenient joy to her cousin. Lucy's mother, the ironmaster's only sibling, had married well—Mr. Morris owned a complex of spinning mills in Utica—and so had escaped the pall that settled on Beecher's Bridge and her family when the old ironmaster made his spectacular exit. Lucy was a few months older than Harriet and had been the dearest friend of her otherwise lonely childhood. They had not seen each other for two years.

The Morrises were very rich, at least in Harriet's perception, and although Uncle Henry had not managed to return to Beecher's Bridge since the day of his wedding, Aunt Rebecca had been a regular visitor, and sent Harriet extravagant presents at Christmas and on her birthday, shawls and fine gloves that made her other clothes seem dingy. Two years ago, on her eighteenth birthday, Harriet had received an elaborately articulated diamond-and-platinum pendant on a velvet choker that had belonged to her grandmother. It lay in a leather case in her top drawer, and whenever Harriet opened the box she thought of her mother, who would have worn the necklace with such delight.

Harriet knew nothing of society beyond Beecher's Bridge, though the trip to Italy would have been a starting point or cornerstone to a different life, had her mother not died, had the affairs of the ironworks flourished in the way the Morris mills had. If . . . If . . . . Harriet had developed an aversion to this word that had such power over her life.

Lucy, on the other hand, knew all about society, having made her debut in Utica and attended the cotillions in New York City. Her letter, which scarcely left time to reply, was an announcement of her intention to visit Beecher's Bridge on her way up to Lenox, where she would be staying for a week at a very grand house party, to be joined there over the weekend by her fiancé. In the meantime, the heat of

Manhattan was unbearable to the point where she could not make any decisions about her wedding, or the dress, or the silver pattern, and so she would leave all that in Mama's hands and escape to her dear cousin in the hills of northwest Connecticut.

Such prattle, thought Harriet, with affection for the girl she used to know. She was a little envious of the ease of her cousin's existence: she wished she could abandon the decisions in her own life so carelessly to another, if only for a while. But the letter was stark proof of how their lives had diverged, and the advantages did not all reside on Lucy's side of the ledger. Could she imagine herself spending a week in Lenox, making the slow circuits of the garden with the other young women and wearing her jewel to dinner for the pleasure of her fiancé? Such refined and exquisite boredom. She tried hard to picture the face of the fiancé. Well, Lucy would tell her all about that, she was quite sure.

It seemed impossible that she and Lucy had, such a short while ago, seemed like sisters, or twins, or even the same being in two bodies. The identity of impulse and experience had been the bond willed by both: if Lucy had read *Little Women*, then Harriet must too. Each copied the other's tricks of fastening or braiding the hair, and for a few months they attempted, by letter, to coordinate their souls in the matter of addressing the Almighty.

The mention of the great house in Lenox set Harriet to worrying what Lucy would find to do in Beecher's Bridge and what she would think of such plain accommodations: no tennis court, no crème brûlée, no servants other than Mrs. Evans and the girl who came in to clean twice a week.

She would clear out the top three drawers and leave this sunny, pleasant room to Lucy, taking a single bed in the guest room. It was only three days: Mrs. Evans's cooking couldn't do much harm in three days. She would have to make time for the Chautauqua Circle, as a diversion for Lucy, and as for the rest of the day, when she must be at the works, well, there were a great many books in the library.

When she had written her reply, Harriet moved her clothes to the guest room and cut some Queen Anne's lace and larkspur for the bull's-eye glass pitcher on the table in the hall. Tonight she would find time to straighten up the rest of the house.

On the basis of Lucy's letter, and because she had not seen her for two years, Harriet had imagined a trajectory for Lucy's personality and appearance that fell quite wide of the mark. There was no awkwardness between them at all, but a great deal of talking, often at the same time as they struggled to find the rhythm of their old exchange. Lucy did not dominate the conversation with details of her own doings or of New York society, but seemed most interested in what had happened in Beecher's Bridge since her last visit. The ironmaster was very pleased to see his niece again, now grown into such a handsome young woman—beautiful, Harriet would have said, in all sincerity—and if Lucy did provide details on her adventures in New York with her mother, it was at Mr. Bigelow's suggestion, his reiterated suggestion, because he wanted to hear every word. Yes, she was beautiful, and Harriet was relieved to find that she did not in the least resent it.

The invitation to dine at Senator Truscott's came as a gift out of the blue to Harriet, for Thursday was an impossibly busy day, and dinner at home would have been anybody's guess. The Chautauqua Circle had gone well enough: Harriet arrived just in time from the ironworks, braking the Packard to a halt and plowing furrows in the pebbles of the Hatchers' drive. Lucy listened to the discussion of *Uncle Tom's Cabin* with an attentive, fixed expression. Afterward, Harriet drove Lucy home and returned to the works to learn that Toma and his crew had cleared the salamander from furnace number 3.

They've done it, was what she heard, and knew exactly what was meant. She stepped out onto the newly cleared road to intercept Toma and was taken aback by his appearance: shirtless, sweating, blackened by soot, flecked with the shrapnel of iron and shards of exploded slag. Some of those glassy fragments had opened wounds so that the sweat running down his chest was tinged with pink, and he carried one shoulder higher than the other.

"Thank you, Toma, thank you," she said as he passed. He smiled at her but did not speak, seemed intent on the single task of walking. "Will you be all right?" She wondered what had become of his shirt, did not like to think of him walking through the works and on to the drummers' hotel as a sort of spectacle. He would need a shirt. He needed someone with water and a cloth and deft fingers to pull those slivers, for the slag would splinter and the wounds might fester. She walked a few paces beside him, her handkerchief useless in her hand, and knew she could do nothing. "Thank you, Toma. Sleep well."

There would be time for a bath if she hurried her father along, and if Mrs. Evans had remembered to make a small fire in the stove to heat those pipes. She thought with a sinking heart of Lucy's new perspective on the bathroom, with that green-and-brown oilcloth on the floor—a desperate attempt at a floral pattern—and those crude pipes jutting through the wainscot below her mother's wallpaper. Lucy had been to Newport, where there were three gleaming taps for each bath: one for hot water, one for cold, and one for water drawn up from the sea.

Her bath was cold, as Lucy's had been, and they laughed about it. More time to dress, said Lucy as she helped Harriet lace her stays.

"Will you wear this?" she asked, pointing to the jeweler's box she had found in the top drawer. "Tonight sounds like a special occasion, and I don't think anyone would be surprised if you *did* wear it. How old do you think he is?" Harriet did not know, had not yet entered into the finer calculations of a relationship that was neither definite nor wholly desired. "If he should by any chance propose to you this evening, you must look your best."

Harriet's best turned out to be more Lucy's idea than her own, and Lucy's clothes too, the black velvet discreetly pruned here and there, and noticeably short to the wearer's eye. Don't worry about it, was her cousin's advice, he won't notice anything but this. She took the pendant from its case, and Harriet saw that the velvets of ribbon and dress were perfectly matched.

Senator Truscott's frank admiration of her appearance, expressed to her father and then to Lucy, did nothing to improve Harriet's mood. What is wrong with me? she wondered. They were the only guests; there was no crowd of constituents or important persons to distract Truscott's attention, no other agenda than the celebration of this moment that had such an odd feel to it, an expectant awkwardness in which her father and Lucy seemed to know their roles. Standing in the library with her glass of iced tea, Harriet felt a prickling in her neck where Lucy had drawn up the hair so the choker and its brilliant pendant might show to better advantage. Had Lucy put her finger on it?

Was this the night? Lucy had experience in such matters, whereas she knew nothing at all.

When they sat down to dinner, Harriet was surprised to find her card at the end of the table rather than the side, so that she was facing her host down that long display of candles and old silver as if she were already the lady of the house. Her sense of unease was raised another notch and she distracted herself by admiring Lucy's hands and the perfection of that ring in the candlelight. Truscott deferred to her father when it came time to say a grace over the chilled Sénégalèse, and after taking a moment to compose his thoughts, the Ironmaster asked for blessings on this house and on the whole town, and on all the inhabitants thereof, concluding with a plea that the Lord should see fit to make rain.

As the fish course was being served, Truscott gave an instruction to the maid, who reappeared with a bottle of champagne wrapped in linen. Harriet was surprised, but she allowed her flute to be filled. Her father declined, saying that water was good enough for him. Lucy was delighted by the champagne, and by Truscott's courtliness. Her merry eyes flashed from one end of the table to the other, as if willing this connection. Truscott tasted his champagne and nodded to Lucy. To Harriet he made his apology.

"I thought we might make an exception to the rule on this special occasion."

He raised his glass to her and offered a toast to the continued good fortune of the ironworks and to the wise management of that operation. He assured his guests that the financial resources of the Iron Bank along with whatever political influence he might possess were all at the disposal of the Bigelow enterprise. It was a difficult undertaking; but risks and Herculean labor were necessary to any ambition, and he was sure they would prevail. He paused and drank.

"And if I might continue on a more personal note . . ."

This he might have done had not Harriet seized the floor with an account of Toma's heroic success in clearing furnace number 3. When she paused for breath she saw a look of puzzlement on Fowler Truscott's face, amusement on Lucy's.

"To the ironworks, then, and to Herculean labors," she said by way of recovery, and drank off a good deal of her own glass.

The conversation never did return to the personal note that Senator Truscott had intended, but his disappointment might have been tempered by observing how animated a conversationalist Harriet became with that swallow of champagne and with the succeeding sips.

Home at last after this very full day, Harriet had turned down the bed and was brushing out her hair when she heard Lucy call out to her.

"Cousin, you are not to leave me alone in this bed. There is loads of room for us both, just as there always was." It was true that they had always shared the same bed wherever they happened to be, and bed was the place where secrets were told. Harriet would rather have kept her thoughts to herself tonight, but it would be silly to make a fuss over such a thing, and unfriendly too.

She settled herself on her side of the bed and without thinking put her arm under Lucy's pillow. This was how the housekeeper used to find them in the morning, after they had talked and read the night away: Harriet on her back and making a whisper of a snore, Lucy curled on her side, pillowed by her cousin's arm.

"I know you did it on purpose."

"What could you be thinking of?" It was no use: Lucy knew her too well, and she felt the beginning of a smile.

"You know very well that Senator Truscott was on the point of proposing marriage to you." Lucy turned her head to study Harriet's face, then tickled her. "You faker . . . admit it!"

"Yes, yes! No, stop, or I shall go away to the other bed and leave you to your nightmares. I just didn't want it to happen. He kissed me."

"Where? I mean when?"

"The other day, in his office. And he didn't ask me, he just did it."

"Well," said Lucy, reflecting on her own broader experience, "it has to start somewhere, and the responsibility does seem to fall heavily upon them. Cecil had to be guided to the mark, though he does it very well now."

"Lucy! I mean you haven't told me a thing, and now . . ."

"I'll tell you all about him later. He's nice, and I'm sure you'll like him. It's just that he's not very interesting in the abstract. Maybe when he's older and has made a success of his career, or, I don't know, been to Africa."

"You mean like Senator Truscott?"

"Well, it was fascinating, the bit about the water buffalo and all the natives falling down and running away, and only President Roosevelt's shot, at the very last minute, to save him. Do you think every word was quite true?"

"Dear Lucy, perhaps it is you who should be marrying Senator Truscott, and give me Cecil, or nobody at all. Something was wrong tonight, and I don't think I can bear to talk about it any more just now."

"Oh, you'll sleep on it and everything will come out right. Anyway, what I really want to know is who this Toma fellow is. He sounds to me like a character from Grimm: desperate and heroic and doomed. And you did positively glow when you were talking about him."

IT WAS A CONVERSATION that could not be exhausted in the course of a single night, unless they were prepared to sleep the following morning away, and Harriet, mindful of all the things waiting on her desk, retreated drowsily before Lucy's cogent questions and concerns, yielding ground to experience and common sense, saying at last—Oh, I'm sure you're right . . . and you are so kind to worry on my behalf. But we'll talk about it tomorrow night, after you have seen him. She fell asleep as she was saying these words, and in her dream the dinner party was replayed, with the dramatic revision of Toma's entrance, an uninvited guest but not unexpected, and when he took her hand and asked her to marry him, no one was surprised.

Meeting Toma in the flesh did not produce the anticipated effect on Cousin Lucy, who arrived at the ironworks shortly after noon, as Harriet had suggested. Toma did not show up until one o'clock. Harriet had been keeping an eye out for him through the long morning at her ledgers, and with Lucy there, admiring the cunning space and seated in Toma's chair, Harriet made an attempt to hide her concern under a show of busywork.

"I won't say a word," said Lucy, and proceeded to make conversation as if someone else had uttered the vow of silence. Harriet bent her head to the ledger and felt an odd sensation in her stomach that she attributed to hunger. Lucy broke off in mid-sentence: "I don't suppose this could be him coming along now."

The window gave onto the dusty yard, which allowed Harriet to keep an eye on the daily routine of the works, the flow of deliveries and expedited goods. As soon as she saw Toma she had a premonition of awkwardness. His face was set in an uncharacteristic expression of ill humor, and there was something about his gait that suggested pain, or the sudden onset of age. Before a word was spoken she began to formulate excuses and lines of defense.

Lucy talked too much and too brightly, Toma hardly at all. He would not eat lunch with them, even though Harriet had sent out for his favorite sandwich of pot-roasted beef. He had no appetite, he explained, for in addition to his great fatigue, he had seen the newspaper in the general store, and the headlines told of the assassination of an Austrian archduke, the crown prince himself, by a conspiracy of criminal Serbs in the city of Sarajevo.

"Sarajevo!" said Lucy with emphasis. "It doesn't sound like a real place at all. Wherever do you suppose it is?" She caught a look on Toma's face that almost silenced her. "Well, I have, of course, heard of Austria, so I suppose this must be something serious."

"Serious, yes. Serious." Toma had turned away from Lucy to gaze at the dust in the yard. "There must be a war. It is what the Austrians want, and now they have their excuse. I would say it is very serious."

"Will you . . . ?"

"No. There is nothing to be done yet, here or there. My friend Harwell will write to me if he can, and I will ask him for news of my people."

There were desultory attempts to lift Toma's gloom, but for the most part the cousins ate their sandwiches in silence, ashamed of their hunger. His distraction gave Harriet the opportunity to study his face as if from behind a screen or through a knothole. Lucy's words, so gaily spoken, came back to her: desperate, heroic, doomed. Never had she felt such empathy for him; never had she felt so far removed.

They retired to bed that night after an early supper. The heat had taken all appetite away, and Amos Bigelow declared that a week of dining with Senator Truscott would kill him. Now, even with the windows wide open and the candles snuffed, the bedroom was oppressive. Harriet was conscious of a sheen of perspiration, a dampening of her sheerest nightgown. They had come to bed not to sleep but to talk.

"He is, it must be admitted, a striking presence." Lucy's words hung in the dark, close air. She giggled. "The strong, silent type, I suppose."

"It was just that he was so tired, and I think he may have hurt himself. And that wretched business in the papers."

"My dear, he's positively monosyllabic. I'm sure I've never met a man with more limited conversation. And on top of it all, I had the distinct impression that he was judging me. Did you see how he turned his back on me?"

"You must make allowances, Lucy; he is not as he seemed today, and I'm sure he likes you."

"That's the silliest thing I have ever heard you say. Ever, ever. There is only one explanation: you are in love."

"I am not."

"Oh, for heaven's sake, Harriet, do you think I wasn't watching? You had calf eyes for him as he sat there and brooded."

"What are they?" asked Harriet, hoping to distract her cousin.

"You know, going all soft inside, lapping up his every word, and looking at him in . . . in invitation."

"Lucy!"

"I'm just telling you how it looked to me, and I think someone must bring you to your senses. Think what you'd be throwing away."

By way of rebuttal, Harriet drew out from under the mattress an envelope that was beginning to show signs of wear and lit her candle. She read to Lucy from Toma's farewell. Not the whole letter, of course, but the paragraph in which he wished her well and spoke in praise of the senator, framing it as a gentle valedictory to his own fallen hopes. Harriet thought the passage was quite exquisite; it reminded her of something she had read, an English writer, perhaps an essayist, though she could not put a name to him.

"That's all very pretty, but I think he's making my point for me, advancing the senator's cause."

"Dear Lucy, I don't want anyone making up my mind for me, not even you. I don't think you can quite see how I feel."

As if responding to a challenge, Lucy reached across and took the candle, holding it close to Harriet's face. Harriet strangled a shriek as the splash of hot wax struck her breast, burning her through the voile.

"Has *he* kissed you as well?" Harriet flushed and could not answer.

"Well, he has, then. You're not fooling me for a minute." Lucy blew out the candle and Harriet drew a long breath in the dark.

After a minute or so, during which Harriet imagined that she was to be abandoned to a sleepless vigil, Lucy spoke again, all sternness gone. "I want you to tell me everything. Will you do that?" Harriet's tongue stuck to the roof of her mouth. She made no reply. "Then it must be worse than I thought, almost," and here Lucy gave a throaty little laugh of complaisance, "almost like that boy in Italy who—"

"Lucy, for the sake of our friendship, do be quiet. Toma *is* the boy from Italy. That is all you need to know."

There was another silence now, and Harriet, having opened the floodgate in her own mind, was afraid that she might, this once, have imposed her will on Lucy. There was something funny about the way she was breathing.

"Lucy?"

Lucy had been weeping, trying to hold it in, and she gave way now to her feelings. She threw her arm over Harriet and buried her face in the pillow, with the result that Harriet was suffocated in the mass of blond hair. Lucy sat up.

"Oh, it's much too hot for this." She was half sobbing and half laughing as she said this. "I can't believe it, Harriet. It's like a novel, a bad novel, I hope."

"Why bad?"

"Because in the good novels everybody ends up dead or unhappy, and in the bad ones . . . do you see? That's why I read the bad ones. And I don't want you to be unhappy. I couldn't bear that. I feel so stupid not remembering that name. I should have known all along."

"It doesn't do any good for you to worry about me. Maybe I'll have a perfectly ordinary life."

"Has he kissed you again, I mean here?"

"Yes."

"Oh, Harriet. I don't think poor Senator Truscott stands a chance. It will be a terrible shock to him."

"Lucy, nothing is happening. It was just once, and it won't happen again."

"I hope you're right, and you must be sure not to let it happen again. The third time would seal it, I think. There would be no going back."

Harriet stared into the dark for a long time. Lucy, fast asleep, lay against her like an ember, and those warnings were like beacons in her mind, leading her to try such disaster and disgrace in the fire of her imagination. Distant flashes lit the sky, and she thought she could drowse off to the sound of rain on the roof. But there was no storm, no echo of thunder, only the distant lightning that kept her from sleep, and much later the whistle of the freight that woke her.

FURNACE NUMBER 3 was charged with charcoal, limestone, and a carload of the Salisbury hematite early the next morning, and by six-thirty P.M., with shadows of tall pines giving some relief to the sweltering workers and the crowd of onlookers, Mr. Brown satisfied himself that the iron—the first batch in forty years—was ready for the casting. Ever a cautious man, he would have preferred to run the first iron off into sows and pigs so that he could be certain of the quality. It was, to him, a new furnace, and any new furnace had its quirks. He wanted the first wheels, and all the wheels, to be perfect. There was the difference of working with the cooler blast to be considered, and the delicacy of achieving the desired degree of hardness, 4 or 4 ½, no more.

But Harriet, with an eye to her inventories and her schedule, persuaded him otherwise. Think of your long experience, Mr. Brown: I have absolute confidence in your abilities. And Horatio added a few words in support of this boldness, though he was less mindful of the foreman's excellence than of the dwindling resource of water and of the fragility of his improvised power train. There had been no time or money to invest in the piping to recycle the hot gases from the stack as was done in the main furnace, but it was known that the slower and less efficient cold-blast furnace yielded the best iron.

The men on the day shift had stayed to see the hearth unplugged and the river of iron run down the sand channel into the casting shed to the waiting molds. No matter how many years a man had been on the job, no matter how tired he was, there was something about the runoff that held his attention as if he were still a boy. The power of that incandescent flow, heralded by a spray of sparks like a comet when the furnace was tapped. How may times had the story been told about the fellow—not here but at a furnace just down the river or over the mountain—who had tripped and fallen across the casting channel, and had lost his arm. Or was it his face? And the mystery of it too, for you never knew for sure what was happening inside the furnace until the plug was tapped.

Mr. Brown, dour fellow that he was, had still some sense of ceremony about these few minutes. The last of the slag was tapped and run off. As it cooled into volutes and spirals of rough glass, he inspected those forms and hues as would a priest the entrails of the sacrifice. When the iron itself was tapped, he attended to the flickering spectrum, read there the traces of those elements that would determine the properties of this particular batch. He nodded his head, satisfied that disaster had been averted.

Toma stood apart from the crew and the townspeople with his back to a white pine. He couldn't hear much over the wheeze of the bellows, but he could see how the onlookers were enveloped in a tide of happiness: backs slapped, hands shaken, pint bottles passed covertly from one pocket to another. This should have been his celebration too, but in the rush of heat and light from the breached furnace he saw only war and death, for this morning, on his way to the works, he had passed by the telegraph office in the depot to hear the news. Sometime in the night the Austrian troops had crossed the border into the Kingdom of Serbia, implementing Plan Yellow, the general mobilization that Harwell had told him about long ago, and by now, for all he knew, they might be at the walls of Belgrade.

He was thinking, then, not of wheels and inventories but of what he must do. Somewhere, back across the sea, boys younger than he were marching through the night or peering over some parapet, imagining the might of Austria that the dawn would reveal. It was his war. Was there not an invisible thread held in the same hand with which Aliye had killed herself, turning first around his mother and the Austrian captain he had slain and now around all those young men yet to die? Harwell, who had brought him through the valley of death on their escape from the Sandžak, from the Austrians, had told him, on the basis of certain and secret knowledge, that the tinderbox of the Balkans, had wanted only the one spark, and now, six years later, another Serb had killed his Austrian.

Surrounded by his ghosts, Toma stared unseeing at the celebration and was surprised by a touch on his arm. Harriet had come to be with him, and stood with her back to his tree. Was she too a ghost? Did she hold in her hand the other end of Aliye's thread?

Feeling his gaze on her, she turned to him. He took her hand and she let him do it, though it was not yet dark.

"I am sorry I cannot stay, but I must take my father home. He has been worrying himself, and this excitement is draining him. But perhaps I could . . ."

"Yes," he said, and saw that it was a mistake to anticipate her thought, for with no visible motion she withdrew from him.

"What I meant, what I would ask, is if you could use your influence on this celebration. See how those dreadful bottles are passed around. Remind them, please, that we must work tomorrow."

In spite of her tone, Harriet walked away from him with such a lingering step that he thought she had more to say, or would turn to look back. But she did neither of these; only her gait betrayed her indecision.

When she had vanished down the dark tunnel of the road to the works with her father, Toma relaxed his shoulders, then stretched. He still felt the effects of his violent labor, but the deep ache in his bones was reassuring to him. He wandered away from the tree, glad for the company of living men, and instead of following his instructions found himself partaking of those offered bottles, the rough whiskey another defense against ghosts and regret.

There was no general drunkenness this evening—the furnace men were not so dissolute as Harriet feared—and Toma felt only contentment as he moved away from the furnace to make water. The stars were bright and near in the black sky, and they seemed almost to flicker at him, for at each resounding groan of the bellows, a column of flame and sparking cinders flew up from the stack and bleached away the firmament.

The slag pile was as old as the furnace, and so concealed in brambles and the eager vines of bindweed that its exact extent could not be determined. In the clearing and rehabilitation of furnace number 3 the contours of the heap had been pushed back, and the glassy chunks, rounded and softened by time, were broken into new forms by rough handling. It was one of these, a dagger of cobalt shot with green streaks, that Toma now stepped on. It slid through the sole of his boot and on through the foot.

Toma fell backward onto the slag, receiving other wounds to his back and scalp. When he was found—and he was lucky to be heard between wheezes of the bellows—it was not immediately apparent what had happened, for the pain so bound his tongue that he was not coherent. Looks like he's been shot, said someone, and Horatio was called for.

"Jesus Christ," said Horatio, "will you look at that. Don't touch it!" The flaming light of the furnace caught the tip of the shard where it had split the tongue of the boot and cut the laces. Toma had recovered his senses somewhat and tried to rise, but Horatio held him down.

"You stand on that and you're going to feel a whole lot worse."

"The hotel . . . Mr. Wright will help me."

"And how is he going to help you, except maybe help you lose the whole damned foot, and then you won't be any use at all." Ignoring Toma's protests, Horatio detailed two burly furnace men to carry the injured man down to the silk mill

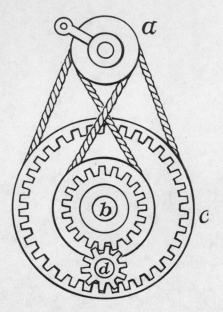

A planetary motion. Revolution of a pinion around its own center and also around the common center of two externally centered gears. a, driving pulley with cross band to gear pulley b, and direct band to gear pulley c. The differential motion revolves the pinion D around its own axis and around its external axis b.

Weeping wounds *Although clean lint is the dressing of choice for any wound, bog moss may be used if properly prepared. Moss should be dried, picked clean, and thoroughly steamed or passed through a solution of corrosive sublimate. When dry—a sterile mangle may be used—moss may be stored for future use. Do not allow moss to touch the wound, but use it as a thick layer between inner and outer windings of muslin, where it will readily absorb any suppuration. Change dressing when saturated or crusted. Muslin may be boiled for 10 minutes and dried. Do not reuse moss. See page 47 for Comfey Leaf Ointment, and page 59 for various Spermaceti Salves.*

—from Ransome's Herbal Remedies, 1867

CHAPTER

SIX

The Royal Victory Hotel
Belgrade, Serbia
18 July 1914

Thomas Peacock
c/o Bigelow
Iron Hill
Beecher's Bridge, Connecticut
United States of America

My Dear Toma:

As Chapman puts it:

"O 'tis a most praise-worthy thing when messengers can tell
(Besides their messages) such things as fit th' occasion well."

In the evenings, having nothing better to do, I distract myself by attempting my own translation of Homer. I am satisfied that my rendering is an improvement on Chapman's accuracy, but I do not have his ear, his musical gift, and so I yield to him here.

Lydia has not been able to travel with me to Belgrade because of her confinement, so I am a bachelor again, though soon to be a father. Thank God she is not in this place. At least she was able to forward your letter of 20 May. I am certain she has already written you with news of your father's and your sister's health.

Hearing from you makes me long for simpler times, but perhaps the attraction of the past is that it is over, and we can make of it what we will. Uncertainty often seems more terrible than any known grief or pain, and this moment in Belgrade answers that description.

You will have read in the papers how Gavrilo Princip, ineptitude notwithstanding, managed to dispatch the Archduke Ferdinand to his eternal reward.

What you may not have heard or read is the confession wrung out of Princip by his captors, the details of the investigation by the Austrian authorities, and the particulars of Austria's summary demands on Serbia. It will come as no surprise to you that the assassins were connected with the Black Hand, so called, and that their aim was to free Bosnia from the oppression of Austrian annexation—a blow struck to further the cause of Greater Serbia. The Serbian government would like to pass all this off as the work of young radicals who have no sanction or support, official or otherwise. But their protestations of innocence are undermined by certain details in the confession, and more significantly by the evidence of the unexploded bombs in possession of the conspirators: they come from the Royal Serbian Arsenal at Kragujevac, this provenance clearly stamped on each device.

I have now a confession to make that will qualify me as a source of advice on the political situation here as it concerns your future. You will remember the occasion on which I made a visit, uninvited, to your quarters in the Hermit's Cave at Stupa Vasiljeva. It was your mother's anxiety over your comings and goings late at night that prompted my mission, for she knew you were too good a hunter to come back night after night empty-handed. When I discovered the secret of your cave I could not bring myself to tell your mother the truth, for she had already lost two sons and you were, perhaps in all innocence, simply honoring your brother by providing a decent burial for his remains. I held my tongue and hoped that I had done no wrong.

But there were other items there besides the body, and I refer to those explosive devices for which he sacrificed his life, the same bombs that Princip carried, I should venture, but quite certainly from the same source at Kragujevac. I have a precise memory of the coat of arms stamped on the metal.

I am not going to argue politics with you, even though the bombs in that case were intended for use against Prince Nikola, now King of Montenegro and my esteemed employer. A king has many friends and many enemies, and must take care for his own safety. But it is your safety that concerns me closely as war gathers so palpably in the Balkans and you sit in a foreign land pondering your course of action. Do not, I beg you, be so foolishly brave as to entertain the thought of returning to answer this crisis of arms. You are still persona non grata in Cetinje, however much the king's courtiers and ministers may approve of your conduct on personal grounds. Your execution of the odious Captain Schellenberg was very nearly a casus belli, and although the Austrians took no punitive military action, they did cut off the subsidy for a certain time—a most serious step in the king's view. And the Schellenberg incident necessarily reminded the government in Cetinje of your brother's complicity in the bomb plot of 1907, that old stain on the family honor. Needless to say, should you fall into the Austrians' hands you can expect no quarter.

I invoke the memory of your mother in urging you to be sensible: she gave her life to get you out of the circle of violence and retribution that is now about to engulf all of Europe, and you must do what she required of you. There is nothing you can achieve here except the losing of your life.

As for myself, I feel no heightened sense of urgency or mortality. There are strong rumors of an imminent Austrian mobilization, and now that they have their excuse, I suppose we shall not have to wait very long to find out what will happen. In the meantime, the youth of Serbia, clothed in finery and ignorance, parade in the streets of Belgrade and are rewarded by maidens who stuff flowers into their rifle bores, and no one except myself perceives any irony in this. They will discover soon enough what war is, and whether flowers have any efficacy against the Austrian artillery. The government, of course, feels no need to demonstrate its heroism, and so to a man they have retreated to Nish, out of harm's way. This withdrawal leaves me, as the Montenegrin trade representative, quite underemployed, and as soon as the ink is dry on this letter I shall depart for Cetinje, there to await the arrival of the presumed son and heir. To what, you may well ask.

Lydia, I know, joins me in sending you warm wishes and prayers for your safety.

Yours, etc.
Auberon Harwell

Toma read the letter twice, wondering, each time, at its swift passage from Belgrade to New York to Beecher's Bridge. Even in the shadow of war, this small miracle. He smiled, imagining Harwell's irritation at another small miracle and at the failure of his prophecy. For the war had started, and despite the terrible rain of the Austrian artillery bombardment, the walls of Belgrade still stood; the flower-spangled defenders, wielding a few old cannons, had turned back the Austrian flotilla with great loss of life, and it was said that not a single Austrian soldier had set foot upon the Serbian bank of the Danube.

He thought about the letter, about what he must do, and his hand went to the silken cross around his neck. Harwell had given him that, and his mother had given it to Harwell. Why? A sign then of something, surely, and a sign of something else now. His eyes roamed the high shadows above the calico curtain and, finding nothing but cobwebs there, came to rest on his elevated foot and the field of snowy linen. His face contracted and darkened as he contemplated this obstacle to his will. Here was his answer and Harwell's reassurance: What use was a cripple when it came to fighting? The foot throbbed in response to his savage thought, and to the despair of his perception was added a drip of irony and the suspicion of cowardice. Had not his father prevailed over his enemies with his shattered leg? Had he not freed himself from the fallen rock with his own *hanjar* and bound the stump? Had he not told this tale to his sons with the evidence of those severed and impaled heads? Toma imagined that he bore yet the imprint of that terrible hand in the flesh of his shoulder: there could be no turning away from that past, or from the future.

He eased himself to the side of the bed, moving the foot last of all. He would stand up, take a few steps, and then think again, on the basis of this experiment, about what must be done. Everything was accomplished soundlessly until he put weight upon his right foot. He did not cry out, but the sound of his falling was unmistakable, even over the murmur of the river. Olivia had been folding laundry at the far end of the mill. When she found him he was unconscious.

THE ROAD, BUILT FOR the slow traffic of carts and drays and long since abandoned to the occasional pedestrian, was a challenge to the Packard and to Harriet Bigelow's confidence in herself. The saplings of the beech wood pressed in from both sides; in that pleasantly dappled, green-gold light, she had trouble gauging the depth of field before her, and the long lateral beech whips, seeking the light of the old roadway, were upon her before she could raise her arm. One of them, deflected off the post of the windscreen, had struck her face, and she was certain it had left a mark. When she flinched at the next grazing of the branches, and shielded her face with her hand, the wheel was jerked from her grasp by a loose boulder and the Packard stalled.

She resented the cargo on the seat behind her and felt foolish for having taken possession of it in such an impulsive way. At the same time, she was anxious for the safety of the portrait—an image of a woman, perhaps a saint—for she knew it was precious to him. Perhaps she should find a frame for it. Perhaps that would seem too familiar a gesture.

The eyes had given her such a shock in the general store when she stopped there on the way to the works. She knew nothing of Toma's accident, and had enjoyed a late breakfast with her father, during which they offered a toast to the success of furnace number 3 with their teacups. She had stopped by Mr. Wright's with her list, asking that the delivery be made after noon, when Mrs. Evans would be finished with her cleaning, and she left an order for the ice man, who kept a notoriously erratic schedule. There was the portrait, askew and staring at her from the back wall, one corner propped on a bag of green coffee, the other on the collapsed mound of his belongings.

"Why is that thing over there?" she demanded rather sharply.

Mr. Wright, who paid superficial attention to his customers or to his lodgers upstairs unless they were in arrears on their accounts, had difficulty in locating the object of Harriet's concern. "I beg your pardon, Miss Bigelow?"

"Where is Mr. Peacock? And what are his clothes and that portrait doing here?"

"Ah, yes, Mr. Peacock. Well, since he won't be using that room for a while, I says to myself: Might as well rent it out to another fella as argue with him over the rent."

"Has he gone, then? And why?"

"Not gone, no. Cut up his foot pretty bad, and the nigger sends word that he'll pick up them things later. That woman of his will look after him, meaning Peacock, down below until he mends up."

Harriet's tone was so clipped that Mr. Wright might have imagined she was annoyed with Peacock for being so careless. "I shall save Mr. Washington the trip if you'll put those things in the automobile for me now. And we are nearly out of ice, so please locate Mr. Beckley, if you can, and alert him."

For two days Harriet debated her course of action, and her cargo fermented in the sun beating down on the Packard, on Beecher's Bridge, and on the dwindling Buttermilk. She tried not to inquire too often after Toma's recovery, and her discretion was matched by the taciturn Horatio, who disclosed only that Toma was in pain and that he would recover. But on the second day Horatio knocked at her door and asked did she want him to take those things in the car.

"Thank you, no, Mr. Washington. I thought I'd bring them myself, and visit with him for a few minutes."

Horatio said nothing and made no motion to leave, as if he were waiting for her to reconsider.

"Has the doctor seen him?"

"No."

"But you said he was in pain."

"Pain doesn't kill a man, and in my experience, Doc Spellman is hasty with the knife. Olivia tends to him. She knows these things."

She stared at him, trying to read his thoughts and betray none of her own.

"Tomorrow, then. Perhaps in the afternoon the heat will have broken." She turned back to the page of her ledger.

TOMORROW CAME AND THE heat did not break, and now she was staring at the eroded gravel of the incline where the road approached the old silk mill from downriver. The turn off the main road was just a few hundred yards beyond the Truscott drive, but what a distance this dank, choked slope was from the clipped lawn rising to the senator's house, then subsiding to the lake she imagined to be paved with golf balls. Not very long ago the thought of the senator and those golf balls would have provoked a smile: all that energy focused upon such silliness. But she had no fond thoughts for the senator today, and had driven past the stone gateposts without so much as a glance at the white house four square on the rise. It had been so much simpler before he had expressed his feelings for her. Why was that? She knew perfectly well what was on his mind, and had Mrs. Evans to remind her in case she forgot. But all was changed now, and though she did not know exactly what she felt for him, the situation between them no longer reflected her wishes or responded to her will. All the same, she knew that Fowler Truscott would not approve of this visit any more than her father, and she hoped that her car had not been seen on the road.

Harriet ended up walking to the silk mill. If she had made a determined run at those ruts she might have forced the Packard to the top of the hill, but caution lightened her foot on the accelerator. Although the rise was not steep, the driving wheels found sand beneath the gravel and the balding treads shot a hail of pebbles into the beech wood as the car began to slow. Too late she found her courage; the engine made a tremendous roar, but the Packard lost all traction and she panicked, turning the steering wheel to the right, where her path lay. She was traveling backward now, losing ground and altitude. The angle of the tires opened the way to disaster, and she ended up on a diagonal across the road with a beech trunk wedged between the tire and fender. The Packard, after a clarion backfire, stalled in this ignominious posture. She sat very still with her hands gripping the wheel. The lever of the spark was in the starting position, eleven o'clock: she must have knocked it with her wrist in the effort to keep the car on the road.

She could not leave his clothes behind. She gathered them into a bundle with one of the cleaner garments as a wrapping, and tucked the portrait under her arm. She walked the few paces to the top of the road and found that she was nearly at the door of the mill.

She knocked. The door opened suddenly and she did not know how she should address the severe, unwelcoming woman who stood before her.

"What is it?"

"I am Harriet Bigelow"

"Yes."

"And I have come to see Toma, Mr. Peacock. Is he well?"

"He is better now. The foot will heal."

"Mr. Washington told me that you have experience with this. Herbs or medicinal plants, I suppose?"

"Do you want to see him?" There was no welcome in Olivia's voice, but a veneer of deference. Harriet noted this and wondered at it, for she had always felt, on the basis of their occasional encounters, that this was a person she would like to know, even have a kind of friendship with.

"If he will see me," she replied.

GAZING ABOUT HER AT the interior of the mill, with the shafts of afternoon light illuminating the disorder of scrap metal and rusted machinery, Harriet wondered how these people lived, and in particular how Toma, the patient, could be accommodated in such chaos. She would not imagine the relationship between Olivia and Horatio, though she knew well enough what was said about them at the works. She paid no mind to it. But here she was confronted with a domestic reality: this was the kitchen, and there the salvaged leather armchair where Horatio no doubt sat, and behind the calico curtain must be where they slept. A clearing of the throat from that corner told her that Toma was awake, and that their chamber, such as it might be, was now his sickroom. What did she know of relations between men and women? Nothing. But she was sorry that Toma was here and not in the spare room at Iron Hill, where she and Mrs. Evans could take proper care of him.

"Oh, how pretty," she said to Olivia, then pointed to the rainbow of silk spools on the far wall when she saw that Olivia had no idea what she meant.

"I guess so. They've always been there; I don't look at them. He's over behind the curtain. I'll be in the laundry if he needs anything."

Toma greeted her warmly, raising himself higher on his pillows and making room for her to sit on the bed, which she did, her face flushing, as there was no chair. He did certainly look the part of the patient, with his bandaged foot and the gauze wound round his forehead, even a seep of blood on the pillowcase.

"You have come to see me," he said with evident pleasure.

"I have brought your clothes. And we owe you so much. I am very grateful."

He took her hand. Though his touch was cool and brief, it reminded her of so many things. She blushed and took her hand back into her lap, thinking: What a prim gesture for a woman sitting on a man's bed here in the middle of nowhere. Why should I not hold his hand?

"And furnace number 3?" He was looking at her with an expression of what might be amusement.

"Furnace number 3 survives. Two days ago the power train failed: the vibrations knocked over a supporting post and some gearing was nearly ruined, so the whole day was a loss. But yesterday we made almost four tons of iron, all told, and cast twenty-three wheels. Horatio is pessimistic about the water, and of course about his machinery. He wants to reduce the rate of the bellows to avoid another mishap, and Mr. Brown will not hear of it. He says his iron will be soft or brittle—I can't remember which—with the most dreadful consequences. I'm sorry to say they had some very sharp words for each other."

Toma looked at his foot, and her eyes followed his gaze. "Here I am talking about machinery and I haven't even asked you how you feel."

"It is better today, but there may be pieces of the glass still in there, so we will see. Horatio thinks some bone has been damaged, perhaps a tendon. For now, I am of no use." He smiled, and she saw the effort that was required.

"But shouldn't the doctor see you?"

"Olivia thinks there is no need. It is in God's hands, as my mother used to say."

"Like the rain, I suppose. I don't see how we shall get on without rain, and unless your foot heals, I shall ask for both things in my prayers, as perhaps you do."

"I do not pray. It was simply an expression that I use because I have heard it so often."

"You do not pray?"

"I have lost the custom of prayer, though there was a time when I believed God heard my prayers and answered them. He delivered my enemy into my hands."

"One must pray for mercy, I think."

"I shall leave that to you. If there is a God, and if he listens to any-one, he will hear you."

"He hears all prayers." It was time to go now. She and her father would have the long, hot walk home from the works, and she would have to find a reason, a false reason, for the absence of the Packard. God would have to hear that too. She stood up.

"I have been meaning to ask you about this portrait that I always seem to end up carrying. Is it someone you know?"

He seemed reluctant to answer. "No. It belonged to a friend, a coun-tryman of mine who was dying, and he urged me to keep it. Perhaps the painter was someone who was remembering the icons in his village church. Or perhaps it is the face of his mother, his sister, his . . . I do not know. It reminds me of my home. Thank you for taking such care."

There was a truth buried somewhere in his words, but she did not know where it lay.

HORATIO WASHINGTON WAS ON his way home after stopping at McCreedy's Saloon, as was his habit on payday; his step was sure on the steep path, and the pitcher of beer had put him in a good mood. The front room of the saloon was a pleasantly lit, smoky, convivial place, and it suited him to make these visits. Was there a man in the works, except the abstainers, who did not stop off here after being paid? Was he not as much a man, and was this not a free country? His private view was that it was not, but all the more reason for him to stand at one end of the bar and drink his pitcher of beer with the chaser of rye offered by McCreedy. He would speak if spoken to, but more often he got a nod and a smile. That was enough for Horatio, who knew, if not his station, at least the limits of tolerance. But he also took satisfaction from the occasional cold stare of a stranger, some man unused to drinking with Negroes and resentful of his presence. There was never a confrontation because when inquiry was made about that nigger down the bar, the man was given no encouragement at all by McCreedy or his patrons, and Horatio didn't have to say a word.

The figure on the path took him by surprise; there were no casual visitors in this steep wood, and even Olivia's laundry had to be picked up or dropped off at the general store. He had not remembered Harriet's intended visit because he had not believed it.

"Oh, Mr. Washington, I am so glad to meet you here. I have left my automobile just by your house, and I shall need a couple of men in the morning, as it is stuck to a tree. Would you help me with that? And not a word to my father?"

Horatio nodded and would have spoken, but she plunged on: "And please thank Mrs. Washington for me, as I'm sorry not to have said good-bye to her." And then she was gone past him up the path with her rapid step, her bright eye, her flushed cheek.

He turned to watch her, weighing in his mind the phrase "Mrs. Washington," which struck him with its sadness. Too late for that now. Was there ever a right time?

He thought again of his power train, jury-rigged through the woods from the wheel to number 3, and imagined revisions to the linkages to reduce the strain and accommodate the low water. In a couple of days he'd have to send someone out to tap the last holding pond up on the side of the mountain.

The sun was down below the line of the trees as he approached the mill, and there was Olivia, the lamp already lit, chopping vegetables with savage strokes of the knife he had made for her. She looked different somehow, but he could not put his finger on it. The severe expression perhaps, or was it just that she was older? It had been a long time since he had looked at her with that eye that could discriminate down to a sixty-fourth of an inch. Perhaps not since the day he had judged her old enough to give him what he needed.

What had he given her in return? He had given her a home, kept her out of trouble, educated her. It was the last that he took pride in, for he knew it was his own education, an act of will and dearly bought, that made him the equal of any man in Beecher's Bridge. You're nothing without that, he had said once, pointing to the book she had thrown down, and had slapped her face, not hard, when she persisted in using "ain't" even when she knew the right way to say it.

He had never told her that he loved her. He had never said that to her mother or to any woman; the words had no place in his careful vocabulary, for they did not signify. But looking at her now, with the suggestion of age in her unsmiling concentration on the task, he thought that he could have said it, and it wouldn't have cost him so much. But it was too late now. The girl was gone, grown up into a woman he didn't quite recognize.

IT HAD BEEN A LONG time since Olivia had been to confession, so long that one priest had retired and another had taken his place. She wondered if there was anyone else she could talk to, as the priest would have to know about everything, and what she cared about was this one thing. She spat on the iron to test its temperature and glared at the red eye of the charcoal in the brazier. The perspiration beaded everywhere on her bare arms, prickled her scalp, turned the pale cloth wound around her hips almost transparent, and the blue flowers looked like tattoos on her thighs. It didn't seem right that the hotter it got the more clothes had to be washed and folks wanted them back sooner. She couldn't go on like this. There was only the priest. He would have to do.

When Horatio had run the pipe up the hill to tap into the top section of the old canal, he wasn't even thinking of her or her laundry. Whatever he said about it now didn't change that, but it did annoy her when he said she shouldn't always be asking him for things. She never asked him for anything because she knew better, and the one thing she had asked for—a real bedroom with walls and a ceiling and a window— well, sometimes he was as good as deaf. She wondered if the man in her bed now was God's way of showing Horatio he should have given her what she wanted. Maybe He had a sense of humor. But the priest probably didn't.

Originally the pipe had run right through her laundry and into Horatio's shop, where he had set up a hand-carved wooden wheel in one corner to run his grindstone or a lathe. At night he would sometimes sit in his chair with a pencil and the paper with a faint blue grid, drawing wheels with whorls and scallops like seashells, or sit at the bench with his carving tools translating from paper to wood. Those were the good evenings, when he did not drink, and he came to her afterward without bitterness. Those were the nights, she now realized, when she almost loved him.

She sighed and shook her head. Drops of her sweat fell on Mr. Breen's drawers and were cooked away with a swipe of the iron. A fire in August. A fucking fire in fucking August: these words she said aloud, and the thrill of Horatio's imagined outrage produced a shiver down her spine.

Horatio, on his own initiative, had rerouted the pipe so that it swooped down into the middle of the laundry room at the far end of the mill, beyond his workshop and junk piles. A present, he said, with a smile that made his face almost unrecognizable. She had no idea of what he meant until he showed her how the cock turned and the jet of water, fine and fierce, shattered and bent on the new-carved vanes of wood, and the axle of the wheel drove those gears salvaged from someplace up on the mountain and the paddles churned the water in the vat to a soapy froth.

Never have to touch that soap again, he said, holding one of her reddened hands in his own, a moment of affection that surprised them both.

The wheel had seemed a miracle, and at a certain hour in the late morning, on a clear day, the angle of the sun through the windows in the roof produced a rainbow where the water jet found the knife-edge of the vanes and was forced back upon itself in two curves like a swan's neck.

But it was a fragile miracle. Leaves or debris got caught on the grating of the intake pipe and she would have to climb all the way up there to clear it, or ask Horatio if he was going that way; sometimes a possum or raccoon drowned in the backwater and rotted away until her laundry stank of sweet death, and she worried that customers might complain of the odd smell of their pillowcases. Horatio had explained to her in a stern voice the danger of taxing the machine with heavy loads and stripping those gears.

She tried to show him in small ways that she was grateful, knowing that being told so would make him uneasy. Then one night—how was she to know he had been drinking all that time?—she emerged from her laundry exhausted and stumbled over a piece of scrap left lying in her path. Maybe her voice sounded angry. She was wondering if she had broken her toe.

The odd thing about Horatio was that it was hard to tell what effect the drink would have on him. Sometimes he did not drink at all, and sometimes he drank and seemed not much changed. She could see no pattern in it. He talked no more than usual, slurred no words if he asked about what she had read or what she needed carried down from the town. The liquor seemed to make him no happier, she thought, but perhaps more attentive to her in a way that was not unpleasant. And there were the other times too, and one thing the drink never did was take away his desire for her. And even if he could not finish—especially if he could not finish, for that must be her fault, her lack of desire for him—he knew how to hurt her, and took his satisfaction from that.

Her angry comment that night had touched some nerve bared by the drink. He laughed in a way she did not recognize, then put his hands on her roughly. She thought he wanted sex, and she made clear that she was having none of it. She slapped his hands away and by accident hit him a glancing, backhand blow on his face. It was the first time she had ever refused him. It was the first time he had ever beaten her.

He hit her with his open hand and with his fist and with the stretcher ripped from a broken chair. He beat her after she stopped struggling or even trying to shield herself, and all without saying a word. No explanation or accusation, as if they both knew what must be done. He tore the shirt from her in an effort to keep her from running, then held her by the throat and slapped her breasts. I won't run, I won't run no more, she said. Go on and fuck me, Horatio, if that's what you want. I don't care. You hear? I don't care. He knocked her down, slamming her head to the floor, and that was the last she knew until she awoke in the dark, aching, her mouth full of blood, lying in her own soil. What had happened to her when she was unconscious? She did not know.

She resolved that all this would be forgotten: it would be as if nothing had happened. Things returned more or less to normal, and there was a kind of peace between them. But one thought remained: that she should, or might, kill him. She was amazed that such a thought could have occurred to her. It was three days later, when her lip was healing and the marks on her face all but vanished, that Toma first came to the mill.

She thought again about the priest, trying to remember his face, for she did not go to church very often. Horatio hated churches the way he hated bad grammar. They were both signs of ignorance, of weakness. I have had sinful thoughts, Father, about killing a man. Your husband? No, he's not . . . And so the conversation, the confession, would wander off into other matters that might concern the priest, or even God, but did not seem urgent to her. She could live with what had happened in the past. She knew her mother was safe and with God. She could even live with Horatio, or thought she could. But something had changed for her the day Toma came to call. And now he was back. Horatio had brought him back.

Horatio liked him, now, not at the beginning; that much was clear. Who else did Horatio like? Nobody.

She had never slept with any man other than Horatio, never kissed one. Her experience and his vigilance had burned that curiosity out of her. But now she was seized with a strong feeling that lay somewhere between love and regret. Regret for what? Something she had lost, or something she had never known? She had said those crazy things to him, made her confession to a man as much a stranger to her as the priest. Then he was gone. And reappeared now in this improbable way. What would she do to keep him? What would she not do?

There had been no time to think at first. She had sent one of the men to the pharmacist with her laundry money for the draught, saying, Wake him up if you have to. When they had got the laudanum into him and he drowsed off, only then did she dare cut the boot off and probe the wound for splinters of the bluish glass before binding it. The next day he slept still, and she washed him, cutting those ragged clothes away until he lay naked on the sheet. She rebandaged the foot, applying the herbs she had gone out to gather at dawn. Now she had time to think.

These thoughts had the terrible power of novelty. Here on her bed, where she had experienced the things that bound her soul, lay a man who might set her free. It was as simple as that. She did not stop to consider the paradox that her bonds had been invisible until a means of escape appeared; neither did she ask if her deliverer were willing.

Toma slept on, with only the rise and fall of his chest as a sign of life. In this heat there was no need to put the sheet back. Washing him was a task like washing the clothes in her tub: something that needed to be done. But because she had not covered him, this moment was suffused with a disquieting intimacy.

She had drawn many things: flowers, buildings, bits of Horatio's scrap, his hands, even his head as he sat in his armchair concentrating on something. Never a figure drawing. But she had taken a drawing class in the library—it was there she had formed her nodding acquaintance with Harriet Bigelow—and had seen those books, so she knew something about the unclothed figure and its aesthetics, if only through the eyes of others.

He is beautiful, she thought. With her hands clasped in her lap, she struggled with the mystery of a new desire. Would it be different with him?

She made a mental inventory of the things Horatio had required of her for his pleasure, acts that had not grazed her imagination until now. That had been sin. But she would give him everything. He would not have to ask, much less compel, because she would know. That was the hidden gift of her sin, and for a moment she could almost forgive Horatio.

Horatio. She imagined Horatio's wrath were he to know her thoughts. How could she hide them from him? She could run away, but where? Or she could kill Horatio. Here was the thought that would drive her to the priest, and she raged at both of them, Horatio and the priest. How could what she felt for Toma have turned so quickly to its opposite? This was madness, as palpable as nausea or a rising fever. She drew the sheet up to cover everything but his face.

Nursing him, sleeping on the floor, the heat. She was worn out. But worst of all was his indifference. She saw no sign that he had any feeling for her other than an awkward gratitude. If anything, he avoided her eye. He seemed angry himself, muttering at the weeping wound in his foot, muttering in his sleep, which disturbed hers and Horatio's too. The only time he seemed happy was when the white woman came to call. After that, even his courtesy became bitter to her, and she hated them all: Horatio, the priest, and now Toma.

Her back was to the door and she did not see it open; neither did she hear it over the hiss of the wheel and the clatter of the paddles. But the sweat was running down her arm now, and when she half turned to find a rag, she saw him out of the corner of her eye. He had a length of two-by-four under his arm as a crutch.

"Didn't I tell you not to be walking around."

"I had to get to the privy."

"This ain't the privy. You didn't see the sign on the door?"

"No."

"It says Keep Out. I tried to keep it simple." His smile broadened. She glanced down at herself, following the momentary flicker of his eyes. The batiste of her camisole was plastered to her chest and the blue flowers of her wrap were the poor sentinels of her modesty. She might as well be naked. She brought one arm up across her breasts. She could smell her own sharp odor. He could probably smell it from where he stood. He was not smiling now.

"I am sorry. I heard your machinery and I did not stop to think. Will I disturb you if I am looking at it?"

"Look all you want."

"Thank you. You will show me how it works?"

She should have told him to turn his back so she could cover herself, but it was done, whatever damage could be done by looking. From his appraisal of her—the movement of his eyes seemed almost accidental—she knew that he was not shocked, knew that he had had other women. It did not matter now. He would not look at her again. There was a hopeless quality to her rage: she wanted at least to be noticed.

She eased the clutch lever forward. The paddles grew still and the wheel, now free, spun faster. He bent over it awkwardly, trying to keep his foot clear of the spray. She began to fish the clothes out of the rinse water.

"You shut that thing off when you're finished. No need to be wasting my water."

They had no further conversation. She put the clothes through the wringer, turned once because she thought he had said something, and saw that he was talking to himself. When she was done with the ironing he was still fussing with the wheel, soaked to the skin, and the bandage on his foot looked like an old mop.

"Come," she said as she shut off the tap. She lifted him to his feet and saw that the bolt of pine lay beyond her reach. He was as meek as a child when she draped his arm around her neck and led him away to the sickbed.

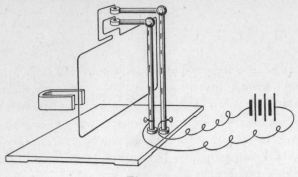

Figure 21

Fig. 21 shows a method by which a wire carrying a current and free to move may be arranged. This is a most important experiment, and, if possible, should be performed by everyone interested in the study of electricity. The experiment shown in Fig. 21 is the fundamental experiment showing why it is that a motor will operate. By reversing the experiment shown in Fig. 21, and by causing the wire to move across the lines of magnetic force, it is possible to generate current in the wire. This is also a fundamental experiment, for it shows in the simplest possible manner how mechanical power can be transformed into electrical power, or how a dynamo works.

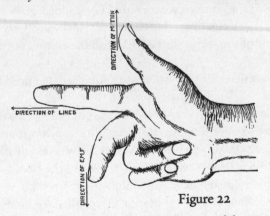

Figure 22

The relations that exist between the direction of motion of the wire, the direction of lines of force and the direction of the current in the wire when moved by hand or by mechanical force, is most easily remembered by extending the thumb, first and second finger of the right hand at right angles to each other, as shown in Fig. 22.

—Practical Electricity,
sixth edition, 1911

CHAPTER

SEVEN

Toma's dream was so pleasant that he awoke laughing. He had constructed a machine that caused all of Mr. Bigelow's wheels to be fabricated in the twinkling of an eye, and when Harriet Bigelow called out his name in those flute tones of the thrush that sings after the rain, he answered her with a question: Which of us shall cross, for see how the river has fallen? She made no answer but disengaged herself, laughing, from the arm of Senator Truscott and then walked across the water without wetting the hem of her skirt.

There was such promise here—interrupted by the inconvenience of his waking—that he tried to reimmerse himself in the details of his dream. What was the exact expression on her face as she passed over the water? Did she step upon stones in the shallows, or was she borne up by the water itself? What was the working of his machine?

Dawn bloomed through the high windows of the monitor and Toma puzzled for a moment over the particular quality of this light. The air was pleasantly cool and the panes of glass glistened. The weather had changed, but there could not have been so much rain or else he would have woken sooner.

He could not capture the creature of his dream—she was both less and more than the woman who had sat on this bed—but he was glad to be awake and alive. He stretched extravagantly, his pent energies coursing to the extremities with an almost epileptic violence, and the yawn was a kind of ecstasy. When he opened his eyes, his gaze fastened upon a five-bladed fan in the shadows above the windows. He blinked, then squinted. Those skeins of cobweb attesting to the fan's disuse suggested the work of a gigantic spider, or . . . He held his breath until the thought should complete itself.

A movement of the calico curtain interrupted this waking dream that had enveloped the earlier one. Dreams within dreams. Olivia noted the strange expression on his face.

"Are you well?"

"Very well, and today will be a special day."

"I brought you coffee. Heard you laughing and knew you'd done sleeping. Here. Mind you keep your foot up."

He took the burning enamel mug from her hand, then laughed, almost scalding himself as he did so.

"What?"

"I believe you are trying to make yourself look ugly. Can't you smile?"

"Why should I smile?" Her expression became more resolutely severe.

"Oh, because the heat has broken, or because my foot is getting better, or just because I ask it of you. What have you done with your hair?"

The slight motion of her head sent a shudder through those countless spirals, a feral message like the bristling of a dog. "Nothing. I washed it and tied it up to be out of my way."

"Yes. There is copper in it that I have not seen before."

"Red, you mean. When I see that I want to cut it all off."

"You must not do that. Come closer?"

She did as he asked, bent down to him. Did he wish to say something to her in confidence? No, only to look closely at the band of plaited silk that bound her hair, that little rainbow that she had fashioned from the spooled thread on the shop wall. He held up to her gaze the silk cross, plaited of fine colored ribbon, that hung at his neck. As if she hadn't noticed.

She said nothing. Of course it had been for him, and what was the use of it if he did not notice? But now that he had seen what he was supposed to see, she felt foolish.

He was sorry that she could not share this feeling, the sense of possibility and fruition glimpsed in the instant of his dream, which was still expanding obscurely within him; and even though he lay perfectly motionless on the bed, he had the odd sensation of being full to bursting with this immanence, of having to concentrate on each breath as if it might be his last.

He thought of the things he would need, for all of which he was dependent on Olivia's goodwill. She must take his telegram to the depot and leave word at the works for Miss Bigelow to send him a particular catalogue, and for Mr. Washington to spare him some time at the end of the afternoon. She agreed readily, and he calculated that she would be gone for a good two hours on these and other errands. Two hours in thrall to this glowing surge was a lifetime: if he survived it he would have mastered the machine in all but its physical execution.

He must be calm in order to work, and when he heard the door close behind her, Toma spent the first five minutes of his two hours trying to slow the racing of his mind and heart. He set his undertaking against Edison's vast achievement and the incandescent musings of Nikola Tesla, his fellow Serb, who would surely scorn the expenditure of precious thought to the end of manufacturing a few iron wheels. He had, with his own eyes, seen the working of Tesla's coil, wherein currents, alternating to the millionth of a second, strove and resonated with each other, magnifying the mystery of the universe, channeling it through the very body of the inventor to produce an unearthly glow in the sealed glass tube clutched in Tesla's hand.

Tesla had talked of the things that could be achieved with his invention—the coil—and by harnessing electrical energy to meet human needs and desires as yet unglimpsed. But it all began with an idea, Toma was quite sure, not with some specific physical challenge—an idea that would quite literally light the way into the future. Judged from the perspective of the task, the making of wheels, his own putative solution was no more than the labor of a mechanician: the water would move a dynamo whose mirror image, the motor, would move the air, and the wheels would pour forth from the furnace mouth. But he had been guided to this electro-mechanical linkage by an idea, and that idea was most simply and thrillingly expressed in the vision of Harriet Bigelow crossing the water toward him. An idea could move the world and anything in it. When he closed his eyes, the fan above him began to turn.

JOHN STEPHENSON 121 WORTH NEW YORK CITY 10 AUGUST 1914
PLEASE SEND BROKEN DYNAMO BODY SHOP STOREROOM AND
VOLTMETER STOP WILL PAY FREIGHT STOP FOOT MENDS SLOWLY
STOP PEACOCK

> c/o Wright's General Store
> Beecher's Bridge, Connecticut
> United States of America
> August 11, 1914

Auberon Harwell, Esq.
The Grand Hotel
Cetinje
Montenegro

My dear Harwell:

I write to you in great excitement.

I was in a very bad way when your letter arrived. I had received a wound in my foot, and also I had heard the news of my homeland. It seemed that the world and my fate conspired to bury me alive in this place so far from my people. But your words recalled me to myself and what I must do.

You would laugh to see me: I am like my father with his wooden leg. Not a real one, but one I made only this morning, with a block under my heel so that I can put no weight on the wound. It is like a very short stilt, and I am lopsided. My nurse could not contain her laughter even as she tried to be angry with me. I do not mind her laughing, for it is pleasant to hear, and in any case I can walk.

And you, my dear English, would laugh also to see what object my genius fastens on, but perhaps a bitter laugh. What a strange education you have given me: Homer for the exercise of the soul; a bit of your peculiar Bible to temper my brutish religion; Macaulay for style and rhetoric; and that crabbed work of science to point the way to my future. You hated that last book because you could not understand it, and you persevered only out of love for my mother, I think. It must have been so, for I heard what you said under your breath, words that were never found in my dictionary. "Sodomite," you called him, poor Professor Drinker, and said that because of his book you must banish all red books from your library. Do you remember telling me that you could not approve of a book that caused you to question your own intelligence?

It was like having a blind man as a guide to an extraordinary landscape, but I am grateful for your trouble, and now more so than ever. I am in mind of something you once said and have probably forgot. It was not long after we had made the dam so that our neighbor's cattle might drink from our stream. And the water when it went through the channel had a great strength to it, causing, from time to time, a little whirlpool or vortex, like a man with his pipe blowing smoke rings. Later that night I was asking you questions about the vortex, puzzling over how one might measure the force of the water there or predict its course in the stream. You tired of these questions that could not be answered, unless perhaps by Professor Drinker, and said this: "When a leaf or a bit of wood is caught in the whirlpool it is real to me for that moment because I can see what happens, and it almost makes sense. But you, Toma, can hold the vortex in your mind without such aid, would make it stand still so that you can measure it, and one day you will be able to summon such things without having seen them at all, and they will be as real to you as the table here or this spoon."

Your prophecy has come to pass. There is a curious device in this place where I am living, a waterwheel fashioned by my host. It is driven not by the river current but by a narrow jet of water under a head of 160 feet. Although the pressure is terrific, the actual flow or expenditure of water is modest: a most ingenious and efficient thing. I have experimented with the positioning of the nozzle and the delivery of water to the blades or cups, making such calculations as are possible without any instruments at all, and trying to fix, first in my imagination and then in the nozzle and the wheel, the perfect flow of water to the blades and its unimpeded escape.

There is an economy to this device, and of all things necessary to the ironworks just now, water is the most scarce. Not only will this wheel produce a mechanical effect, but also an electrical potential, and if I can adapt this source to my task of iron making I shall have done something clever. Yes, it is only a trick, or might seem so, and such wheels have been used for some years in the great mountains of the west, where a simple sluiceway can deliver hundreds of feet of head to power machinery or make electricity. But I can tell you there is something about this wheel that will not let me rest, something that defies the mind's grasp, and at night I see in my dreaming the vortex—perfect but for the friction and gravity—formed by the water jet as it is shaped by the wheel's vanes. There is perfection in this, somewhere, could I but see it and seize it, and I am haunted by it, by the turning of perfect wheels.

Do you know—of course you do not—that the connection between mechani-

cal motion and electrical impulse—one producing the other, or vice versa—arises from a circularity similar to what you observed with the leaf in the vortex? Put a current through a wire and you produce concentric rings of a magnetic field circling that wire: magic indeed. Wind that wire into a coil—it is called a helix, but vortex would mean much the same—and you have made a magnet, with poles, north and south, at either end of the coil. Or wind your wire on an iron core and place it between the poles of a large magnet, and you have either a dynamo to make electricity or a motor to produce mechanical rotation. In either case, motion or electricity is produced as these little circular fields around the core wires, acting in concert, react to the field of the embracing magnet. Force the core to revolve in that field and you will produce electricity; or run a current through the same core—reverse your process—and you will produce mechanical rotation.

There is a beautiful simplicity in all this. Perhaps you will take my word, for I am speaking of a mystery that no one truly understands. But if you were here in Connecticut I could show you the workings I have described and you would at least appreciate the symmetries. The helix and the vortex, the flow of water or electricity . . . perhaps it is all one if properly understood.

Such elusive perfection, such fertile mystery viewed from the small space of the mind. I have fallen into a madness that is like the madness of love, and it is hard to think about anything else. It is the madness of love, for, as I have written you before, I must have this woman, Harriet Bigelow, who is the mover of my labors.

I shall do what I can, and I shall write to you of my success if that is to be. My thoughts are with you in your own great undertaking: may any daughter have the grace and courage of her mother, and may any son grow tall and be in all things a proper English.

> My affectionate regards to you both,
> Toma

PS: I have made such a compression of my thoughts in this letter that when I read it over I scarcely understand my own words. And I have left out something that is puzzling to me, something that I must understand. My host, the maker of the wheel, has a black skin. He must know something of my feelings for Miss Bigelow, for he mocks me, and himself, by saying that we are the same: not brothers, but alike. We are not, and can never be, equal to good people like the Bigelows. He is a proud, bitter man who has thought much on these things. You once told me that your family and Lydia's were not of the same circle, which was *why you spoke the same language in different ways. Does this mean that you and Lydia cannot live in England? As you know well, Aliye could not live with my people, nor I with hers. It was only when I came away from Montenegro that I saw her as I see her now. What does this mean for my present hope? Here is another subject in which you can instruct me.*

TOMA SAT AT THE BENCH with his head in his hands, the Cleveland Armature Works manual open before him. He turned back to the first page of Chapter XVI: "Diseases of Dynamos and Motors: their symptoms and how to cure them." On the bench beside the book lay the yellowed enamel of the Weston voltmeter with its obdurate and unmoving pointer. It had been a long day. It would be a long night.

He remembered the day the dynamo had died, or at least been buried, and it was he who had called the cascade of sparks to Mr. Burden's attention. "Kill it," he said. "Commutators or brushes are fucked, maybe both. Nothing but trouble it's been, long as I can remember, and who knows if it's worth fixing. Put it somewhere for a rainy day, and tell the boys they'll have to get on by hand." Burden laughed. "You know, son, that thing's older than you by a long shot. Don't owe us a thing. I'll talk to the old man about it."

Mr. Stephenson was in no hurry to throw anything out, so the old Edison machine gathered dust in the storeroom and passed from the memory of Mr. Burden and his crew, who had more than enough to do without tending to such antiquities. The rainy day never came.

It sat now on Horatio's bench, a hundredweight and more of iron sculpture with its casing removed, its shadow ballooning on the wall in the unsteady light. And it was, as far as Toma could determine, comfortable in its retirement and deaf to his call.

He had trued the commutators and buffed them with a fine abrasive to remove the grooves worn by the sparking brushes. Copper on copper: it was indeed an old machine. Then he trimmed the ragged ends of the brushes to the curve of the commutator rings and set the springs so that there was the gentlest contact. Still plenty of copper left to work with, and he would need it all, for even if he were successful—especially if he were successful—the dynamo would be running sixteen or eighteen hours a day, sparking all the while, each tiny arc fusing the tip of the brush to the copper of the whirling commutator, throwing off an infinitesimal dust of copper that would wear like water on stone until the rings must be polished again, the brushes trimmed and reset. And still the current would not flow.

The machine was an old one, running on direct current, and quaintly shaped, with the identification EDISON ELECTRIC CO. in heavy cast lettering along the base. But it was not so old as to have been created in ignorance of the advantages, including beautiful simplicity, of alternating current in all its applications. Early in his career, when he was yet a student, Tesla had devised an experiment to demonstrate the elegance and feasibility of alternating current, and by inference its superiority to direct current. By means of that alternating current the poles of electromagnets set on the circumference of an iron plate were excited in sequence, and on the plate an iron egg responded to this revolving polarity by performing its own revolutions, faster and faster, obedient to the flickering currents and to Tesla's will, until at last it stood upon its end, offering that perfection of form, motion and stasis, in the same instant.

Toma had replayed this scene in his mind often, sometimes arraying himself in the colors of Tesla's genius, sometimes delving into the dismay of the professor or the amazement of Tesla's fellows. But the interesting point now was that the dynamo Tesla used to produce his magic show ran without the nuisance of sparking. Every dynamo under the sun produced alternating current as the wires on the drum revolved through the magnetic field—north, south, north . . . this was in the nature of things. The troublesome brushes and commutator converted the current, forcing it to flow all in one direction—direct current—because that was a concept more easily grasped by lesser minds. Tesla had dismissed all that—thrown away the brushes and the commutator and shown the back of his hand to lesser minds.

And yet here was this machine in front of him, a monument to direct current and the weight of custom, and if Thomas Edison could not be called a lesser mind, he could be called worse things. For Edison, who by exercise of a mere fraction of his intellect must have seen the advantages of alternating current, had not only ignored the genius of Tesla but spent millions contesting the issue with Tesla's employer, Westinghouse, staking his fortune and reputation on the effort to shore up the direct-current technology, whose days were numbered.

And why would he do this? Because of the even greater number of millions already sunk in the enterprise, in those cable conduits that ran under the streets of New York; in the machinery itself, layer upon layer of it, an entire system, a kind of theology written in steel and copper, and all dedicated to a single false assumption. The theology of a failed god. Edison must have seen the widening gap between the old technology and the new; but because he was shackled to his own success he could not jump, or chose not to.

Another element to Toma's discontent was this: he was, as Horatio had so pointedly observed, an outsider and almost an outcast here for all the talk about opportunity and however high the welcoming statue in the harbor of New York held her torch. Was not Tesla's otherness held against him? Did it not explain how slowly and grudgingly capital had flowed in the direction of his ideas? And, he thought, flipping the dead switch in merciless repetition, how much greater the resistance to feeling? His dream of Harriet coming to him over the water was no more than a wish, a very pretty wish with the elements of fable. And here was he, Tesla's sorry kinsman, mired in the real world.

He had fallen asleep, and Olivia touched his arm.

"I brought you some coffee, seeing how you fixing to sit up all night."

"I hope not, but thank you."

"You been sitting here a long time, not a sound, not a shadow on the roof, and I'm thinking: the candles burn all the way down, who knows what he's got lying on that bench?"

"I promise I shall not burn you up in your sleep."

"I wasn't asleep." She jerked her head to the side, in the direction of the erratic stertor behind the curtain. "Horatio be sleeping hard enough for both of us. I think you wore him out."

She stood in her nightclothes. A new moth crashed against the screen and he turned the talk to Horatio's extraordinary efforts with the wheel and the jet and a new arrangement of belting to drive the dynamo. Olivia nodded her head. She might or might not have been listening to his every word.

"What I want to know is when do I get my laundry back. Mrs. Bryce's boy is due to drop off her things tomorrow, and I heard her family has been visiting with her."

"Not soon. I cannot tell you a lie. Not soon unless I fail."

She looked down at him, and he up at her, measuring each other. He had no authority other than Horatio's to do what he was doing, and Horatio was fast asleep.

"Drink your coffee," she said, laying her hand on his arm. "And explain why what you do is more important."

"Well." He drank, buying himself time, and as he set the mug down, a thought about the dead machine tickled the edge of his mind and vanished. "This machine, this dynamo, will make electricity, and if I do my work as well as Horatio has done his, I can make the electricity generate a draft for furnace number 3, and Mr. Bigelow's contract for the wheels may be fulfilled. If that does not happen, perhaps Horatio will have no job. So you see, we want the same things, you and I."

She listened carefully to this explanation, making no superfluous motions of agreement, and allowed his conclusion to hang in a moment of silence.

"Except that your machine ain't working."

"Yes, but I have not lost hope."

"And that thing with the wires on it? The whatchum. Don't that make the electric?"

Toma laughed. The battery, which was necessary to the operation of the Bigelow Packard, had also been appropriated—like Olivia's wheel—but under a subterfuge, and thanks to Horatio's sly disconnection of the positive lead.

"Yes, it does, but not enough for this purpose. For now it helps me investigate the problem, the sickness of the dynamo. Afterward it will supply the little portion of electricity to excite the workings of the dynamo, like the stone that starts an avalanche, or a lucifer to light a fire."

"Can you show me the electric?"

"You can't see it; you can only see what it does. Here, watch the dial of the meter." He took the leads of the battery, with which he had been trying to make a circuit through the various parts of the dynamo, and touched them to either end of a heavy paper resistor. The needle on the meter jumped almost to the end of its scale.

"Can I feel it?" she asked, her voice slow with wonder.

"No, wait." He made a quick twist of two wires to incorporate the resistor and cushion the current to her. He offered the innocent tips of the wires. "One finger on each. You will feel a jolt, perhaps like touching the stove."

"Only a fool does that on purpose."

He smiled at her. "You are afraid of finding out?"

"I ain't afraid to find out." She touched the wires without hesitation and took the current, which wrung from her a long breath like a sigh or a groan. She looked at him not with reproach but with calculation, rubbing her tingling fingertips against her thumbs.

He dropped his eyes from her gaze and saw the distinct outlines of her risen nipples beneath the thin stuff of her nightgown. He cleared his throat and made as if he would stand. She put her hands on his shoulders.

"What about you? Are you afraid to find out?" Before he could answer she kissed him. It was an awkward gesture, as she had so little experience of seduction or tenderness. She watched his face for a moment before she turned away and disappeared through the curtain.

He sat back in his chair, trying to direct his thoughts to the unfinished business on the bench. He reached absently for his mug. The scent of the coffee, which had been reheated over a candle from this morning's brewing, put him in mind of an odor he could not place until this moment: the odor, very faint, of burnt insulation. That was it: the sparking of the dynamo had been so extreme, the rogue currents so out of phase and so violent, that the windings on the armature must have fused and shorted out.

It took him only a few moments to find the spot where the damage had occurred. By careful manipulation of the copper he restored the wires there to their original dimension and uniformity, and with a few careful twists of silk from the far wall he was able to reinsulate the wires. He thought of the same silk wound into Olivia's freshly washed hair, her arms around his neck.

When the armature was reassembled he again applied the leads of the battery and found that the voltmeter responded as hoped at every point: the circuits were complete. He went to bed. But, tired as he was, he did not soon fall asleep, nor could he will again the vision of Harriet's acceptance of him. Instead he turned over in his mind the possible consequences of his careless electrical jest.

CHAPTER

EIGHT

From certain signs, including Horatio Washington's virtual disappearance from the ironworks, Harriet Bigelow had an instinct that something was afoot down below in Power City. She was not aware of the delivery of the dynamo, even though the crate had come from the siding right through the yard of the works. But the particular catalogue Toma had requested—page upon page of electrical fittings, gauges, capacitors, and windings—was one clue, and the disappearance of the battery was another. Of course a battery may fail, but Horatio's demeanor, the uncharacteristic evasiveness of his gaze, made her immediately suspicious of his explanation.

It would be simple enough to ask Toma what he was about. But Toma could not come to her, nor could she, having made the one uninvited call to the silk mill, go to him again.

She was in the act of writing a note to Toma when her father called out to her: "Harriet, my dear, what do you know about a length of cable from Mr. Stephenson?"

Harriet went to him, as she must do in order to be heard. He held up the telegram. "Twenty-five hundred feet of electrical cable. What can he mean?" There was confusion in his eyes and a gathering anger in his voice.

"It must be a mistake."

"Well, I don't know about that. Mr. Stephenson is a man of business, and this would be a very odd sort of mistake. You must make the matter clear to him, treading softly, of course. Electrical cable indeed, as if I could make wheels by black magic. Perhaps you should have a word with your friend, Stephenson's young man?"

"I shall take care of this, Papa."

"I know you will. You have a way with letters and a very neat hand too."

Harriet returned to her desk with the sense that events were unfolding in a way she could not control. Wasn't this what she had wanted? Hadn't she asked Toma to save the situation? What right then had she to question the means? It had seemed, in the shadows of that bedroom above the stable, exactly the right thing to say: it was on the one hand true—the Bigelow Iron Company must be saved—and it also had the virtue of redirecting the energy of that moment, the current of feeling between them that she was honest enough to admit she both felt and encouraged.

Harriet was more easily seduced by the happy eventuality than by imaginings of disaster, and liable to minimize any difficulties intervening between the present and some pleasant future. Could she have guessed that Toma's solution to the problems of the ironworks might involve a bold technical stroke? Perhaps. Could she represent to herself the reservations of her father about such a course? She did not want to. But now she had no choice but to acknowledge that her father's suspicious objection—though he knew nothing—was very forceful, and that she was engaged in an act of deception.

Finding little satisfaction in the prospect of corresponding with Mr. Stephenson—what was there to say that would not compound the awkwardness?—Harriet turned back to her half-written letter, hoping to find vindication of her course. But she found nothing of the sort: perhaps the shock of the Stephenson telegram had cleared her vision. The words she had written to Toma were inadequate. She had asked no direct questions. Of course she trusted Toma to do what was right and to exert himself to the utmost; that much she had seen in his eyes at the moment of her asking. But there was also the possibility of failure despite all extreme efforts. Who, after all, could change the weather? Or foresee an injury? She was prepared to be surprised by triumph; failure was another matter.

But something else had found its way into her letter. As a preface to her remarks about the progress of the casting—that part of the letter would have so little pleasure in it—she had described her garden to him, the garden he had helped her plant. For the amusement of the invalid she painted a deprecating portrait of its little corners and general aspect, so yellowed and fallen from the green glories of April when each new shoot had promised an earthly paradise. She thought this would cheer him up, because it was clear from her visit that he was melancholic. But beneath the wry flourishes she saw the ghost of her own regret. Might he not conclude from this letter that she missed him, and that her garden drooped in his absence? She stared at her handwriting and was reminded of a comment by Lucy, spoken very softly and with the mildest exasperation: My dear Harriet, I think you do not know yourself.

Harriet sifted through the other correspondence in her box until she came upon the Iron Bank stationery, an envelope addressed to her in Senator Truscott's hand. Was it his hand? The clerk's writing did bear a strong resemblance. She puzzled over this annoying ambiguity: How could she not know his writing? Also, she compared the unopened letter to an imaginary one, the one that Toma might compose in response to her own.

Senator Truscott and the letter in hand represented a kind of insurance. She would never mistake Toma's writing for any other, and she could summon a feeling, almost a physical sensation, simply by thinking about his response to her letter. Fowler Truscott's letter evoked no corresponding emotion, but it did, even unread, convey his benevolent attention. If she would but trust in him—thus spake the envelope—a way might be found out of these awkward circumstances, a wide and pleasant way that led, there could be no doubt, to that impressive white house with the lawn descending to the lake.

Harriet sighed. She would not destroy her musings to Toma—what harm could there be in them?—but would complete the letter on a different tack. These men were both her suitors; but while she had read enough popular fiction to know that a case might be made for either one, she had no experience or encouragement to place herself at the center of the drama. Such lessons as she had learned from life persuaded her that caring and coping and self-improvement were the natural channels for her energies, and it was almost an embarrassment to consider too closely the question of what she might feel for a man who would be her husband, or to balance the claims of the candidates. She sealed her envelope with no sense of doing any wrong: she was protecting, as best she knew how, the things that were familiar and nearest her heart.

A commotion in the yard caught her attention. Several workmen from the idled forge descended the steps from the railway siding, linked to one another like mountain climbers. The cable had arrived.

She went to stand between her father and the window, rearranging the papers on his desk to distract him. "That would have been the eleven-twenty freight, then," he said, commenting with satisfaction on the whistle of the train's departure. Any sound that reached him was to be celebrated.

"Yes, Papa, it must have been."

"Are you feeling well?" he asked, gazing up at her. "You do not seem quite yourself today."

THERE WERE MANY FOLK in Beecher's Bridge apart from Harriet Bigelow who had a curiosity and some inkling of what might be afoot in the underworld of Power City.

Amos Bigelow's aversion to that place, coupled with his position as the town's largest employer, had the effect, over time, of rendering anonymous the land below the falls. Even though the large maps in the post office and the bank still carried the designation Power City, the name had dropped out of the vernacular of Beecher's Bridge, and that quarter was most often referred to as Down There.

Nothing had happened Down There in the last fifty years to arouse any curiosity. It is true that Horatio Washington and Olivia Toussaint—the Darkie and his Yellow Woman to those grown bold over a second pint of beer—lived in the silk mill. But they had no visitors and the place was all but inaccessible by road: the only souls who ventured there were boys old enough to be entrusted with an urgent bundle of laundry, and they generally congratulated themselves, upon their return, for having survived manifold threats of vague description.

But the Stephenson contract was a turning point in the dusty affairs of Beecher's Bridge and in how Power City was perceived. The men employed at the ironworks came soon to understand—as did their wives and the sharper children—how much was riding on this one venture, and they knew they were all in it together. No man had to be told twice, and when Horatio called out for a Stilson wrench or Mr. Brown for a puddling iron, there was a competition of eager hands for the task. The lamps in the kitchens were lit a few minutes earlier so that no shift should be delayed by the tardiness of the man of the house. Children were possibly more receptive to instruction by their elders.

Although the anxieties of a continued drought could never be put entirely out of mind, the infusion of hard currency coinciding with the signing of the contract had a wonderful effect upon commerce and optimism in Beecher's Bridge. Accounts at the general store were nearly current, and Mr. Wright was further encouraged by a flurry of sales from his jewelry case, which had been gathering dust for months. At the saloon, McCreedy noted that he was having to restock the premium ale sometimes twice a week.

By virtue of his efforts in opening up furnace number 3 for operation, Toma had earned the unspoken awe of his fellows at the ironworks. Now he was recuperating in seclusion and the water level in the Buttermilk was dropping still. Great things are expected of heroes, even wounded ones, and it was an interesting coincidence—or no coincidence at all—that the two men who might save the contract were living under one roof, putting their heads together Down There.

Nobody knew for sure what was going on in the silk mill, but curiosity and speculation more than made up for the want of fact. "Scientific" became a ready word to those who could not afford to be without information or opinion, and when uttered with a thoughtful expression usually sufficed to satisfy casual inquiries. Martin Flaherty entertained the pleasing fantasy that the Yellow Woman, who was said to come from New Orleans, was performing rain dances and wearing nothing whatever. And Mrs. Vernacci, who lived along the Bottom, which is not to be confused with Down There, but close enough to it, reported to her neighbors that she had heard a kind of crackling accompanied by erratic flashes in the crowns of the trees when she went to the outhouse well after midnight. Mrs. Ogden, her very prim and reliable neighbor, confirmed this story from her own experience. Mrs. Vernacci and Mrs. Ogden were not friendly, had not exchanged words since the former intemperately expressed her belief that the Ogden tool shed infringed upon her backyard by some two feet. Mrs. Ogden's verification was thus as independent as Mrs. Vernacci could wish, though she regretted that this marvelous vision had not been granted solely to her. Opinion was roughly divided between those who thought that the Devil himself was at work in Power City and those who assigned the lights and the sound to some scientific experiment.

Fowler Truscott saw no flickering portents and no experimental noises disturbed his sleep. Mrs. Vernacci's story would, in some version, eventually reach his ears, but in the meantime he had access to all those papers relating to the finances of the ironworks and to his politician's instinct for which way the wind blew.

The summer had been a pleasant one for him, in spite of the heat and the drought, for he was able to imagine how much less bearable Washington would be in this season. Here he had his garden, somewhat seared, and the lake upon which he took early exercise in his single scull, with his bulldog Sousa perched precariously upon the bow platform keeping a lookout for fish. The morning was the senator's time for the newspapers and for his correspondence, and in the afternoon he attended to the affairs of the bank and to the perfection of his golf swing.

One of the affairs of the Iron Bank, of course, was its relationship with the Bigelow Iron Company, a connection now almost exactly defined by his personal interest in Miss Harriet Bigelow. The senator was not quite sure how or why this had happened. He had known the family for many years, and the iron company had always been an important client. But until last summer he had not seen Harriet as more than a charming and accomplished child.

The first tremor came with the accidental discovery that she was not merely the scribe but the author of all correspondence from the ironworks. He marveled at the efficiency of her thinking, at her command of each detail of production and inventory, at the sure leap of her mind from such details to their economic consequences. Most impressive, and most reassuring, was her deference to age and authority in the person of her father. This modesty, continually deflecting praise or even acknowledgement, had the effect, in his eyes, of redoubling every other charm of her person or character. He had turned these thoughts over in his mind during the nine months when he was mainly in Washington, and had come to Beecher's Bridge in June with a determination to win the hand of Harriet Bigelow.

The senator was not a simple or coarse man, and he did not imagine that this enchanting girl's affection was to be purchased. Nor could he flatter himself that he might sweep her off her feet by the force of his personality or his physical charm. Once—and here he had a delightful recollection of another girl and that giddy fortnight following the triumphant conclusion of Yale's rowing season in 1884—once, but not now.

There were two mirrors in the senator's bathroom, one on the medicine cabinet and the other swivel-mounted on posts atop the vanity. A few weeks ago he had caught a view of himself in the mirrors, two views, one familiar and the other not. The unfamiliar reflection showed the withered flank and the tentative posture of a man approaching the limit of his middle age. He shifted his weight to the leg he could see but there was little satisfaction there. Could that possibly be his body? He drew himself up and considered the contours of the chest and belly, which were not shocking to him, for all that they could be improved by the stiff bosom and white waistcoat of evening dress. Mornings on the lake, he said aloud to the panting Souza. Do us both good, old fellow.

The exercise had made him feel more vigorous than he had for quite some time, made him feel almost young. But although the senator was inclined to excuse himself from the full rigor of examination and analysis that he applied elsewhere, there were certain signs that he could not ignore, signs that his suit could not succeed along the lines familiar from his youth. That kiss, to take the most obvious example, had not been well received. Should he have asked for permission? He did not know. The moment had seemed propitious and he had yielded to his impulse. Would she have responded differently to the twenty-two-year-old Fowler Truscott, stroke and captain of the victorious crew? He thought again of that girl whose every particular he remembered except her name.

But he had other things to offer than brash youth and well-turned legs. During the congressional season, when he had seen Harriet only twice during holidays, they had corresponded, ostensibly about the management and fortunes of the iron business. He knew, or had a strong instinct, that he occupied a special place in her life—the mother dead, the father distracted—and she was so young. The tone of her letters had become somewhat more familiar. While she still addressed him as Dear Senator Truscott, she entered into the pleasant fiction that she was his eyes and ears, and recorded the extraordinary hue of the turning swamp maples, the distant cry of loons (not sighted), and the early breakup of ice on his pond: all those little things that the country man in exile might long for. From the elegiac tone of these observations as much as from any details of iron manufacture and shipments, he deduced two things: that the business, in spite of her energy, was not going well, and that her responsibilities weighed upon her. And this third thing as well: she had, if only so slightly, and perhaps without knowing it, opened her heart to him.

It might be that the Stephenson contract could still be saved, but that would depend upon the weather. He had paid a ceremonial visit to the works after the opening of the old furnace, and from the evidence of his own eyes as well as from the anxious, eager explanations of the foremen, he understood that the enterprise hung by a thread. He hoped for the best, of course, but in strict banking terms the Bigelow Iron Company account would have to be seen as a bad debt, and Harriet Bigelow might be the sole remaining asset. Whether the crisis occurred now or a little further down the road was a matter of a few dollars. He tried to take a long view of what seemed an economic reality: The Bigelow Iron Company, lone survivor of the industry in these hills, must inevitably yield to the brute efficiency of the coal-fired empires of Pittsburgh. And something else would take its place here, though he was not so wise as to know what that enterprise might be. As his friend Mr. Coffin had commented, that fellow Darwin made a better economist than a biologist.

On a particular afternoon in late August the senator sat in his office at the bank with Miss Bigelow, who had responded to his note, and with the senior clerk, who may have wondered at such enthusiastic attention being devoted to such dismal figures.

"Nothing will change, you can depend on that," was the senator's conclusion. "We stand behind you and have the utmost confidence in your success." He said this, and might have noted the wondering abstraction of his clerk's expression except that he was watching Harriet.

There came a knock at the door to announce an urgent visitor for Miss Bigelow. "Who is it?" he asked. Who would dare? he thought. Her identity was not known, but she had been sent by Mr. Peacock with instructions to find Miss Bigelow. It was Olivia, hair askew and streaming perspiration, who entered and would look only at the carpet.

"He says to give you this. He says to read it now."

And Harriet read to the accompaniment of Olivia's ragged breathing: "We are halfway home and confident of success. Tell me what money you can spare."

"MOTHER OF GOD," muttered Toma, "will you look at the price of these things!" The lines of Horatio Washington's mouth tightened as he scanned the catalogue pages.

"Perhaps they are too fancy?"

"A motor is a simple thing. They are too expensive, that's all."

"And the others?" Horatio nodded at the stack of catalogues on the bench.

"The same. Cleveland Armature, Onan Generator . . . a matter of a dollar or two. I had no idea."

"And Miss Bigelow says?"

"Fifty dollars. The payroll must be met on Friday. Fifty dollars, and I have another twenty."

"What will you do? Without the motor all you can do with your dynamo is make sparks."

Toma looked at the dynamo, which sat now on its separate bench, connected to the wheel by a belt running through a hole in the wall of the laundry. Horatio's collection of parts and scrap had been pushed back piece by piece to the east wall, and that space was now occupied by the coils of Stephenson's cable.

"I am thinking what you can do."

"You would have to ask Olivia. She handles that, but I doubt she's got much saved."

"I don't mean money. I want you to make me a motor."

Horatio considered his left hand: two fingers were still numb from the jolt of touching the wrong part of the dynamo. "I don't know anything about that."

"You don't need to know anything. You simply have to make a copy of the dynamo. An exact copy."

"You have a dynamo. What would you do with another?"

"You are forgetting. They are the same thing. If I could apply enough electricity to the dynamo, and adjust the brushes, it would produce motion, mechanical energy. It would be a motor. One is the mirror to the other."

Horatio said nothing. Toma continued, in the tone one might use to an obstinate child. "You take the dynamo apart, carefully, and see how it is made. I will purchase the wire for the windings and the brushes. There is enough money for that."

Horatio sighed. "I'm tired. I don't understand your God-damned machine, and I don't trust it any more than I would a snake. What happens if we fail?"

"The same as if we don't try: You're out of a job." They glared at one another. Two days ago Mr. Brown had ordered number 3 shut down, as there was not enough water to produce a blast for both furnaces. Horatio had set his men to working the tub bellows by hand, trying to keep the main furnace and number 3 in operation. It could not be done, not in this heat, not without killing someone.

"How long do I have?"

"Three days, if we place the order now. I'll be ready by Friday to test it and to string the cable."

"And you think it will work? You think you can do this?"

"I think *you* can do it, Horatio. This is what you are good at: you told me so yourself. Think of the Springfield Armory. Think of all those interchangeable parts. That is what you must do now, the same job, the interchangeable parts."

Horatio's eyes moved to his piles of scrap against the wall and Toma knew that he had won. "It might work," said Horatio, "but it won't be much to look at."

"One thing more. Would you speak to Olivia about the money? I must have certain measuring devices. Everything up to now has been guesswork."

Horatio grunted, and Toma held out his hand. "Thank you, Horatio."
"I know why you're in this."
"Perhaps you do."

ON AUGUST 30, because it was a Friday, Amos Bigelow began tidying his desk at eleven o'clock, putting on the far left corner any items on which action might be deferred until the afternoon, or perhaps tomorrow. He did note that there were two pieces of correspondence from Mr. Stephenson in this pile. He and Harriet would have to put their heads together and come up with some answers that would ease the gentleman's anxiety. With his handkerchief he wiped away the fine dust that seemed to be everywhere these days.

The spirit level assured him that his surface was truly horizontal, and so he laid out his pocket watch and the old leather book in which he recorded the variations of chronometry along with his observations of temperature and weather, morning and evening. There was always a pleasant anticipation of noon in the sun's reflected progress across his ceiling. Rafter by rafter the muted image crept from west to east until at last it struck the second mirror fixed above his desk and was bent down to his purpose. On a good day the noon whistle would sound when the reflection of the sun was bisected by the dark crack in the surface of Amos Bigelow's desk.

It wasn't a perfect system, and he regretted that his hand was no longer steady enough to take these readings with the quadrant. He regretted as well, when he remembered to do so, that he could no longer hear the whistle from Titusville, which, being four miles downstream to the southwest, must necessarily have its own separate noon. But Horatio, that excellent fellow, had arranged these mirrors for him, and adjusted the exterior one seasonally, and it was in a way more convenient, for he could more readily observe the variance of watch and whistle from God's true time.

He knew from his reading of the newspapers that there was strong public opinion and growing legislative sentiment in favor of what was

euphemistically called Standard Time. He knew from Fowler Truscott
that sooner or later the bill would pass, cleaving the country into four
vast zones, time zones. Why would one wish for such a thing? Why
tamper with such a simple principle that mirrored the divine order?
How was a man to be sure of anything at all if noon were not noon?
The senator's answer about efficiency and the requirements of the
transcontinental railroads came so readily and casually that Bigelow
perceived his partisanship and affected not to hear the explanation.
One thing Amos Bigelow wished to avoid at almost any cost was a re-
opening of the old antagonism between the two families.

As the hour approached, anticipation acquired an edge of nervous
energy, for there were three observations vying for his attention: the
transit of the sun, the variance of his watch, and the timing of the
whistle. The tension gathered in his shoulders; his right hand was
poised with the pen above his note book; and the left hand rose slowly,
palm open to the heavens, as a conductor might summon the brass section to a triumphant chord.

Today had the makings of a very good day, with the curve of the
bright disk just grazing the mark and the second hand of his watch at a
promising angle. But it was not to be. There was a disturbance at the
edge of his vision that he tried to ignore.

"Go away!" It was the woman from Down There, Horatio's woman.

Olivia startled at this bellow and was only too ready to obey, but
first she must put the envelope, Toma's envelope, where it would be
seen, and since Amos Bigelow seemed to be staring fixedly at a particular point in the center of his desk, that seemed to be the sensible
choice.

"Agghhh!" The whistle coincided with this cry of despair, and in
swatting at the offending envelope Amos Bigelow managed to send his
watch skidding to the edge of the desk, where Olivia intercepted it.
There would be no observation today, no record of his efforts.

"Is this from Horatio?" Bigelow was already tearing at the envelope
in his fury before he had looked at the writing.

"No," said Olivia, "and it ain't for you. Toma sent me to find Miss
Harriet, but I don't know where she's at. It's for her."

"Yes, yes . . ." But Amos Bigelow unfolded the single sheet anyway
and was baffled by the message, a single word: Tomorrow.

Harriet Bigelow affected bewilderment and indifference to the note. This was for her father's benefit, but she really did not know what to make of it. Could it be a joke of some kind?

Throughout the afternoon she sustained a deliberate lack of curiosity about the meaning of the message, about what might happen tomorrow. Her father was too upset by the ruin of his chronometry to pursue the matter. In a way it could have been worse. Toma might have written her in much more explicit detail, or even about other things. Such a letter, suffering the same fate as the actual one, would have required a great deal of awkward explanation.

She and her father dined early, as usual, and afterward sat in the parlor, where Amos Bigelow liked to listen to Harriet's playing of the harmonium—hymns and popular tunes, for the most part—or to her reading aloud from Trollope or Dickens.

They were both tired, an effect of the heavy but rainless fog that had descended on Beecher's Bridge in mid-afternoon. She played the organ this evening, "Rock of Ages" and a Sousa march for her father, a bit of Schubert for herself, but she found her attention was drawn to a small vase of flowers on the table by her father's chair. She was a good soul, Mrs. Evans, and the dusty blooms were a kindly forethought. But Harriet was annoyed by the flowers, annoyed by the inclusion of those ghastly flesh-toned zinnias, which ought to be weeded out of the garden altogether. She remembered with an almost painful clarity the arrangement of bleeding heart and purple columbine that Toma had set in that very place, in the same vase, and how the flowers held such promise. Thus was the theme of hope quite innocently threaded back into her thoughts.

They retired to bed after going out onto the porch to observe how the glow of the unseen moon irradiated the fog, and when she sat down in her nightgown in front of the glass, she found that the damp air it had already curled the pages of her music—now rendered her hair unresponsive to the brush. She was not flattered by her reflection in the glass, nor was she reassured by this ritual

The interruption of his noon observation had preoccupied Amos Bigelow to a degree that his daughter found disturbing; and even more distressing was the way he kept introducing the incident into conversation as if it were an entirely fresh subject. Of course she hoped that he might be more himself tomorrow. If he could be persuaded to take another reading, as he would in the case of bad weather, then today's disaster might be downgraded to an inconvenience. But she was enough of a realist to read the future of such odd behavior, her own future as well as his. Might not the horizon of her life be reduced to the care of this one soul? Tonight this idea, which had occurred to her before, presented itself not as an abstraction but as a foregone conclusion whose only uncertainty lay in its timing. And who then would tend to the affairs of the ironworks? There was only the one reflection in her glass, and those bare shoulders spoke only of frailty.

She went to bed with these thoughts and did not fall asleep as she had expected to do. In the end it was the fond thought of Toma—now forgiven—and what he might achieve tomorrow that brought her peace.

THE FOG HAD NOT lifted by morning and the sun could not be seen. Mrs. Evans commented on the strangeness of this weather and remembered that such a gloomy damp had been the harbinger of a violent hurricane some twenty years earlier, the same year Harriet had been born.

"I am sure we do not need a hurricane, Mrs. Evans," said Harriet, "only a little rain. A persistent rain, but not violent."

"We can't choose, dear, now can we?"

"No. That is simply my hope." She stopped short of adding that it was her prayer as well, for there the thought or wish must be expressed in a less particular way, and God could answer her prayers in any way He saw fit. Her remark had turned sour on her. She saw that her father had not been following the conversation.

"Time to be going now." He pushed his plate away. "That boy's up to something." Here he fixed his daughter with an odd, momentary glance that seemed to go right through her without really seeing her.

It was apparent, once they reached the ironworks, that nearly everyone from the swampers and puddlers to the machinists had reached the same conclusion as Amos Bigelow. There was no one about in the yard, no sound of industry in the forge, no casual banter of men about to go on shift. They saw the square figure of Mr. Brown hurrying off in the direction of number 3.

"Good morning to you, sir! Good morning, miss!" he called out in uncharacteristic exuberance, and then the fog swallowed him.

"By God, will you look!" exclaimed Amos Bigelow. Harriet looked: three black lines slicing diagonally through the thick air, and with the swallows haphazardly perched there, her first thought was for a tipped sheet of music.

The life of the mill was ahead of them now as they hastened along the uneven path, the power train stilled and silent beside them, the black cables converging on their route.

"Don't touch it, Papa."

Was it her imagination, or had the forest already begun to reclaim the clearing in the few days that number 3 had been shut down? Or was it this odd half-light? The furnace was fired and ready, though with both shifts on hand there seemed to be a great confusion up above on the charging platform and many shouted inquiries addressed either to Mr. Brown or to Horatio Washington, who tended the ugly rust-mottled box that received the cables. He paid no attention to the workmen pressing up as close as they dared to the device.

"I had a cousin once, in Hartford, and he was near killed by the electric when it went wrong," said one.

"Hmm . . ." said his friend wisely, "and there's them in this very town as has been struck by lightning. Will this thing make lightning, then, Mr. Washington?"

Horatio did not answer, but struck the metal box with his hammer and held up his hand for silence. He pulled three times on a cord, and all eyes followed the cables down to their vanishing point.

Harriet kept her father by her at the edge of the clearing, away from the confusion and the questions.

"Are you frightened then, my dear?" He wondered at the grip of her restraining hand.

"It looks almost like a holiday, don't you think? Or the Independence Day picnic."

"I think everyone but me knows what's going on here. Can you explain this thing to me? Is Horatio in it then?"

Harriet was never so glad to see Senator Truscott, who now came to stand beside them. What did he know? and how?

"By a single stroke of genius is the world reordered." Truscott was quoting someone, perhaps himself.

"What?"

"Never mind, Papa. It's about to happen, I think."

And indeed it did happen, so soon after the answering signal from below—a small bell tied to a tree near the box—that the first thing she noticed was the changing light, a growing illumination like a second dawn as the driven air was fed into the tuyeres by the hidden fan and the flames leapt up from the stack. The motor's whine rose through this spectacle and leveled off at the very edge of her hearing, and the roar of the fan now drowned the cheering.

Could he hear it down there? she wondered. Could he know? She wanted to bolt down the steep path and bring him his triumph like the runner from Marathon.

Fowler Truscott noted the expression on her face, a kind of transfigured beauty, and was reminded of something: yes, that moment in his office so recently. He put his lips very close to her ear.

"Oh, well done . . . how very well done indeed."

CHAPTER

NINE

". . . and although I am flattered by your reference to the genius of Mr. Edison, I must also . . ." Here Toma wiped the pen on a scrap of newsprint and put it down. Senator Truscott's note, elegant, and generous, and obtuse, was propped against the battery. The battery . . . damnation: he would have to find another one somewhere. Must also what?

The senator's communication was remarkable for its courtesy and timeliness, having been delivered by Harriet Bigelow in person, to the evident displeasure of Olivia. Horatio, as Harriet explained succinctly, was too occupied with the amazing device to come down himself. "And I long to see your wheel." Her phrase "your wheel" struck a deep chord of pleasure in him. The same phrase, repeated in the senator's note, had an ironic echo.

Of course he had obliged her. She had a knowing smile for the battery and an awed appreciation of the dynamo. They walked together along the belting that linked the dynamo to the waterwheel standing in the wreckage of Olivia's laundry. He gave her his hand to help her through the access hole. She marveled at the spectacle of the wheel enveloped in its own mist and running at full throttle; he would not look at the machine, but at her.

"I cannot tell you . . ." she began. "Horatio said I should be very proud of you. It is such a miracle, this thing. Mr. Brown is beside himself, and promises us twenty-five wheels a day from number 3 alone. Will you show me how it works?"

He nodded in agreement. He noticed that the spray had made a dew on the front of her dress. He put out his hand as if to wipe it away. "H . . ." he said, as she caught his hand in hers.

She glanced down at herself and laughed. "Do I look positively drowned?" Then, not looking at him but at his hand: "Do you remember when you first called me H?"

"I remember everything." The question and the pressure of her hand must be an invitation, and so he took her in his arms, sweating and work-stained, and found her mouth.

"Your dress," he murmured.

"It is already ruined. It does not matter."

TOMA FOUND SENATOR TRUSCOTT'S letter unaccountably naïve. Flattering, perhaps, but only to a fool. He had invented nothing, and this talk of Edison, the genius of the junk pile, was very wide of the mark. One device to make running water produce electricity, another to make that electricity move the air and feed it into the furnace. The two connected by lengths of borrowed cable. His contribution was no invention, but an application, nothing more than the overcoming of circumstance: Horatio's unwillingness, his own physical limitations, the lack of money, the crudeness of equipment. This is what had tempered his thinking, even in that transcendent moment when the connection of the two wheels had come to him, one for water and one for air. There was tremendous excitement in the enterprise and the accomplishment, but it must not be mistaken for genius.

This was how he understood the matter. He had made no claim for himself or for this solution, had avoided even a description of it in his note to Harriet, not because he was modest but because he was proud: one day he would put his hand and his name to something that would be deserving of such praise. The senator's note, betraying such profound ignorance, was an insult, or so Toma came to feel.

The other awkward point was the reference to "your wheel." He regretted that he had not corrected Harriet's mistake. It was not his wheel, but Horatio's, and all he had done was tinker with it, adjusting the delivery of the jet to extract the maximum mechanical advantage, reinforcing the timbers supporting the axle to reduce distortion at high speed. And because of his injury and lack of balance, he had not even been able to do this on his own. Again, it was Horatio, with his fine eye and those huge, steady hands, who brought the wheel to its new position.

Toma stood up and made his way through the shop to the laundry, putting some weight on the foot that was almost healed, trying not to limp. Even at rest the wheel was an undeniably beautiful thing. He set it in motion with a touch and it was as if he had willed some part of his own body to move, so eerily familiar to his hand, such effortless response in spite of the mass.

It seemed as if the spinning might have no end, as if the natural law governing bodies in motion had been defied. There was no sound to it, and only by the quality of reflected light did he know that the wheel was slowing down. The circumference, which had appeared as solid as one of Mr. Brown's iron wheels, resolved itself into the sculpted cups— eighteen of them—that received the jet and threw the water back upon itself; the central disk where those corrugations of wood spiraled and tapered toward the axle became a vortex to the eye, more distinct, more mysterious as its speed ebbed. He stopped the wheel with his hand.

Horatio had used a straight and tight-grained beech for his work, preserving it with corrosive sublimate, then tempering it in an oil bath for weeks, gradually increasing the temperature until the water content of the wood was driven out and replaced by the oil. Each piece he had polished, taking care, he said, for his true edges, then were his eighteen pieces laid down in a circle, the heavy cups outermost and the arcing tails like old pipe stems laid toward the center. The splined dowels were seated with a glue that would hold despite the oil, and the whole drawn into a perfect circle by a perimeter belt. When he was done, said Horatio, with a rare animation, as if it had been a contest of strength, when he had executed this one final step that must succeed or fail without reprieve, there was not so much as a drop of expressed glue to wipe away. It was done, and it was perfect.

Horatio knew the quality of his work, and Toma, running his finger in the spiral groove from cup to axle, could find no seam in the wood, though he knew it was there. It was almost as if Horatio had imagined this thing and willed it into existence. Could he make Truscott understand? or Harriet? Did he himself grasp the idea in its entirety? He did not wish to claim the wheel as his own. He was humbled by it,

awed by his sense that there might be properties and potentialities
here that he had not yet explored.

A bell sounded in the shop. That would be Horatio's signal. He
opened the jet valve and levered the belt into position on the axle. It
was a matter of a few steps to get to the dynamo, by which time he
could hear that the wheel was approaching the threshold speed. With
two sharp yanks on the cord he answered Horatio, and groped without
looking for the clutch lever. His eyes were fixed on the dial and on his
crude system of variable resistance. Better to start high than have the
motor's coil burnt out by the first rush of unanswered voltage. He
clamped the switch to close his circuits and eased the lever to engage
the free pulley to the dynamo. The stuttering hum of the wheel was the
bass to the dynamo's treble whine, a chord that told him as much as any
of the meters arrayed on the bench.

MUCH LATER, IN THE DAYS and weeks after he had made his attempts
to give an account of the fatal evening, he came back to questions no
one else had thought to ask.

The evening was to be a celebration; Olivia had purchased a fine
standing roast and had taken the afternoon off in order to cook it, but
the heat of the oven made the living quarters of the mill and the shop
unbearable. Toma was glad to stand in the spray of the wheel, and
when he went back to the shop to check the meters and the sparking of
the dynamo, he broke the wary silence to suggest that she come away to
the relative cool of the laundry.

"When I'm done," she replied, intent on paring potatoes. "Horatio
is going to want to eat when he comes home."

At four o'clock, with the clouds already gathering, she walked past
the open window of the laundry, unbuttoning her shirt—Horatio's
shirt—as if he could not see her, or perhaps she did not care that he
did. He moved to the window to watch, knowing where she was
headed, and if she did not care there seemed no harm in it. She kept
her back to him as she shucked her clothes and lowered herself in to
the pool. She had a bit of soap and she washed, still with her back to
him, but when she rose from the pool she made no effort to cover herself. She brushed the water away with her hands and made a beautiful

arc of her body to reach her legs, then stood perfectly still to let the air do its work. She wrapped herself in the blue-flowered cloth and walked up past his window without ever once meeting his eyes. He smiled, thinking what a lucky man Horatio was.

They sat down to eat at five-thirty, and Toma poured from the straw-covered flagon of wine that he had asked Olivia to buy with the last dollar he had in his pocket. A thunderclap above Great Mountain drowned Toma's toast to Horatio, and before they had finished the meal the storm broke upon them. Horatio raised his glass to the rain: the water was insurance, he said. Let's hope it doesn't stop.

The bottle of whiskey was put on the table by Olivia after the plates were cleared, and Toma was surprised to see that she took a glass for herself. He had never seen her drink before this evening, and yet she had taken her share of the wine. They were all exhausted: she because the laundry had reverted to punishing hand work; Horatio because the hauling of the cable had come on top of his labor on the motor; Toma because he could only doze, never sleep, while the machinery was running. So the rain was not only insurance: by the time the whiskey was poured there was probably enough water in the Buttermilk to run the main wheel at the works, and Toma could send a signal via the bell-pull. Why didn't they just turn the machinery off and go to bed?

At eight o'clock a messenger with a dead lantern arrived with a message from Mr. Brown that the casting shed had flooded and he was banking down the furnace for the night. By this time Horatio and Toma had moved to the bench to continue, with the help of illustration, a discussion of the Pelton wheel's design and its possible improvement. Whenever Toma caught Olivia in the corner of his eye, she seemed to be looking at him, her arms crossed on her breast and the glass in hand.

Bewick, who had fallen on the path, was glad to take a glass of whiskey while Olivia worked to revive his drowned lantern. He was a Scot, a puddler of many years' experience, and he chose his words carefully. He did not comment on the contents of the glass other than to murmur his thanks. He was more forthcoming in relaying Mr. Brown's opinion of the wheels, and how disappointed he was to have such a fine run of the hearth interrupted.

"But at least there's a good night's sleep in it for you," he said, raising his glass to Horatio. "We were talking it over, you know, wondering how much longer you could carry on. It's not as if you're a young man, no more'n I am myself. Not like Peacock here." He drained his glass, nodded at Toma, and belched. "I'll be off now. Mr. Brown had a boy ready to go but I wanted to come and pay my respects. Thank you, missy," he said, taking the lantern, "I don't know as it will see me all the way home in this rain, but thank you anyway." Olivia shut the door behind him with unusual emphasis. She had knocked over the lantern twice while threading a dry wick.

The rain drummed on the roof, not in a steady pattern but fitfully—now drizzle, now downpour. A leak in the roof sent a cascade down onto Horatio's junk pile, and he told Olivia to put a bucket there. The lightning was more constant than the rain, intent on the destruction of the scarred outcropping at the end of Great Mountain. "Lightning Knob," murmured Horatio. "A betting man could win money on it, if he found a fool to take the bet."

The temperature had dropped ten or fifteen degrees since they had sat down to dinner. Toma was exhilarated as much by the gift of rain and the electrical display as by the whiskey, but he saw that every time the lightning struck Olivia flinched, and after one particularly violent bolt she crossed herself.

"You know I don't hold with that," said Horatio.

"Maybe we all going to die," she answered, looking squarely at him as she drank again.

"Nobody's going to die." Toma pushed back his chair and went to the bench, to Horatio's rendering of the wheel. "Horatio, will you come with me? We'll need light. I want to show you something, and I want to ask you a question about your wheel."

"I'm tired, boy."

"You can sleep tomorrow, as long as you like."

He had been thinking about the wheel all afternoon, listening to it and rearranging it in his mind, embroidering upon its apparent perfection. He did not think that Horatio saw this thing as anything other than a convenience that had bought him peace with Olivia, a device now turned to another practical purpose.

They took two lanterns each and went to the laundry, and because she would not be left alone, Olivia followed them carrying the bottle. She offered it to him and he refused. He removed the driving belt and spun the wheel with his hand.

"If you stand here, Horatio, you will not get so wet."

"What am I supposed to be seeing?"

"You are going to see how fast the wheel can go with no load on it and the cock open all the way."

"I don't need to see anything. What good does that do?"

"I don't know. It will be like watching a horse to see how fast it can go. What good is there in that?"

"I was in the cavalry once. Got a medal, and as far as I remember, that didn't do me any good either. Go fast when you need to. Go slow when you don't. You break this thing, you'll have an awful lot of disappointed folks."

"I want to see how fast the horse will go," said Olivia.

"Give me that bottle, girl." Horatio took it and set it down out of her reach. He turned back to Toma. "You know, there's trouble in this thing if you run it too fast. If you'd ever worked a lathe you'd know what I mean."

"Here." Toma handed him the coils of the slack driving belt. "If the axle starts to vibrate you can ease it down. But I think you'll see that I was right and the wheel will find its own limit."

Horatio took the belting and wrapped it around his forearm to make a short noose that he could bring to bear as a friction brake if need be. Toma opened the cock partway. The wheel began to turn. In a matter of seconds it built to that familiar pitch, and then he turned the handle as far as it would go.

There were two adjustments that could be made to the jet, one to advance it toward the cupped blades, the other to alter its angle of access, and thus the trajectory of the exit water. The closer the jet, the greater force it imparted, but at such a rotational speed the tips of the cups deflected the water as if from a solid rim. Elevating the jet would allow it to clear the tips of the blades, would alter the vectors delivered to Horatio's parabolas. All of this could be calculated if he had the time and the right instruments.

Toma eased the right-hand crank from noon to two o'clock and the greased gearing elevated the jet by a couple of degrees. He could see almost nothing because of the dense spray, but his ears told him what he wanted to know.

"How is it, Horatio?"

"Well, it seems—"

"Wait, wait." Toma backed away from the cranks, away from the spray, and bumped against Olivia. How long had she been standing there? He needed a clear view of the exit water, so that he could compare it to Horatio's precise renderings of the blades. She stumbled against him as he turned and did not pull away. One arm around his waist, hot whiskey breath on his face.

"Horatio, I'm coming." He unwound Olivia's arm and gave her the metal rail as a support. "And don't you touch anything. Stand here."

Horatio's stance spoke to his doubt: braced against some startling of the animal on the other end of his tether. "I'd say you've had your fun. Feel that." Toma put his fingers to the belt, saw how it lay barely grazing the pulley, felt its hummingbird pulse. "I say we quit. I have to pull on this belt, there's no telling what happens to that shaft."

"Give me just a minute and we'll shut it down. I need to—" Did she stumble against the cranks? Did she do it out of boredom? He could see nothing other than the path of the exit water from this new angle, and heard no alteration until the metal of the nozzle hit the wheel, and one of the cups struck him on the face and knocked him down.

He did not know, then or afterward, whether he might have been unconscious for a matter of moments, but when he was again aware of himself and of the blow to his head, so much had changed that it was hard to find sequence or order in his surroundings. One of the lanterns had been kicked over and Horatio directed a steady flow of invective at Olivia and at the wheel. He heard the woman screaming, or sobbing, "I can't! I can't!" and then the wheel, its pitch so altered that he had not located it there at the edge of his hearing. On either side of the wheel the exit water funneled out almost horizontally, a pair of spiral horns enveloping the axle and bearings, smashing into spray against the framing timbers. Were all the blades gone, then?

"Shut it off! You hear me? Olivia!" There was a pleading tone in Horatio's voice now, and as Toma darted through the spray at the other side of the wheel—away from Horatio and the writhing belt—the eccentric treble of the axle sounded an alarm in his ear.

"It's going . . . can't hold it!" Horatio's cry was followed by a splintering as the shimmying axle tore from its bearings and stood on end, a vast and lethal top attached only to Horatio's belting. The water from the jet splashed harmlessly on the floor. Olivia's eyes were as wide and white as fried eggs. What did she see?

She saw Horatio talking to the wheel as if he might gentle it, saw the furious axle, as it found imperfections in the cement floor, begin to hop and skitter to a punctuation of piercing notes, the distress of tuned metal. Higher now each jolt in the erratic jig, and Horatio following it, trying to keep the belt clear of the wheel, muttering, "No . . . no . . ." as it made a stubborn gyroscopic progress across the floor. And when it reached a certain seam in the cement, well known to the soles of Olivia's feet, the wheel made a fantastic bound, the axle almost achieving the horizontal. The belt was caught at this angle, or looped upon itself, and when the axle touched the ground for the last time the wheel shot sideways through the wall of silk bobbins, bearing Horatio away into the night. It was so sudden that they were not sure what they had seen, what to believe or hope. There was his shoe on the floor, there the gaping hole in the wall. They could see nothing but rain beyond the splintered wood.

Perhaps they already knew that he was dead, though they pretended otherwise. Perhaps on another night with the help of a moon or even the stars they would have found him. But the lamp Toma held out into the rain was of no use even before it was drowned.

"Bring me a candle, anything. That thing on the nail by the stove."

When she returned with the hurricane lantern he was sitting on the floor trying to jam his foot into the shoe Horatio had left behind. It was the wrong shoe and the foot was still swollen.

"You can't put a shoe on that foot yet. You can't go out."

"You go then."

She might have obeyed him but for the lightning strike. She dropped the lantern and he caught it in midair, burning his hand on the hot glass.

"I can't."

"Then I'm going. We must do something."

"If he ain't dead, he'll come back. He's a hard man, Horatio, hard to kill. Don't you go out there."

Olivia watched as he dragged himself to the door, and when he had worked his way around to the drop-off she moved near the gap in the boards to watch his light. She heard him calling out the name, over and over, saw the light swerve and vanish in the tinkling of glass. There was no answer that she could hear. She set the remaining lamps on the floor out of the rain, one by the door, the other by the hole so he could see his way back. She waited, wondering if any of them would live through this night.

Toma appeared in the doorway on his hands and knees looking more than half-dead. She took him up in her arms, kept him from falling. "He's gone. Take those wet things off and come to bed. Don't let me sleep alone tonight."

HE SLEPT LIKE A dead man in the clean sheets, slept through the wet, enfeebled daybreak, and would have slept longer but for a knocking at the door. He was trapped under the languorous warmth of her thigh across his, and his first thought was that Horatio had come back. Galvanized by this possibility, he struggled free, lifting the dead weight of her leg and flopping her ungently onto her back. She groaned but did not wake. He made to cover her with the sheet, then remembered his own nakedness and took it for himself.

It was not Horatio at the door but Mrs. Breen's boy, a red-haired lad on the cusp of adolescence with a head too small for his body. Judging by the bundle he carried, his journey down the path had been an adventure. The boy scraped the fresh mud from the laundry with his nails, would not meet Toma's eye.

"She says, my mother says, that she wants it all back day after tomorrow latest, or . . ."

"Or?"

"Well, that's when she wants it back, is all." The boy thrust the bundle at Toma. "And, sir?"

"What?"

"It's about the darkie, I mean Mr. Washington."

"What about him?" The sound of his own voice was making Toma's head ache.

"Is he dead or somethin'?"

"You saw him? Where?"

"I seen him up a tree and he ain't movin', though he seed me, and . . ." The boy's round-eyed narrative came to a halt.

"And what?" Toma shook him until his head bobbled like a flower on a broken stalk.

"And he ain't got no pants on, I mean you can . . ." Young Breen's courage failed him in the face of this awful comedy. He bolted from Toma's grip, scrambling up the path with remarkable agility, driven by terror of the darkie, dead or alive, and of the white man, dressed like an angel of vengeance, who stood bellowing for Olivia to come.

Jamie Breen would in time achieve a privileged status as the first witness to the Darkie's Last Ride, as the event came to be known in the town, would be able to describe every detail, down to the shimmer of silk threaded into snags and shrubs along the river, bright colors that suggested a celebration. In later years he sometimes varied the telling to put himself more or less on that path as the tragedy unfolded, and when his friends told the story for the benefit of some new visitor to McCreedy's Saloon, why, Jamie himself had seen the darkie flying out of the mill in his cloud of silk thread, and had heard his fatal groan as he lodged in the tree.

But Jamie's thought as he hurried away was to find his friends so that he could retail his unembellished news. Perhaps they wouldn't believe him at first; perhaps they would have to see for themselves that Horatio Washington was indeed stuck up a tree, buck-naked, and you could see his black thing. He wouldn't mind going back himself in the safety of numbers, in broad daylight. But nothing in the world could induce Jamie Breen to go back to Power City alone. He'd heard it said often enough that anything could happen down there, and now he knew that it was so.

SEVERAL DAYS LATER, after the excitement had run its course like a fever through Beecher's Bridge, Harriet sent a carefully worded note to the bank. In response to Truscott's repeated requests, she managed the salutation "Dear Fowler." The words looked odd to her, but she had neither time nor sheets of paper to waste and she needed Truscott's undivided attention.

The silence from the silk mill was palpable and inexplicable; her mind fed on it as it would on an obstinate physical symptom. She had already written twice to Toma, first a note of sympathy for the loss of his friend and collaborator, and then a message of concern about the schedule of repairs and her hope that she would see him at his earliest convenience. She could not visit the mill herself. She had written her condolence note to Olivia, and did not know her well enough to intrude on her mourning.

And so she turned to Fowler Truscott: no one else knew so thoroughly the affairs of the ironworks apart from Toma. But it was awkward sending him on this errand. What would they say to each other, or read into the other's response? She colored, glowing in the reflection of this dangerous, flattering speculation.

She finished the letter, signed it, sealed it. The weather had turned hot and dry; every day the level of the Buttermilk fell an inch or two.

Truscott, the letter safe in the pocket next to his heart, made a cheerful progress from the ironworks down to the silk mill. Though the path was now dry he had a staff in one hand; the *Wall Street Journal* served him as fan and flyswatter. This exertion in the sun, even going with the hill, had brought two very bright spots to his cheeks, and his linen jacket, cut to the Norfolk pattern, was already soaked through under his arms. But he did not mind, for the jacket now fit him quite comfortably. How these trees had grown up since he hunted here as a boy. He reflected on the common thread of natural progression, in trees, in himself, in human enterprise. It pleased him to think in terms of progress rather than aging.

Toma answered his knock with the air of a man deeply preoccupied, and for the briefest moment—until Toma thanked him for his letter—Truscott wondered if he had even been recognized.

"May I, Mr. Peacock?" Because his host was barefoot and shirtless, the senator thought he might remove his jacket.

"What? Oh, of course. We are not so formal in this place, as you can see. Will you come in?"

"Yes, yes, if it is no interruption. And if I might have a glass of water?"

"Olivia, some water."

"I ain't decent yet." The voice came from behind the calico curtain. Toma wiped a mug with a rag, filled it from the bucket, and offered it to Truscott, who had been surveying the shop. It reminded him of a train wreck, or what he imagined one must look like, and there was no evidence of a wheel. That other device there, with the wires running away and up through the gable, must be the electrical device.

"I offer you my condolences on the loss of Mr. Washington. I did not know him, except by sight, but Miss Bigelow has explained his importance to the ironworks. I hope, to put it delicately, that his expertise is not irreplaceable?"

"You speak of the wheel?"

"Exactly so. The wheel here in particular, the one that was implicated in your friend's death."

"I have her letter." Toma shrugged.

"Something stands in your way? You must excuse my ignorance of the substance of your work."

"Something," said Toma, hobbling to the bench. "You could say that something has come up." He stared down at an untidy sheaf of papers, on which designs—quite abstract to Truscott's eye—were overwritten with calculations.

"Is it perhaps a matter of the shock? The accident must have . . ."

"Yes, yes . . . the accident, exactly so. The accident has changed everything. I see now what must be done." He took from the benchtop a bit of wood curiously curved and broken at the heavy end.

"This is good news, then. Miss Bigelow will be happy to hear it."

"Do you think so?" The unfocused gaze that accompanied these words had the effect of arresting the smile on Truscott's face before it had run its course. "I don't."

"Unhappy, then? But what . . . Sir, in what sense do you speak?" Truscott had divined a depth in the connection of Harriet to this man. His ground was uncertain.

"It is a technical thing, and therefore perhaps difficult for you. Do you see this?" Toma handed him the wooden object. "This is the largest remaining fragment of the wheel, Horatio's wheel. It is the only clue I have."

"Clue!" Truscott made an effort to control himself. "My dear fellow, try to understand what is at stake here. It is imperative that you rebuild that wheel. As I am sure you are aware, the future of the Bigelow Iron Company depends on fulfilling the Stephenson contract, which success, in turn, depends on reconstructing that wheel. Is it a question of money, perhaps?" Truscott's question had a taint of anger. He was aware that he was losing his temper, losing an argument to which he was the sole party. Toma's manner, his distraction, was most aggravating.

"Will you listen? Something happened to the wheel in the accident, even before the accident."

Toma looked away to the calico curtain, and so Truscott looked too. There was the woman, carefully dressed, as if for church. How long she had been there he did not know. No words were spoken between them, and Truscott found the silence oppressive. A strange business, this. If it had been an affair of white people there would have been an inquiry of some sort. He cleared his throat.

"About the wheel?"

"We were experimenting with the system and there was an event, an accident, that altered the wheel. It was a mistake."

"So: a pointless experiment leads to a lethal mistake. A man's life is wasted, and while the fate of the Bigelow Iron Company hangs in the balance, you carry on as if nothing had happened. Have you no shame, sir?"

Toma glanced up and spoke very slowly, as if he doubted Truscott's understanding. "You will not speak to me of shame nor teach me how to grieve. I am responsible for the accident but sorrow will not raise Horatio from the dead, and so I ask myself: Why did he die? Because the wheel, without those blades, or cups, went faster than before. You had only to listen. So fast that its vibration broke through the frame. Then Horatio danced with the wheel and was gone."

"And he died, as everyone knows. So . . ."

"So now the idea of the wheel lives. The sound of it is in my head as if I am the measuring device; and lives, or very nearly, somewhere on my papers there. When its secret is known to me, then I will need your money."

Now Toma smiled as if some weight of indecision had been lifted from him. Truscott was on the point of responding to this visionary impertinence when suddenly he saw his path converging with Toma's. It never pays, he thought, to get angry. When he spoke now he sounded much more like himself.

"You will build this new thing, then, whatever it is, and not the old one?"

"Yes. If not now, then never. It will be lost. All will be lost, and Horatio's death will mean nothing."

Truscott's mind raced ahead of his understanding. From a certain point of view, all was lost right here, right now. What might be salvaged? "Are you saying, in effect, that the hand of God came down and altered the wheel, made it perfect, and in so doing killed Mr. Washington?"

"I do not say it was the hand of God."

"You do realize that Miss Bigelow will be disappointed?"

"I can do nothing about that. Perhaps she will understand the importance of this new work."

"We must hope so. But in the meantime she will see only loss in your resolve." While he spoke, the senator was making rudimentary calculations of his own losses, to be offset by the prize. This was going to be a very expensive matter. "Well, I've done my best here, all I could do. You are determined on this?"

"I am."

"And, so that I might explain it better to Miss Bigelow, what benefit or improvement did the accident confer?"

"Ten percent, I am sure, perhaps as much as fifteen, judging from the song of the wheel."

"Fifteen percent. I say."

"Perhaps. The acceleration is along the curve that you hold there in your hand."

Truscott considered the wood with blank amiability. "My dear sir, do not confuse me with technical matters. I must take you at your word. But if you are correct, I do know some persons of influence who will most certainly understand. We shall talk again. And in the meantime?"

"For now I need nothing, only time."

"I got to go." Olivia put her hat on.

The senator was pleased to find his jacket somewhat drier than before. "Then we shall go up together, Mrs. Washington, and may I express my deepest sympathies for your loss." Olivia stared at him without expression, and so he turned to Toma. "Good luck to you. I hope to hear from you soon. I am at your disposal."

On his way back up the hill Senator Truscott followed Olivia in silence and at a respectful distance. But, being a man, he could not help noticing the provocative grace of the figure ahead—her buttocks were more or less at his eye level—and he wondered about the curious tragedy that had befallen her. Past the ironworks they went in this configuration and out onto the road. They parted without acknowledgement—how could he address her back?—she heading toward the pink stucco pile of her church, and he to the hewn stone of his bank. His final reflection was that she must be roughly the same age as Harriet or perhaps a bit older—it was hard to tell with these people—and that Horatio might have been as old, or as young, as he.

"I DON'T UNDERSTAND," said Amos Bigelow. "Everything was working well, and now this. It is an uncivil letter, and from an old friend."

"Mr. Stephenson is only exercising his judgement as a businessman, and his right. The fact is that we did not, could not, deliver the wheels as we had contracted to do."

"But he has enough to start? We ship every week's production to him. Can there be such bother about an unavoidable delay?"

"The contract, I fear, was specific on this point. There is a penalty for nondelivery of any part of the order. I suppose he has contracts and obligations as well, perhaps with penalties."

"And Mr. Brown?"

"He has done his best under the circumstances."

"That boy Peacock? Why hasn't he done something?"

Harriet could find nothing to say.

"What a mistake it was to put any faith in him. Well, well, it's done now and the fat is in the fire. Tell me, my dear, what I must do."

"I will write to Senator Truscott of this development. He will know what must be done."

PART TWO

1916

CHAPTER

TEN

The wooded environs of Great Mountain are a most pleasant adjunct to the civilized charms of Beecher's Bridge, and we make no doubt that the growing reputation of our town as a summer resort—we cannot quite call it a spa—is enhanced by the bracing propinquity of such apparent wilderness.

The air, of course, has always been refreshing, and is now, with the suspension of enterprise at the Bigelow works, more so than ever. A second hotel, the Mountain View, has been erected and does an excellent business—especially during the high season—in friendly competition with Mr. Shepherd's older establishment. The table at the Mountain View is certainly noteworthy, and Monsieur Boule, the chef, has set his hand to dishes that would be more familiar to the citizens of Paris than to our native New Englanders. Mr. Shepherd has not swerved from his plain fare of roasts, puddings, and local produce—you will never encounter the bleached asparagus or the hothouse grape on his table—but he has responded in other ways. What visitor can fail to be impressed by the recent renovation of the Shepherd's public rooms, including those dramatic Tiffany windows in the entrance hall and on the stair landing, the splendid girandoles blazing in the evening, and the impressively carved and upholstered items of furniture in the lounge? (The proprietor of the Mountain View has referred to these with uncharitable humor as "Pope-ish thrones.") And the one thing that adherents of either establishment can agree on is the sense of relief that their repose is untroubled by the distant hammerings of the forge, and that the snowy aspect of a starched collar or lace cuff is not under constant threat from industrial soot. There was much to be regretted in the passing of the Bigelow Iron Company, but much to be gained as well. The Lord giveth, and the Lord taketh away.

We are a little in advance of that high season just now, this being only the middle of May, but there are guests enough at the Shepherd even so. Some are en route to the Berkshires; some are resting before the season in New York; there is a gentleman from Concord who can tell you a great deal about the niceties of Congregational Church architecture . . . in fact he *will* tell you, unless you are deaf; and there are two botanizing ladies whose knowledge of our flora puts the local amateurs quite to shame. Well, we must make the best of any situation, and there is the prospect of a rubber of bridge after dinner or at least a decent cigar and a game of billiards with the proprietor.

The excellence of the standing roast coupled with dread of the Concord encyclopedia have occasioned this energetic outing in the direction of the mountain, by that scenic carriage route known as the Five Mile Drive. A spirited mare from Mr. Moore's livery steps out as if the stanhope were of no weight or consequence. In passing the triangular green and the Congregational Church we noted with approval the new construction of rustic bentwood trellises and gazebos that will shade the strollers in high summer, and saw that the protective winter sheathing of Mr. Stanford White's splendid bronze and granite fountain has been removed so that we may once again marvel at those tritons and spouting dolphins.

But now, at about the midpoint of our circuit, we stop and tie the mare to a stone post that marks the beginning of a foot trail leading up the mountain into the wilderness.

Wilderness is a euphemism when applied here or anywhere in the state of Connecticut. There may be pockets of the aboriginal forest, usually in those steep descents where the raggy or the tanner—whose quarry was the hemlock bark—knew better than to risk injury to himself or his horses. But here we see the old stone walls running beside the road in the shade of substantial pines and occasionally caroming off into the shade and out of sight. This is no wilderness but the abandon-

ment of human labor and habitation, the relinquishing of an old economy of field and pasture.

What lesson is there in this history? Ezekiel tells us that all is vanity; an extreme view, perhaps, but irony is certainly a useful tool to the
historian.

We have previously noted the ambitious scheme of the Grand
Canal, so called, and Power City, and the troublesome legacy of Aaron
Bigelow's ambition. No doubt Mr. Amos Bigelow sees himself as a victim of history. Well, our mountain has other victims as well, and not
just individuals who hoped foolishly or dared too much, but entire
communities that have failed.

Beyond that ridgeline there, on the northeastern flank of Great
Mountain and just at the limits of our township, was situated the hamlet of Meekertown, at a distance of some seven miles from the center
of Beecher's Bridge. Not much is known about Meekertown or its inhabitants, and even its exact location is a subject for speculation. We
imagine it to have been a simple farming community, well watered, but
with no advantage of soil, as the early settlers avoided the rich river
bottoms in favor of hilltops, fearing the damp and vapors. But it was
not poverty of soil that doomed Meekertown, rather the poor opinion
of its neighbors.

The simple farmers of Meekertown had no post office and no
church. There may have been a general store, but if so it was a modest
one. For all needs beyond the most basic, then, a pilgrimage to
Beecher's Bridge was required, and seven miles is a considerable journey in these hills, especially in winter. What we have to go on here are
the tithe books of the Congregational Church, holographs of two sermons by Dr. Robbins—they were not included in his *Collected Sermons*—
and several diary entries by Mrs. Hoover's great-grandmother, a lady
with an omnivorous curiosity and some decidedly Old Testament instincts.

It would seem that the inhabitants of Meekertown gradually fell
away from that strict and enthusiastic observance of the Sabbath required in the early days of the past century, and so earned the censure
of the people of the town, for whom the service entailed only a stroll
across the green, or a brief ride in carriage or sleigh. The decline in

attendance seems to have been gradual rather than precipitous, and more pronounced in those grim winter months. We have some sympathy for their situation—practical needs could not be addressed on the Sabbath, and what if the horse were lame?—but the right-minded citizens of Beecher's Bridge had none. Mrs. Hoover's ancestress made note of each empty pew, and the Reverend Robbins had harsh words for Meekertown and its people, even a reference to Sodom and Gomorrah.

Did the townspeople recoil from contact with such slack spirituality? Were lines of credit at the general store and the bank closed down? We cannot help but take the charitable view that the farmers of Meekertown were not so much degenerates as they were victims of geography.

Of Meekertown itself there remains no trace and the property records were destroyed many years ago in a fire in our town hall. The last remaining inhabitant of that vicinity, a Mrs. Wilms, died in 1896, with the taxes on her farm several years in arrears. She was almost never seen in town. It was said that she had a set of wooden teeth and that she would cut the toes off her hens to keep them from scratching in her yard, where there were a few flowers. We visited her a year or so before her death in an effort to ascertain the exact location of the original hamlet. (The report of her dental equipment seemed accurate, but there was not a chicken or flower in sight.) Unfortunately, age and the years of isolation had taken a toll on her mental process, and she could not recall that there had ever been any other inhabitants on that part of the mountain. The one clear thought in her head was that she had been struck by lightning in a hailstorm in the summer of 1851. The second time she told us this she pushed back the sleeve of her shapeless woolen garment to show a faint but unmistakable fern-leaf pattern on the withered flesh. We had heard of such a marking of lightning's victims, but had never before seen the evidence.

The property in the area of Meekertown was acquired piecemeal by Aaron Bigelow for the outstanding taxes, and became part of that extensive charcoal-cutting preserve known as the Bigelow Plantation. And so the tragedy of Meekertown is folded into that larger historical narrative of which Amos Bigelow feels himself to be the inheritor and the victim.

It is just as well that Mr. Bigelow resides in Washington just now; otherwise this damp glory of our spring must depress him, for the relatively mild winter and the torrents of April would have been encouraging to iron production. See how the trail ascends here! And do you mark the music of falling water just ahead?

If we will look upon history as a catalogue of vanished communities and failed enterprise, then its study must be as discouraging as the face of that old woman who remembered nothing, not even the name of her deceased husband. But would not the sensible writer or philosopher also take note of a parallel history, consisting of those invisible yet tenacious motors of progress that we have referred to as dreams? And what a rich and colorful vista presents itself to us now, as subtle in its interweaving of the mutable and the eternal as the very landscape before us, where new shoots and flowers proceed from stumps that have slept through the winter.

Communities as well as individuals have their formative dreams, and we need look no further than our own town to find that this is so. For Beecher's Bridge has not withered away with the passing of the ironworks, though no doubt there is economic distress in many a household along the Bottom. Instead, and with the active encouragement of Senator Truscott and his bride, we have embraced a higher or at least more refined idea than mere manufacture: the promotion of tourism upon the pillars of healthful recreation.

Consider these improvements of the past two years: there is the splendid new organ in the Congregational Church, and a most accomplished organ master, both funded by generous gifts from the senator; we are now the seat of the Litchfield Choral Society, with concerts twice weekly during our summer season; and perhaps most significantly, there is an agreement with the great university in New Haven that the music school—one of whose professors holds the recently endowed Truscott Chair—will hold its summer session in Beecher's Bridge, a trial arrangement that has every likelihood of becoming a permanent feature of our summers. The wanderer in such pleasant seclusion where we now find ourselves may, in the coming months, be entertained by the distant strain of a flute in the Greenwoods.

There are varying degrees of enthusiasm for this new direction in the affairs of Beecher's Bridge. Amos Bigelow, for example, cannot be expected to embrace this new possibility, any more than would the idled furnace man who cannot play the flute. How do the dreams or strivings of individuals interact with one another or circumstance to form the general or communal thing? Well, this theory of the parallel history of dreams is the fruit of this very outing, and, like anything newborn, must not be tested too soon or too severely.

Now that we have arrived at our destination, this glen with its picturesque falls so near the highest reach of the mountain, we observe that we are not alone. For here, seated by the falls, staring at the tumbling water, is Mr. Thomas Peacock, late of the ironworks and now engaged in researches that may in time redirect the fortunes of Beecher's Bridge. Were we to engage him in conversation, no doubt he could shed light on the lines of our inquiry, for he is a man with his own fierce aspirations . . . dreams, if you will. But there is an unwritten etiquette of the Greenwoods, and people will come here with various ends, some best pursued in silence. If he has seen us he makes no sign, and so, rather than risk an encounter that is not mutually welcome, we shall withdraw. By the time we reach the carriage there will be a slight chill in the air, and the impatient mare will carry us home to tea.

THE GULLY IS KNOWN as Rachel's Leap. A little way down the mountain the watercourse is shaded by old-growth hemlock trees, and the steeples of rock are humid and green. There is little light or air, and no view at all.

Near the top, the growth is mostly scrub oak, and from the first waterfall—Pothole Falls—there is an impressive view out over the valley of the Buttermilk. But Toma is lost in his thoughts and has scarcely raised his eyes from the water. This has long been a popular spot for courting couples, and the irony is not lost on Toma; in fact it has everything to do with his being here. Today is his birthday, his twenty-fourth, and exactly a year ago he left the silk mill in the morning and walked up the mountain to these falls to be alone with his thoughts and mark this day. Why this place? He had found it on his own in the course of one of his scavenging trips—Horatio had a map of old mill sites on the mountain, with an inventory of their equipment—and something about the landscape reminded him of Montenegro, and so of his family and Harwell and Lydia too, who were the only ones who might remember the significance of this day.

To his great surprise, he found that he was not alone at the falls, and the woman on the far side, who had apparently arrived by a different path, was Harriet Bigelow. He had not seen her at first, and even then did not recognize her. But when she threw back her shawl and turned her face to the sun, he knew her. They had not spoken since the failure of the ironworks.

"Toma!"

He smiled and made an awkward half bow in her direction.

"Well? Are we never to speak again? Or are you waiting for me to come to you?"

There was still snowmelt to swell the stream and Toma could not, as he might have done in August, simply step across on the large rocks. He hopped once, twice, with perfect luck, but he fell short on the third, which would have brought him safe and dry to her side. She laughed at him, or with him, as he emptied out his boot.

"That was almost perfect."

"I was too ready to obey. I should take my boots off to wade. But there, you see, I could not." He pointed to the purple scar on his naked foot.

"Oh! I am so stupid. How could I not have remembered? Did you hurt it again just now?"

"No, it is nothing. But it is ugly to see."

"Yes. Your perfection is quite spoilt." Her tone was mocking, but her eyes were warm. "I should not have asked you to do it."

He did not know where to begin. "I hope your father is well."

"He is well enough, thank you, though he is sad. He does not know quite what to do with himself."

"I am sorry."

"Oh, I don't think there was anything to be done, in spite of all we had hoped. We must not dwell on it." Her kindness was a punishment. She too now seemed at a loss for words, but, caught in the corner of his eye, how she glowed. Was she blushing?

"What a happy accident that we should meet here. I thought we might never find a time, you see."

"Yes," he said, though he had no idea what she meant.

"I thought you would not want to speak to me." She was looking away from him now, her profile chiseled against the trellis of new oak, the hair loosening in its prison of pins.

"And why would that be?"

"Well . . .," and now she was certainly blushing.

"Well?"

She looked at him. The blush and the radiance had vanished. She was angry. At him? "Will you make me say it? Is it of no consequence to you that I will marry someone else?" He said nothing. "But surely you knew?"

He took her hand. "Do you remember when I told you this would happen?"

"I didn't believe you. I didn't know."

"Now you know." He stood up and helped her to her feet. Then he kissed her on either cheek. "It is as it must be."

Now, a year later in the spring of 1916, Toma sits in exactly the same place and stares at the water, with the same scene running through his mind over and over, or fragments of it, as if he might by a concentration of will bring it to some different conclusion. What might he have said to make her realize that she would not be happy with this man, and that her purgatory would be the mirror to his own? In some reconstructions of their encounter all barriers are thrown down and the consummation of longing takes place by the brook, with her shawl for a bed on the tiny flowers. But by whatever route they arrive at that moment there is no surprise or discovery in the unveiling of her flesh, the convergence of their pleasure, but instead a sense of connection with something known. Home, he thinks at this unlikely moment, home.

Three months after their chance encounter, Toma attended the wedding of Harriet Bigelow and Fowler Truscott. The note enclosed with his invitation made it clear that he must not fail to come.

The event was agony for him. Dressed in Horatio's black suit and in a white shirt borrowed from Mrs. Glatt's bundle of laundry, Toma felt light-headed in the church. At the reception, he found that the pain of smiling could be eased by champagne. He observed the other guests, saw that the distance between two people engaged in casual conversation was greater than in his own country. Why had he never noticed this before? He took particular note of the gentlemen—Senator Truscott's friends—and of the senator himself. He thought of Harwell, thought: He would know how to do this . . and I shall learn.

Later, after more champagne, Toma had a conversation with the groom, who was in an expansive mood. Truscott asked after progress on the wheel, and Toma was able to report that he had a prototype and some encouraging readings from the newly acquired gauges. The senator's face was flushed, but Toma's answer clearly interested him. "We shall speak soon," said Truscott, pressing his shoulder.

Yes, thought Toma, but not before your wedding trip. He raised his glass. "Your health, sir. Or as it would be said in my country, *ziveo.*" They both drank.

He did not wait for the departure of the bride and groom. The champagne was beginning to lose its anaesthetizing effect. But as he passed through the doorway onto the verandah he saw the cousin, Lucy, disengaging herself from two young men with the promise of a swift return. "Be a dear, Cecil, and hold this glass for me? I will look in for a moment on little Caroline." She must pass within inches of him, and he stood his ground.

"Mr. Peacock, what a pleasure to see you again."

"It is an honor to me, Miss Lucy. You are an important person on this day, yes? The . . . maid of honor."

"No, Mr. Peacock, the matron of honor, as I have won the race to the altar with my dear cousin."

"Yes, of course. I forgot that you were to be married. I congratulate you."

"Not only married, but a mother, too. And now Harriet. Did she not look like an angel today? Quite unbearably beautiful?"

"You have found the perfect word."

"What I meant . . ."

"Yes. It does not matter now. And if it is proper to say it, you were a fitting companion to her."

"How kind of you, Mr. Peacock. May I introduce you to my . . . ?"

"Another time, perhaps. I must go. Good-bye."

When he got back to the silk mill he gave his clothes to Olivia, who had no curiosity about the wedding. Horatio's suit was brushed and swathed in an old sheet. Mr. Glatt's shirt was subjected to examination.

"Hope you didn't put anything on this I can't get off."

THERE ARE SEVERAL TRAILS leading down the mountain from Pothole Falls, some no more than silent thoroughfares of the white-tailed deer, and the one chosen by Toma this day was an indirect route back to the silk mill. Down through the cathedral of great hemlocks and tumbled stone he went, then veered left, and in a few minutes he climbed out onto the scarred eminence of Lightning Knob. From this height he could see part of the town, the lines of the river and the railroad, the idled works, and practically beneath him, the Truscott house, which had been the object of renovation in the months since the closing of the ironworks.

Toma had marked the progress of the glass and iron addition, a conservatory that extended the house in the direction of the mountain. The work had begun in the fall, but could not be completed before the onset of winter owing to a late change in plans. Mrs. Truscott had decided that the new room must accommodate exotic houseplants as well as the grand piano, and adjustments to the temperature and humidity required the installation of a new furnace.

The workmen were back at it now, having got an early start after the mild winter. A week, perhaps two, and they would be finished, well before the Truscotts returned from Washington for the summer.

Olivia was waiting for him at the door of the silk mill. She handed him the envelope that Mr. Watrous, obligated by the ostentatious display of postage, had carried down from the post office, special delivery.

"Aren't you going to open it?" There was a tone in her voice that suggested an imminent argument. He had heard it more often lately.

"I will take a mug of water first and see how Stefan is coming along with the new couplings. The senator can wait for a few minutes."

The silk mill had undergone a transformation since Horatio's death. A new bay had been opened out to the south. It was a sunny, pleasant space, despite the confusion of wires, and the new wheel, the gleaming metal prototype, sat in its well. Stefan Sazlo, an acquaintance from Toma's evenings at the Franklin Institute, had brought a crucial skill in metalworking to the job. He was a quiet, sober man of middle years; he grew excited only when Olivia preempted the water supply in the middle of one of his tests.

"Well, Stefan? Any happiness?" It was almost a joke between them, for if Stefan were to discover happiness in any sphere, he would be at pains to disguise the fact.

"Some progress, my friend, that is all. In an hour or so I shall need your advice or opinion on the couplings." He continued in a lower tone: "But it is good you are back. I think you were expected sooner."

All the improvements to this place, and all the instruments—apart from those that Mr Stephenson's loan had provided—came through the generosity of Senator Truscott. He, Toma, would frame the request in writing, with the briefest explanation, and Truscott would send the money. Although there was always a provision for Stefan's wages, it was understood that Toma's living expenses would not be part of this accounting. Olivia was the only source of real income in the household.

What might be in the envelope he did not know. He had not asked for money, and would not until he had run a complete set of tests on the new prototype. But there had been an evolution in Truscott's letters from the original disclaimer of technical incompetence toward an intimate knowledge of the project and some sophisticated questions. Was it another obscure point of American manners to so thoroughly disguise one's intelligence?

The letter was brief and it enclosed a sheaf of crisp currency.

"What's he say?" Olivia asked.

"He wants a report on the progress of the machine."

"And that money?"

"He wants me to report in person. I am to go to Washington to meet someone very important, a Mr. Coffin."

"I never heard of him."

"I think Truscott mentioned him before."

"What does he say about his wife?"

"Nothing, except that she sends her regards."

"Regards. What does that mean?"

"Nothing. It is a way of being polite."

"Will you take me with you? To Washington?"

Toma shrugged. He was thinking of the two technical points raised in the letter as topics for the upcoming meeting, and wondered how Truscott could make head or tail out of such a discussion.

But Olivia had taken the shrug as a yes, and her mind was working through the details of what must be done in order to get away, of the train trip to Washington—which must go through New York—and even to where they might stay in the nation's capital.

"Always wanted to go somewhere, anywhere, just to get away from here. I did ask Horatio, asked him until he told me to quit because he was done traveling, nothing more he wanted to see. But I ain't seen anything. And you know what I want? Are you minding me?"

"Yes."

"I want to sleep on sheets that I don't have to wash. I want to sleep in a real hotel."

"A hotel," Toma repeated. His own experience of such places was limited. "I don't know the cost."

"The cost . . ." She made a dismissive sound with her lips. "Look at all that money there in your hand. Seems to me you'll be staying in a hotel." Now she looked at his face and saw that she had won, or nearly so. "You can tell them I'm a white woman."

With one hand she pulled the mass of her hair up and held it there for him to admire. She glanced in the direction of the bay where Stefan worked, then smiled at Toma and with her other hand began to undo the buttons of her shirt.

HE IS LODGED SO deep in her that even when he is perfectly still she feels the heat of him like ice in her spine, and piercing chills ripple through her. He puts his hand over her mouth to silence her and she fights him, thrashing side to side, hips arching clear of the sheets to meet him, holding him aloft on the bow of her body until he finishes. This time, like every other time, it is like finding something she didn't know she'd lost. All she'd been trying to say was I love you.

He rolls away, leaving her with a slick of sweat on her belly and cold air between her legs. She listens to his breathing, wondering if he is asleep or just faking it, and she wants to touch him, run her hand down over his stomach, the thought and the smell of him filling the pool of her desire. She likes the second time better. Slow, deliberate, almost tender. She thinks that in one of these moments he will tell her that he loves her.

The silence is what she hates. If he would only talk to her so that what they have just done is more than the coupling of beasts, so that she doesn't have to think about Horatio.

She has told him about her mother because she thought he would want to know what she had been through. All these years of holding it in, wondering how God could have let her mother die in Cuba—the shell landing in the laundry cauldron that nearly killed her too—and how He could have left her to the mercy of a man who would rape her every day, or nearly, from the age of twelve on. Now that she is safe from all this, now that he has saved her, doesn't he understand how she loves him?

However she frames these questions, the answer does not come out right, and there is no door in the blank wall of his silence. He does not love her: there is her answer, and this knowledge deadens her mind even as she feels him growing hard in her hand. She bends and takes his nipple in her teeth, feeling the jolt run clear through him like the time he made her touch the wires. He's more than ready now and so she impales herself, rocking back and forth, using her fingernails like knives, until she tears the seed out of him again.

Such ferocity, though it is her own, makes her think again of Horatio. She falls back from him and wraps herself in the sheet. "At least," she says, "at least I didn't love him."

"... after the credit crisis of 1912 was negotiated and Coffin struck the balance between financial conservatism and entrepreneurial daring, there was no more effective manager of personnel and resources to be found on our shores. Both in his admirable personal life and in the standards and goals he established at General Electric, Mr. Coffin became the model of corporate success in our new century, the true face, we might say, of American Capitalism."

—from "A Tribute to Charles Albert Coffin," *Almanac of Electrical Engineering*, vol. 28, no. 3, 1926

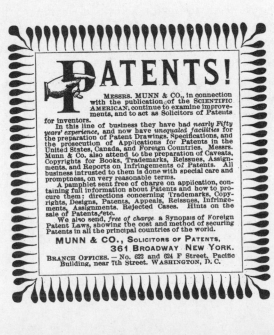

CHAPTER

ELEVEN

Toma slept for most of the train journey from Beecher's Bridge to
Washington. He was glad that he had the two seats to himself because
he was coming down with a cold, the same one that had laid Olivia up
in bed for three days with fevers and night sweats, so that she could not
make the trip.

"You are going without me?"

"Yes. I must."

"Send him a telegram. Ask him can't he wait two days."

"The date is fixed; it cannot be changed. Mr. Coffin has important
business in Panama."

"Take care of yourself, then, like you took care of me. And don't
you spend all that money."

He was anxious about the time. He did not carry a pocket watch—
did not own one—and he had been awakened by the train's squealing
halt. Where was Truscott? The concourse of Union Station was illuminated, but the gas lamps were reduced to insignificance by the scale of
this space and the dark vault of its roof, starless smoke-blackened cof-
fers like a threatening sky.

The minutes passed, and he wandered from the center of the floor to
the stalls of the curio sellers. He was turning over in his hands a plaster
model of the Washington Monument, when he heard Truscott's voice.

"My apologies. We had a rough time of it this afternoon, or this
evening rather, and only at the last minute did we reach agreement on

the wording of the bill in committee. Otherwise we were headed for a filibuster, and I might not have been able to meet you at all."

Toma wondered at the word. "It is a curious system. I hope someday to understand it."

"Oh, a clever fellow like you, it wouldn't take long. But now we are off to see Mr. Coffin."

"Now? You said . . ."

"Yes, yes." Truscott consulted his gold hunter. "But Mr. Coffin sent word this afternoon that his plans are changed, and he must leave at two A.M. Follow me."

Truscott set off at a strong pace, not in the direction of the cab rank but back through the gate. At the far end of the platform, beyond the last marked track, several rough steps took them down to the level of the rails. The senator stumbled over a cross tie and steadied himself, with an oath, on Toma's shoulder. A gas light flared to life not twenty feet from them, illuminating the white collar and cuffs of a very black porter.

"Over here, Senator, over here."

The porter helped them up the steps and into the car and they were greeted by a puckish gentleman of late middle age, dwarfed by his visitors in the confines of the vestibule.

"Well, Senator, how good of you to come to me on such short notice, and had I the sense to light the lamps in time, you would not have had to take the Lord's name in vain. And this is our guest who has traveled so far to meet with us? Come in, Mr. Peacock, I beg you. Do come in."

Toma had never seen such a chamber as they now entered, never even imagined it. Here everything was compressed perfectly and effortlessly so that no motion or corner would be wasted. There was Mr. Coffin's desk, there the leather chairs and upholstered settee where they would sit. Portraits, to an appropriate scale, hung against the red damask; next to the settee, a vase of yellow roses; and on the opposite side a cabinet opened out flat against the wall to show the racks of bottles and glasses secure against any motion of the car. It seemed to Toma that he was looking through a lens into Mr. Coffin's dollhouse.

"Please do not judge me by the extravagance of my friend Mr. Huntington." Coffin's voice was kindly and soft. He had read the expression on Toma's face. "I would have preferred something much plainer, but Mr. Huntington was bound in the opposite direction, and what you see here had begun to seem shabby to him. I bought it as an act of friendship. But it has been a great convenience, a very great convenience. By noon tomorrow I shall be in Tampa, with the ship waiting for us, and in another thirty-six hours or so, Panama, and all without having to leave this car."

"This car will go to Panama?"

"In the ship, yes."

"Ah."

"And do you see, when I am in Washington, or Panama City, I have no need of a hotel. The world comes to me, just as you and Senator Truscott have. Again, Fowler, thank you for your flexibility and your forbearance. The timetables of the Southern Railroad are beyond my control."

"It is always a pleasure, Mr. Coffin, never an inconvenience."

"You are kind. Now, William, would you show Mr. Peacock to the dressing room? I'm sure he has had a very long journey. And if he needs anything, of course . . ."

The porter led Toma down the narrow corridor to the second door.

"Please, sir."

Toma eyed the expanse of marble and the gilded fixtures; William turned on the taps and held out the linen towels with Huntington's embroidered monogram. Through the half-open interior door Toma saw a carved bedstead and another splendid Turkey carpet. He wondered if his boots were clean enough for such finery.

"We haven't much time, sir, as Mr. Coffin will want to dine before ten." He put a clean white shirt on the marble beside the towels. "If you'll give me your coat I'll see what can be done. And if you need anything else in the meantime, the bell cord is just there, beside the basin."

Toma stripped to the waist and used the soap, the towels, and the brushes. The shirt was soft and fine and smelled faintly of lavender. The gilt and crystal bottle next to the soap dish contained a clear, stinging liquid of the same scent. Well, he thought, why not?

William reappeared just as Toma was fastening the last button of his trousers. The coat had been brushed; more than that, its wrinkles were gone. William held out a cravat of dark gray silk, and before Toma

had a chance to protest, he had slipped it deftly under a stiff white collar and fastened the collar to the studs in the shirt.

"Mr. Coffin is not a formal man, but . . ." When he had finished
tying the cravat, William knelt and with his brushes transformed
Toma's boots. "There. I think we are ready now."

". . . A MATTER OF TIME, Fowler, but otherwise a foregone conclusion.
Of course I speak from the vantage of Wall Street, more or less, and
have not the broader view of your . . . Mr. Peacock, do sit down with us
and have something to drink. We will eat in just a few minutes.
William, some sherry, please. Or do you take liquor, Mr. Peacock?"

"No, sir. The sherry, please." He saw that Coffin drank nothing and
that Truscott had a tumbler of whisky with a tall glass of water beside it.

"I cannot tell you, Mr. Peacock, how intriguing I find your work, of
which the senator has been kind enough to keep me informed. And in
such unlikely circumstances, as I understand it. How is it, if I may ask,
that you came to the idea of the several wheels yoked together? Fowler
has not managed to clarify this for me."

Toma glanced at Truscott, who seemed preoccupied with his tumbler of whisky. "Sir, the values there, the results on the multiple wheels,
are . . . uncertain. I do not want you to think that . . ."

"Yes, yes, I know how you experimental fellows are, wanting to
dot the *i* and cross the *t*. But from what I know, and simply from the
schematics, that does seem the avenue of commercial application,
and so . . ."

"Excuse me, sir, but have you seen the drawings?"

"Of course I have; why else do you think we are here?"

"Mr. Coffin, I am embarrassed to speak. Will you tell me what is
your work?"

"My work?" Coffin was amused but courteous. "I can see that there
has been a lapse in our communication. A glass of water, please,
William." Truscott cleared his throat and would have spoken, but Coffin cut him off.

"My job is that I am the chairman of the General Electric Corporation. And your job is to complete the work on your turbine, which, if

I am any judge of such matters, will have a lasting impact on our business, and perhaps upon the supply of domestic energy in the event of a prolonged conflict with Germany."

"America is at peace, Mr. Coffin." Toma seized upon the one part of Coffin's statement that he understood unequivocally.

"We have not yet declared war, that is true. But it is also my job to look ahead, on behalf of our shareholders and our employees at General Electric. We will be at war within a year, you may count on it."

Toma felt foolish and also resentful of Truscott, who had never explained anything of this connection. He felt the cold coming upon him more strongly now. He fumbled in his pocket but found no handkerchief. He spoke intemperately.

"And am I one of your employees?"

"William, a handkerchief for our guest, please. No, Mr. Peacock, our connection has been informal to this point. But I assure you that we take your work very seriously." Coffin sat back in his chair to look, without expression, at Fowler Truscott. "And William, when you can, some more liquor for Senator Truscott. Thank you."

"I had meant to have a discussion with him before the meeting," said Truscott, "but that was impossible, given the timing."

"Yes. I have brought this on myself. Or rather on you, Mr. Peacock, and I apologize for the confusion. Perhaps, under the circumstances, I should ask if there is anything I can tell you that would speed the work, or clear the air?"

"Only this. What is the connection between my work and the war that you say is to come?"

"A very fair question. Our committee on long-range planning, which has a very close connection to the National Research Council, projects a serious shortage in electrical generating capacity beginning about three months after the declaration of war."

"I see. I am sorry, I do *not* see. How can you know this?"

"Do you know how gunpowder is made?"

"I do not."

"Well, neither do I. But I do know that it cannot be done without an ample, cheap supply of nitrate. Senator, will you tell our guest where we obtain our nitrates?"

"We get them from Chile, from the offshore guano deposits."

"Guano? What is guano?"

"Bird shit, Mr. Peacock," said Coffin, taking delight in this scandalous phrase, "whole mountains of it. Is that not so, Fowler?"

"Indeed. It would seem that the pelagic fowl of that region have nested on the same islands for centuries, even millennia, and so . . ."

"And so the mountains of bird shit that constitute our cheap source of both fertilizer and explosives."

"Yes. But . . ."

"But in the case of war with the Germans, given the strength of their ties to South America, our access to the guano is uncertain."

"Then what?"

"Well, it would be very inconvenient to fight a war without ammunition, explosives, and so forth, and so we must find a way around."

"An alternative source," interjected Truscott.

"Now the Germans, it seems, have developed a sensible process for the fixing or conversion of atmospheric nitrogen: the Haber-Bosch method. But we do not have access to this information, which is very closely guarded. What we have is a different process."

"And?"

"And that process requires an extraordinary amount of electrical energy. I'm afraid it is quite wasteful. Am I making any sense to you, Mr. Peacock?"

"Yes."

"Good. And on the strength of that may I suggest we dine? George gets very cross with me if I am late to the table. We'll just go along into the next car." Coffin rose stiffly to his feet. He seemed quite tired.

"It has been a long day for me, and I'm an old fellow. If I leave any questions unanswered, you can always ask Steinmetz. He's a great deal more competent in the technical area than I am."

"I do not know Steinmetz."

"Oh, but you will. I can assure you of that."

AT 9:45 THE FOLLOWING MORNING, following Truscott's written instructions, Toma presented himself at the United States Patent Office and asked to see Mr. Frederick Flaten. The day had broken very clear and fair, as Coffin had predicted, and Truscott's note was precise to the minute as to how long it would take to walk to the Commerce Department building from the hotel.

Frederick Flaten was a small man, youngish, with sandy hair and very bright cheeks. His effusive manner was surprising to Toma; from their preliminary correspondence on the patent application he had imagined a sober bureaucrat.

"Well, Mr. Peacock, I have been so anxious to meet you. One has no idea, does one? I mean from your letter . . . well, perhaps if I were an expert in handwriting I could have imagined you as you are."

"As I am . . . yes. And from your letters I would be guessing that you are older, and perhaps more . . . more serious, if that is the right word."

Flaten blushed and unrolled the drawing, anchoring it with his inkwell and other objects on his desk. "We are very solemn here. Rather like a funeral parlor, I'm afraid." Flaten spread his arms deprecatingly so that Toma could appreciate the somber black of his coat and waistcoat, the subdued stripe of his trousers. He also saw the precision of cuff and collar, the arc of the watch chain interrupted by a buttonhole, and the discreet show of colored silk in the breast pocket. Flaten smiled reassuringly, as if to say that solemnity could not claim all of him.

"It is an honor to me that my turbine has come to the attention of an assistant primary examiner. Is this not so?"

"Yes, yes, the Applications Branch has done the proper thing in bringing this"—he tapped the drawing—"to Division Eight, and specifically to my desk. It's not so much an honor, you see, as proper procedure, and recognition of one's interests, that is to say my interests. I find your work utterly fascinating." Flaten fixed his eyes on Toma's.

"But your letter . . . ?"

"The first action, as we call it. Well, there are very few perfect patent applications, just as there are very few perfect human beings. There is usually some discussion, some back-and-forth, either to clarify the specifications or to modify what is claimed as novelty. It would have been better, perhaps, if you had consulted an experienced attorney in formulating the application. It is not necessary, strictly speaking, but I often advise applicants to do so."

"There is a problem in the wording then?"

"Yes, originally. It seemed to me on first reading, and even more so after refreshing my memory in the Search Room, that there is a risk here of ambiguity vis-à-vis the Tesla Bladeless Turbine."

"I have read about Tesla's machine, and it is entirely different to mine. And besides, it doesn't work. The metal, at such a rate of revolution, becomes deformed."

"My dear Mr. Peacock, Tesla's difficulty in fabrication, or in production and marketing, is no concern of ours. A patent is a patent is a patent. He owns the *idea* of his machine, whether or not he can build it, and it is my job to protect his idea, or his rights to it."

"I tell you that my machine and his are different, which I can demonstrate with no difficulty. Is this the only problem?"

Flaten cleared his throat behind his hand, and was about to answer when he glanced down at the drawing of the wheel. "A very beautiful drawing, this. Somewhat unorthodox, but quite exquisitely done. It is the part of my job that I like best."

"Thank you, but it is not my drawing. It was done by my friend."

"Well, well. Yes, on the other matter, there is a more substantive problem, though the overlap with Tesla's design is hardly trivial."

"And that would be?" Toma thought it curious that Flaten's letter had made no reference to a second difficulty.

"After I had written to you—the first action—it came to my attention . . . that is to say a colleague, my superior, had a word with me about your application."

"Is this a normal procedure?"

"I cannot say that it is, though I have heard of precedents in other divisions."

"And what are those things, those precedents?"

"They are matters pertaining to the national safety."

"You mean the war?"

"Yes, my dear Mr. Peacock, the war." There was no expansiveness about Flaten now, no smile or display of the handsome watch chain. He rubbed his hands together and gazed at Toma, or through him, without expression.

"Everyone I have met in Washington seems to think I have invented a new weapon and called it the Peacock Turbine."

Flaten smiled weakly. "I'm afraid this is out of my hands. There are firm guidelines in these circumstances, and restrictions that apply so long as the application is placed under security."

"This is ridiculous, a joke."

"I assure you it is not."

"Then I demand an explanation," said Toma, his voice rising. "I shall appeal to your superior, who seems to have authority here." He pushed back his chair and Flaten grasped his wrist.

"Please, I beg you, sit down. There is no right of appeal in these cases; in fact, you are forbidden to discuss your invention with anyone."

"Forbidden to discuss it? How am I to work? How am I to live?"

Frederick Flaten's face registered an expression of such sympathetic distress that Toma could not doubt his sincerity. Flaten patted the back of Toma's hand reassuringly. "I think there is a way. But you must understand that anything I say now is in an unofficial capacity, because I am your friend."

"Yes," said Toma, as if he understood.

"There would be no objection to your carrying on the work, further experimentation and refinement, and so on."

"But how will I . . . ?"

"And if there were a coinventor, then you would be free to discuss with him the most intimate details of your work, but only with him."

"There is no such person. You have read my application."

Flaten paused and looked again, with uncomfortable emphasis, into Toma's eyes. "And if, either before or after the application, you had assigned your rights in the device to a third party, partially or entirely, then you would have free intercourse with the assignee, and the right to compensation. It would be better if the assignment predated the security intervention, but I think that can probably be arranged."

Toma's anger drained away, and at ten-thirty in the morning he felt suddenly exhausted. Flaten looked anxiously at him, awaiting his response.

"As my friend, then, can you tell me where I should turn?"

A smile tugged at one side of Flaten's lip, as if they were playing a game; but he did not speak. So Toma took the pen from the holder on the desk and dipped it in the inkwell. His hand hovered over the blotter and Flaten quickly supplied a sheet of paper. Toma scrawled the initials GE; Flaten's face was illuminated with relief and unfeigned happiness. It was really, thought Toma, a very nice smile.

Flaten crumpled the paper and threw it away. "That name did come up in my discussion with . . ." Here he inclined his head toward the frosted glass partition in the corner of the room. "They have a natural interest in such matters, of course, and their involvement may even smooth the way for the application."

"It would seem I have no choice, if I want to eat. But tell me, if you can, what you know about Dr. Steinmetz, Dr. Charles Proteus Steinmetz."

"Steinmetz? I should think that nearly everyone in this building knows Dr. Steinmetz."

"And do you know him?"

"Yes. Well . . . in a way." Flaten's face looked like pale wax. "No. I mean I have nothing against him, but he almost cost me my job."

"You may tell me, if you will."

"I am allergic to smoke, you see, always have been, and one day this cloud of smoke billows over the partition—this is when I was just an assistant examiner, and I was sitting right next to the chief's office— and I was trying not to make any noise coughing. Then this little man walks out of the chief's office smoking the most *enormous* cigar, and the chief shows him out. When he comes back I am literally weeping and struggling to control my breathing, and the chief is furious at me because he thinks I am laughing at Steinmetz."

"And is Steinmetz funny, then?"

"No, I mean he is a genius, everybody knows that. But . . ." and here Frederick Flaten had to suppress a nervous giggle, "but he is a dwarf, so it could go either way. And the trouble was that as soon as I understood that the chief was angry, and why, I *did* start to laugh. It was awful. I was sick afterward in the wastebasket. Oh, you must think I am awful . . . I do apologize."

Toma spoke carefully. "No, I do not think you are awful. It was a mistake, as the chief must realize, for you are no longer merely his assistant. Is this not so?"

The sun shone again on the assistant primary examiner of Division Eight. "Yes, that's true, though I thought it would never happen. I thought my chances here were finished." He looked at Toma and sighed.

"I say, you're not by any chance free for lunch? I'd be very pleased . . ."

"Another time, perhaps. The rain . . . ?"

"Check."

"Yes, the raincheck. My mind is too full now of this other matter." Toma rose and took his hat.

"Of course it is, and you must write to me if you need further advice. But will you tell me one thing—and perhaps this has a bearing on the Tesla design, perhaps not—but where did the idea of the multiple wheels come from?"

Nothing in Washington was what it seemed, and Toma looked carefully at Flaten, wondering what guile lay behind the question. None, he decided. "It is strange that Mr. Coffin asked me the same thing just last night. But if you will promise to keep the secret, I will show you. It began with one wheel, then it became two. How it happened is like a child's game, embarrassingly simple."

He took the pen and dipped it again, and Flaten supplied the paper. "It was late at night and I was thinking about two matters at once: the mechanical features or design of my wheel, and the formula for determining the effects of turbulence and friction along these spiral grooves. I drew a wheel." Toma drew a wheel. "And then I had an idea about the equation, so I folded my paper." Toma folded the paper. Flaten followed these moves as he would a magician's. "And I wrote my equations on the back, like this."

"And?"

"And in the morning . . . well, here, you open it." Toma handed him the slip, and Flaten unfolded it to the two wheels.

"Really?"

"That's all there is to it, I'm afraid. The second wheel, mirror to the first, was a great step forward in the design, and if I had waited a few seconds before folding the paper, I might have missed it altogether."

"May I keep this?"

"Of course. But it is our secret."

TOMA HAD INTENDED TO leave the Patent Office and clear his head with a walk through the cherry trees and lawns near the great obelisk. But on his way down the stairs he saw an arrowed sign pointing to the

Search Room and the Library. Sooner or later he would have to do this. Why not now? He followed the arrows, thinking of the money he had wasted on that fool of a patent agent.

It was a pleasant room: long tables of inlaid wood, leather chairs, and high sunny windows. The clerk brought him the file on patent #1,061,206, the Tesla Bladeless Turbine, and Toma spread out on the table the description and the specifications and the drawings. Not only was the machine elegant and compact—so compact, he had heard it said, that it would fit in your hat—but there was the mystery, thrilling to him, that Tesla's own hand had written these words and drawn these lines. He laid his hands flat on the pages for a moment.

As he began to read, awe and reverence gave way to a small sense of pride, and to hope. His wheel, his turbine, was indeed different from Tesla's design, and at one point he muttered aloud: "With all due respect, Mr. Tesla, you do not own these concepts."

When he had finished reading Tesla's application, he turned to the official remarks on the folder itself. Someone had expressed doubt that it was really practical to run a turbine at such speeds. Still, the patent had been granted.

Toma, after consultation with the clerk, was soon hemmed in by a semicircle of folders, and he spent the afternoon reading through them, making notes to himself. He could tell at a glance which of these machines would work in a useful way. Some of what he read was nonsense cloaked in elegant expression. Occasionally there was an insight of startling purity and originality.

Near the end of the afternoon the words began to swim on the page, and he closed his eyes. He dozed, imagining himself in a forest of great trees. His feet knew the way and he was walking toward a light at the edge of the woods.

A bell rang and the clerk began collecting folders scattered on the long tables. It was a quarter to four. Toma stood and stretched, clearing his head with a mighty yawn. He was ready for Steinmetz. In fact, he looked forward to meeting him.

ON THE LONG WALK to Georgetown he stopped often to admire a building or a gated garden; he knew that he must not arrive before the appointed hour, but also he was struggling to contain his excitement. He stopped on a certain corner where a colorfully dressed African man was selling bits of skewered meat that perfumed the whole block.

"Where are you from?"

"Nigeria, sah."

"What are you doing here?"

"Just selling meat, sah. You like?" The meat was delicious, though it stung his mouth.

"Yes, I am very hungry, and I like. What is it?"

"Goat, sah. I de kill dis goat an' take he meat, den I pound 'im wi' de bottle an' put 'em some ground nut meal an pepe for hot. Goat meat make you very strong, sah, pass all strong for woman." At this the man smiled so splendidly that Toma had to laugh.

"You go buy one more time?"

"Thank you, my friend. I will buy another. No, two more, and I will eat them on my way."

He walked on, tearing at the meat on the bamboo sliver, taking care not to stain Mr. Coffin's fine shirt. When he had finished, he ducked into the next tavern and washed his hands and face with the strong brown soap. Standing at the urinal, glancing down at himself, he repeated, in the vendor's patois: Strong for woman . . . yes, I am very strong for woman. At the bar, after finishing his beer, he took a handful of peppermints to sweeten his breath.

The house was set back from the street and almost invisible for the hedge of candleberries and the yellow climbing roses that threaded their way through the wrought iron.

The gate was a puzzle to him: there was the bar, which rose from its catch when he lifted, and still it would not yield. He pulled on the bell, feeling foolish. Harriet herself answered and he had those few moments of her approach down the brick walk to observe her. She kept her eyes cast down to the path and seemed not to see him. The impatient quickness of her step was measured now, but he would recognize anywhere the carriage of her shoulders and those two bright spots of color in her cheeks that embarrassed her because she seemed to blush.

"Toma?" She tried to screen the sun's glare with her hand, and he had the sensation of being invisible to those familiar gray eyes, gray shading to green at the edge. "Is it really you?" The light glanced off the many little diamonds at her wrist and filled the much larger stone on her finger. He had never seen these things before.

"Yes, it is Toma. You would think that a great inventor could open the gate without help."

"I am sorry. It is only . . . well . . ." She took a large key from the folds of her skirt and inserted it into a mechanism hidden in the ivy on the gatepost. "Fowler does complain about this, and of course he won't carry such a key."

"There are thiefs here?"

"No. There is the bolt on the door for them. It is Papa . . . he can't be trusted to stay." She sighed and took his hands in hers. "You have come all this way, and I am so very glad to see you."

He followed her up the path to her door. The calm of the evening was marred by a few clanging blows from the back of the house that sounded oddly familiar, though out of place on this quiet street.

They sat in the front parlor, a formal room, oval in shape, with gray walls trimmed in gilt and yellow silk upholstery. Harriet called for tea. To the maid she said in a low, urgent voice: "Tell Powers that he must go to the shed. I cannot bear that noise." And to Toma she said: "I am sorry. I hope it will not spoil your visit."

Toma shook his head and occupied himself with his tea. He had not wanted her to be unhappy in this way. It was difficult now to recall the elation that had borne him from the Patent Office to this house.

"Has your visit to Washington gone well? Fowler never mentions your work without praising it. He says that great things may come of it."

"He is generous. If not for him I don't know how I could have gone on after what happened."

"Yes, we all had to go on. And I think generous is the best word to describe my husband. He has been very tolerant of Papa and his whims. Now, then, your day? And afterward I long for news of Beecher's Bridge."

They talked as the tea cooled and the twilight in the room thickened. She did not call for light, and still there was no sign of Fowler Truscott. When he told her of the arrow in the Patent Office that had pointed his way, she mistook his meaning.

"To Georgetown? That can't be true!"

He laughed aloud, remembering the time they had spent in her closet of an office and how her earnest habit of mind had often led her into the ambush of his humor. "No, no . . . the road to my success. I spent the afternoon in that temple of invention, and it was shown to me that I have a place there. I believe I shall be rich someday. That is why I am glad to visit your home. I must gather ideas on how to spend my wealth."

It was a stupid thing to say, whether he was hoping to impress her or hoping to make her laugh. She said nothing at all, and because she sat in the striped chair with her back to the garden and the dying light, her face was hidden. Was she looking at him, or at the fine objects and materials in these shadows? Or did her fingers seek the reassurance of that great stone in her ring?

"And may I not joke with you now that you are married?"

"Of course you may. I am out of practice, that is all. I thought for a moment that you were laughing at me. Please go on. I don't understand what it was that you saw."

"I think it will sound foolish if I try to tell you, so now you must promise not to laugh at me."

"Go on."

"It was like being in a wood and knowing where I must go, because I could see there was a light beyond the wood. And the great trees that I must not touch are the designs of Tesla, of Parsons, of Curtis . . . all of them inventors."

"And what was the light, in this dream of yours?"

"The light? I didn't get there, so I cannot tell you. If I had to guess, it is the Peacock Turbine, crowned with success and radiant. What else could it be?"

"If I had seen such a thing, and had to guess what lay beyond the wood, I think it must have something to do with holiness, or salvation."

"Perhaps. Salvation is a good enough word. But here we are, speaking of such things, and sitting in darkness, which may stand for sin in your way of thinking. Shall I call for light?"

"No, please, not now. Powers will light the dining room when it is time for supper, and I do dislike Mr. Edison's lamps, though Fowler says we must have them. Do you remember how we would keep the one lamp trimmed to save the expense?"

"Of course I do. And did I not tell you that even the one lamp seemed wasteful, and that in my home we could go for weeks without lighting one?"

"So you did." He could tell from her voice that the memory pleased her. "In the dark this seems more like home."

"You will be back there soon?"

"Yes, soon enough."

"I forgot to tell you: just yesterday, at the depot, I saw a crate with your name on it, and it was half the size of this room."

"The piano . . . I had forgotten the piano."

"And the new room is almost finished."

"I'm sure it will be wonderful, and that I shall grow to love it in time. But what I remember is our own home."

He had no lighthearted comment to make. His fingers were clenched on the teacup. He groped for the tray to put it down.

"Do you ever wish, Toma, that we could go back?"

"Go back?"

"To the way things were."

"Did you not say we had to go forward? I think perhaps you have forgotten the way things were."

"Some days it seems I can do little else but remember. Is this not true for you?"

"I remember that you once asked me to do something, and I tried to do it because that was the only chance I had . . . for you. But I failed, and we both knew what the consequences would be, even if we could not speak about it. The rules were simple. You were the prize I did not win."

The harshness of these words caused a catch in her breath whose meaning he knew. He went to her and took her hand. He knew her face was turned up to him, for he felt the sweetness of her breath.

"And now?"

"And now I have my work, which is my life, and if I think about what might have been I cannot go forward."

"You do not think of me?" If he turned his hand in hers his palm would lie against her cheek. But she released his hand abruptly and stood. "I hear Powers in the pantry. You must give me a moment. There are matches and a candle there where you were sitting."

Powers came, and the Edison lamps were lit, and they went through to their supper. In the dim second parlor, Toma laid his hand admiringly on the case of the grand piano.

"Yes," said Harriet, without enthusiasm, "Fowler has encouraged me greatly in my music. Shall I sing for you afterward?"

"If you will. That was one of the pleasures of the old days."

As the soup was being served, Harriet caught him glancing at the third place setting.

"We won't wait for him. There is no telling when he will come, or if he will come, though he did so want to see you. He is very busy now. He will call by ten if he has to stay in town."

"Perhaps your father will dine with us?"

The glare of the electric lamp made her look pale, and sharp. "I think not. Surely you see how it is? He takes his meals in the shed out there to save time, otherwise they will never be ready. Oh." She put her spoon down. "It is unbearable."

"They? Is he still making the wheels?"

She nodded, staring at her soup. "We cannot live in town. And my husband no longer feels that he can entertain here. It is part of his job, you see."

"But you are doing what you must do. You cannot doubt yourself."

They ate in silence, taking no pleasure in the cold capon or the jellied veal. At one point, Harriet laid down her knife and her fork and cast her eyes around the room, as if looking for something that was not in its place.

"Do you still live in the silk mill?"

"I do."

"And . . . ?"

"Olivia sends her regards."

"And mine to her, of course."

Toma had been filling his glass with Madeira from the decanter. Now he pushed it with his forefinger across the polished mahogany until it rested by her water goblet. "Could you think of this as medicine?"

She drank once and gave a little sigh of surrender, then finished the whole glass. "I would never have done that on my own."

"I could not leave you in such low spirits."

"Are you going, then?"

"Soon."

"Could you not stay until Fowler returns? Or until he calls?"

When the plates were cleared they went to the second parlor, where she lit the candlesticks on the piano and the gas jet in the sconce beside her bench. "Mr. Edison is not welcome in my music room. What shall I play for you?"

"Come." He held out his hand and she took it. Out through the dining room and the pantry and the kitchen they went, then onto the back porch and down into the garden. In the shed, surrounded by a clutter of tools and bits of iron scrap, they found the old man asleep in his chair, a flurry of insects around his lamp.

Amos Bigelow did not know Toma, but he knew his daughter; and although he complained about his lost hammer, he allowed himself to be led to the music room and seated in the curve of the piano, under the dark canopy of the lid.

"Now, play what you think he would like to hear," suggested Toma.

Play she did: a march, then a mazurka, and finally, when it was clear that the old man was keeping himself awake by an effort of will, a lullaby, with which she sang him to sleep. Toma was no judge of music, or of singing, but he was moved by this performance. When the last chord settled on them, she folded her hands in her lap and they looked at one another without attempting a conversation.

The telephone rang once in a distant room. "That will be Fowler to say he is not coming home. I'll turn on the light at the gate to summon a cab."

When they were saying good night, out on the curb, he asked: "Will you be long in coming to Beecher's Bridge?"

"I have not even wanted to think about the move. There is so much to do. Three weeks, I think."

"And how long will you stay?"

"As long as I can."

"The change will do you good."

"Yes. Now good night." Instead of the dry peck on the cheek he might have expected, or her hand, she gave him her mouth, full and soft, if only for a moment.

THE HORSEHAIR UPHOLSTERY was unyielding and the carriage smelled of mold. The jolting of the cobbles cleared his mind. He had spent an evening alone with her, and ended up wishing that her husband would return and deliver them from their pantomime of courtship. He had embarrassed her with an ill-chosen remark about becoming rich, words that seemed to mock the emptiness of her life.

What good had been accomplished? He would have the rest of the night and all his tomorrows to reflect on the things that would not change. There was that moment in the darkened parlor when a slight pressure of his hand would have resulted, perhaps, in a blind, hopeless, compromising embrace. Hopeless, that was the word. He must remember to buy that plaster mold of the Washington Monument on his way through the station tomorrow. Olivia would know that he had thought of her when he was away.

"MODERN JOVE HURLS LIGHTNING AT WILL— MILLION-HORSE-POWER FORKED TONGUES CRACKLE AND FLASH IN LABORATORY

Schenectady has a modern Jove who sits on his throne in a laboratory of the General Electric Company and hurls thunderbolts at will. He is Dr. Charles Proteus Steinmetz, electrical wizard, who announced today he has succeeded in producing and controlling indoor thunderbolts with all the characteristics of its natural brother except the thunder clouds."

—*The New York Times*, March 3, 1922

Charles P. Steinmetz

CHAPTER

TWELVE

Consulting Engineering Dept.
General Electric
Schenectady, New York
May 15, 1916

Thomas Peacock
P. O. Box 97
Beecher's Bridge, Connecticut

Dear Sir:

I write in the understanding that the arrangements between General Electric and yourself are in place and wanting only certain formalities. I offer my profound congratulations upon your ambitious design. Perhaps the situation with the patent examiners aggravates you, but it is only a temporary difficulty, and also a tribute to the importance of your device. Energy, in all its forms, is the preoccupation of the General Electric Corporation. No country can be truly great without the foundation of an ample energy supply coupled with a ruthless ingenuity in its exploitation. Germany is the best model here, and we in America have much to learn from her about social and industrial organization, a fact that is obscured by all this ill-informed talk about war.

So much for general observations. Perhaps when we meet we may discuss such matters at length. But for the time being, and until my work in Schenectady allows me to visit your laboratory, I am in urgent need of particulars. I hope you *will not take it amiss if I say that the specifications in the patent application seem rather vague to me, as they are accompanied by no detailed measurements of the wheel. There is no reference, either in the patent documents or in the ancillary materials supplied by Senator Truscott, to the formulae by which you derived the proper curvature of the vanes or structural members . . . thus I have no conception of the theory by which you are guided in your researches.*

Certainly there may have been some error or omission in the papers supplied by Senator Truscott, who is not a technical man. And I myself am not so thoroughly grounded in your line of hydrodynamic research. Therefore, in order that we may work together efficiently, would you kindly supply, at your very earliest convenience, and in your own hand, the measurement, data, and preliminary test results on the attached list. In addition, I would suggest the following lines of experimental inquiry as necessary to a more complete understanding of the turbine's potential efficiency. . . .

Very truly yours,
C. P. Steinmetz

"And what do you make of our friend's letter, Stefan?"

"Do you really think he will come here?" Stefan's equine features, normally so inexpressive, struggled to accommodate this extraordinary possibility.

"I am certain of it."

Stefan looked around the shop. "See what a mess this place is."

"How long will it take us to jump through all his hoops?"

"I do what I am told, boss. I am used to jumping through the hoops. It'll take me a while to measure and check and run through these sets of tests. But I think you must worry about the other, ja?"

"You mean the mathematical questions."

"That and his 'theory' . . . if only he knew."

"Well, I will come up with something to satisfy him."

"I don't think you understand, boss, about Dr. Steinmetz. Have you ever seen one of his books?"

"No, have you?"

"Certainly. Why else do I ask this question? It is one equation after another, more numbers than words."

"Tell me, Stefan, what is his field of expertise?"

"Ach, whatever he wants he can do. He starts in motors, alternating-current motors, and sometime in the nineties General Electric buys out old man Eichmeyer's company to get their hands on Steinmetz and his patents, otherwise he is killing them with his streetcar motors. Then he goes into the problems of high-voltage transmission that nobody else can touch, like eddy currents, magnetic leakage, hysteresis."

"And now?"

Stefan paused to spit out his tobacco plug and replace it with an equivalent chew of Mr. Wright's driest and most pungent salami. He seemed to live on this stuff, and the reek of it overpowered the smell of new pine construction. He held the knife ready to cut another piece.

"Thank you, no."

"So now Dr. Steinmetz has his own little part of the General Electric Company, and when some engineer has a problem with this or that, he comes hat and hand to him."

"Hat *in* hand."

"Ja, okay, and when he is left to himself he thinks about lightning."

"How do you know that?"

"I read the magazines, what do you think? Every few months he is writing something about transient currents and arresters, which are the protection devices. This is a big headache, I can tell you, if lightning hits the line."

"I see."

"Anything else, boss?"

"If you have those magazines I would like to see them."

"Sure, sure. I have them, I give them to you."

Toma left Stefan to his meal and went to the kitchen end of the mill. Olivia ladled cold beans into a tin plate. This was a long way from being rich.

"You stop by the store to see if my things come yet?"

"No, I forgot."

"You wouldn't forget if they was yours. You'll be sorry, maybe."

She said this with a smile. The Washington Monument had been a fine idea. Even more welcome was his report of Patent Examiner Flaten's praise of her drawings.

"You talk to the lawyer about those papers?"

"No. The patent agent took my money and gave me bad advice, as I found out almost too late. He puts his hand in my pocket and steals like a thief. So now I keep my eyes open and rely on no man."

"Just so you know, that was my money that got stole. And I bet you the General Electric knows some things that you don't, even if it is your machine."

"The money will come now every month, and when the patent is granted, there will be more. Read his letter if you want."

Olivia smoothed the paper of the letter on the table and read, sounding the words aloud as she did so. It made Toma think of Horatio to see this, and he laid his hand gently across the back of her neck.

"Well?"

"At least you know where he stands."

"And how shall I answer him?"

"You don't need to be wasting time on that. Just do what he says."

Toma sighed. It was a bad day when Stefan and Olivia agreed on anything.

Toma finished what was on his plate, and when Olivia went back to the laundry he poured himself a cup of cold coffee and took out the other letter that had arrived that morning, the one he had already read twice.

> *1822 Q Street, N. W.*
> *Washington, District of Columbia*
> *May 15, 1916*

Mr. T. Peacock
P. O. Box 97
Beecher's Bridge, Connecticut

My dear Toma:

It is now ten days since your visit, and I realize I must write you this letter to correct some impressions you may have taken away from that evening.

It is very, very early in the morning, which is the only time I have to myself, and the time I feel most alive. As I used to do at Iron Hill, I creep downstairs, unwilling to disturb that almost-light with a match or a candle, and in the kitchen—darker yet—I work as silently as an Indian, wanting just the pot of tea for the perfection of this moment. Do you remember when you surprised me there, thinking it must be Mrs. Evans? I must have looked a fright when you lit the candle. I think you were shocked to imagine that anyone in the household was an earlier riser than you.

The parlor where we sat seems quite changed now, its fine curtains swathed in old linens against the summer sun and all the furniture covered too. Perhaps this is to remind me that those things are not so important, and I must not grow too attached to them for they may be taken away. The shrouds make it easier for me to reflect on what is important, and the light begins to fill the garden. Would that I were a garden, to be filled with such a light.

The simplicity of that light is what I want for myself. No choices, no distractions, no cares can prevail against the one obligation, which is to be filled with light. So often in the real world we are borne away from the light, not toward it, and I do not fear sin as I do confusion.

You caught me at a low point, when my worries about Papa had reached a kind of crisis, and I saw my life being given over to this one care that would consume all the rest. (By the way, thank you for your inspiration of bringing him to hear the music: he was quite cheerful the next day and hardly missed his hammer at all.) It was my distress over Papa that prompted me to recall those old days that seem sweeter and simpler.

That was a mistake, and when I think what impression Powers might have had of us, I go quite cold and anxious. Of course if my husband had not been so tied up with his work we never would have been sitting in the dark talking of old times, and our table conversation would have been filled with his account of the doings of the Senate, and he would have drawn you out about your work, as I could not. He is remarkable in his ability to get to the heart of the matter in even the briefest of conversations, and is in every respect the most perfect husband. He is so very good to me.

It is hard to bring my thoughts to focus here, harder to make myself understood. May we, in the name of friendship, have no more confusion about what is past? Nor about the future? I cannot imagine coming back to Beecher's Bridge if this were not agreed between us. Let us preserve what was by honoring what is and what must be. There: a challenge, certainly, but an unambiguous one, and if we see clearly we shall rise to it.

I hope you will not mind my speaking my heart to you. If there was ever anyone who understood my feelings it is you, and may it always be so. I have been much eased in my mind by going to our church here every morning—not a

Congregational Church, but it is very near—and I shall walk there as soon as I lay down my pen.

> *Yours ever,*
> *H*

BILLINGS LEANED ON his shovel. He was a short, sturdy man and his years as a stoker at the Bigelow works had made him an expert in the employment of that tool. But now he was dissatisfied, for this was not dignified work, nor was he working at his own pace.

"Does it ever occur to you, Sandy, that these folk have their heads up their asses, for all the money they've got?"

"And spending it too, which is the important bit to you and me." Foster thought that it was more tiring to listen to Billings complain than to keep shoveling. "A house as big as this one is a bugger. Always something to fix, which is why I wouldn't have it if you paid me. But if she wants a new drain, I'll dig it for her, because I get paid." As an afterthought he added, "Which is more'n I can say for you, and you don't get on with it."

Still Billings did not move. The day was just getting warm, and although he had stripped to his undershirt, the sweat made a dark mat of the hair on his shoulders and chest. "But it makes no sense, man. First it's a kind of greenhouse thing, then it's someplace you sit and play music where you can look at the sky, I suppose, and now it's both at the same time, and needs a furnace and I don't know what all. You ask me, the poor woman don't know what she wants. Hasn't the faintest idea."

"Nobody asked you, Billings. Now for Christ's sake dig."

Harriet Truscott, at her desk, looked out the window and knew she must speak to the workmen again or they would never be finished in time, never get the sod back in place and the dirt swept up. As it was, the construction looked raw enough, in spite of the new planting of shrubbery around its edge. But she would not go outside and engage in conversation with that half-naked man who looked like a bear. How odd it was, she thought. Fowler, though she had never seen him thus, was not so . . . hairy. In fact . . . She opened the window enough to be heard.

"Mr. Foster, I beg you to hurry. The train comes at eleven, and I want everything to look perfect. I am sorry to disturb you."

"Yes, missus. I'm sure we'll have her done by then."

She shut the window again and moved her chair so that she could not see the hairy man. But she had a sudden concern for his wife. What did one do if one's husband were like that? It was Lucy's fault that she was thinking such thoughts. Eleven o'clock. She must finish her letter and then see to the arrangements for lunch. It might be days before she found another opportunity to write. Had she foreseen how much fuss was involved in Dr. Steinmetz's visit, she would have planted in Fowler's mind the suggestion that he stay in one of the hotels.

Her cousin Lucy, she felt, must have grown bored, or bold, or both, to write such things, using as an excuse the familiarity of their girlhood, that fond and distant memory.

"You will never guess," began Lucy, "what I have come across after all these years. You will remember the party we had for New Year's and your papa allowed you to come because your mother was so ill? It must have been just after your trip to Italy. What fun that was, and the snow so perfect for days on end, and the men had shoveled the snow off the entire pond to the black ice below. We could have skated all night by the light of the bonfire if we had been allowed to. And on the Eve of the New Year, as was the custom, the lead was melted in the fire for fortune-telling, and all the unmarried girls—even we, who were hardly of an age for such things—must cast for our husbands.

"Mary Parkhurst, you remember her, was such a timid girl and her hand holding the door key shook when she tried to pour the ladle of lead through it. A drop of it spattered on her wrist and she let everything fall into the pan of water and made such a noise. But when we fished it out, there was something that looked very like a book, and in the end she did marry a minister, so I suppose it really does work. I got only drops of no shape at all, and they said I probably would not marry, or that my husband would have no particular calling, and I said Poo to that. And now that I *am* married—and more proof, would you believe it, due in October—and Cecil doing so well in his uncle's office, I see that all those little sprinklings of lead were so many coins, and I am vindicated after all.

"You were the last one of all to take the ladle, and with your customary bravery you held your hand steady and let a great dollop of lead through the hole in the key. When we fished it out of the water it was the strangest thing to look at, for it did rather resemble a man, but with a great bundle on his back, and as no one could solve the riddle I called out that Harriet must marry a hunchback. You were quite cross with me. Later, when we were in bed together, and perhaps a little merry with the champagne Papa had allowed us, I tried to make amends. I showed you your bit of lead, which I had put in my pocket, and pointed out that the creature had three legs. 'And do you know what that is, Harriet?' I asked, pointing to the middle one. And you said 'No' so very quickly, and turned such a shade of scarlet that I knew perfectly well you knew, but I couldn't get another word out of you.

"Well, dear Harriet, I have found your little man again, wrapped in cotton wool in the very back of my drawer, when we visited my parents at Easter. I laughed to see him, and laughed again to think of how you must blush now, for there is no question of your not knowing, though I would be eager to know how you have solved the rest of your puzzle. I will question you no more, for I certainly don't wish you to be vexed all over again by this silly thing. But I do hope to come and see you before it becomes too difficult to travel, and I shall bring your treasure with me. Have you news for me in any way?"

No news, thought Harriet, and placed her hand on her belly in an effort to imagine what such news would actually feel like. She was not cross with her cousin—it would not change Lucy at all to be cross with her—but she was not to be drawn into the dialogue that Lucy seemed to have in mind. She was pleased to find a way of answering the letter that neither ignored Lucy's text nor surrendered to the impropriety of it. The hump on the back of the figure turned out to be a most telling augury, for she had married a man who had the cares of the world on his back, and she rejoiced in that, for who better to bear such a burden? She made no answer or mention of the other. What could Lucy possibly want to know about that? And what could she bear to tell?

She was silent, too, on the matter of "news." She was not ready to share with Lucy or anyone else the possibility that God might not bless her marriage in that way. And if she dwelled rather long on her new room, and her piano, and the progress she made in her singing, it was at least partly in response to the knowledge that Lucy herself could not sing a note.

There was the stamp of feet at the door, though she had not heard the sound of the motor. She sealed her letter and went down.

HE IS NOT A DWARF at all, thought Harriet as she poured coffee for Dr. Steinmetz. He was quite short, in fact very short, and he did certainly have a hump on his back, which was unfortunate. But he also had the most beautiful manners, and very lively eyes too.

"Thank you, Mrs. Truscott, for my coffee and for this exquisite meal. May I smoke?"

"Of course you may. Coffee, Mr. Peacock? Fowler?" Toma had barely spoken in the course of the meal and seemed anxious to her.

"Thank you my dear. And if Dr. Steinmetz is going to indulge, then I might also. Sir, you do me great honor, and a very elegant cigar, too. Is it true, by the way, that story one has heard so often?" Fowler Truscott held up his unlit cigar and Steinmetz shrugged and pursed his lips, as if to say: I will not dispute it.

Harriet looked inquiringly at her husband.

"Oh, nothing improper, Harriet, just that Dr. Steinmetz is a kind of legend in Schenectady on account of his cigars."

"It was a small thing. . . ."

"They thought to banish smoking from the General Electric premises, and they put up a sign. Then Dr. Steinmetz disappears for five days, and no one knows what is wrong. A vice president of the firm is sent to his house to find out why he has stayed home. Is he ill? No. The reason is simply this: No Smoking, No Steinmetz." The senator laughed, Harriet smiled, and Steinmetz shook his head.

"This has become a kind of folk story. I don't believe I spoke those words."

"The words may have been altered to make a better story," said Harriet, "but I am sure the part about your importance to the firm is true."

"Thank you, Mrs. Truscott. I am pleased to accept your kind exaggeration."

"But seriously, Dr. Steinmetz, to touch again on our earlier subject, and hyperbole aside, may we not interpret your presence in Beecher's Bridge as a mark of your corporation's commitment to this project?

Might we not hope, one day, to have an installation, perhaps an entire division, of General Electric right here in Beecher's Bridge?" It never failed to impress Harriet how her husband could pluck such connections out of the air in mid-phrase, the way her horse on one lead would make a flying change to the other.

Steinmetz chuckled. "You speak of 'my corporation,' but I belong to it rather than the other way around. I am only an engineer, and so it is only proper that I should come. This is a most pleasant town, I think. Who knows what comes after?"

"Oh, but, Dr. Steinmetz," the words burst from Harriet. She was overwhelmed by the thought of Power City, rising like the phoenix, and the strength of her feeling made her blush. "It is quite thrilling to think that it might happen. Toma . . . ?"

Toma smiled and said nothing. Steinmetz inclined his head to acknowledge Harriet's enthusiasm, and he bestowed a glance on Toma. "You see that our young friend does not commit himself, wisely I think. You are speaking as if an invention, or even a patent, is a reason to build a factory, and I can only say: Perhaps. What is certain is that the job of the engineer is more complicated. I don't want to bore you. . . ."

"Never," said Harriet. "Please go on."

"First we find out that a thing exists—and here is Mr. Peacock with such a thing, his machine. Then we must get to the general theory, which is nothing but the phenomenon as it would exist under ideal conditions. And the last part is to adapt those general theories to the specific conditions under investigation. You can see, then, that we are now only at the beginning."

"Oh yes, I quite see, now that you have explained it. But you must not take away my hope, and my husband's, that something wonderful and useful shall be accomplished right here."

Again Steinmetz made his courtly, seated bow, a gesture that emphasized the relative hugeness of his head. He smiled up at the senator, who had poured him a small glass of cognac.

"Thank you. My life in Schenectady will seem dull after this." He turned back to Harriet. "Senator Truscott was telling me, on the way from the station, of your family's long involvement with industry here, so I understand your enthusiasm. But if Mr. Peacock's turbine wheel is successful, it will not be the achievement of one man or one town, it will be part of a new way of thinking, of doing, which is energy and industry together, each element interconnected, so that the coal burned at the mouth of the mine in West Virginia can light the city of Philadelphia; or the high mountain stream, which is particularly adapted to the function of this turbine, can power, at a distance of many hundreds of miles, the factories of Mr. Ford."

"Good heavens," murmured Harriet.

"Splendid!" exclaimed Senator Truscott. "A vision of the future. And what do you call this thing, this arrangement?"

Steinmetz pressed his palms together, then turned his hands perpendicular to one another. "I sometimes think of it this way: the grid . . . for the lines of electrical transmission will leave a mark on the map like a gridiron. Every part contributes and cooperates. Mrs. Truscott, have I distressed you?"

"No, no. It is extraordinary, what you say." She stared at the tobacco-stained fingers. "But I can't help thinking that it doesn't sound very much like . . . well, like America."

Steinmetz was delighted by this observation. "Mrs. Truscott, you have seen the essence of the matter. Exactly so: this is not a description of America, not now, but as she may be, with luck. At this time, it is more an accurate description of Germany."

"Fascinating, fascinating." Fowler Truscott's tone announced another flying change. "And would you have time to see the rest of Beecher's Bridge today? I think a little air would be just the thing."

Steinmetz rose and offered Harriet his arm, ignoring the difference of height. "I think I must attend to Mr. Peacock's business, yes? But first, if I may see the new music room? Really, Mrs. Truscott, I am overwhelmed. The soul of an artist, but the mind like an engineer's. If only other women were like you."

THE BRANDY AFTER LUNCH had given Charles Proteus Steinmetz a headache, and he was in a less generous frame of mind as he and Toma made their tour of the silk mill. It was a glorious afternoon, and the little yard by the door was filled with fluttering sheets set out to dry in the updraft from the river.

Inside, the kitchen was as orderly as Toma had ever seen it, with not a frying pan or a dish in sight. Even the calico curtain seemed to have been washed and ironed. Stefan sat at his bench in the new bay, trying to look very busy, but overcome by the urge to stare at Steinmetz. The collection of scrap and machine parts had been picked up piece by piece, wiped with rags, and set down against the wall. Toma and Stefan had scoured the floor, but while everything seemed a good deal cleaner, there is no way to disguise a junk pile.

"Do you find this material useful?" Steinmetz waved his cigar at the pile.

"Sometimes, yes, particularly so in the early stages of rebuilding the wheel, and we have been able to adapt some of the gears from the old ironworks." Steinmetz said nothing; he nodded as if he were already thinking of something else. Toma remembered Horatio's passion for these articles, and that long, rambling lecture. "Do you know what Mr. Edison says about a junk pile? He says that invention—"

"Please, please!" Steinmetz put his hand to his forehead. "Do not talk to me about Edison's junk pile . . . such nonsense, and I don't believe that he said that any more than I believe myself to be the author of my famous phrase. You know, Mr. Edison has done some wonderful things, but he is a man of the last century, no matter how much the newspapers love him. And why? Because he thinks only of inventions and not of systems. This is a lesson for a young man to learn."

Toma nodded respectfully, but added, almost in an undertone, "Yes, sir, but I think of myself as an inventor."

"Well, well, I suppose we must always have inventors. And as long as we have inventors, they will be waiting for the world to reward them for the better mouse trap, or the improved turbine, ja?" He turned away and walked the length of the bench to the sunny spot where Stefan worked. "And what is this, my friend?"

Stefan realized that the great Steinmetz was addressing him, and he could hardly answer. "The wheel, Dr. Steinmetz, that is the wheel."

"Yes, yes, of course, and my compliments on your work. But where is your notebook?"

"My . . . ?"

"Your working papers, your observations. . . ."

Stefan reached behind the wheel for the dog-eared composition book in which he made his calculations and kept records of the wheel's performance. Sitting squarely in the crease of the open book was the unconsumed portion of his daily sausage. Stefan uttered a moan of dismay and pushed the book to the edge of the table, where the trash barrel stood.

"No, no, my friend, the sausage is innocent, and that would be a waste. I will try some if you please?" Stefan cut a piece with his penknife, and Steinmetz ate, nodding his approval. "Much too good to throw away."

"Es tut mir leid, herr Doktor, es sollte nicht geschehen."

Steinmetz's frown relaxed at the sound of his native tongue, and he replied in German. Toma did not catch what was said, but Steinmetz tapped the paper where the sausage had left a corona of grease. Stefan smiled up at him, knowing he had been let off lightly.

Steinmetz took Toma by the arm and walked to the far end of the mill. He spoke in a confidential tone. "Now, my friend, we must have a little chat about our problem."

"And what is that?"

"Problem is a strong word. Perhaps there is a better one."

"Yes?"

"Let me see if I can explain. You are a young man, clever and energetic. And out of this chaos"—here Steinmetz encompassed the silk mill with a small gesture of his hand and cigar—"out of this chaos you have made your marvelous machine, with perhaps a little good luck too."

Toma did not reply, but nodded, acknowledging the compliment, if that's what it was.

"So far, so good. But now you are no longer the independent operator, living from hand to mouth. You have sold your machine, or the controlling interest, to General Electric. So what happens now?"

"We perfect the machine, we manufacture it, we sell it. There are many uses for the Peacock Turbine. . . ."

"Ah, the Peacock Turbine. There it is: the statement of the problem."

"But that is the name, as the patent application states."

"Yes, indeed. That will not change. But my point is that your thinking is all for the machine, your invention, and nothing beyond. I suppose Edison is your hero?"

"No . . . I would name Tesla, Nikola Tesla." Toma spoke the name with pride.

"Even worse. You have taken as your model the most arrogant, intractable, and egotistical man that was ever put on this earth, or at least in the category of scientist. Shall I tell you who my hero is?"

"If you please."

"Well, he is a man with not a single patent to his name, and you will certainly never find his photograph in any newspaper, and probably not a single article."

"Then how should I know him?"

"Because you have already met him. It is Mr. Coffin of whom I speak."

"Mr. Coffin?"

"Yes. What do you think he is?"

"I think he is the chairman . . . no, a capitalist."

"He is a system builder, and Mr. Insull, who directs the great electric utility in Chicago, is another. They look not at one invention or another, but ahead to the time when everything is interconnected, every resource is exploited intelligently and officiently, and—"

"It is what you were saying at lunch. The grid, you called it."

"Very good. You begin to understand. The grid is the interconnection of all energy and all enterprise, and the system that Mr. Coffin builds at General Electric is to hasten the day when that is possible."

"And the machine, my machine, is a piece of that system."

"Exactly so. It is not an end in itself, or not in the eyes of the General Electric Corporation."

Toma nodded. He thought this might be the end of their chat, but Steinmetz's expression of inquisitive attention told him otherwise.

"I am ready to do whatever is necessary, anything that is in my power."

"Anything, you say? Well, a very big first step would be to take everything of importance here"—again Steinmetz made the gesture with his cigar, and the trail of smoke hung in the air—"and move it to Schenectady."

"With all due respect, Dr. Steinmetz, that is not necessary, and not reasonable. There is no waterfall in Schenectady of any importance, let alone a head of one hundred sixty feet."

"Well, well, a waterfall is not such an important thing. Do you know, we have almost perfected a system for making artificial lightning in the research laboratory there, to test my lightning arresters? A matter of months, perhaps. And if we can do that, I assure you we can make a waterfall too, though not such an elegant one. A few pumps, and—"

Toma cut him off, speaking very low. He was afraid he might lose his temper if he spoke in a normal tone of voice. "Neither is it possible. I am sorry, but that has all been decided. It is stipulated in the contract."

Steinmetz found that his cigar had gone out and asked for a match. "I know about that piece of paper, of course. It is discouraging that a matter of scientific importance has been left in the hands of lawyers. But I was thinking of the inconvenience of this arrangement. I am in Schenectady, you are here. The equipment must be manufactured in Schenectady and shipped here. If it is not right, it must be sent back. Yes, I know what the contract says, but I was hoping you would change your mind. You can understand my disappointment?"

"I understand how it must seem to you. Ask me for anything else."

Steinmetz sighed. "I scarcely know where to begin. I will send a couple of men down from Schenectady who will be useful to you. They know how things are done at General Electric. We will see. Perhaps I have overestimated the difficulties. I am sure you are not afraid of hard work. So we roll up the sleeves, ja?" Steinmetz smiled at Toma, pleased with his own turn of phrase. He walked along the wall a few paces and stopped by the door that bore Olivia's sign, its message underlined by the crudeness of the lettering.

"And here is the laundry, I suppose?"

"That is Olivia's room."

"I think I know the smell of bleach, and sheets do not grow on trees, even in Beecher's Bridge."

"Yes, it is a laundry."

"Can you imagine, Mr. Peacock, if I send my engineers down to work in a laundry? You must get rid of that, or we will be the laughingstock of Schenectady."

THE VISIT TO BEECHER'S BRIDGE of the Wizard of Schenectady coincided with a snap of glorious weather that unfurled over the Berkshires and the North West Corner like a fine new flag. The long, damp spring had caused farmers and gentlemen of the town to consult their almanacs or pocket diaries of seasons past, and left them wondering whether things were quite right. Conditions in March had been nearly perfect for the making of maple syrup, but that was a small comfort if you couldn't plow a furrow and get the crop down in April: 1884 was well within living memory, and the newspapers said later that the sunless summer had been caused by the eruption of Krakatoa, an island on the other side of the world. Perhaps the damned thing had gone off again like a Roman candle? And further back, not within living memory, but no less vivid for that, was the terrible year of 1816, or Eighteen Hundred and Froze to Death, as they called it back then, when cruel frosts came down in every month of the year, and the wolves walked the main street of town, right past the Congregational Church. Of these facts people were as sure as they were of the Bible itself, or nearly, for their authority was the printed texts of Dr. Robbins's sermons, in which the wolves were used to very good effect.

But now all that had been forgiven and nearly forgotten, and the soft wind—a perfect temperature, day and night—touched the land and released a season of bloom that was a kind of eruption. From the Truscotts' broad lawn one could see how the mountain laurel made its progress up the side of Great Mountain: the white glowing of full blossom at the swampy margins of the lake; the pink of opening flowers on the slopes; and far above, where the bushes were stunted and the dark green leaves rimmed patches of bald rock, a sprinkling of hard red buds. On the last day of his visit, Saturday, Dr. Steinmetz was persuaded by Harriet to come out before breakfast to find the yellow warblers along the lake, and she had given him her bird glasses so that he could see for himself how the laurel, blossom and bud, told a story about the climate of Great Mountain.

"Yes, I see it. It is a kind of litmus paper, yes? For the temperature."

"And today, Dr. Steinmetz, we shall take our picnic up there. No excuses."

"No, no, I would not miss it."

For two days Toma had watched Steinmetz work, and had been

impressed by the restless curiosity, the almost manic energy. He was remarkably spry as well, and Toma had seen him throw himself under the wheel to get a better view of things. A variety of gauges and measuring devices sprouted from the pockets of his coat; he was forever asking Stefan to take down the notations he called out; and he could evidently solve equations in his head without having them written out.

To Toma he was polite, even cordial, and no allusion was made to the conversation of the first day. Stefan followed him around like a dog, hoping to be rewarded by some task, or a scrap of German. He even got on well with Olivia, who had no inkling of the fate of her laundry.

"Mr. Steinmetz, you have been lying in those puddles again. Let me take your coat before it soaks you through." She had it off his back before he could protest, and for the rest of the morning Steinmetz wore a woolen shawl draped on his shoulders while his coat flapped outside with the other drying articles.

At last he pronounced his satisfaction—or acknowledged that no more progress could be made with the equipment at hand. He consulted his watch. "Nearly eleven. I think we must not keep Mrs. Truscott waiting."

The picnic party gathered on the drive in front of the Truscott house and Harriet made a last appeal to her husband.

"Fowler, this is such a day. Look! Look! It is an eagle, I think. There, he's gone behind the mountain. Can't you come with us? We could try wrapping it in a bandage."

"Nothing would give me greater pleasure, I assure you, but the knee does not want to go up the mountain, and it most certainly would not want to come back down. You take care of our guest. I think Toma may have to carry everything, but he's a young, strong fellow."

She suggested they take the car around by the Five Mile Drive to give them a boost up the side of the mountain, but Steinmetz would not hear of it. "In my youth, you know, I climbed in the mountains, though you might not think so. And when the weather is acceptable, I ride my bicycle to work, even now. All summer long I am in my canoe at Camp Mohawk. Do not worry on my account." He made an effort to stand taller, more upright, as he spoke his boast, and even made a joking pantomime of flexing his bicep.

Steinmetz's vigor on the trail, even under the weight of the small pack he insisted on carrying, was no surprise to Toma, although they had to stop often for the little man to catch his breath. His cigars, he said ruefully, were catching up with him. Then he laughed and admitted that he was looking forward to the pleasure of a smoke once they made it to the top. He was anxious to press on so that they might have another sighting of the eagle.

"I have never seen an eagle in Schenectady."

They talked about birds, perhaps in anticipation of the eagle, and Steinmetz recounted the story of his pet crows. They were wild crows but they came to his window to be fed, and he talked with them, or at least came to know something of their language. The end was sad, though, as one of the crows, feeling a false sense of security, was ambushed and killed by the raccoon, which had somehow got out of his cage. The other crow had not long survived this grief. "But I have them both stuffed, so they are still with me. They are sitting on my bookcase now."

By the time they had climbed up through the dark evergreens of Rachel's Leap into the sunlit clearing of the falls, they had passed from ornithology to botany. Steinmetz, in enumerating the treasures of his garden, mentioned his prized patch of *Cypripedium*. Harriet gave a little shriek and seized him by the hand to drag him away off the path and into the underbrush of laurel and scrub oak.

"Look there, Dr. Steinmetz! And was ever the ladyslipper in more perfect bloom?"

"It is the very same." Steinmetz's voice ceded nothing to hers in enthusiasm. "And if I did not know better, I would think I am in my very own garden."

They came back to the clearing still holding hands and stopped near the bank of the stream, with Steinmetz on a low hummock, so that he was nearly of an equal stature to Harriet. She seemed to be blushing; it might have been the exertion of the climb, or the happiness of her botanical discovery. And notwithstanding all the reasonable arguments to the contrary, one might suspect that the little man was in love with her, or at least with the idea of her.

Steinmetz went off with the binoculars and a cigar in search of his eagle, leaving Toma and Harriet to lay the cloth. She knelt now where she had stood with Steinmetz, the same spot where she had earlier broken Toma's heart, and gave him a smile of generous and transcendent sweetness.

They began to tear at the chicken, and when Toma turned his back to dip a cup in the stream, Steinmetz cried out: "No, my friend, we can do better than that." He drew from his pack a slender-necked bottle of hock and three stemmed glasses, each wrapped in a dish towel. He poured the wine and Harriet drank without a murmur, though she would not let him fill her glass again. After lunch, and after Steinmetz had smoked the other half of his cigar, they lay back, shaded their faces with the dish towels, and slept.

"I wonder where all this water comes from." Steinmetz was awake and writing in his pocket notebook. He had his boots off and was bathing his feet in the water, still cold with snowmelt. "We are very near the top of your mountain, no?"

"Very near," said Harriet, stretching but not yet risen from her spot on the grass. "The water must come from Dead Man's Lake, which is supposed to be very deep."

"A lake on top of a mountain . . ." Steinmetz pursed his lips and cocked his head, then muttered a phrase in German that ended with the word *Walchensee*. He turned to Harriet. "And you have not been there?"

"Never."

"And you, Mr. Peacock?"

"I think no one goes to Dead Man's Lake. There was a man at the works who said there was nothing to see, and damned hard to get there."

"Then I will bet you he never went. We will follow the stream. What could be difficult in that? Come. We leave all this here for now."

The Steinmetz expedition made a brave attempt on the lake: good progress at first along the open bank of the stream, then slower as they stooped under the boughs, then the trees became so thick they had to clamber down into the streambed. They had been climbing by degrees, but the stream had been slowing to their pace. Now they entered a zone where the water widened out into a dense growth of alders, and the current was imperceptible. But for the sun they would soon have been lost, for there were no landmarks here. In fact there was no land at all. They were apparently in Dead Man's Lake even though they could not yet see it.

They felt their way cautiously along the bottom—rocks giving way now to an unpleasant ooze—using the narrow alders to support themselves. Harriet had abandoned her skirt to the water in order to have both hands free. Steinmetz, still leading the way, was soaked nearly to the top of his trousers, and no one had mentioned the temperature of the water, which was little better than freezing. Harriet looked back at Toma with a question in her eyes, and he made a violent thrusting motion with his head, which she took as encouragement to speak.

"Dr. Steinmetz, I am afraid I cannot go on. Forgive me."

"Ah," he said, concerned but still cheerful. "I think the mountain has beaten us today, yes? But it was good that we tried. Oh! I am sorry for your clothes. Will you lead us back, sir?"

In half an hour they were back at the clearing trying to warm themselves. Harriet murmured an apology and began to remove her shoes. Steinmetz turned his back, but Toma was not quick enough, or did not understand, and when he glanced up she had taken one stocking off and was beginning on the other. He saw that the flesh from ankle to mid-thigh was bluish white and he took the tablecloth, warm from the sun, and used it to towel her dry. She did not flinch or think to protest. When Steinmetz turned, it was as if nothing had happened; his attention was focused on his cigar.

"Thank goodness this is still dry. At moments like these . . . Ah, another surprise." And from his coat pocket—the same coat pocket, Toma could have sworn, that held the micrometer—he produced a small silver flask. "We always carried this in the mountains."

He offered the first sip to Harriet. "Please, a good swallow, or it will have no effect at all." Then to Toma, and he took the last gulp himself. "Now if only we had dry stockings. I am very afraid of making blisters on Mrs. Truscott's feet."

They set off down the mountain, feeling the effects of the long day and the jolt of cognac. On the pretext of resting and warming themselves in the westering sun, Toma led them out onto the bare top of Lightning Knob, and Steinmetz was delighted to see the Truscott mansion, set like a doll's house below them.

"Is that not my host there?" inquired Steinmetz, and without waiting for an answer launched a vigorous "Hallooo!" that ricocheted off
the side of the mountain and caused Fowler Truscott to stop in mid-
swing. He waved back at the party above.

"This mountain has many wonders. And what is this pleasant little
peak called?"

"Lightning Knob," replied Harriet, her face suffused with the color
of the late-afternoon sun. Steinmetz repeated her words as if trying to
grasp her meaning.

"Is there a reason for this name, I wonder?"

"Oh, I believe so, Dr. Steinmetz. The stories that are told in
town. . . . And in the short time I have lived in my husband's house I
have been impressed, and sometimes fearful. Or I was, until I saw that
it does not strike the house itself."

Steinmetz turned to Toma and raised his eyebrows. "Is it so? I cannot doubt Mrs. Truscott, but is there an explanation?"

"Perhaps. I did once see, among the papers of Mr. Bigelow, who
was—is—Mrs. Truscott's father, a geological survey that noted the extraordinary incidence of magnetite in the rock of Great Mountain,
which accounts, I believe, for the uselessness of the compass in these
parts."

"So? Magnetite? I know the magnetite, it was long ago the basis of
a patent of mine, for the magnetite arc lamp. I don't recall the number
now, but it burns with a most pleasing light." He knelt to examine the
rock, brushing away the litter of mica chips and tearing at the dwarf
blueberry bushes growing in a crevice. Out of his pack he produced a
geologist's pick and began to attack the rock until he had prized away
several chunks of it. Then he wrote in his pocket book.

They left the Knob soon after that, and for the rest of the way
down the mountain Steinmetz seemed happily isolated in his own
thoughts.

When they reached the bottom of Great Mountain, they were
tired, but their clothes were almost dry, and Steinmetz was in an excellent mood.

"Such a day . . . such a day. If only I had seen the eagle."

Magic Annihilator.—To make 1 gross 8-ounce bottles; Aqua ammonia 1 gallon, soft water 8 gallons, best white soap 4 pounds, saltpetre 8 ounces; shave the soap fine, add the water, boil until the soap is dissolved, let it get cold, then add the saltpetre, stirring until dissolved. Now strain, let the suds settle, skim off the dry suds, add the ammonia, bottle and cork at once.

WHAT IT WILL DO.—It will remove all kinds of grease and oil spots from every variety of wearing apparel such as coats, pants, vests, dress goods, carpets, etc., without injury to the finest silks or laces.

—*from* Lee's Priceless Recipes, *1895*

FLOATING

. . . the friendly hand, held under the back of the head, is a great aid to a beginner. . . . Lying on your back, legs straight before you and feet together, arms close at your sides and head thrown back—all that is necessary to keep afloat is a constant rotary motion of your hands under water. Very soon even this movement may be dispensed with, and you may lie as easily on the water as on your bed.

—*from* The American Girl's Handy Book, *1898*

THIRTEEN

The summer of 1916 was a time of feverish activity in Beecher's Bridge. First there was the arrival of the two consulting engineers from Schenectady: a Swede, slab-faced and phlegmatic, named Larssen, and his polar opposite, Piccolomini, a sharp-faced man with the metabolism of a shrew.

Almost immediately, and on the basis of detailed instructions addressed by Steinmetz to Toma as manager of the Experimental Site, construction began on a substantial stone-and-reinforced-concrete extension of the mill to the north, and the woods rang with the hammering of the stonecutters. The new building would house the production model of the Peacock Turbine, whenever that should become reality, and would place the machine more directly under the source of its power, the reservoir that Horatio Washington had tapped into. The masons' job was less onerous than it might have been thanks to the ready supply of stone available in the ruins of Power City. The silk mill itself was henceforth to be known as the Experimental Site.

From the foot of the falls the improving work began its march uphill. New piping was installed—a gleaming black pair in eight-inch cast iron—and Horatio's salvaged plumbing became another relic of the mountain. Word soon got around that at full blast the jet of water from the nozzle would withstand the blow of a sledge and rip it out of a man's hands. The new pipes were strongly reinforced to withstand the pressure of that column of water. It was fitting and ironic that this highly specialized and expensive pipe had been laid down within spitting distance of the old ironmaster's violent exit from the world.

The Bigelow works, already falling into ruin, were the next to be transformed, for as Steinmetz had foreseen, there was hardly room down at the Experimental Site for any important manufacturing operation, even adequate storage and warehousing facilities, and no convenient access from the railway line. The buildings of the old ironworks were torn down or modified to their new purpose. Toma was installed in Amos Bigelow's old office. A telephone line was his connection to the wheel.

All this was change enough to keep the conversation going at McCreedy's Saloon for years to come. And, as in those boom days of the Bigelow Rifle, there was money too: the new construction and the influx of General Electric personnel were the salvation of many a household, and certainly of the saloon, which had been nearly derelict two years after the closing of the ironworks. Not much was known about the work up there on the crown of Lightning Knob, where a team of engineers had hauled drums of fuel and some outlandish equipment. The deep core samples of rock were crated up and sent to Dr. Steinmetz in Schenectady, New York. Business was business, and the Schenectady men were good customers, but McCreedy's opinion was that there was plenty of rock lying about for the asking in Beecher's Bridge, so why would anyone go to such trouble?

In mid-June a small item appeared in the local weekly newspaper, near the end of a column entitled "Events in Beecher's Bridge," announcing the relocation of Olivia Toussaint's laundry from the old silk mill to South Side Road. All pickups and deliveries, without exception, were to be made at Wright's General Store. A new schedule of prices would be available soon. The reason for the instruction in the article was that the new location of the laundry coincided exactly with the Truscott mansion, and it would hardly do to have Mrs. Breen's boy traipsing up and down the drive.

After the unpleasant shock of her eviction from the silk mill, Olivia had come to accept this new arrangement, and she had driven a hard bargain. Here she had conveniences that were previously unknown and unimaginable. Somewhere outside, and not too close to the house, there was a gasoline-driven dynamo that was attended by the chauffeur between the hours of nine and three. The engine not only provided light in her basement space but powered both the washing machine and the mangle. As Mrs. Breen's sheets or Mr. Breen's drawers could not be displayed on the Truscott lawn, a special gas-heated drying unit was brought by rail from New York, and clothes or sheets laid over those heated tubes were dry in a fraction of the time, come rain or come shine. Olivia did not abandon her old charcoal-heated irons to some new technology, but that was the only holdover from the laundry in the silk mill.

On this warm day at the beginning of August, she was glad to turn off the switches and pull the cord to signal the chauffeur that the dynamo might be shut down. The dryer was doing its work, and the charcoal glowed merrily in the corner. Sweat gathered in beads on her brow almost as fast as she could wipe it away with the cool linen hand towel. But no matter how hot it got, she certainly wasn't going to shuck off her shirt here, as she would once have done without a second thought. She wondered now what would have happened—or not happened—if he hadn't got himself a good long look at her that day. He had only pretended not to look. Olivia climbed the stairs into the house, where porches and awnings kept everything dim and cool.

In the hall the smell of phlox was strong, and a vase of the white spires had been set on the table beside the tall clock. Where everybody was, she could not guess, for it was very still. They might both have gone out in the car, and she would not have heard it over the noise in her laundry. Up the main staircase she went, slowly so as not to break a sweat again, and she trailed one hand along the banister, the other grazing the dark panels. Her feet made no sound on the carpeted treads. She liked the smell here—wax and flowers and settled dust— and the fragments of colored light falling from the high chandelier reminded her of the window in the church behind the altar.

She must check now on her linens. What was the use of all her effort down below if the towels hung crooked or a pile of the master's shirts listed to one side? There were many different monograms, generations of the Truscott women and the Bigelow women, and they must not be carelessly mixed. Did the upstairs girl, Lily, even know her alphabet? Then too there were the stains, and as her mother had taught her, the earlier you attended to them the better. Bleach would destroy the linen over time, but if you laid the washed sheet or garment on freshly cut grass in the sunlight, that would take care of most stains, even blood. Harriet Truscott could look out on the lawn on a warm summer day and feel well cared for. There was her best nightgown, the one trimmed with lace eyelets, lying on the cut grass like a fallen angel.

At Harriet's dressing table Olivia paused now to look at the array of beautiful objects—the cunning hooks, brushes backed in ivory, little blue glass bottles with silver wrapped around them like tendrils of a vine—and to see her own reflection, head to toe, in the pier glass, an object she had never seen before she entered this room. She touched what lay there, and then took up the earrings. Moonstone and sapphire they were, in a setting that seemed very old-fashioned. These, she thought, must be Harriet's mother's; but whatever they were that slut of a maid should have put them back where they belonged. She held them to her ears and stood before the mirror, lifting her head and turning so that her hair fell just beside the earring. It was too hot for this. She put the earrings down.

It had started with the earrings. Not these earrings, but another pair of simple gold ones, a leaf pattern of some sort with a tiny dot of emerald in the center, like a bud. They were far in the back of the box, and she thought they would not be missed, at least for a day. In her imagination these were earrings for a young woman, perhaps a girl, perhaps the first pair of earrings Harriet had ever worn. When would that have been, she wondered, before or after he knew her? She had put them in her apron, one in each pocket so they would make no noise, and she had taken them home. Yes, he had noticed, though he said nothing.

She had gone on to borrow other things: other earrings, a scarf, and then a drop of perfume. That was when he knew. She said Harriet had allowed her to try it. She could tell that he did not believe the lie, but neither did he challenge her, and their complicity was sealed in sex. After he had finished in her it took almost no time to get him hard again, and when she was on top of him and could tell how near he was, she leaned down with her breasts over his face and buried him in the valley where she had put the stolen scent.

The perfume always worked, and it was perfectly safe. All she had to do was make sure that Harriet had already used it that day. Once, just after she had helped herself, she got a funny look from the upstairs girl. But Lily was lazy and no match for Olivia, and at least she had the sense to know it.

A laundress knows things about a woman—her time of the month, what she wears under her clothes—and one day Olivia came across a gossamer undergarment in the back of the press that she had never seen in the wash. She put her hand inside to feel the fabric, saw the shadow of her skin through the airy stuff. She put two drops of perfume on the silk, and hid it in her apron, where it made no show at all. On her way back down the stairs to the laundry, she felt faint with desire.

Tuesday was the night that they both bathed, and when she was finished she slipped into the silk and put on her robe, then emptied two more kettles into the metal tub for him. She brought him a tin cup of whiskey and sat behind him on the stool, kneading his shoulders as he lay there like a dead man. She had had a long day herself, but this was something she never tired of. When she began to soap him he started to grow hard until it floated there in the murky water like an old cottonmouth in the bayou. She rinsed him off and made him stand on the braided rags to be dried, ignoring that insolent thing staring her in the face as she knelt down for his feet, pretended that it was an accident that her cheek grazed it on the way back up, and then with a good grip on his buttocks she took him in her mouth until he grew completely hard and it like to have choked her. Now she held it to one side and took his balls in her mouth, very gently, the way Horatio had showed her, with his hand wrapped in her hair to hurt her if she did it wrong. The skin was soft from the heat of the bath and they were as slippery as oysters in her mouth.

When he was good and ready she stood and held her arms out and down.

"Take it off me." The robe dropped to the floor and she could see that he was startled by the silk, then shocked as he made the connection for himself.

"Where did you get that?"

"You know."

"This is crazy. . . ."

"Ain't nothing crazy." He put his hand to her and she leaned against it, whispering in his ear, "You tear this, I'll have to hurt you," and began to laugh.

They got to the bed and she made him wait, taking her sweet time as she inched the silk down, him staring like a madman, and then he finished, just like that, shooting it all over her, and she laughed again. "Who you think you're with, honey?"

He was quiet then, and she did not ask him what he was thinking. He was always quiet afterward. Maybe he was thinking that she had gone too far, but she wasn't finished yet, could not leave him alone. The next time really was better, for now the silk smelled of them both, and of her.

"WHAT IS IT, OLIVIA?"

"Nothing, ma'am, I was just checking like I usually do when the laundry is drying. Mr Truscott see those things, the plus fours, and how the grass come out?"

"He did when I brought it to his attention. Thank you. I doubt he has any idea of the work in a household, but I certainly do. I can't think how we got along before you came."

Olivia looked down at the floor as she murmured her thanks, and Harriet had cause, again, to remark on how beauty often seemed an accident of circumstance or feeling.

"Mrs. Truscott?"

"Yes, Olivia?"

"If you don't mind me asking, which of these beds do you use?"

"I sleep in my own, of course."

"Yes, but I meant . . ."

"Oh."

They looked at each other, Harriet chewing her lip. She could not answer the question; she did not want to give offense. Perhaps she had misunderstood.

"Why do you ask?"

"It's just I can't tell, and I do know that sometimes a sheet wants changing afterwards; get to the stains before they set. I do that in my own house, though it means extra work. I'm not carrying tales, but Lily isn't always careful about things."

"I don't think I follow you. Is there a problem with Lily?"

"I don't want to start trouble. I just want everything to be right for you, and it's no good my ripping up both beds to see. You have such nice things, and things don't keep themselves unless there's somebody looking after them."

"Thank you, Olivia. I am sure this is meant kindly, but I cannot . . . I cannot answer your question. I suppose I shall have to make it clear to Lily when the sheets . . . when the bed . . . somehow. Oh." Harriet took a handkerchief from her pocket, though she was blushing furiously rather than crying.

"I didn't mean to upset you, Mrs. Truscott. It's just that men, like you said, they don't notice things. But a woman does. I do. So if you change your mind, you let me know. It's not that I mind the work."

She was gone then, and Harriet was left staring at the dressing table. The question she could not bring herself to address had a perfectly clear answer. They had "used" both beds, twice in each one, to be exact, and twice in her bed in Washington. This accounting was memorably simple, the more so because she had dropped the gentlest of hints to her husband that she hoped very much to have children for her father's sake. Fowler had kissed her brow, as if rewarding her bravery, but things hadn't changed much. And there had been the time, too, on their honeymoon, but that didn't count because . . . well, as Fowler had said, it had been a very strenuous day, walking all those miles to see the great cataract of Niagara from every possible point of view.

She had not known what to expect, though Lucy, given half an opportunity, would surely have told her everything she needed to know and much more besides. She supposed things were "normal" between Fowler and herself, but she could not know for certain. It was pleasant to have him there in her bed, and the scent of fresh talc with the deeper layer of pine tar soap was reassuring. She liked it when he fell asleep afterward, and sometimes they spent the whole of the night together, or at least until he got up to find the bathroom.

Although she would not dwell on the specifics of her intimacy with

Fowler, this conversation had forced upon her the realization that whatever "normal" might mean to her, it meant something else to Olivia. Her face burned with the knowledge that Olivia's definition must be based on her experience with Toma.

She would find a way to ask someone, Lucy, as a last resort. Or she would find a book. Surely, in these times, doctors addressed such issues frankly, steering a course between evasion and impropriety? But how would she get such a book? Mrs. Hawley at the library could not be trusted to keep this information to herself. She was sure that her rela-tions—conjugal relations, in that hideous term—were adequate, even if what she liked best came before, and afterward. But she would have given anything to have access to a wise person of her own sex, someone she did not know, or who had a voice and no face, someone who could relieve her of this burden and explain what Olivia was talking about. What stains?

Harriet closed her eyes. When she opened them again she saw that her earrings were not where she had put them down last night, and where she had seen them only an hour ago. She was absolutely certain of this.

THE STACK OF MAIL on Toma's desk had dwindled to this one tattered item: the address in Cetinje, the fierce profile of Prince—now King—Nikola, and Lydia Harwell's neat italic hand. There were two folds of paper within, and he read first the one that fell out most readily.

July 22, 1916

My Dear Brother:
   Our father is dead. That is how I must begin, and I have started this letter so many times since the day but I did not have the courage. Also I am afraid for my own life, but now I am safe in Cetinje, and Lydia tells me she will correct the errors in my writing.
   The memory of it is a thing that is not touched except with pain, so I will tell it simply. I went home during the summer break because I hear nothing from him in months, we hear only about the fighting. There is no news, only rumor,

and I cannot know unless I see for myself. I went with Janika, a friend who is a teacher here like me, and so we are not afraid of the roads, but we keep our eyes open and we go like thiefs in the night.

He is well, Papi, though the leg always gives him trouble. The boy who lives with him now, from the monastery, does the hard work for him and even cooks when he can, though a dog would not eat it. And so Janika and I are cooking and cleaning and making them have a bath after so long, and he is happy, I think. Janika is a little in love with him, or the valley, and he puts his hand on her head and calls her daughter.

Then they come. Papi sees them and tells us to get in the house and not come out for anything. We must hide. They are taking the horses for the army, and as the oxen are not gone to the high country, they take them too. Papi says nothing, and I can hear the boy crying, though there is no shooting.

I do not understand their language well, but I think they have been here before, because one of them asks, "How is your wife?" in the mocking voice of the fiend. And still he makes no answer. Then the same voice says, "Kiss the flag and you may live." Maybe the boy does that, but Papi will never do it. "So," says the voice, and there is a shot. "Now you will not be so proud." I do not know if they shot him in the good leg or the wooden one, but both were broken when we found him. He fell, I could hear that, but he did not cry out, and he did not speak to them. Then they rode over him, and back, and back again. I did not know you could make a horse step on a man, so they must train them for this.

When they were gone, we came out and ran to where he lay, but there is no breath left in him. The boy was hurt too, but he will live.

I am sorry to bring you this news. We spoke of you only the night before, and he was proud of you. The monks somehow heard what happened, for they came and buried him by the ruin of the stupa, and said prayers over him.

Your loving sister,
Natalia
Cetinje
August 4, 1916

Dear Toma:

There are no words for the sorrow I feel, or only poor ones. I grieve less for your father, God rest him, than for Natalia, and when I think of her bravery in setting off as she did I am seized with outrage that her reward was to witness

THE LIGHTNING KEEPER

such a thing. I keep myself from going mad by repeating, like an idiot who knows only one thing, "It could have been worse." Brutes who trample a crippled man would be capable of any atrocity. She is still a child, Natalia, though she teaches in the primary school, and I thank God for her safe return. You would probably find her quite grown up after these eight years, and her resemblance to your mother's photograph is striking. I plan to keep her here with me for the time being, and she is very good company for Sophie, who is such a talkative creature that she wears me out. Natalia has drawn a portrait of you in pencil that is quite fine, and if Sophie passes near it she must tell me about Uncle Toma.

My own news is not so good. The fighting goes on, far to the south, though what the Serbs use for bullets and food, I do not know. Bron was wounded in the leg in the retreat into the mountains of Albania, with the Austrians herding them to destruction. The leg has gone septic on him, he writes, and of course there are no medicines to be had for any amount of money. He spares me the worst and jokes that if he could only find a pretty nurse he would be on his feet in no time. But the fact is that he cannot possibly walk, and though he talks of being carried to the sea and safety in a litter, I don't see how starving, desperate men can be expected to do that. I must prepare myself for worse news.

His sense of humor is the same as ever, and he says he plans to write to you if he can beg more paper. In any case he sends you his love. I have not yet told Natalia how things stand.

There was a knock, which he ignored, and Harriet opened the door. "I am not disturbing you, I hope?"

"No, please come in." He put the pages back in the envelope and made an effort to smile at her.

"Fowler told me what was happening here at the works, and that you had taken this office. Everything is so changed."

"Not everything. I told them that they are to do nothing to this building."

"I am glad. And here is the famous photograph of my grandfather."

"As I say, nothing has changed. A little cleaning is all. Will you sit down?"

"Thank you. I have come to invite you to dinner with Dr. Steinmetz."

"Dr. Steinmetz writes to me nearly every day, but not to tell me he is coming back to Beecher's Bridge."

"Oh, but he is. And it was such a success last time. Please say you'll come. I hardly ever see you any more, except by accident."

"It was you who were the success, I think."

"Is it hard for you to appreciate his good qualities?"

"Ours is a professional relationship. Perhaps I see another side of him."

"He writes the most charming letters. This morning I received a little package with two little cuttings from his cactus house wrapped in cotton wool, and very specific instructions on how to get them started. He writes that one will have a yellow flower, and the other scarlet, and I am hoping that they shall have their first tiny roots by the time he gets here. He has an idea of how my glass house might accommodate both orchids and cacti. Wouldn't that be wonderful?"

He said nothing.

"Oh, Toma, it is almost as if you were jealous of Dr. Steinmetz." It was a curious thing for her to say, and the word hung in the air.

"I know him differently, that is all. He does not write to me of his cactus plants or his crows."

"I think you judge him too harshly. He has the sweetest nature."

"What else does he send you?"

"Let me think. There was a picture of him and a child—a step-grandchild, I think, though I am not clear on the connection. It almost broke my heart: they are practically the same size, at least in the picture. Also a book about lightning." She could see the bitter line of his mouth. "Imagine, Toma, how lonely his life must be."

He fastened his eyes on hers. "I have known loneliness."

"Of course you have, but not his kind of loneliness, his . . . deformity."

Toma's fingers began to drum on the envelope. "Did I ever tell you about my father?"

"Yes, of course. Such a brave man. And to live without a leg, I suppose that is like a deformity."

"He is dead." Toma pointed to the letter. "I have just learned of it."

"You are angry at me. I am sorry about your father." She rose from her chair and he from his.

"Please sit down. I should have said it differently."

"And I—" She dropped into her chair. "Here I am going on and on

about dinner parties and Dr. Steinmetz. Will you tell me what happened?"

He saw how close she was to tears, and he could not answer her
question. "He was old. That is reason enough. Let us talk about something else." He put the letter in the breast pocket of his jacket.

"Well. You are looking very smart. I remember bringing your
clothes to the silk mill, and I don't remember these."

He looked down at his jacket and the plain black silk of his tie
against the white shirt. "No, these are all new. I belong to General
Electric, as Steinmetz would say."

"And he told you to buy these clothes?"

"No, it was the engineers, practically the first words they spoke
when they got here. It would never do, when it came to hiring workmen, for the manager to be dressed like the stone mason. These were
the exact words."

"The manager. Well, it suits you, I think. But look at all these letters! How do you keep up with them?"

"It is all I do, and most of it is from one office or another at Schenectady. I sometimes think they have stolen my wheel and left me to
do the paperwork."

She laughed. "You do sound just like Papa complaining about his
paperwork, and of course he didn't really know how much there was."

"Alas, I have no secret helper."

"Perhaps I . . ." She shook her head and did not finish the sentence.
"Surely all this construction means that things are going well?"

"I am very busy, it is true, so busy that I must leave the work on the
wheel to Larssen and Piccolomini, and they push it in a direction I do
not understand. Testing the parameters of scale, they call it, which
means Let's see how big we can make it. I sign off on everything, but it
is their work. And they are working for Steinmetz, not for me."

"Toma, you make it sound as if he were your enemy."

Toma sat back in his chair and stared at her. The letter in his
pocket was like a live coal. "Harriet, do you not know that my people
are at war with his?"

"But he is not a soldier, you cannot blame the war on him!"

"And he has written newspaper articles about the war, saying that it
would be good for Europe if Germany wins."

"I have not seen them. But I am sure he means no harm to you."

"I am not thinking of myself, and one can do great harm without meaning to."

"Toma, this is America, not Europe, and Dr. Steinmetz is an American, as he told me himself, with an emotion he could not conceal. And if there is anything I can do . . . perhaps I can speak to him?"

"Oh, Steinmetz is a scientist, an engineer."

"He is a man, Toma." Her face wore an expression almost of reproof, but she went on in a gentler tone, "I think that for a start you should call him Dr. Steinmetz."

"All right, I will. And what shall I call you?"

"You must call me what you used to call me. I don't see why there must be any awkwardness between us just because I am married." Her smile was encouraging, but it lacked conviction. She hurried on, "And please say you will come next Friday?"

"I will come. And I will be charming to Dr. Steinmetz."

"I hope it will not be awkward for you to come alone?"

"No."

"At seven then?"

"At seven."

"Toma?" They stood by the door now. She had her hand on the knob, and she was not looking at him, but at the floor, at the familiar worn planks. "I am curious to know . . ."

"Know what?"

"Will you marry her?"

"No."

She said good-bye without looking at him. On her way into town to do her errands, she thought about the letter she would write to Dr. Steinmetz acknowledging the book on lightning he had sent. Her appreciation must be expressed in general terms, as she could not claim to have understood everything she had read; but the letter would be embellished with her own observations of that phenomenon. Some instances were fresh in her mind—the limb of an exploded scrub oak that had sailed down like a boomerang to plunge into the Truscott lawn, or the balls of pale fire she had seen circling the crown of Lightning Knob like ghosts or emissaries from another planet. Others were dim memories: when she was six or seven years old lightning had struck the church during the service, melting the lead in the stained glass, taking away the left arm of Jesus along with several of His lambs. Such recollections were hardly scientific, but she was sure they would be of interest to her friend.

AT THE END OF the day Harriet relaxed in a cooling bath. Had she the energy, she might have walked down to the lake for a swim, for this was the perfect time, when a long light flooded the valley of the Buttermilk, and even after the sun had set on the lake and the house, it still lay on the mountain above her. When that too had faded she would gaze at those darkening shapes and feel a strange suspension, as if the twilight as well as the water had received her, and on the walk back up the slope the clumps of white phlox would be like beacons along the edge of the mown grass.

This evening she was exhausted, and besides, Fowler was there, hitting his golf balls in the direction she would walk. She did not want to spoil his fun. She was so used to the sound of it now that when she heard the particular music of a well-struck shot she found herself listening for the distant splash. And when she heard the other one she might smile, for Fowler would be muttering things under his breath that he would never allow her to hear.

It had been simply too hot in the music room, as she now called the new glass and iron structure, even though the rolling shades had been let down and the side windows opened. She had gone to check on the cactus cuttings to make sure they seemed . . . well, happy was a silly word to use for a plant, but it would never do for them to seem *un*happy when Dr. Steinmetz arrived. And although she knew that the cuttings could not have set roots in so short a time, still she was disappointed to see that they had not. She stayed afterward to do her scales, though she was already perspiring, for she was determined she must practice both in the morning and at the end of the day. Labor Day was almost upon her and she must justify Mr. Blunden's confidence in giving the solo to her. Also, and more pressing still, Dr. Steinmetz had flattered her with the request that his second visit to Beecher's Bridge should not pass without the pleasure of hearing her sing. Very softly now she hummed the descant, hearing in her mind all those voices swelling and rising to hers. It is the perfect summer, she murmured after the last chord.

She heard the chime of the big clock; had she been that long in the bath? She wanted to be ready for Fowler when he came down. They would not dress for dinner tonight, but would have supper served on the verandah looking out over the lawn and the lake, an escape from the heat of the dining room. She had begun to count the days. They always dressed for dinner in Washington.

She opened the press to find the linen she would wear, and it did not matter that she could not quite see what she was doing, for it was as if Olivia read her mind. There on top of the pile of blouses was the one she wanted; she knew it by the tiny, perfect pleats. The towel slipped as she was powdering herself and she caught sight of a pale form in the pier glass, and for a moment there was someone else in the room, someone else who was also Harriet Truscott. She lit the lamp to find her earrings and that little necklace that Fowler admired, and the room was again familiar.

She heard Fowler humming to himself in his dressing room as she went to the stairs, and so she had a few moments to look in on her father, who would now be finishing up his supper with Mrs. Evans in the kitchen. He rarely stayed up long past the setting of the sun, and shook his head despairingly if she or Mrs. Evans or the cook tried to light a candle or lamp for him. Anything that would make him comfortable, any reasonable thing, must be done. It was very hard to make him understand that someone else now lived in Iron Hill, in fact he would *not* understand, which was why it was a blessing to have Mrs. Evans here for so much of the day. She had a way with him, and was fond of him too. Mrs. Evans, unfortunately, had made it clear that neither love nor money could persuade her to move to Washington.

"Did the work go well today, Papa?" She could not be sure that he heard what she said, but it was a familiar question, and a familiar answer.

"Pretty well, pretty well. I hope they'll be ready in time." He barely looked up from his plate. She patted his thin shoulder and spoke over his head to Mrs. Evans. "Perhaps tomorrow, if he's had a good day, he might eat with us? It would be a nice change for him."

"I'm not sure it will make much of a difference one way or the other, child, but we can try if you like."

"Change, my foot," said the cook when Harriet was gone. "Beef and potatoes today, and the same tomorrow. It's a wonder it don't kill him in this heat, nor me too. There, Mrs. Evans, he's spilled it down his front again."

It was much more pleasant outside, and by the time they finished their supper it might almost be cool. The days were getting so short now. She had always been saddened by the long diminuendo from the solstice, but this year it affected her particularly and she resented the fact that such a clumsy metaphor had lodged in her mind. She picked a sprig of mint for her tea and stood looking out over the lake, trying to draw its peace into herself.

She heard Fowler humming at the cabinet where he kept the liquor, heard the ice going into the glass and the whiskey being poured. Here was another inevitability. It was something they did not speak about, for what was there for her to say without sounding shrill, and to what effect? She hated the smell of it, and she knew it was not rational. The only helpful thing was to attach the fault to herself rather than to him. She was thinking about her father in those dark old days of his grief when her husband came up and kissed the top of her head.

He held the chair for her and she took her place at the little wicker table. The supper was already set out, and the champagne bottle was beaded with dew. She put out her hand and touched it.

"May I pour you a glass?"

"No. No, thank you. I have my iced tea." She remembered with pleasure the wine she had taken out of courtesy to Dr. Steinmetz on the mountain and the fiery sweetness of the Madeira she had drunk with Toma on that troubling evening in Washington. She did not see how she could explain this contradiction to Fowler, but neither was she comfortable with the idea of keeping things from him.

"I stopped by to see Toma this afternoon on my way to town."

"And how did you find him?"

"Well enough, I suppose. Looking very much the bright new penny in those old surroundings."

"He is making his way in the world. A young man to watch."

"He worries much, I think."

"I can't imagine why. He could hardly be in better hands, or have a more promising connection. General Electric, after all."

"I do wish I understood it all a little more clearly. Everything seems to have happened almost overnight."

"That is the way a business must be run, my dear, and how a politician flourishes, for that matter: one seizes the opportunity. There are other fellows out there, you see, with their eyes on the same prize, and so an organization like General Electric, and certainly a fellow like Coffin, must waste no time and spare no effort."

Harriet set down her fork. She thought all this sounded very like the senator's recent remarks to the chamber of commerce in Torrington. "I'm sure you are right. But can you explain the particular urgency here? Or the prize they seek?"

Fowler Truscott refilled his glass and looked affectionately at the dance of the little bubbles in the candlelight. "As I understand it, and you must make allowances for my speaking in broad terms, Toma's machine represents an advance in a certain area of GE's business, which is the making of electricity where the water can be carried to the apparatus at a considerable height, and therefore at great pressure."

"Such as the height of our Great Falls?"

"Oh, yes, and much more. There are the turbines they have perfected for the big, slow rivers that we have generally in these parts, the Connecticut, say, or the Hudson. But there are rivers elsewhere, in the great mountains of the west, for example, or Europe, or Canada, even South America, where you have many hundreds of feet of altitude and tremendous pressures of water at your disposal, and an entirely different machine is required. Perhaps Toma's turbine will replace all those operating in such circumstances. And then, as you heard Dr. Steinmetz explain, you have the elements of a system, his power grid, that knits all enterprise together, delivering electricity wherever it is needed. You will see factories and mills freed from the constraints of geography, and you will see every farm across the United States run by electricity. You may depend on it. An astonishing prospect, and one that should provide the foundation of a new Republican consensus, once this business in Europe is out of the way. One might say that Steinmetz's ideas will reenergize us, ha ha."

"I cannot conceive of Dr. Steinmetz as a political man."

"I should hope not. I have been told that he has some rather odd ideas, socialism, you know, and the less said about that the better."

"And do you think that Toma has anything to fear from Dr. Steinmetz, or any reason to be uneasy about his situation?"

"Fiddlesticks. The boy should be on top of the world. He has to understand that he is part of a huge enterprise and not out on his own, but that should be a comfort. Wouldn't do to rock the boat just now."

"I'm afraid Toma may be under a great deal of stress, and has had some bad news from home. So perhaps when Dr. Steinmetz comes to visit you could . . ."

"I think I understand. Get the lion to lie down with the lamb. That sort of thing?"

"Yes. You always find the perfect words."

They sat in silence for a few moments after the table was cleared, and Fowler drank off the champagne. Harriet thought that if she were alone she would have liked to have that last glass for herself.

"Are you feeling well, my dear? You haven't seemed quite yourself for the last couple of days."

"I think it must be the heat, and perhaps a little nervous anticipation of the concert."

"I'm sure that's it."

"Do you ever think what it would be like if we lived here?"

"But we do live here."

"No, we live in Washington. But I have never been so happy as we have been this summer, and I was thinking . . ."

"Come, Harriet, we cannot simply think of ourselves. There is my work to consider, not to mention the election, and the war, which we'll have to sort out sooner or later, and that rascal Wilson. No, no, I can't imagine jumping ship under these circumstances. I should lose my self-respect."

"Yes, Fowler, I see how it is. I was being foolish, and selfish."

They took a turn on the lawn then, with the dew wetting their shoes, and after reading for a while in the stuffy parlor they went up to bed. He kissed her forehead at the door of her bedroom and wished her a good night.

Her foolish idea, combined and compounded with several others, kept Harriet awake long after she had blown out her candle. It would never come right by itself, she thought, and her efforts had come to nothing. Prayer, too, had been a dead end. For the second time in her life she wondered if there were any use in getting down on one's knees. Whether, in fact, anyone was listening. She got up and found her way in the dark to her husband's bed. He was asleep. She eased herself in beside him.

"Mmmm. Hello, my little hen, what is it?"

"Fowler . . ." She did not want to weep so she stopped and drew a great breath. "You must tell me what to do."

"Tell you what? Perhaps in the morning?"

"I shall never get to sleep tonight unless all this is settled."

"Settle what?"

"I cannot go to Washington and leave Papa here, and I cannot bear to take him back there. He was so unhappy. That is why I thought, why I asked if . . ."

"I see, yes, of course."

"And my duty is to you, I know that, but it doesn't help me to see what I must do. It is you who must decide."

He stroked her hair and held her against his shoulder. When he spoke, the rumbling in his chest sounded very much like the words of an oracle, or of God Himself.

"Here is what I think must happen. You will stay here as long as you must, and I shall go to Washington. I shall miss you, of course, but I shall not resent your absence."

"But how shall I explain it? It will seem like the end of our marriage."

"It is your duty to your parent. And I have my own duty. It is really as simple as that, and in any case it won't be for very long."

In a small voice, she asked, "How can one know such a thing?"

He went on in the same tone of calm assurance, with his hand making the same maddening motion on her hair. "It stands to reason, my dear. One has only to look and mark the decline, almost from one day to the next. In one sense it will be a mercy when God takes him, and for you too."

She was quiet then, too shocked for tears, and at the back of her mind was the quite awful possibility that he might interpret this initiative of hers as a prelude to intimacy, and she could not bear to think about that now. So she feigned the rhythms of sleep while her mind went round and round the finality of his words like an animal in a cage with a lump of poisoned meat. Eventually his hand was still and she heard that he slept. She was trapped there with his arm around her. It did not seem possible that she would ever get to sleep.

Perhaps it would have been better not to have slept. In her dream she was lying in bed with her father to comfort him as his life ebbed away; she was trying not to sleep, for she was the line by which he clung to life, and if she closed her eyes he would be gone. She awoke with a start before dawn in a cold, anxious sweat to find that it was her husband she lay with, and he was still alive.

I AM ELECTRICITY
THE FARMER'S HANDY ANDY

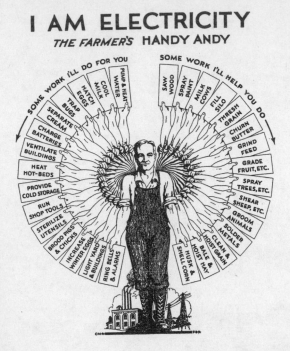

SOME WORK I'LL DO FOR YOU

PUMP & HEAT WATER
COOL MILK
HATCH EGGS
TRAP BUGS
SEPARATE CREAM
CHARGE BATTERIES
VENTILATE BUILDINGS
HEAT HOT-BEDS
PROVIDE COLD STORAGE
RUN SHOP TOOLS
STERILIZE UTENSILS
BROOD PIGS & CHICKS
INCREASE WINTER EGGS
LIGHT YARD & BUILDINGS
RING BELLS & ALARMS

SOME WORK I'LL HELP YOU DO

SAW WOOD
SPRAY PAINT
MILK COWS
FILL SILO
THRESH GRAIN
CHURN BUTTER
GRIND FEED
GRADE FRUIT, ETC.
SPRAY TREES, ETC.
SHEAR SHEEP, ETC.
GROOM ANIMALS
SOLDER METALS
CLEAN & HOIST GRAIN
BALE & HOIST HAY
HUSK & SHELL CORN

I AM ELECTRICITY
THE FARMWIFE'S HANDY ANNIE

SOME WORK I'LL DO FOR YOU

LIGHT HOME
PUMP WATER
HEAT WATER
MAKE ICE
RUN RADIO
TELL TIME
RUN FANS
RUN HEATERS
HEAT PAD
FREEZE ICE CREAM
COOL KITCHEN
REFRIGERATE FOOD
LIGHT SUN-LAMP
PUMP CELLAR DRY
COOK WAFFLES

SOME WORK I'LL HELP YOU DO

WASH CLOTHES
IRON CLOTHES
MIX FOOD
COOK & BAKE
WASH DISHES
TEST EGGS
BOIL EGGS AT TABLE
TOAST AT TABLE
MAKE COFFEE AT TABLE
EXTRACT FRUIT JUICE
VACUUM CLEAN HOUSE
MASSAGE FACE & SCALP
DRY & CURL HAIR
GRIND MEAT
RUN SEWING MACHINE

CHAPTER

FOURTEEN

From his new residence in the Bottom, it took Toma only five minutes
to walk from his breakfast table to his desk, which gave him a good
jump on the day, on the box overflowing with correspondence, requisitions, and reports. Much of the paperwork resulted from the geographical separation of the Experimental Site from the headquarters in
Schenectady. Toma knew this perfectly well. It was as Steinmetz had
predicted on his first visit to Beecher's Bridge, or as the General Electric lawyer had warned in the original negotiations. Toma could not
wander down a corridor to ask a hypothetical question or borrow a
wrench any more than Steinmetz could drop in to see and hear for
himself how things were going. Each tool or question or scrap of information required paper, many pieces of paper. It must be the same for
Steinmetz, Toma realized, though there was never a hint of reproach in
his letters.

Sometimes, when he worried about this matter, or felt inclined to
pity himself, he would glance for reassurance at the sturdy post just a
few feet beyond his desk. It had been salvaged from some earlier construction, for its several mortises and peg holes bore no relation to its
present function. Behind it was the door to Harriet Bigelow's office.
He remembered the chipped mouth of the green bottle found near the
silk mill, which served as a vase on the windowsill; he remembered that
the ledgers lying flat on their narrow shelf came within a half inch of
interrupting the arc of the door. These things were as familiar, as pre-

sent to him, as the pattern on his mother's apron or the three books on the shelf over her kitchen table. He had many vivid memories, and some led to sadness or rage; but the green bottle summoned hope. That is what Lydia had told him in the postscript to her letter: Defend your hope, whatever it may be, for it is all you have.

On this morning, August 27, Toma was up earlier than usual; he was anxious about the visit of Steinmetz, which, for all he knew, was a deliberate surprise. Olivia saw him to the door, and she made certain that the red cufflinks she had given him were secure and right-side up. "Uneeda" was the legend in tiny white lettering, as if he were a walking advertisement for a tin of biscuits.

"Do you really like them?"

"I wear them every day."

She put her arms around him and her head to his chest. He held her there, not wanting to be the one who drew away, unable to escape the odor of her hair: the red jar—Society Cream—to straighten it, the brown bottle to hide the red highlights. She had told him what it felt like to have Harriet's hair in her hands, how she had shown her what might be done with its weight and texture. And the other day, in the midden, he found what at first seemed to be a wig, a tangle of hair that turned out to be Olivia's. These were not trimmings but thinnings, long strands shorn at the scalp or yanked out by the roots.

The bulk of the mountain shielded this neighborhood of Beecher's Bridge from the early sun, and Toma's route past the iron-works to the Experimental Site was all downhill. How pleasant it was, and how different from the journey at the end of the day.

Beyond the ironworks, where the path grew steep, he stopped by a maple tree; it was from here that he had first glimpsed the ruin of furnace No. 3. He looked for it now and saw the girdle of brambles and a tracery of weeds sprouting from the fitted stones; it was being absorbed back into the forest. What if he had not seen the furnace?

The traffic up and down this path had fallen off since the telephone between Toma's office and the silk mill had been installed, and it looked more familiar to him now. But the whole aspect of the silk mill had changed, the old building disappearing as new structures sprouted from it. A gravel road led to the east gable, and what had been their bedroom and kitchen was now the loading dock. To the right was the new stone fortress of the turbine wing. From this angle and elevation the rooflines came together and formed a notch framing the tree where Horatio's body had hung. What if he had not seen the furnace?

This persistent thought was connected, as if by an arrangement of mismatched gears, to his embrace of Olivia. There was no explanation of why things had happened as they had, no plot, as there would be in a story, no motives. All he could say was that there was a connection, with logic but no meaning, like a mechanical sequence.

Stefan was already at his bench. Toma looked at his pocket watch, another gift from Olivia. "How long have you been here?"

"I am the early worm, boss. This is when I can do my work without someone asking me for another thing every ten minutes. And you?"

"I thought I'd get here early just to look around. I have to send that report by tomorrow. I am hoping you have time to run one last series today."

"That's what I mean. That's why I am here now. They don't give me time to do what wants doing before there's some big new rush. Why don't they wait until they know something before they change it?"

"The materials division says the alloy isn't stable. They are looking for something else."

"German silver isn't good enough for them?"

"German silver is the reason Tesla's turbine failed. They aren't complete idiots over there."

"Why don't they let me make the turbine rotors, then? I'll do it right."

"Stefan, I'm afraid we're beyond that stage. Wait till you see what's coming today."

"What?"

"Just wait. I don't want to spoil your surprise."

Toma wondered at the changes. The bay he and Stefan had built was now partitioned off with metal doors and a small sign that read Restricted Area. Windows flanking the loading dock admitted the morning light. New cabinets, new shelving, new benches. The monitor along the ridge of the roof was a landmark, its dust and cobwebs undisturbed since Horatio had climbed up there to salvage the old fan.

What he would have wanted was a strong cup of coffee and several hours to himself with Horatio's vanished pile of scrap.

"Stefan, would you have a couple of men pull the old turbine out from under the bench there and get it up the hill? I don't think anything is safe here."

"Can't do that."

"Why not?"

"Every so often they want me to hook it up again, run the test, like maybe I cheated the last time."

"I know nothing of this."

"Listen, boss, I don't want any trouble, but I'm telling you it drives them crazy that the new prototype doesn't give them what they want, so they think something must be wrong with the figures, the tests on the old one there. Larssen just shakes his head and stares at the work sheets until I'm almost sorry for him. The other one, Piccolomini, I don't talk to, but he knows that I built the old one, just the way you told me, and I know that the new one is a piece of shit. He knows that too, but it's his piece of shit, so I don't care."

"And why have I heard nothing about this from you?"

Stefan kept his eyes on the bench and tapped the work sheets with his pencil, leaving a random pattern of dots. "I know it's not right, but they show me a piece of paper from Dr. Steinmetz, so what do you want me to do?"

Toma put his hand on Stefan's shoulder. "Do what they tell you, Stefan. And then you tell me, okay?"

"You know me, boss. I'm no engineer, I just build things, and I do what I'm told. But I'm no dummy either, and if you ask me what's wrong with this thing I can tell you right out: it's too big. What do you think?"

"I think you may be right. And I think it does not matter what you think, or what I think."

"But this is not reasonable. They must be crazy."

"I didn't say that. We see the thing differently, that's all."

"Well, if I say this paper is white, and you tell me it is black, one of us is crazy."

"You know, if I close my eyes I can still see a waterwheel that I saw when I was a child. The man who made it was a genius, but he did not know it. All he wanted was a better way to grind barley in his trickle of water. And the wheel that Horatio built, why did he go to that trouble? So his woman can wash clothes, that is all. And both those wheels, like the turbine under your bench there, you can put your arms around them. Tesla's machine? The bladeless turbine? You could put it in your hat."

"This story of yours . . . what is the point?"

"I don't know, Stefan, I am just thinking out loud."

"So who's right and who's wrong?"

"I don't know. But your friend Dr. Steinmetz sees something else when he closes his eyes. He sees an empire, and for that you need a very big wheel indeed. Make the big wheel and you'll be a hero, just like Steinmetz." He clapped Stefan on the shoulder and laughed.

"Tell me, what was your wheel for?" Toma had never seen Stefan smile so. He had no ready answer. "I am thinking this story of yours is really about a woman?"

"Yes, Stefan, it is about a woman."

"Are you staying while I run that test?"

"No, just until the freight comes in. I'll be over by the dynamo if you need me. I haven't seen those new gauges yet."

At eight o'clock the morning shift arrived, and Toma greeted them with nods, or by name if they had worked with him in the old days at the furnace. At the same time, the Schenectady men emerged from their restricted area and issued orders to Stefan and the technicians. Toma nodded at them as well, thinking that he should make, or should have made, more of an effort. The tension between Piccolomini and Stefan was immediately obvious. But Toma had observed that Piccolomini held himself aloof from the other Italian immigrants, of whom there were many among the stonecutters and the masons. His contempt for the harsh dialect they spoke could be read on his face.

At the sound of the freight whistle men started to gather at the doors of the loading dock, and Toma went to stand near the engineers.

"This is an important day, I think." Larssen was looking into the air a few inches above Toma's head as he spoke. Piccolomini was rocking back and forth on his heels.

"Important one way or the other," said Toma pleasantly.

"You must not make jokes."

"Indeed not. I hope for the best."

The horn of the truck put an end to the small talk, and the doors swung open, revealing a huge wooden crate.

"Here. Set it down here, and gently, gently," Larssen instructed the porters. He took a wrecking bar from one of the men and made short work of the crate. The axle for the new turbine—the third prototype as it was to be called—gleamed through the excelsior, and the smell of shaved pine filled the air. Larssen groaned in rapture. Piccolomini crossed himself.

It was not as massive an object as the axle to the Curtis turbine that Steinmetz had described, but it was larger than any machined part Toma had ever seen. He wondered if the new turbine shed would be adequate to contain this thing when fitted out with its rotors. Stefan's face was a study in shock: the eyebrows raised, the mouth working soundlessly. Toma caught his eye and smiled.

CHARLES PROTEUS STEINMETZ was not a heavy sleeper under any circumstances, and the instantaneous flash and report of a lightning strike so near the Truscott house was the final straw. He had been careful to drink only two glasses of wine with dinner, for the drowsiness induced by alcohol was a fleeting phenomenon, and his sleep, like everything else, must be carefully managed. But here he was, wide awake and staring at the ceiling. He might as well get up. He would find a book.

A tension had been building in him all day, and he could not quite put his finger on it. It was pleasant to have the company of Mrs. Truscott, who was so gracious and attentive, who took such pleasure in serious conversation. In the afternoon he had asked her to sing for him, and she had obliged. At dinner he had shocked her by explaining his vision of the future, the part of it pertaining to electricity and the total utilization of hydroelectric resources.

"Now that we have so many uses for electricity we must collect all the power which there is in the watercourses of this country. When that is done, there will be no more rapid creeks and rivers, but the streams which furnish electric power will be slow-moving pools connected with one another by power stations."

"Even here?"

"Certainly here."

"All the water, you say?"

"Yes, yes, every drop. I tell you that a great mistake was made at
Niagara Falls because they diverted only a part of that great flow
through the power station. An opportunity lost."

"But surely you cannot mean to take it all away? The people . . ."

He saw how the idea distressed her, and he took her hand. "My
dear Mrs. Truscott, I am not such a monster. On the weekends we will
turn the machines off and you shall have your waterfall."

He remembered now the sensation of her skin against his and the
pressure of her large and exquisitely proportioned hand.

But it was not any thought of Harriet Truscott that kept him
awake. All day long he had felt the mountain at his back. He had been
distracted—in his calculations, in conversations with Peacock or the
engineers—and from time to time he had stolen a glance at it. When
he had launched into his soliloquy with his hostess he had been extrap-
olating from his earlier thoughts, his awareness of the mountain. He
knew this feeling, though not for years had he experienced it so acutely.
He would have to be patient.

The lightning struck again near the house and he went to the window, shivering in the warm night. His room faced out over the lake, but
if he opened the sash he might get a glimpse of the mountain. Now the
rain began to fall in fat drops driven by the wind. He found his robe on
the bedpost and went out to the stairwell.

The electrical storm seemed to be caught on Great Mountain like
a ship upon a shoal, and he had several bursts of illumination to help
him down the dark stairs. One tremendous thunderclap seemed to rat-
tle the house and he heard, or imagined, an echoing resonance in the
stairwell that made him smile; it was like being inside a percussion instrument. Even without the lightning he would have been guided to
the glass house by the damp odor of foliage. The door had been left
open.

He had once taken a train trip across the country to California and
witnessed a splendid electrical disturbance miles and miles away to the
south across the Great Plains. He spent that night in the observation
car at the tail end of the train, where the glass panels on the side and
roof gave an unobstructed view of the display. He sent the porter to

bed after asking for a bottle of Riesling, and for several hours he sat in a swiveling velvet chair, transfixed by those bolts as various as snowflakes, calculating the energy required to produce such a marvel. There was no rain to blur or distort his perception of the lightning, only the gusting smoke of the locomotive. He took pleasure in the thought that one day, perhaps soon, these monstrously dirty machines would be replaced by locomotives running on the "white coal" of electricity produced in the mountains of the west, or even by these same lightning bolts. Indeed, why not with the aid of the lightning? There was not so very much useful energy in the individual bolt, but the destructive power of lightning must in any case be tamed, and some use might as well be found for it.

Tonight was a different experience altogether. He was directly beneath the storm and the rain fell so fast that the slanting glass roof might be a river and he a fish. When the lightning struck again on the height just above the house he heard a sound, a sigh, and out of the corner of his eye caught sight of Harriet Truscott, her bare arms folded across her breast, her mouth forming a perfect circle. He fumbled in the pocket of his dressing gown and lit a match to announce his presence.

She seemed to welcome his company. "It is thrilling, is it not? Would we be safer inside?"

"I think we are safe enough here. Your Lightning Knob is our guardian." As if to demonstrate the point, the lightning struck the Knob again, and the outline of the mountain swam in the water on the roof. She took his arm, and he felt the warmth of her breast pressing against his shoulder.

He took off his linen robe and held it out to her. "Please put this on. I can tell you are feeling a little chill."

"Are you sure? Will you be all right?"

"Yes. But take care with the cigar in the pocket."

"If you wish to smoke now you may do so."

"Thank you. An admirable solution."

At the next lightning strike, still on the Knob, she took his arm again, then laughed, as if embarrassed by her reaction to the storm. "Have you no improving lecture for me on the subject of our mutual interest?"

"What?"

"The lightning. We have talked about it and written about it, and here it is."

"No. I can think of nothing to say. I find it humbling."

She gave a little squeeze to his arm and whispered, "Dr. Steinmetz, I think you must be the wisest man I have ever met, and the kindest."

"And you, my dear Mrs. Truscott, are the soul of the world."

They lapsed into a comfortable silence, but his mind was more restless than ever. The mountain, at last, was speaking to him in the language of creation, a language he thought might be lost to him. He wanted a pen and his notebook. He needed to write down these thoughts before they faded. A great work lay ahead of him, a final challenge that would require everything he knew and all his remaining strength. He had not felt this way for years.

THREE MEN GATHERED on the first tee of the Beecher's Bridge Golf Club at ten o'clock the next morning. It was a cool, breezy day that married summer and fall. The caddy master had made note of Senator Truscott's guests and wondered whether the gentleman in the long coat intended to play, or if he would simply watch, in which case the guest fee could be waived.

"No, no, Dr. Steinmetz has given his word, and a good game of golf does wonders for a man. Just the thing after a hard night."

It had been a hard night. In response to his wife's request, the senator made an extra effort at cocktails and dinner to draw out both Steinmetz and young Peacock, for when men got to know each other, and broke bread together, almost any difference could be smoothed over. That was the way things worked in the Senate, and in the Bible too, when he came to think of it, but it was a thirsty business, especially because the burden fell on him. It had gone well, he thought, but he did feel a little worse for wear this morning. Harriet, too, had seemed tired at the breakfast table, and when he asked her if she had slept well, she said, Yes, dear, well enough, by which he knew that she had not. Well, a man could not help it if he snored.

The first tee, just below the windows of the dining room, looked out over a broad green vista comprising the fairways of the first and ninth holes, with a strip of the original rough meadow lying between them. To the left was the line of the evergreen forest, and in the distance was another fairway and a round, bright patch of green with a yellow flag on it.

Dr. Steinmetz was given the honor, though he protested that he had never played the game, had no idea how to proceed.

"Like this, Doctor, like this." Senator Truscott took his driver and demonstrated in slow motion the mechanical principles of the golf swing. "Just hit it as straight as you can for now, and we'll fine-tune it later."

The caddy, a young man with an old face, handed Steinmetz a club. "You'll do better with the spoon. More loft to it." He showed Steinmetz where to stand and how to grip the shaft, then teed up a new ball for him.

On his first two attempts Steinmetz missed the ball altogether, and Truscott murmured soothingly, Practice, just practice. On his third effort he produced a soft squib that rolled to the edge of the tee and fell away out of sight. Much better, said Truscott, we'll call that your mulligan.

"My what?"

"A shot that is not counted against your score. Gentlemen's rules."

Steinmetz put another ball on his tee, muttering in German. This time he struck beneath the ball, tearing a long strip out of the lawn. The ball rose precipitously and came down on a patch of bright green atop a rise not forty yards away.

"There!" he cried in satisfaction. "Would that be what you call the green?"

"No," said Truscott, "that is the ladies' tee, but a fine beginning all the same."

Toma watched carefully as the caddy demonstrated the correct grip on the shaft, with the interlocking of certain fingers and the left thumb nestled in the right palm. But when he took the club himself it was one hand above the other, a baseball grip.

"Where is the green then? That yellow flag out there?"

"No, sir," answered the caddy, "that'd be the fourth coming back. The one you want is beyond the trees and around to the left."

"Must I aim over the trees?"

"Heavens, no!" exclaimed Truscott, "it's much too far. We are al-

lowed three strokes to reach this green, but a well-placed drive, just beyond the corner there, allows the scratch golfer to attempt it in two."

"Thank you."

Toma swung the club once, horizontally, as if he held a bat and not
the driver. He addressed the ball, tapping the grass six inches behind it.
Truscott was about to offer advice when Toma swung awkwardly but
with tremendous energy. The ball soared away somewhat off-line in
the direction of the fourth green, and then the rotation took purchase
and it veered left, climbing still, and came to rest on a distant rise many
yards beyond where the evergreens bent away.

"Prodigious, simply prodigious. I think you may have a gift for the
game." The senator's own shot was a pale mirror image of Toma's. It
started off straight, then drifted weakly to the right, away from the hidden green. "Ah well, business as usual, I see."

"Might have been the wind, sir," said the caddy, "but do keep that
arm straight."

Progress toward the green was slow. Steinmetz climbed his hill with
a different club, a mashie, and it took him three shots down the long
slope to reach Toma's ball. They waited there for Truscott and the caddy.

"My friend, if I had hit such a ball, and on such a day, I should re-
joice. But you are distracted from your achievement." Steinmetz was beginning to find the young man interesting. Had he not just quoted, last
night, a passage from Homer in response to his own pontifical remark
on the intellectual foundations of engineering? Had the boy not suggested a link between the deposits of magnetite on the mountain and his
own research on this substance? That was years ago, but his patent on
the magnetic arc lamp was still a source of pride and satisfaction.

"I am thinking about the work, sir, and wishing it went as well as
the golf shot."

"Like all inventors, you are impatient. In time you may learn the
virtues of the engineer."

"I think . . ."

"Oh, oh, here is our host. Now you must think only of the golf."

Truscott's third shot had landed not far from the green but in a
sand trap. It was Toma's turn to hit, and when the caddy handed him
the spoon, he asked for the driver again.

"If you hit a shot like the last one I don't know that we'll ever find it."

Toma thanked him for his advice but took the driver, and against all odds hit a ball that followed almost the same trajectory as the first. It bounced once on the green and caromed off sideways, down into a shrubby hollow marked with white stakes.

"Oh, what bad luck," cried Truscott cheerfully. "That's out of bounds. It will cost you a stroke even if you manage to find it. You're up, Doctor."

By the time Toma had hacked out of the brush, and taken his penalty, and hit a wedge to the green, he lay seven. Truscott, after several humbling strokes from the sand, also lay seven on the green. Steinmetz, as near as could be determined, had taken a dozen strokes.

"Perhaps now I shall distinguish myself." It was certainly true that Steinmetz had been successful on the practice putting green, although he insisted on facing the hole and holding his club as if it were a croquet mallet. Now, however, his ball lay on the fringe above the flag.

"Very gently, Doctor, would be my advice. Just try to get it near the hole."

His coat flapping in the breeze, Steinmetz stood at the top of the green and gave brief consideration to the factors that would affect the outcome of his stroke. He started the ball on its long, twisting descent, and after some twenty feet, traveling at a dangerous speed, it hit a beetle and gave a little hop to the left, right into the cup.

"Brilliant!" cried Truscott, "simply brilliant. Who would have thought it possible?"

"Almost anything is possible," replied Steinmetz in a perfectly neutral tone.

It took Truscott and Toma two putts each to hole out. The senator came very near with his first, but Toma was deceived by the slope of the green and ended up farther away than he began.

"Fiendish, these fellows who make golf courses. A flat putting surface wouldn't be asking too much after a hole like this one." The senator's ebullient empathy was muted when Toma sank the long putt coming back. "Good. Well, that's one hole down."

"And how many have we?" asked Steinmetz.

"Nine, Doctor, nine."

"I will watch, then. Otherwise we shall never finish, and I fear for my back."

"But my dear sir, you were brilliant on the green."

"Thank you, I was. So . . . I shall play the greens, and you play the rest. Yes?"

"That's it. I have been thinking how we might arrange this as a match, with the three of us and our varying experience. One must be competitive or the game loses its salt."

"I wouldn't know."

"What I propose is that Mr. Peacock and I play from the tees, and if we reach the green in a tie, then you put your ball on the green too, and whoever putts best wins. What do you say?"

"By such accounting I have won this hole. Would that be fair?"

"Fair enough. Mr. Peacock and I did little to distinguish ourselves."

"And the two of you play, how do you say, equally?"

"You mean a handicap? I shouldn't think that Mr. Peacock needs any help in that way."

The next hole was a short one, about one hundred and sixty yards to an elevated green, with pasture in between and trees right and left.

"Tell me," muttered Toma to the caddy, "how do I hit it so that it goes straight?" The caddy again showed Toma the arrangement of hands and fingers on the shaft.

The ball flew straight and true to the green with that sweet sound that Truscott so admired.

"There," said Toma.

"Yes. A very good shot."

"The advantage of good advice," observed Steinmetz.

Truscott's good humor suffered another setback when his shot—again that weak fade—landed in a trap short and to the right of the green. He set off without comment up the fairway, leaving his guests to make their own way. Steinmetz swung his putter as he walked, scything dry timothy and umbels of Queen Anne's lace now folding up into green, ribbed purses. He bent to retrieve an old ball, and when he stood up, there was the mountain again, rising above the white pines.

"I do not tire of looking at it."

"What?"

Steinmetz pointed with the putter. The golf course was on the west bank of the Buttermilk, downstream from the falls, and from this distance and angle the crown of Lightning Knob was aligned with the dark green of the watercourse from the lake on the height of the mountain.

"We shall make another trip up there tomorrow."

"I'm sure Mrs. Truscott would welcome that."

"No, just the two of us, and perhaps one of my men from Schenectady."

"Not a picnic, then."

"No, I have been thinking about the next step."

Truscott's wedge shot from the sand struck the flagstick halfway up and dropped straight down into the hole. The author of this miracle raised his arms in triumph.

"Couldn't do it again if my life depended on it. In the darkest moments, a ray of light. Perhaps there is a connection to divine providence, Doctor?"

"None that I can see."

Toma missed his putt.

The third hole was an easy par four if played with confidence. The flag could not be seen from the tee, but a well-struck drive would land on the rise about one hundred eighty yards out and bounce down to the hidden green. It was quite possible to make a hole-in-one here.

But in front of the tee the land dropped away into a steep hole with knobs of grass on its slopes and a growth of bracken at the bottom. Along the left side, close to the line that the ball must take, was a wall of trees with several branches overhanging the fairway.

"I call it the Slough of Despond," Truscott remarked, staring down into the pit. The caddy reminded him of his recent success here and again mentioned the straight left arm. "Let us hope I can set a good example."

Perhaps he followed the advice too carefully. The ball started well and was beyond the Slough when it bent left and struck one of those branches with a sound such as David's stone must have made on Goliath's forehead. Straight back it bounced and vanished down into the hole.

"Damn and blast! I shouldn't be surprised if there's water down there."

Toma's shot was unimpressive but adequate, a low screaming mishit into the face of the slope. He could easily have joined Truscott down in the pit, but his ball skittered uphill and lodged in the short grass on the rim.

"You fellows play on to the green. I might be some time down here."

They watched for a while as Truscott and the caddy trolled the bracken for the missing ball, watched Truscott fall and be helped to his feet. His right leg was soaked to the thigh with an oily ooze.

"What a curious geography you have here," observed Steinmetz. "Perhaps we had better go on."

Toma took a club from the bag and executed a lusty practice swing.

"Gently, my friend. I think it is not so far to the hole."

Toma shortened his stroke and lifted the ball over the rise. When they came to the green they saw it lying on the far edge, just short of a crescent-shaped sand trap.

"I think I need your advice." Toma spoke in a low voice, with his eyes fixed on the ball.

"I would hit it with the putter, but not too strongly."

"Advice on something else."

"A professional matter?"

"Yes." Toma tapped his ball; it stopped halfway to the hole. He went to stand over it. "I think I must resign my job."

"Please finish what you are doing. When your ball goes in the hole I shall discuss the other matter."

Toma putted twice more, narrowly missing the hole each time.

"I cannot take this game seriously. If not for the senator I should go back to my office."

"To your office? But you have just spoken of resigning. You must take pleasure somewhere."

"I took great pleasure in my machine, but that seems so long ago. Now I must find something else."

"Spoken like an inventor. It goes back to what I was saying last night, about engineering. Someday, by the way, I hope you will tell me how you came by your Homer. But as for the job . . ."

"I am no use to you. And I think the wheel is a failure. What do you think?" Toma tapped his ball into the cup.

Steinmetz did not reply, but put his own ball on the green. "Just for practice." His ball went straight into the cup. "Ah, if only I had your strength and your youth I might have to take up this game in earnest. You feel that you have failed?"

"Ask your engineers."

"I don't need to do that. I know the numbers. But this is now an engineering problem, and one must always expect the setbacks, have patience with them. The inventor, by nature, sees only perfection. He has no patience with these difficulties. In the long run, I have no doubt of our success. The Peacock Turbine will make you famous."

"That sounds rather empty to me."

"You need another challenge. Fortunately, I have some ideas on that."

They were interrupted by the thump of Truscott's ball on the green. It rolled to within three feet of the hole.

"Our host will be pleased."

Truscott's pleasure was muted by the recollection of several strokes lost in the bracken. Toma had won the hole handily, and the match was now even.

The hint dropped by Steinmetz had an unfortunate effect on Toma's concentration, and the assurance of his early efforts was now mired in thought. His ball seemed to follow whatever line Truscott's took, or vice versa, so that there were no opportunities to pursue the conversation that preoccupied him. Truscott, thanks to his experience around the greens, won two of the next three holes, Steinmetz the other.

The flaw in Senator Truscott's golf game was that he did not understand his limitations. He stood on the seventh tee and took a deep breath, disturbing the argyll pattern of his sleeveless pullover. "The driver please, caddy." He held out his hand, but his eyes were fixed on the Long Water, and the flag beyond.

"The driver, sir?" The safe shot here was to the right, where the fairway bent around the water hazard.

"The driver."

He put two balls in the water, both well struck, both falling just a few yards short of the far bank.

"How I detest this water. All right, then, the spoon." He swung recklessly, and the ball faded far right, into the trees. "Not my best effort. But at least it's not out of bounds."

Toma followed the caddy's advice and hit an iron down the right side. He and Steinmetz stood in the fairway, waiting on the search for Truscott's ball.

"The Experimental Site must be expanded." Steinmetz spoke abruptly, and Toma's first thought was that he was talking to himself. "A tower on the Knob will lift the receptors clear of competition from the mountain, and if we tap into the magnetite the existing lines of electromagnetic conversion will be concentrated. What do you think?"

"I have no opinion, Dr. Steinmetz. What are you talking about?"

"Up there." Steinmetz pointed with the putter. "We shall build the lightning laboratory. The first in the world."

"What has this to do with the work on the turbine?"

"It is all the same work. Were you not listening last night? The turbine is merely an engine to produce energy. Lightning is the same energy, but in a destructive incarnation. Unless we tame it there can be no significant progress toward the goal, because the grid will always be vulnerable to the lightning. That is clear, I hope?"

"Yes."

"Now, suppose we are playing our game of golf, and a storm comes up. I stand over there, with my feet in the water, and I make so." Steinmetz raised the putter straight up at the heavens. "What do you think?"

"I would say you are mad."

"Unless?"

"Unless . . . unless you wish to be struck."

"Exactly so. That is the object of my plan. I want the lightning to come to me."

"And what have I to do with this?"

"You are young. You are strong. And, as you were telling last night, you have experience with tunnels. The iron cores must be sunk into the magnetite like the roots of a tree."

Toma said nothing.

"This is your new work, or the work I can suggest to you. You will be part of something important, very important. You will be my lightning keeper."

"I don't know what to say. I must think."

"Good, you will think, then. I see the senator has found his ball."

"Fore!"

The senator played onto the green. He was not in a mood for small talk or encouragement. Steinmetz whispered to Toma, "You cannot lose this hole except by foolishness. Be patient."

Toma hit his ball with the same club. It bounced twice and rolled to the front edge of the putting surface. A little pitch put him within two feet of the flag.

"I'll give you that one," said Truscott. "That way I won't have to count up my own score."

Steinmetz won the eighth hole, another par three with a steeply sloped green. Truscott and Toma, having driven the green, both took three putts. Steinmetz placed his ball several feet behind Truscott's and watched carefully what happened to his host's first putt. He did not make the same mistake. He was home in two.

Victory on the final hole seemed to be in Senator Truscott's grasp. He hit two fine straight shots to the green below the first tee. Toma, short and in the deep grass, took the cleek and swung as he had at the beginning of the round. His ball soared over the green and rolled back down the hill.

"You have done me a favor, I think," said Steinmetz.

Truscott overheard the remark. "We shall have to see. The ball may not be on the putting surface proper."

But it was, and so Steinmetz was entitled to play his ball. "Where shall I drop it, sir?"

"Oh, anywhere you like. I'm afraid it won't make much difference."

Indeed it did not. Steinmetz needed only the one putt, and Truscott's par counted for nothing.

Harriet was waiting for them at the top of the hill. "Fowler, your leg. I hope you didn't hurt yourself again."

"No, I won't use that as an excuse. It was a fine game, but I shall have to change. I don't think they'd let me in the dining room looking like this." He walked off, favoring his right leg, in the direction of the locker room.

"And you, Doctor, did you enjoy yourself?"

"Yes, a strange game of course, but in fact"—and here he glanced at Toma—"I think I am the winner. And now I am famished."

ON THE TUESDAY after Labor Day, the Truscotts stood on the platform, waiting for the 10:23 from Pittsfield. There had been a frost the night before, and the senator saw scarlet and yellow everywhere he looked. Could this have happened overnight? There were spots of color in Harriet's cheeks. He thought she looked particularly beautiful.

"Ah, the Icebox of Connecticut."

"My father used to say that."

"Did he? Please give him my kind regards. I'm sorry I did not have time to say good-bye to him."

"Yes, of course. Fowler, see how beautiful the trees on the mountain are, and the swamp maples along the river. I do wish you were staying."

"I wish I could. It will be quite different in Washington."

She thought of that drawing room swathed in white, a room of ghosts. How would he manage?

He took her hand as if he read her thoughts. "Don't worry. Powers and the staff will know what to do, and we'll muddle through until you come." She looked down at her hand in his, at the green stone that caught the sun.

The senator drew a deep breath. "You must be pleased. Everyone I have met in the past two days has complimented me on your singing, as if I had anything to do with it."

"I am glad it is over. It loomed so large beforehand, and now it doesn't seem very important at all."

"You have been preoccupied this whole week, understandably so. But now that's over. Oh, and Dr. Steinmetz sends you his compliments. He was sorry to have missed the event."

"You have had a letter?"

"Yes. The arrangements to do with the lease on Lightning Knob. I said they could have it for a dollar a year, provided he does not beat me at golf again. Ha ha!"

"Dear Dr. Steinmetz."

"Yes. He is welcome, of course, whenever the lightning business calls him here. I should have asked you, but I knew you would be pleased."

"At first I was of two minds about what is to come. I did not like the idea of anything being built up there, but Dr. Steinmetz was so persuasive about it. I have never felt quite safe with the lightning so near, and especially if you are away in Washington. But now all the lightning must strike the Knob, and that is good. I will be glad for his company. I am glad, too, that Toma has taken to the idea."

The senator looked at his watch. "Should have been here already."

"Will you sit down?"

"Thank you, no. The knee doesn't bother me now."

"When will you come back?"

"When I can, when I can. Perhaps Thanksgiving. Certainly for Christmas."

"I shall write to you every day, boring letters I'm afraid."

"You have written me letters when I was there and you here, and I was not bored at all."

"Yes, but that was . . . well, I shall make them as interesting as I can."

"Beecher's Bridge will not be duller for my absence. I shall be glad to hear how the work goes along up there, and I expect you will have Dr. Steinmetz to entertain from time to time. There is no need to play the widow just because I am in Washington." His words were meant to cheer her up, but they had the effect of reminding her that they would not live as man and wife until her father died, and that she had chosen this.

"Fowler, you know that I would never do anything you didn't approve of."

"Of course you wouldn't, Harriet." He gave her hand a reassuring squeeze and bent down to kiss her cheek. "Of course you wouldn't."

PART THREE

1917

"When alternating currents had finally been conquered, and alternating current transmission-lines began to spread all over the country, an old enemy became more and more formidable—lightning. And for many years the great problem upon which depended the further successful development of electrical engineering was that of protection from lightning."

—Charles Proteus Steinmetz

CHAPTER

FIFTEEN

The colorful place name is catnip to the amateur historian. The more colorful the better; and the more lurid the surrounding tale, the more urgently he embraces his self-appointed task of verification, a task that, in most cases and for one reason or another, will end in failure. It is, often, like chasing a will-o'-the-wisp.

Let us start on a positive note at the top of the mountain. The etymology of Dead Man's Lake is secure. Josef Vereinskellen was a Revolutionary War veteran who had been invalided out after an encounter with a cannonball at the battle of Monmouth. The ball had taken off his left ear and a bit of his cheek and scalp, and deafened him because he was so close to the cannon's mouth. He was a woodcutter and lived a solitary life up on the mountain; one of his pleasures was ice fishing perhaps it reminded him of home. There was no witness to the critical event, but the old soldier stopped making his weekly runs to the general store in February 1792, and in the spring a couple of boys reported seeing his fishing shack floating in the lake. It should be Vereinskellen's Lake, of course, but the name hardly trips off the tongue.

A little further down we come to Rachel's Leap, and no one alive can state with confidence who Rachel was and why she jumped. There is no relevant piece of paper in the archives of Beecher's Bridge, and no such name on a headstone in our cemeteries. Well, in fact there are two, but they lived to such ripe old ages—seventy-four and eighty-eight—that one has difficulty imagining them as candidates. Perhaps someday a document, or a letter, or a diary will turn up that sheds light on this. But more likely not. In the meantime, the name of that spot is enshrined, and Rachel and her unhappiness are as real to the people of the town as if she walked among us today.

In any case, the historian has few tools in a contest against entrenched opinion. Were it possible to prove beyond doubt that Rachel merely sprained an ankle, or that her name was really Rebecca, it would make no difference. People will believe what they want to believe. But still it is a matter of honor and of personal satisfaction to make the attempt at precision. I have searched in vain for Jack's Rock, said to stand up out of the swamps south of the mountain, where a solitary fellow was found dead. Who was he? Why was he there? How did he die? These questions elicit many blank stares, and any answers forthcoming hardly inspire confidence. Even the topographical maps are mute: there is no bundling of contour lines to suggest the whereabouts of this fabled rock.

Or consider the matter of the alleged Viking graves. On a low rise overlooking an old beaver meadow two graves are laid out, with weathered stones marking the head and the foot. One, having less than four feet of grass between the stones, belongs to a child; the other is over seven feet long. They were a famously tall race, the Vikings, and Elmer Brown claims to be able to discern a runic inscription on the headstone of the larger grave. But Mr. Brown says many things to entertain the patrons at the saloon, and that is no forum for rigorous thinking.

What would the poor Vikings be doing here anyway, so far from the sea and the safety of their ships? A forensic dig, with myself and a qualified fellow from the University of Connecticut directing the work, turned up no supporting evidence in the way of artifacts, and the skeletons did not seem to have been in the ground for hundreds of years. The adult was a woman, certainly tall, and young enough to be the child's mother. The rise and its beaver meadow are not far from where Meekertown is thought to have been located, and the tithe records at the church indicate that a man named Halverson farmed in Meekertown for several years just after the Revolutionary War, long enough to have come to this grief.

Local history, by the long or the short way, leads us back to questions about human nature. No doubt Mr. Brown's audience at the saloon would choose the Viking warrior over poor Mrs. Halverson. It adds mystery or dignity to their lives to believe in the Viking. As for Rachel, I often wonder if the sprained ankle isn't a perfectly likely scenario. Perhaps she was out with friends on an excursion and came to a point of rock where she made a show of bravado.

"You wouldn't dare," one calls out.

"But I would!" cries Rachel, jumping and landing awkwardly. It could have been much worse.

The incident would have been reported with humor and admiration, and perhaps the friend said to his friend in jest, "I thought she meant to do away with herself." Time passes and the tale or the name is passed on. The exact exchange of words is blurred or lost, and the circumstances too. Someone who has never known Rachel hears the story, someone with disappointments of her own: from that point on Rachel is alone on the mountain with her sorrow, and it is bleak November, not springtime. What motive would there be for such an alteration? Perhaps none at all. The story she has heard touches the listener in a strange way: she knows what she would have done in Rachel's place, and thereafter their stories are entwined.

All this is speculation. There are no facts beyond the name of the place, and I am filling in the blank canvas to amuse myself. How unfortunate that one can hardly utter the word "speculation" without qualifying it as idle.

Peacock's Folly is quite a different kettle of fish. The half-finished building—a stout tower when complete—sits on the crown of Lightning Knob and even at this stage may be seen from almost any part of Beecher's Bridge. Its official name, the Lightning Laboratory of the Experimental Site, is a cumbersome one. Its popular name was given before the first stone was laid, in a meeting of the town selectmen. Ordinarily there would not be any such meeting: the Truscotts might erect whatever they please on their property. But it was Mr. Peacock's plan to utilize the abundant cut and dressed stone available in the various ruins of Power City, and the cartage was in progress when someone asked whose stone it was. The answer, owing to the situation of taxes long unpaid, was that at least some of the stone was the property of the town. Mr. Peacock made a vigorous presentation to the selectmen of the scientific principle and the economic benefit involved. The

second item the selectmen grasped perfectly well; but in response to
the first, one gentleman whispered the phrase that took on a life of its
own.

Peacock's Folly it is, then, and one cannot imagine that such a mis-
chievously colorful name will soon be abandoned. But what exactly is
meant?

Connecticut could hardly have achieved its reputation for invention if every initiative, every effort to expand our scientific frontiers,
were treated thus.

Why such sudden judgement? Some allowance must be made for
the apprehensions of our people. Many families, having worked at the
Bigelow foundry for generations, suffered as a result of its demise. The
iron company, like the church on the green—and the Catholic Church
too, of course—seemed to be part of our bedrock, an institution that
could not fail. Fail it did, however, thanks in part to the efforts or omis-
sions of Mr. Peacock. The Bigelow bankruptcy gave advantage to those
who had always said that it was the Devil's work being carried on down
below the falls.

The principal engine of our local prosperity is now, as Senator
Truscott had hoped, the engagement of the General Electric Company
in matters of research. That activity has taken a new course. The work
below the falls was one thing: waterwheels are familiar objects, after all,
and anyone who reads a newspaper or a magazine must be aware of the
potential benefits of electrical service. But given the long history of
lightning in Beecher's Bridge, the collective memory of fatal or near-
fatal incidents, of herds on the mountain driven mad in the storm and
plunging to their death, can anyone look on this tower with a neutral
eye? Where many of us hold our breath and hope that the disturbance
will pass us by, Mr. Peacock's scheme is to bring the lightning to us, to
make it play over Lightning Knob like the tamed lion. The more the
better, he says, while assuring us that it is all perfectly safe. And some
of us respond with mutterings about the Devil's work.

Still, the economic activity is real enough. An old charcoal cutters'
road has been cleared up the eastern slope of the Lightning Knob so
that the stone may be hauled up from Power City to within a few hundred feet of the crest. From that point a railed hoist and a gasoline
motor lift the blocks up to the construction site.

The same equipment runs the compressor, the pump, and the hydraulic system necessary to the Bucyrus Excavator boring vertically into the mountain to house Dr. Steinmetz's aerial, or lightning rod. One would have to be a man of science to understand all the details, but Dr. Steinmetz, on his visits to Beecher's Bridge, is not shy about saying that great things will come of this work. Word has it that his nickname in Schenectady is *Loki*, after the pagan Norse divinity associated with lightning.

Mr. Peacock is relentless in directing this activity, calling on that same energy with which he once attacked the obstruction in furnace number 3. If the excavator should balk, he will fix it; and if an instant repair is not possible he will lead the men down into the shaft with picks and buckets rather than wait on the new part. The work must go on. At the end of such a day he comes down to his office in the old ironworks to deal with his correspondence.

One cannot help admiring such single-mindedness; perhaps it is necessary to the accomplishment of a great work. But to those of us who aspire to no greatness there is something unsettling in Mr. Peacock's refusal to acknowledge either fatigue or the notion of his own mortality. Might this be the surest etymology, after the fact, of the name Peacock's Folly? It is generally unwise, and certainly unwelcome, to opine on the condition of our neighbor's soul, but who can glimpse Mr. Peacock in his nocturnal comings and goings—the haggard abstraction of those features in the lantern's glare—and not wonder if this be the face of a man possessed?

HE AWOKE TO THE perfect peace of the mountain. It was past the season of birdsong. At dusk he would listen for the raven and the migrating geese; at night sometimes an owl would wake him; and at noon, when the excavator shut down, the red-tail's solitary shriek would skewer the silence.

He had claimed this angle of the construction as his campsite, and depending on the progress of the work he would have to move his things in a day or two. He liked sleeping where he could see the stars; if it rained he could shift the pieces of corrugated metal to keep himself dry.

He rolled over and sat up with his back against the stone wall. When he buttoned his coat and pulled the hat down tight he wasn't much colder than he had been on the pallet. In a few minutes he would light the sticks already laid under the pot of water and add a handful of coffee, but for now he wanted nothing. He waited, looking down at the lake and the lawns and the dark outline of the house, waited until he saw the soft flare of light in that second-storey window.

When the coffee had come almost to a boil he set the pot aside and put a pan with a little butter over the coals. He had heard one of the older hands in the forge, a man who had spent a winter on the mountain with the raggies cutting and splitting hardwood for charcoal, boast about living on whiskey and eggs—a dozen at a sitting. He couldn't eat a dozen eggs, but as he looked in the box and saw only four, he wondered if it would be enough. He threw a couple of shells into the coffee to settle the grounds.

He ate deliberately, scraping the pan with bits of broken bread. He wondered if she ate her breakfast alone, as in the old days, or if someone brought it to her bed. He looked over at what passed for his own bed and imagined her sitting there with the disreputable blankets drawn up around her shoulders, putting forth her hand to accept the scalding coffee, trying to keep her hair out of it as she drank.

Her light had become his clock. When it went out at night he felt his strength fade; he awoke in expectation of it. He wondered now if he had been dreaming of her again, or had the light in the window put these things in his mind?

It was the accident of her singing that sent him to the mountain. He had known nothing of the choral society event until Steinmetz mentioned it at the end of a long afternoon of discussing the lightning project. He was working day and night on the specifications and the costing of the project, and he would not have bothered to go if Steinmetz had not asked him to save a copy of the program.

The price of the ticket surprised him—this was a fund-raising affair for the fire department—and as he settled into his seat at the back of the library the evening seemed more an obligation than a pleasure. He sighed and sat back in his chair to admire the barrel vault of the roof and the wooden galleries just below. There was an element of ostentation in this architecture: a town the size of Beecher's Bridge needed no such building to service its literary curiosity, but the Truscott family had money enough to memorialize its enthusiasms. The senator's father had erected this monument to his wife's love of books, or at least the idea of books. From these shelves had Harriet Bigelow borrowed the volumes on metallurgy that Toma must read; in this same great hall or reading room had Harriet formed her nodding acquaintance with Olivia Toussaint while exercising her gift for the still life in pencil and charcoal. In a few moments another Mrs. Truscott, that same Harriet, would sing for him. Toma shifted his legs to find a more comfortable position.

The names in the program meant nothing to him; but that fellow Schubert must be a German, which perhaps explained Steinmetz's interest. The thought of her singing a German song brought a smile to his lips, and he made a little snorting noise to frame this irony. The older gentleman to his left turned to look at him.

When Toma raised his eyes, the chorus had filed onto the makeshift stage. Harriet Truscott, in her green velvet, was among those in the front row. He had never before seen so much of her throat and shoulders. It was the line of those shoulders and the expressionless set of her features that betrayed her uneasiness. What was wrong? He stared at her, and if he had not been so aware of his neighbor he might have muttered encouragement, as if she were a horse lagging the field.

Was it possible, with all the people gathered there, that she could have felt such intensity radiating from the back of the hall? That is what he came to believe. When her eyes found his her expression changed, and in the same moment the hardness he had brought with him melted away.

The program was an odd mix of styles and periods: something for everyone. When Harriet stepped forward to sing the Schubert there was a respectful, apprehensive silence. Toma held his breath until he realized that he knew this song, had heard it from her own lips. But during the more popular tunes the audience was encouraged to join in, and those who could not sing stamped their feet, sending tremors through the joists of the oak floor. And even over such a din Toma could distinguish one clear voice, at times half hidden, now soaring above the others.

"What is that?" he asked his stern neighbor at the end of the final number, before the applause died away.

"Sir, it is the 'Battle Hymn of the Republic.' Do you not know it?"

"Yes, the song. But what is that . . . ?" Here Toma's vocabulary failed, and with his hand he mimed a tremulous rise, a long swooping descent, the flight of the lark.

"Ah, the descant. That is called the descant, and very prettily done."

"Thank you." Toma closed his eyes, trying to fix the memory of light in the high note, that moment of joy tethered and drawn down to the embrace of other voices in the final chord. There was something so moving in this that he felt tears start in his eyes. People, still applauding, surged toward the stage, but he could not face her. He stood abruptly and left.

What was happening to him? He had heard her sing, not for the first time, and now there was no familiar footing for his thoughts.

The night was cold. He began to sweat as if he had been running or working with the sledge. He sat down on a stone wall, hoping this anxiety would pass. Olivia. She would be waiting up for him and would want to hear about the music. Harriet's voice, this night, was a forbidden fruit, and he was obscurely shamed by it. How could he explain any of this to Olivia, how the singing, or just that one high note, had broken something in him or set something free and he could not now bear the thought of touching her, or sleeping with her, or even being under the same roof. Better to spend the night on this rock than to face the ruin of her hope.

. . . That is really all my news, and what poor entertainment this letter must be. With Fowler away in Washington, and not to return until the holidays, I am left to my own devices. It is amazing how one can feel alone in a house full of people. I do not imagine that you have any recent experience of this, and perhaps you envy my solitude, surrounded as you are by the happy cares of motherhood.

I do wish you would come visit me in Beecher's Bridge in spite of the bother involved. I would come to you, but for reasons which you know, I cannot. Whenever you manage it will be convenient for me, but the sooner the better. After all, how am I to know if I would be a fitting godmother to baby Clara if I have not even met her?

Yours in haste,
my love to all,
Harriet

Well, thought Harriet as she laid down the pen, it hasn't taken me very long to come to complaint and self-pity. Shrewishness will be next. She licked the envelope, sealed it, and applied the stamp with a thump of her fist. Fowler had been gone only six weeks, and already the routine of her day was like a sentence, something to be obeyed without pleasure or hope of escape. She knew she must not put off her letter to Washington.

It did not help that this situation was of her choosing. She tried to keep up with the running of the house on Q Street, sending off the metal crate of eggs every two weeks and writing out instructions on storage of the summer furnishings. But the eggs would probably be eaten by the servants, and the advice was just a way of filling up the pages. She felt older in the absence of her husband and missed those little flatteries that had punctuated their daily discourse. Was it her imagination or were there more mirrors in the house than she remembered? Why should it matter, she argued with herself, have I not married an old man?

The letter she now wrote to her husband struck the usual cheerful tone. Her hand committed white lies to the paper, but her mind was free of the task. She tried to imagine herself living in Washington, in which case her father must be dead, or with her there, or here in the care of someone else. All summer long she had wandered among these choices like a person dreaming of a maze. Today she saw that there was a different aspect to the problem, which was that she had no wish to live in Washington under any circumstances. She shook her head violently and stared at the words she had just written about a storm that had stripped the swamp maples and littered the lake with brilliant colors, about the sweet smell of apple wood in her fireplace. Would he even bother to read these words? What did she want, then? She wondered if she had time to catch the post with these two letters.

"You going out, ma'am?"

"Yes. Will you tell Mrs. Evans? I shouldn't be long." Harriet had expected to find the cook and Mrs. Evans in the kitchen, but instead it was Olivia, and that curious odor was the rock salt she had scattered on the cooking surface of the coal range.

"Where is Ingrid?"

"Oh, cook says the smell gives her a headache, but I tell her it must be done. Look." She held out for Harriet's inspection the egret feathers she had been passing back and forth in the smoke. "Don't they look like new?" Beyond her was a pile of dark feathers that Harriet recognized as the collar to one of her coats.

"Yes, they are much improved, but it's a great deal of trouble to take over clothes I never wear."

"When the master comes back you must look your best for him. It will all be resewn by tomorrow."

"There is no hurry, Olivia, but thank you. Please tell Ingrid we'll have to eat at six, with the days getting so short. Otherwise he won't eat his dinner."

"Yes, ma'am."

The business of the feathers stayed with Harriet all during her walk into town. Not just the feathers, of course, but the inexorable progress Olivia was making through her wardrobe, working to a standard of unsettling perfection, as if the house were a museum and she, Harriet, a doll or wax figure. The sharp odors of rectified spirits and sulfuric ether meant that Olivia was cleaning her silks, and in any room of the house, on any day, there was likely to be an undercurrent of silver polish. At the end of each week Olivia submitted a bill for her work in the laundry, which Harriet paid out of the household account. That amount had not varied by more than a dollar or two for months. Everything else was unpaid labor. Harriet knew this was not right, but her efforts to raise the subject with Olivia had been turned aside.

It was good to be out of the house—Mrs. Evans had become almost tiresome with her gentle suggestions about this—and now she did not want to go back. The mornings in Beecher's Bridge were late on account of the mountain, but for the same reason the evenings were long. After the sun went down behind the hills across the Buttermilk to the west, light gathered on the wall of the mountain, rising mist took the color of the clouds, and slow ripples in the current of the river glowed like dark mother-of-pearl.

She had bolted from the house in a coat that was too thin and shoes that were wrong for anything but a good road. She didn't mind the chill; she would be warm soon enough. Down along the river she went, on the road through the Bottom, wondering which of these houses Toma and Olivia lived in. Would she be able to tell? Probably not. It would be an ordinary house.

Another few minutes and she came to the gate of the ironworks, standing just opposite the saloon. It was about that time when the lamps might be lit, or not, and she could not tell if Toma was in the office. She had written a note to him asking if she might have one of the old ledgers. She would use it as she used old photographs or household objects, to get a conversation started with her father, or at least to get him talking. She had not had a reply, and it would be much the simplest thing if she could ask Toma directly.

A couple of men she did not recognize tipped their hats to her in the yard. They did not know if Mr. Peacock was about; they had not seen him today. She knocked and there was no answer. The door was a splintered, heavy thing that wanted a bump with the shoulder because it had settled against the frame. Had it been any less familiar she might have thought twice.

How long had it been since he was last here? A day or two? A week? A dish of something lay in the center of the desk. Whatever it was, the mice had found it. She needed light. There were the matches, and on the other table she found a lamp with a cracked chimney. The precarious weight of kerosene was reassuring. Maybe things weren't as bad as they had seemed at first.

She worked steadily at the papers, stopping to deal with the mouse droppings or to coax the wick into a better position. The lazy curl of black smoke from the cracked glass made her think of Aladdin's lamp, but it also stung her eyes.

When she had the papers arranged by date into two piles—these opened, those not—she swept up as best she could, using pieces of cardboard as her broom and pan. The dish she could do nothing about, so she put it on the far table. The clock struck five.

First she read through the opened letters and put aside two that seemed urgent. Then she opened the other letters and made nota-tions of their importance on the envelope. The one from Dr. Stein-metz she had to read twice: there was a hint of frustration that he had not had regular reports on progress up above, but the tone was cordial. That was the most important letter.

When she heard the half chime of the Congregational Church she

knew she must finish. On the back of a discarded envelope she left him
a message explaining what she had done, adding her hope that this help
was welcome. She would stop by tomorrow to see if he had left word
about the ledger. She signed the note "in haste, H." It was not a real
letter, and she saw no harm in the familiarity.

The image that stayed in her mind as she walked home was the
dish, with its suggestion of misery. How can it have come to this? she
asked herself. At her own house, where the many lamps were lit and
the air in the front hall was heavy with Ingrid's pot roast, she was met
by Mrs. Evans. Only now did she remember the letters in her pocket.

"Wherever did you get to? Your father has been asking after his
dinner these last fifteen minutes."

"I'm sorry to have worried you," Harriet said evenly. "I was helping
a friend and I lost track of the time."

THE WORK ON LIGHTNING KNOB in the autumn of 1916 attracted
not only humorous attention but real visitors as well. There was no
ground-breaking ceremony, and the first few visitors were stragglers
who thought there was work to be had if they were enterprising
enough to climb the mountain on speculation; or boys who were willing to run errands, though their real interest was in the machine of
monstrous proportions that would, in the course of a very few days, eat
its way into the ground and out of sight.

There were no unskilled jobs on offer, however, and precious few
errands either, but that did not stop the traffic of onlookers. Men who
had nothing better to do made themselves comfortable against the
blocks of stone warmed by the sun of an Indian summer, and made educated guesses about the design and consequences of the Steinmetz
Aerial, as the lightning attractor had come to be known. Some worried
about all that lightning upsetting the cows and souring the milk, others
that business and visitors would be down.

The boys soon found that they could manufacture an errand in advance, and save themselves an extra trip, by hauling a couple of buckets
of beer up the mountain, where it could be sold at a premium. The
speculative conversation among them was influenced by talk of war,
which they had from their elders, and by lurid technological improba-

bilities absorbed from popular magazines. One thought that the machine in the hole could chew its way straight through to the other side of the world and grab the Kaiser off his gold throne. Another said that the stored-up lightning would fly out at the touch of a button and destroy any German airplanes or submarines within a hundred miles of Beecher's Bridge.

Women came too, borrowing their husbands' boots for the expedition; their interest was neither the burrowing machine nor the rising tower, but rather the one completed structure on that dome of scarred rock: a modest board-and-batten affair that might have been a single-hole privy but was said to contain a telephone.

It is true that the telephone never gave any evidence of its existence—they did not know quite what to expect—and no one ever entered the shed, which had a sign to discourage curiosity. All they had to go on was rumor and the black line that came all the way up from down below.

Toma was deaf to suggestions that he demonstrate the workings of this marvelous instrument. It is not a toy, he would say, or, It doesn't belong to me. He did not point out, as he might have, that with the noise of the excavator and its attendant gasoline engine and compressor, any demonstration of the marvelous telephone was impossible anyway.

The telephone came into its own in the hours before and after the operation of the excavator. At seven o'clock, morning and evening, Stefan would be waiting within reach of a phone, in case Toma needed to talk to him.

On this particular day, a Saturday in mid-October, Toma was looking forward to the peace of the afternoon, for the crew only worked until noon. He had his eye on some of the lesser blocks of stone piled for the tower, and also on the weathered slabs that had long ago broken off the shelving rock of the Knob and lay scattered in the scrub oaks below. Winter would come long before the tower was finished, and he thought he could make a shelter for himself like a Montenegrin shepherd's hut, with a hearth at one end and a blanket hung to keep out the cold, or maybe a canvas tarp thrown over the whole thing.

The noon whistle sounded, and the men cleared out either to the saloon or to a good dinner at home. Toma had moved one block to his site, heaving it end over end, but the other, a dark brute shot with streaks of quartz, was simply too heavy for him. He was glad and surprised to hear Stefan on the road below the crown, talking to himself as he usually did.

"Hurry up!" called Toma, "I need a hand here."

"Hurry up . . . always hurry up. Even to the top of this mountain Piccolomini is following me."

Toma let the rock fall back and stood up. Stefan made the last few steps up onto the crown, carrying a carton more or less the size of Toma's rock.

"Here it is, everything, I think. You won't starve and you won't freeze, at least not before Monday."

"Thank you, Stefan, but why didn't you let one of the young fellows carry this for you?"

"Ah, the exercise is good for me." Toma smiled at this unlikely thought. "And I want to see for myself how goes this wonder of the world. There are seven of those, ja?"

"Yes."

"So this is the number eight. Maybe I call it that and Piccolomini has no idea. He listens, you know?"

"Listens to what?"

"The telephone, when you call me."

"He is spying on my groceries?"

"I'm just telling you what I know, so be careful what you say."

"This is your first time up here, I think?"

"Yes. I am curious to understand, but it looks like a mess to me. Too many things going on at once. Can't you get rid of some of these rocks?"

"Those are the blocks for the tower."

"No, the little pieces there."

Toma looked where Stefan was looking, at the hill of broken stone that the excavator had spat out of the hole.

"That's nothing. I can rig a drag line and it will be gone in half a morning, over the edge and out of sight. You should have seen the subway tunnels in New York when we were blasting under the river. What do you do with a carload of dirt that's maybe one hundred twenty-five feet down? This is nothing."

After they had moved the block of stone Stefan settled himself against it with his sausage in one hand and a piece of bread in the other. Toma rummaged in the box.

"I ran into your friend at the store when I was getting this stuff for you. She didn't speak to me, but she gives me a look, and I'm sure she knows exactly what I'm doing. I am hoping she doesn't look at me. What do I say?"

"Maybe there is nothing to say."

"If I have a woman like that I don't throw her away."

"I didn't throw her away. I am just staying up here so the work is done right, and as soon as it can be."

"And you have been up here how long now?"

"Five weeks? Six, I think."

"The way she looked at me, I bet you haven't seen her in that time."

"No. Stefan, I have lived without a woman before. You live without a woman. This is good for me. I am thinking very clearly."

"About a woman?"

"No. About the work here."

"You need to think about this? What's to think? Steinmetz is the one who does the thinking."

"Most of it, but he has other things that concern him, and he is not so practical a fellow. He wanted to put an iron pole one hundred feet high up here."

Stefan looked up, trying to imagine the top of the pole in the clear sky, and shook his head.

"I told him it would not be stable, and he shows me his notebook full of figures, and down at the bottom of the page there is a box drawn around the number one hundred. That's what he needs."

"So you told him no?"

"I told him if he will sink the pole in the ground he can have more than one hundred, and so we dig."

"And he was happy?"

"The thought of more lightning makes him very happy. His head shakes as if he is having a little fit, then he says to me, 'You shall be my lightning keeper.'"

"And what will you do with all this lightning you catch?"

"That is for Steinmetz to say, but I can tell you it's not what you're

hearing in town. You can't keep it, or store it. It is simply a way of testing equipment."

"I tell you what I hear, and I don't have to go to the saloon to hear
it. Piccolomini says it's all a waste of time and money, and the only reason for all this nonsense is that Dr. Steinmetz is in love with the lady,
Mrs. Truscott."

Toma's eyes slid away from Stefan's and down to the Truscott
house, where a car was just pulling up to the door. "The man has a foul
mouth. In my country, in the old days, the blasphemer's tongue was cut
out of his head to make him pure in the sight of God. Perhaps you
should tell this to your friend."

Stefan dismissed the suggestion and the thought of Piccolomini
with a wave of his hand. "Do you have a blueprint of this thing you are
building, or an elevation?"

Toma went to his pallet and reached under the corrugated metal
sheet for a roll of papers, wrapped in oilcloth. Stefan wiped his hands
and anchored the drawings with bits of rock. He worked his way
through the stack, talking to himself in German, then returned to the
section rendering showing the tower rising above Lightning Knob and
the iron embedded in the rock beneath.

Toma spoke first. "I don't think the final structure will resemble
this very closely."

"You know what this thing looks like to me?"

"A bad idea?"

"No. I am not making a joke. Think: where have you seen such a
thing before?"

"A tower?"

"Not just a tower. Here . . ." and Stefan took from his pocket a pencil end. Before Toma could protest, he had drawn several boldly
crooked lines suggesting a great energy emanating from the tower, or
perhaps attacking it.

"There. Now what do you see?"

Toma turned the papers to put the tower right-side up. He looked,
then drew a deep breath. "It seems that wherever I go, Dr. Tesla is
looking over my shoulder, or I over his. This is Wardenclyffe, you are
thinking?"

"You cannot deny the likeness, even if your purpose is different from his."

There was a long silence between them now, during which they reflected on the great disappointment named Wardenclyffe, a technological dry hole that had consumed hundreds of thousands of dollars—much of it J. P. Morgan's—in pursuit of Tesla's dream, the wireless transmission of energy in limitless quantities from his tower on Long Island to any other point on the face of the earth. No one but Tesla understood exactly how it would all work, how that great spike in the earth would tune the magnifying transmitter aloft to the geophysical resonance of the terrestrial globe, augmenting and channeling that energy the way one may increase the loudness of a well-cast bell by tapping it at a precise and accelerating rhythm.

In the end it hadn't worked, or at least the money ran out, and perhaps something died in Tesla along with this dream. The derelict tower on Long Island still stood, a mockery of brave ambition, and the laboratories had been vandalized.

Stefan spoke first. "I did not mean to discourage you."

"I am not discouraged." He tapped the drawing. "There was something else . . . tunnels of some sort?"

"Yes, the radiating spokes of the buried antenna. I guess if you are going to ground the wire, you might do it right, ja? But it didn't work, did it? He was just a Croat with a big idea that didn't work."

Toma was staring at the drawing. "What do you have on it?"

"On what?"

"On Tesla's tower, Wardenclyffe. You have a book, some drawings?"

"I look around. An article, maybe. The papers were full of it. Maybe *Scientific American*. I bring you what I find." Stefan took a folded piece of paper from his pocket and started to write on it. "Oh, sorry . . . this is for you. On your desk this morning when I went in to check. A lady, perhaps?"

Toma glanced at the note just long enough to recognize Harriet's hand, then put it away. "Good." He stood up. "Thank you for this, and for the box."

"My pleasure, boss. I come again if I find something, or I leave it on the desk?"

"The desk is good. And, Stefan—" Toma put his hand on his friend's shoulder—"Tesla is a Serb, not a Croat. A Serb."

"Ja, okay. If it makes a difference."

"And he invented, or discovered, the applications of alternating current, among other things."

"Sorry, okay. He was a great man."

"And he is not dead."

A SATURDAY IN THE Truscott household was like any other day, except that letters had to be at the post office by noon and one of the maids, upstairs or downstairs, would have the afternoon off. Harriet had no letters to write, and found nothing of interest in the mail on the table in the front hall. An invitation to tea, which she might accept, and another to dinner, which she would decline. In the afternoon there would be callers, but the maid would say that Mrs. Truscott was not at home, and put the white calling cards in the silver tray on the same table, each to be answered with a note early in the week. Harriet did not know how she would get through the hours until . . . until it was time to go. She would do something with her hair.

She hardly touched her lunch, and her father surprised her by taking notice.

"You're not eating."

"Of course I am, Papa. Look." And she made a show of cutting her chicken breast into many pieces, of which she ate two. "There. I shall hope to have a surprise for you this evening."

"What?"

"A surprise. You'll have to wait." There was no harm in this, she thought. If she came back without the ledger he would have forgotten anyway.

She left the house at the same time she had left the day before, and it pleased Mrs. Evans to see that her advice was taking hold.

"You are looking better, dear, with that bit of color in your cheeks. You must do this every day."

Harriet smiled and slipped out the door, grateful that she had not seen Olivia.

She did not know if she was too late or too early, or if he even came down from the mountain at all. From the condition of the office, it would be foolish to count on anything. She thought of the ledger again, and wondered if it was a foolish idea. Perhaps her father would be upset to see it. Perhaps it was too soon to awaken those particular memories, though he seemed now to have no sense of time, and even called her by her mother's name, which gave her a little shock that was disturbing but not entirely unpleasant. And then she was there, in front of the door.

She knocked and heard no reply, so she entered again, hoping to find a note in answer to hers. The desk, which had been dusted or wiped clean, was bare except for a ledger and the green bottle that used to sit on the window ledge in her office. She went to the desk and picked it up. She could not remember if she had brought it for him or the other way round, only that it sat there against the light as they pored over the ledgers, struggling with those pitiless numbers.

"You do not approve of Stefan's housekeeping, then?"

She startled, but stopped herself from turning around.

"Are you in the habit of spying on people, then frightening them?" She put the bottle down.

"Are you in the habit of breaking and entering?"

"I broke nothing."

"That is true, and thank you for your help. But must I speak to your back? There, that's better. You are looking very well."

"And you." It was true. He was clean and shaved and wearing a fresh white shirt. She had expected something more in keeping with the state of the office as she had found it.

"You must not stare at me as if I had two heads. Mrs. McCreedy, who is my source of hot meals, allows me the use of her tub, and I keep a few clean clothes there."

"I see. But what about . . . ?"

She did not finish her question and he ignored it, taking a chair and placing it near the desk. He held it for her. "Will you sit?"

He took his own chair—in fact her father's chair—and his suppressed smile hinted at some advantage or superior knowledge.

"You are staring at me again. Is this good manners?"

"Did you not stare at me the last time we saw each other?"

"It was normal, no? Everyone else did the same. I must congratulate you. It was very fine, the whole performance, but yours in particular."

"If it pleased you so, why did I not see you afterward? I felt certain you would come, if only for a moment."

"I could not." The irritating half smile was gone now.

She put her hand on the ledger. "I did not expect to see you today. I thought you would send word about this. May I?"

"Of course. I wonder who actually owns it. Perhaps it is really yours anyway."

"Why?"

"Because your husband bought everything."

"Yes. You are right, but I wish you hadn't said it. Of course you are right. It seems so long ago, and I don't like to think about it."

"Nor I, so what shall we talk about?"

She looked at her lap and remembered how she had once worried about the charcoal dust in the creases of her knuckles that exaggerated the size of her hands. "We never used to have this problem, wondering what to talk about."

"In those days . . . in those days we had only the future to consider, what might happen. Now we know what has happened, and cannot pretend otherwise."

"For Heaven's sake, Toma! You make it sound as if everything is over, your life and mine. I don't believe that, do you?"

"No." He spoke with his eyes cast down, and might as well have said yes.

"You have a great work to accomplish, a work that Dr. Steinmetz has placed in your hands. That is your future now, and if there is anything I can do to help . . ." She couldn't go on. She had said too much already.

"It sounds to me as if you want a job. I think you proved yesterday that you are up to the task. Well?"

"I only want to help if I can. You and Dr. Steinmetz. Of course I know nothing about lightning, except that it frightens me."

"And I know only what Steinmetz has told me. We shall learn together, yes?" He was smiling at her now, in a way that reminded her of the old Toma.

"Yes, Toma, yes. You will tell me what must be done here. I think Dr. Steinmetz will be surprised."

"And very happy, too. He will see a great improvement in the correspondence."

Harriet was silent for a moment. She was thinking of the letter she must write to Fowler. Would she have to ask his permission?

"Toma, you must not hope for too much, for things that cannot be."

Toma took up the green bottle and began to flip it in the air from one hand to the other.

"I would be sorry if you broke that."

"This?" he asked, turning to look at her while he caught the bottle backhanded in mid-arc. "I won't break it. I used to do this with a knife." He set the bottle down on the ledger. "And don't worry about the other."

"Thank you. Then I won't." She felt herself blushing. They were talking, indirectly, about what must not happen, and even this was a kind of intimacy.

"I should go. I'll stay longer next time, after I have made arrangements."

"And when will that be?"

"Not tomorrow, and not Monday, as I have invited people to tea. Tuesday?"

"Fine. I'll leave a list of what needs doing, and you'll bring the tea?"

He was joking with her, but she didn't mind now. "Yes, a thermos. And soon there will have to be some thought of a fire. It is very cold in here. Had you noticed?"

"Yes. Cold in here and cold on the mountain. Stefan will be glad to make fires and leave the correspondence to you. I think he has no gift for that."

She stood up to go. "Will you stay up there all winter?"

He nodded. "It is better that way. Don't forget your ledger."

THERE WAS TIME BEFORE dinner to show the ledger to her father. He looked at the pages and smoothed them with his hands. She did not know if he had understood anything or even recognized the book.

"Is this the surprise?"

"Yes, Papa. I thought you would like it. Did you like it?"

"Oh yes, but . . ."

"But you thought it would be something else?"

He looked up at her with wavering trust. "I thought it would be a baby."

Turbine shell casting, 1923

Only a rock wall separated the Walchensee from the flat land; the bottom of the lake behind this natural barrier reached to the level of the plateau. The situation invited development, for a tunnel could be dug through the rock at a point a small distance below the surface, and large pipes, or penstocks, could then carry the water rushing down the slopes to turbines in a powerhouse nestled against the slope. . . .

Consulting engineers like [Oskar] von Miller usually do not themselves invent and develop technology, but instead depend on manufacturers to fulfill design specifications. Furthermore, large projects like the Walchenseewerk . . . are often designed to take advantage of the state of the art rather than to advance far beyond it. The challenge for von Miller . . . was artfully to adapt . . . technologies to particular local conditions.

— description of the Walchensee (Bavaria)
generation & distribution project, completed 1924.
Thomas P. Hughes, *Networks of Power*

SIXTEEN

When she heard the thump and the wailing cry, Harriet had a pretty exact idea of what had happened, and her first reaction, despairing and ungenerous, was "Oh, not now!"

Mrs. Evans had fallen. She was in the dining room, trying to entertain Amos Bigelow and set the table for the Thanksgiving dinner at the same time. Harriet was in the kitchen, basting the bird one last time, and wondering if it was done. Both the cook and the pantry maid were down with a nasty flu, and Dr. and Mrs. Crowell, old and understanding friends of the family, were in the parlor. Harriet nearly dropped the bird and the pan to the floor. She thrust the baster and the potholders at the scullery girl, whose eyes were round with apprehension.

In the dining room Mrs. Evans, in her best black, lay in a litter of cranberry sauce, and the clothes gave up a strong smell of urine. Dr. Crowell knelt by her and held her hand. Her soft moaning was overridden by his louder complaint about the absence of his medical bag.

"It was right there by the door, and all I had to do was put out my hand. You'd think after forty years that I'd have more sense."

"Is it the hip, then?"

"Yes, almost certainly. We shall have to get her to a bed."

"Of course. Father, go sit with Mrs. Crowley."

The old man stood with his back to the fire, and so close that she could smell the singed wool, which was what drew her attention to him. He wrung his hands, bleating, "Oh, oh, oh . . ."

"Mrs. Crowley," Harriet said very distinctly, "go and sit with Mrs. Crowley." She gave him a gentle push, and like a toy boat he drifted off in the direction of the parlor.

"We'll need help getting a blanket under her. Has she her own bed here?"

"Yes, but I'm afraid it's upstairs. Lily!" she spoke sharply to the hovering maid, "don't just stand there. See if you can find Carpenter. He should be in his room over the garage."

Harriet put her hand on Mrs. Evans's forehead, which seemed to quiet her.

"Will she be all right?"

"Probably so, but she's had a terrible shock. Would you have a sleeping draft, a sedative of any sort?"

"No."

"Then I shall just have to drive home and back, but that will take some time, and I'd like to have her in bed first."

An anxious white face appeared in the pantry door. "Begging pardon, ma'am."

"Yes, Sarah, what is it?"

"The bird, ma'am. Maybe it's burning."

"For Heaven's sake take it out, then!" Sarah vanished.

Dr. Crowell actually smiled at her. "You have your hands full today. You should have told us."

"I am so glad you are here, and so sorry about the dinner."

Lily burst into the room, and behind her, in the shadow of the stairwell, stood Olivia. Harriet had not even known she was in the house.

"He's not there, mum."

"Where is he?"

"I'm sure I don't know, mum."

"And the stable boy?"

"Him neither. Gone the both of them, maybe to town."

"Well, get a blanket then, and stay with Mr. Bigelow and Mrs. Crowell."

"I can help," said Olivia from her station.

Harriet, Olivia, and Dr. Crowell managed to get Mrs. Evans up the stairs and into her bed, with a couple of old blankets and a torn sheet under her. Harriet began to fumble with the fastenings of the skirt and Olivia put a hand on her arm.

"I will take care of this."

The doctor stood back from the bed while they worked. He seemed to be more concerned about Harriet.

"I say again, you have your hands full, and not just today."

"What?" Her mind was wandering: to the kitchen, where Sarah would be doing something with the turkey; to the parlor, where Lily would be on pins and needles. Her father, she knew, made Lily very anxious even under the best of circumstances.

"I think it is time that you took some care for the other situation, and even some strong measures."

"This is not about Mrs. Evans."

"No, but this fall will make it impossible for her to help your father, to tend to him. You cannot do this yourself, not all of it. It is too great a burden."

She protested that she was strong and determined and she could always call upon Carpenter, the chauffeur.

Dr. Crowley said nothing. He raised his eyebrows.

"What are you saying?"

"Amos is an old, old friend, as you must know, but I think it is time, for his own safekeeping."

"You mean the Home?"

"Yes." The word sounded in her ear like the closing of a door.

The Home was a universal shorthand for the Connecticut Home for the Incompetent, located on the outskirts of Billingsford, not a dozen miles away. She had twice visited that forbidding stone building in the course of her work with the Ladies' Auxiliary, and had come away with a chill in her bones that had nothing to do with the weather.

"Please don't." Her voice was faint.

"Harriet, try to think clearly about this, for his sake and your own."

"It is the most dreadful place. . . ." She remembered, too late, Dr. Crowell's connection to the Home as a member of the advisory board, but her memory of particular smells gave her the courage to go on. "Please don't let us talk of this. However sensible the suggestion may be, it is not acceptable to me. He must stay here. I will find the strength."

"I'm afraid I have seen other cases like his, an early descent into . . . well, too early. I'm afraid you have little idea of the sacrifice you will make of yourself, of your domestic happiness."

Harriet, with her eyes cast down, seemed to be reflecting on the wisdom of his words, but she was instead taking an inventory of those blessings. "It is too late, Doctor. Those sacrifices have already been made. I should be in Washington with my husband. But I am here, and this accident will not change my mind about what I must do."

"Well, then," Dr. Crowell made a tactical retreat, "let me see to my patient."

Harriet seemed intent on the dumb show of the doctor's ritual: checking the pulse against the gold pocket watch, bending over the bed to hear the respiration. She was thinking of the office, of those afternoons that began with such bright purpose and ended in the languorous dusk with her staring at a crack in the stove, a necklace of fire, all animation now suspended until his footfall should break the spell.

Olivia said something to her that she did not hear clearly.

"What?"

"She is old. She will be in bed for weeks, and maybe then a cripple. I will take care of your father."

She took Olivia's hand in her own and held it, not briefly, as one might expect, but with a firm, lasting, and fervent pressure.

Portledge
Dec. 6, 1916

Dr. C. P. Steinmetz
Consulting Engineering Department
General Electric
Schenectady, New York

Dear Dr. Steinmetz:
    You are kind to keep me abreast of developments in Beecher's Bridge when you are dealing with so much else. I am sorry for the burst pipes in your cactus conservatory; I hope you have not lost every specimen. Can the temperature really have reached minus eight degrees so early in December? As for the burden

of providing information to Senator Truscott's committee, I urge patience and foresight as the only remedies.

Patience because Senator Truscott's requests are not idle ones: he and his fellows must manage, more or less by stealth, to make the country ready for a war it wishes not to fight. By the way, I congratulate you on your recent statements affirming allegiance to your adopted country. Surely this clears the air. There will be a war, I am certain of it, but there will also be a peace, may I live to see it; and our great company, which you have done so much to establish, must be ready to prevail in that chaos of redirected priorities. Our opportunities shall then be doubled, at least, if we can increase our stake in harnessing those energy resources about which Senator Truscott inquires. He is, as you know, a friend to our enterprise, so we owe him more than courtesy.

Would you be so kind as to enlarge on the information in your last paragraph? Something, I gather, about a great new work on the mountain. But you have again forgot how far your mind leaps ahead of common understanding, and I think your excitement led to illegibility there. How does this "work" connect to either the experimental generating station or the lightning research? And what will it cost?

In closing, I share some good news with you. Thanks to the efforts of our legal staff in Washington, the patent application on Mr. Peacock's device has cleared the final hurdle. I shall write to him myself and congratulate him.

With warm wishes,
C. A. Coffin

Dec. 18, 1916

To: Dr. C. P. Steinmetz
From: T. Peacock (HBT)
Re: Progress on excavation; core samples; transverse tunnels and shafting reconsidered; other business

The work has now reached the specified depth of 150 feet. Experimental steel shaft sections received Tuesday. Prefer eight-foot lengths to twelves, as hoist is inadequate for the latter. Suggest that freestanding aerial above the ground be fashioned of one forged piece in tapering design for stability in high wind. If welded, wind stress and flexion will require external guy wires, creating potential grounds.

Core samples of the rock dispatched this A.M. Great variation here, as you will see, with veins of the purer magnetite occurring almost at random in the granite schist (sample A). Footing of aerial is similar in composition to sample B, but lateral extent and depth of magnetite there not known or easily determined.

In view of uncertainty of rock composition, the surest result—best connection of aerial to electromagnetic potential of mountain—will be obtained by pursuing plan of transverse tunnels per design sketches previously forwarded. Horizontal "legs" of the aerial to be of same specifications as vertical shaft, to be laid in sections and set into tunnel floors. Cost estimates to be available for discussion after Christmas. All excavation to be completed by March/April, laboratory building by May. Aerial to be functional by June, pending tests, in time for its work during the season of electrical disturbances.

Other business: Please advise how pumping equipment should be insulated from ambient voltages of lightning strikes. Estimates of seepage are provisional; situation to be reassessed after thaw in April. Please advise as to date of arrival and suggest when you wish to review plans and worksite.

Best wishes for a Merry Christmas.

Schenectady
December 20, 1916

Mrs. Fowler Truscott
The Manor
Beecher's Bridge, Connecticut

Dear Mrs. Truscott:

Thank you for your kind note. I see your hand everywhere these days. I shall not be able to join you until the 27th, as I cannot, it seems, rush away from Christmas here in Schenectady. The cactus conservatory is rising again from its ruins; I had forgotten how expensive relatively simple plumbing repairs can be. The collection itself will take longer to rebuild, and some of the specimens can only be replaced by the kindness of friends in far places. Do, by all means, attempt to propagate the Frailea castanea and the Mammillaria senilis.

Though my arrival will be somewhat delayed, I have arranged my schedule

*in that I shall be able to spend four or five days with you over the New Year, and
it will be a pleasure to see Senator Truscott in less formal circumstances. And also
yourself—though I should say particularly yourself. There is much work to be
done, and my grasp of the situation is much clearer thanks to your timely
intervention. As for the recreations you promise, I will be a disappointment to
you. I must leave ice-skating to the young.*

*There is a matter of importance that I wish to discuss with you when we find
a moment, and it connects to our earlier discussions about the grid or the network
of power that must bind and connect all. It is a plan that has been growing in my
mind. I will not say more about it now except to observe that in the abstract,
great scientific works have the power and beauty of music, and this idea resonates
in my breast like a symphony.*

Yours most cordially,
C. P. Steinmetz

CIRCUMSTANCE HAD SCHOOLED Olivia Toussaint in many things, but
to the subject of love she came late and at a disadvantage. Her mother
had been taken at such an early age that she was not sure, now, what
she remembered and what she imagined. She had never known a
grandmother, an aunt, an older sister. She did not know if her mother
had a family: no letters survived, not a single photograph. At the funeral the plain pine box had been nailed shut on whatever was left, and
the priest gave her a pasteboard card with the Ave on one side and on
the other a brightly robed and smiling Virgin, who would become the
image and metaphor of her mother.

Had she loved Horatio before he put his hand on her and made
her lie with him? Afterward, all that remained was obedience, his need
an unyielding, inescapable fact, the anvil on which her life was to be
shaped.

At first she paid little mind to Amos Bigelow, who differed from
people she had doctored only in that there was no chance of improvement in his condition. He would not speak to her, and asked every day,
in her hearing, when Mrs. Evans would be coming back. He had forgotten that Mrs. Evans lay in a bed directly above the servants' dining
room, where he took his meals, and that his daughter had taken him up
to see her.

Where Mrs. Evans had persuaded with gentle common sense,

Olivia presided with silent strength. She could, if necessary, resort to force: it was a lesson he had not forgotten. Olivia took over at noon when Harriet went into town, and Amos Bigelow had refused to eat with this strange woman as his companion.

"Where is she?" he wanted to know. Olivia did not reply. She went on cutting his food very small, as Harriet had told her she must do, but she did not care whether the old man ate. He hit the edge of his plate—perhaps an accident—sending the meat flying, along with gouts of gravy that spattered her. She wiped her face and asked him please to pick up his plate. It was as if she had not spoken.

How long must she sit there waiting on this defiant child? She took his fingers in her grip and squeezed. She did not intend to hurt him, but she knew of the arthritis there, had seen his daughter rubbing his hands with ointment of arnica. "Do as I ask, Mr. Bigelow. Do it now." From that moment he did as he was told, but in silence, and always with his eyes averted, as if the sight of her might do him harm.

She no longer worked in the laundry but supervised the new girl hired there, and was a stern critic of hasty folds, hints of damp. She was given a room on the third floor on the servants' side, warmed by the rising heat of the kitchen. It had a view out over the frozen lake and another window on the end so she would have a cross draft come summer. The old man often dozed during the day and his nights were restless. She left her door open when she went to bed and also the door through to the main staircase, so that she could hear when he stirred. If it sounded as if he was trying to put his clothes on, she would go down, put ten minims of the belladonna tincture in the cup of milk left to warm on the radiator, and make him drink it. Sometimes Harriet came, a ghost in her nightgown, to stand with her as the old man sank back into sleep.

"You are very good with him," she might whisper, and Olivia would climb the stairs to her bed and try to find sleep. The scent of the other woman made her think of Toma, and of the many nights in her own bed when she had waited for him.

During the day she sat in a small room between the kitchen and the back door that had been equipped with a bench and certain tools, where Amos Bigelow indulged his obsession with work, perfecting in his mind the wheels that had been his undoing. The clanging was acutely aggravating to the cook, a dour alcoholic Finn who held Olivia responsible for this chaos.

When she saw he had exhausted himself and he rubbed his knuckles in a certain way, she made him put away the tools and sit in the comfortable chair. There she wrapped his hands in lint impregnated with capsicum, spirits of turpentine, gum camphor, and sulfuric ether, a liniment known as King of Pain that she had found in a book.

There were always a few minutes at the beginning and end of Olivia's shift when she overlapped with Harriet, and it would have been impossible not to notice the effect of the daughter's presence on the old man.

They might be playing a last hand of cards, and if she had to correct him—"No, Papa, that is not a trump card. You need the other red one, the diamond"—a furtive delight transformed his vacant expression: he had nearly succeeded in outwitting her. Or she might be reading to him in a very loud voice, sometimes from Scott but more often from the Bible, and when she came to a familiar passage she would pause in mid-sentence and let him recite from memory.

"See how he remembers the Word," she said to Olivia in a whisper. "Will you read it to him after I leave?" Olivia nodded, but did not keep her promise. Later, when the old man dozed in his chair, she took the heavy volume in her lap and ran her hands over the gilded leather. She had never held such a thing. She opened it, and there on the first page was a list of Bigelow forebears, starting with Increase, born three hundred years earlier in Litchfield, in the parish of Berkswich. What impressed her more than lineage was the fact that these people had dared to write their names in the holy book.

She saw also how, at the end of the day, the daughter took delight in the sight of her father, that querulous, unresponsive old man in Olivia's keeping, a delight that could not be feigned. The currents of feeling and caring were as mysterious to the silent witness as the operation of electricity itself.

Olivia had discovered, thanks to the careless gossip of the cook, where Harriet spent her afternoons, and had these hours to turn the matter over in her mind and impale herself upon possibilities. Although she knew nothing of what happened in the office—not even, to a certainty, that Toma was there—she could imagine almost anything.

She considered and rejected the idea that they were physically intimate. Each day she made an inventory of her rival's dress and appearance, just as she would check a shirtfront for stains.

If not that, then what? The expectation of it? She did not hate Harriet, though she had tried. But if she could understand, she might know what to do.

THE WEATHER IN Beecher's Bridge, famously unpredictable, continued clear and cold through December, as the *Farmer's Almanac* had suggested it might. The planes and angles of stone on the face of Great Mountain had yet to be softened by a snowfall; the fields were petrified wastes of windblown stubble; and on every pond and tributary stream an armor of black ice had settled, so translucent that little fishes in the shallows could be seen to wriggle between the invisible ice and the mud, caught in that vise. Only the river ran free.

The cold made little difference to Toma; his stone shelter was warm enough when he made a fire. Down in the shaft of the excavation, out of the wind, the temperature was above freezing, and a man could break a sweat in his shirtsleeves. The work continued on schedule, the only absentees being the uninvited onlookers, who had no shelter from the wind.

December 25, a Monday, was a bleak day on Great Mountain, the brilliant cold weather of the past week having given way to damp lowering clouds that promised snow before evening.

The excavation of the vertical shaft had been completed on the sixteenth, and at eleven o'clock this morning the last nail had been driven in the rough staircase that hugged the side walls and allowed access to a point about eight feet above the floor of the pit. Below the last platform the tunnels would fan out in four directions, and the men, like moles, would probe the mountain with pneumatic hammers. Once the compressor was in place and its ventilation pipe secured, he sent the men home to their holiday. He waited for them at the top of the shaft, under the metal roof, and shook each one by the hand, wishing him a Merry Christmas. But not too merry, he said, for he also passed out the envelopes. The work was on schedule: each man received a note and a gold eagle, a personal expression of thanks from Steinmetz himself.

"What about you, chief?" asked Hawley, the foreman.

"I'll be all right," said Toma, his eyes on the last envelope, the one with his name on it.

"Would you like to have supper with us? We're a crowd anyway, no trouble."

"I have other plans, thank you, but you are kind to think of me."

"All right then, I'll be off. Merry Christmas, and if it comes down heavy, stay put somewhere. I always think of old Anderson's fingers, and how he lost 'em drunk in a snowdrift on Christmas Eve."

"I'll be careful."

Toma had no plans other than dinner in the saloon with a good scrubbing beforehand. He didn't want any reminders of Christmas. His companions tonight would be a like-minded crowd.

He made preparations for his return. He carried an axe to the stream coming down between the Knob and the mountain from Rachel's Leap: it was easier to chop ice from the rocks than to get his pail into the hidden water. He set the ice on the edge of his hearth and emptied the kettle into a bottle, which he wrapped in the down quilt Mrs. McCreedy had given him. A snow of feathers eddied and settled: he would sew up the hole tomorrow. The bottle would not keep his bed warm, but neither would it freeze.

In Montenegro, in the high valley of the crazed monk Vasili, the winters had been hard, and the daily rituals of fire and water were familiar to him. The animals must be watered, and many times he had helped his father chop ice for them. The fire must be tended, and if the wood ran short they would remove the wheels from the cart to make a kind of sledge, and hitch the oxen to it. Down into the sparse forest of the Sandžak they went, and when they had cut as much wood as the team could manage, they fitted the oxen with clumsy, iron-spiked wooden shoes to give them purchase on the grade. His father walked ahead with the reins in his hand, and Toma struggled along in the unbroken snow at the side, with his hand on the brake lever, just in case.

At Christmas they would walk to the monastery at Moraca to hear mass, stopping for the night with relatives near Kolasin. An ox carried

their belongings and the presents they brought, and Natalia also when
the snow was too high for her. Occasionally his mother would persuade
Danilo to ride, to rest the stump of his leg. She never rode, and neither
would Toma. A heavy snow had come down on them once, and they
could not make it to Kolasin or to any shelter. Danilo took the packs
from the ox and made him lie down in the snow. With one canvas he
covered the ox; the larger one he laid out for them, and they dozed
until dawn, packed together like salt fish, wrapped first in the canvas
and then in the snow.

The office was stone cold, yesterday's ashes in the stove, but there
was plenty of kindling and wood. He remembered the formality that
had descended on them yesterday, when she announced she would
have to leave half an hour early to meet the senator's train. That was
how she always referred to him. She didn't know exactly which day she
would be able to return, but with Dr. Steinmetz arriving on the
twenty-eighth it probably wouldn't be until after the New Year.

"You will be all right, won't you?" she asked when she got up to
leave.

"Why not? It's only a few days, and if Steinmetz is with you he
won't bother me very much."

"No . . . I meant because it's Christmas, and you are alone."

"Yes. Well, under the circumstances . . ."

She gave him her restless hand. "I must be off. One never knows if
the train might be a minute or two early."

He held the thermos out to her. "You did not drink your tea."

"Thank you, no." She eyed the thermos warily. "You finish it, and
I'll fetch it later."

The thermos stood where he had left it in the middle of the desk.
When he had laid the fire and lit it, he went to pour a cup of the cold
tea. The desk was bare of fresh correspondence—Stefan must have
dealt with whatever had come in this morning—but tucked under the
thermos was a blue envelope. The color of the paper lifted his spirits,
but on top there was a scrap of white paper, and in Stefan's hand:
"Sorry, boss." Sorry?

The envelope had his name on it, but it was not Harriet's handwriting. Whose then? He remembered the crude lettering on the door
of the laundry, Olivia's laundry.

"Merry Christmas from Olivia. Hoping your work goes well, and that we can be together soon." The childish lettering and the ornate capitals filled the page.

He scanned the shelves and cabinets hoping that there might be another blue envelope. He opened the drawers of the desk. Nothing. He drank the tea and put the letter in the fire, where it was consumed in a greenish flame. He buried the ash with a fresh log and pulled a chair close to the heat.

He woke to the whistle of a train. It was dark and the snow had begun.

In the front room of the tavern Mrs. McCreedy had made an attempt at holiday cheer with red and green bunting over the long mirror, and Toma told her that it looked nice.

"More like flowers at a funeral, wouldn't you say?" There were only a few other patrons, and no talk: they were looking off into the smoke or into their glasses.

"And you, dear, you look like you've seen a ghost. What can I get for you? Something strong, I think." Mrs. McCreedy was a red-haired woman, sturdy, cheerful, and observant, but what Toma most appreciated was the fact that she never asked questions.

"Something strong, and a bath if possible. What is your dinner this evening?"

"We've got a stew, nothing fancy, but I told the girl to put parsnips in it so it'll be a little different. And there's mince pie. I made them myself. Not a proper Christmas dinner, but it'll see you through until tomorrow."

Toma stepped out of the bath glowing with the pleasure of the hot water and unsteady on his feet. The strong drink that Mrs. McCreedy had in mind was a toddy of whiskey, lemon, hot water, and maple sugar, and she had filled the glass again without being asked.

"Second one on the house, seeing as it's Christmas."

He felt through his pockets before pulling on the clean clothes she had laid out for him, and so he came upon the envelope he had forgotten since this morning. No gold coin for him.

Mr. Coffin's congratulatory note was brief and to the point, thanking him warmly for his efforts in keeping the work on the mountain on schedule. Furthermore, in light of the very favorable progress on adapting the Peacock Turbine to commercial requirements, the board had authorized a payment of $20,000 against participation in several licensing agreements recently negotiated. Dr. Steinmetz joined him in expressing wishes for a happy Christmas and a prosperous New Year.

The folded cheque had fallen to the floor while Toma read the note. There was Coffin's signature, and there the notation of the amount. He wondered if this meant that he was rich.

When he had finished his second slice of mince pie, and chased it with a glass of fiery apple brandy, he asked if the snow had stopped falling.

"It has, dear, but we've a bed for you if you want. Perhaps you'd better stay if you're onto the applejack."

Should he tell her his news? Instead he took her hand and said, "If you could see how we drink the plum brandy in my country you would have no fear for me. My supper was a feast. Thank you."

He paid his bill and left five dollars, which he said was for the bath and for his clean clothes. That's too much, she protested, much too much. And your kindness, he said.

The stars and a crescent moon lighted his way up the mountain, and the leather webbing set with screws that he had put over his boots gave him sure footing in the snow. Near the top he glanced back at the lights of the Truscott house below and wondered how much it had cost to build.

HARRIET TRUSCOTT LAY IN bed beside her husband, who had fallen asleep. If she could go back to her own bed and her own room she would be more likely to fall asleep, but Fowler would wake sometime in the night to find her gone and be puzzled, or disappointed, or offended. All she knew was that she was stuck here for the next eight hours owing to her own foolish expectations. She should know better than to misinterpret his expansive pleasure in the dinner, the embrace of his home, her company. It did seem to her that he drank more now, and made no excuse for it. The pressures of work must be overwhelming, she thought, making his excuse for him.

She had the book of Emerson's essays open and propped up on the little pillow, but she could not read any more than she could fall asleep.

She was preoccupied with the logistics of Lucy's arrival three days hence. Lucy and Cecil and the baby would have to have her bedroom, with Caroline and the nurse in the yellow room. The single bedroom with the writing table must be kept for Dr. Steinmetz, as he had expressed such satisfaction with that mattress and his view of the pond. It wasn't perfect, but there it was. If Olivia were not so necccsary she might be sent home and the nurse could go upstairs, Lucy to the yellow room, and she would have her own bed. A week sharing Fowler's bed should not be a hardship, she told herself. But it crossed her mind how much easier it would be in some ways if he were called back to Washington.

When she had juggled these possibilities several times her mind drifted back to her parting from Toma. She regretted having raised the subject of his solitary Christmas, because that could only make matters worse, and it might appear that she was prying. The day before she had asked Olivia if she needed to go home—be away was how she put it—over the holidays and the answer was simply no. And then she had left the office so abruptly, quite like a guilty person.

The mountain rose just beyond her window, cowled in new snow. How many paces would it be from where she lay to the top of the Knob?

She got up and went to the window, easing it open, taking the sharp air on her flesh like a penance. There was no light on the crest as there sometimes was, and she thought: What if he could see me here in my nightgown, looking up to him? Well, what of it? She might as well be honest with herself.

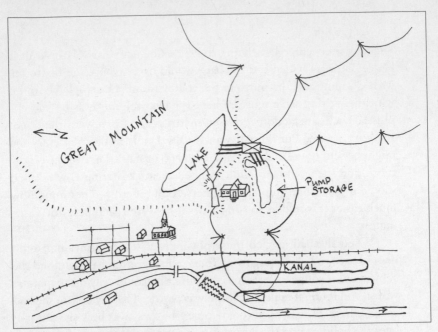

Steinmetz's sketch of Great Mountain

Inside the boathouse

CHAPTER

SEVENTEEN

Despite her careful plans, and her middle-of-the-night revisions to those plans, Harriet's imagination of the New Year's house party did not prepare her for the reality.

Dr. Steinmetz was the good news: his humor and patience were more than equal to the trial of Lucy's children and Amos Bigelow. In the morning, while Fowler was dressing and long before Lucy had stirred, he went down in his slippers and robe to fetch a pot of coffee, then retired to his room to read and smoke. At the table he sat next to Amos Bigelow and made gallant, unrewarded conversation. And Caroline, a temperamental and irritating child, was charmed to silence when Dr. Steinmetz, with the lamp at his back, made shadow shapes of animals on the wall. Afterward, Caroline sat in the corner, her hands clasped, practicing her own shapes.

The odd thing was how little pleasure Harriet took in Lucy's company. Having a new baby and a toddler was exhausting—You can have no idea, said Lucy—but she did have the resources of the nurse, her maid, and also Cecil, who, whatever else might be said of him, was attentive to the children. In the early morning he would walk the baby up and down the hall while his wife slept.

Lucy's peevishness was not to be appeased. She could not sleep properly in that bed: she and Cecil had twin beds. She complained of Caroline's behavior, but left others to deal with her, and she seemed rather short with Cecil himself. When he ventured a comment at the table Lucy, as often as not, cut him off as if he had not spoken. Harriet did not find Cecil interesting, nor was he energetic, except in the matter of walking the baby, but she liked him well enough, and felt sorry for him.

It was difficult to find any time for those long talks that Harriet remembered and looked forward to, and it seemed to her that Lucy might have tried a little harder to create the opportunity. Perhaps those confidences were something they had now, at last, outgrown. The one chat they'd had hardly rose to the level of the meaningful: Lucy was preoccupied with her sore nipples. Harriet suggested she consult Olivia, who was knowledgeable about home remedies and herbal treatments.

"Oh, *her*," said Lucy, with arch emphasis. "I did wonder where she came from. Very striking; too striking, I think, and a bit surly. Perhaps you should have a word with her." And that was the end of their conversation.

Fowler Truscott was in an odd humor, and Harriet, in her few moments of idleness, tried to put her finger on what had changed in him. The least drastic interpretation was that he had put on the mask of the jolly innkeeper as a defense against the number and variety of his guests. Certainly when it came to filling glasses and supplying cigars he was perfect. He and Dr. Steinmetz had a long conversation one morning in the library, with the door half-closed, but apart from that he did not seem to engage with his guests. He had a courtly, bantering manner with Lucy that in another man Harriet might have read as flirtation— Lucy was still very pretty, and Fowler would have seen, or noticed, little of her shrewish side. With Cecil, a recent convert to golf, he chatted about niblicks, mashies, and spoons. The children seemed to make no impression on him at all. Dr. Steinmetz took the fussing baby from Lucy one morning after breakfast and circled the dining room humming and muttering to her in German. He stopped next to his host, who was reading the newspaper.

"Hmmm?" queried Fowler Truscott when he looked up, and Dr. Steinmetz offered him the child. "Oh, oh, I couldn't . . . no, I think you're the man for the job. Carry on." The remark stuck in Harriet's mind, and even more so the attitude of aversion. Men were not expected to be gifted in these matters: Cecil and Dr. Steinmetz were exceptions to the rule. Still, there was something sorrowful in that moment, which Harriet had to resist. If she gave in to it she could not preserve the hope that she too might be blessed with a child.

What had seemed at first to be the understandable fatigue of a man who had been working under great pressure came, after several days of doing nothing more strenuous than lifting his glass and the newspaper, to suggest a chronic condition, perhaps illness, perhaps age. The least acceptable reflection was that her husband, during these months of their separation, had drifted away, or drifted back, back to the habits of mind and feeling that governed his life before courtship and marriage. A question presented itself to her for the first time: if a man does not marry until the age of fifty-three, would it not be sensible to conclude that he had some reservation about the state of matrimony, perhaps an aversion to it? Harriet had always managed to imagine—because Fowler had told her so—that he had simply bided his time until the perfect woman came into his life. Now Harriet was caught short whenever Fowler Truscott paid tribute to his perfect wife. The compliment was delivered in a tone of utmost sincerity, and still it grated on her, and she had to force herself to maintain the smile, the expression, the mask of the perfect wife.

By the obvious measures, Harriet's house party was a success: her guests were well fed, no one fell ill or quarreled, and the predicted snowfall went elsewhere. The weather was clear and not too cold. If it held like this they would be able to skate on the pond on New Year's Eve. But if nothing had gone wrong, neither did Harriet take any great pleasure in her achievement. She found it absolutely necessary to get out of the house whenever she could, away from all this merrymaking.

The day after Christmas, after her restless night, she had gone out for a walk with her husband. After about fifteen minutes Fowler asked if she was ready to go home—head back to the fire was how he put it. No, she said, she really needed to stretch her legs, otherwise she would have no appetite for dinner. Well, said he, you'll know where to find me.

Harriet walked on, straight to the office. It had come to her last night, when she was thinking about Toma anyway, that she must invite him to dinner on New Year's Eve. Dr. Steinmetz would welcome the opportunity for fresh conversation: she was worried that he might find Lucy and Cecil a bit limited. She should have mentioned the party when she had last seen him, but she had not been thinking clearly, and now the ink was frozen, not a pencil to be found.

The telephone sat on a table that had once supported Amos Bigelow's collection of catalogues. She knew that one turn of the crank would produce one ring, his signal. Why had she never dared to do this before? He answered on the fourth ring, just as she began to wonder what she would say if someone else picked up the phone down at the Experimental Site.

"Yes. Is that you, Stefan?" The voice, scratchy and blurred by a clicking like cicadas on a summer night, did not sound very much like Toma.

"Hello?"

"Who is this?"

"It is Harriet, Harriet Truscott."

"Oh?" There was a flurry of the clicks, followed by what sounded like the word "Christmas."

"And to you. Will you come down for New Year's Eve?"

"I can be there in twenty minutes."

"No, not now, on New Year's Eve, at our house."

"New Year's Eve. Yes."

"At seven?"

"Seven o'clock. Yes."

"Well . . . good-bye."

She put the earpiece back on its brass cradle and then sat down because she felt faint. She had meant to tell him about the skating party and to apologize for her abrupt departure. It was so hard to hear anything; but that was not the matter. The bad connection had almost caused him to run down the mountain to meet her, which would have been an awkward misunderstanding, a misunderstanding that pursued her on her walk home.

She tried to reason her way through: Did they not meet almost every day in that office? Why should it be different on this day? But it was no use. She felt the difference in her bones, acknowledged it in her conscience. If she had not spoken so quickly?

She slowed her pace to let what might have been play itself out. He would arrive, in fifteen minutes, not twenty, ruddy and winded by his exertion. She would explain and he would smile and ask: Have I come in vain? And she would flush and reply: Yes, it was my mistake, but I am glad to see you. She would wish she had something to give him, a plate of biscuits or that pretty box of chocolates Fowler had brought her, forgetting that she did not like marzipan. There would be a silence that she would attempt to fill, talking of this and that, and then she would be off, walking home as she was now, filled with the same uneasy excitement, the same dread of those lights ahead.

WHEN THE HOUSE PARTY was in full swing, it was Dr. Steinmetz rather than her husband or Lucy who accompanied Harriet on these necessary outings. She chose different routes for the sake of variety. One day they visited the Experimental Site, and while Steinmetz conferred briefly with Piccolomini and the Swedish engineer, Harriet gazed around her at the transformation of the old mill, remembering Horatio and her father in the old days. She could look forward to telling Toma that she had seen his great wheel in action.

On another day, he on her old pony, she on the new mare, they rode out on a road beneath the mountain. Fingers of the afternoon sun pierced the cloud cover, and when one grazed the mountain, making an irresistible brilliance on the snow and cliffs, she looked up, shading her eyes with her hand, and asked if he must keep her in suspense: she longed to know what he had intimated in his letter.

"Does it have something to do with the mountain? Or did I imagine that?"

"It does, and much more. It would be best if I draw it for you. That would make clear everything. Shall we go back?"

The house was quiet, except for Caroline's complaint somewhere away in the staff wing. The others had gone off in the car with Fowler at the wheel.

"Where shall we sit? We can call for some tea."

He chose the library for its desk. Harriet knelt to light the fire, and when she stood up, Steinmetz had helped himself to a glass of Fowler's whiskey.

"No tea for me, thank you. Will you take something?"

First she said no, then changed her mind, and Steinmetz poured sherry into a tumbler. They drank to each other's health, and she said how glad she was to have his friendship. They drank to friendship.

"Dear Doctor, we must get down to business soon, or I will not be able to follow a word you say."

Harriet pulled a chair close to the desk so she could watch the swift sure strokes of his pen.

"That must be the mountain, and the river, and . . . the railroad." She named things as he drew them, and sometimes he labeled them.

"How do you spell 'canal'? Do I have it right?"

"It doesn't matter. You haven't lost me yet. And what is that?"

"That is the tower on top of Lightning Knob, as it will be when Mr. Peacock has finished his work."

He began to draw lines that she could not make sense of, a dotted one encircling the Truscott pond, and broad, bold ones descending from Great Mountain.

"What are these?"

"Just a minute, my dear, and I am finished."

The swooping lines were added at last, and some odd boxes that resembled nothing in nature or on any map she had ever seen.

"There. I think that is enough."

"More than enough for me. I have lost the thread here."

"Do you remember, when I came here first, we spoke about the grid, the universal electrical interconnection, and about the part that Mr. Peacock's turbine might play in harnessing the water of the high mountains?"

"Yes."

"Good. And thanks partly to your help and fine hand Mr. Peacock has come far toward our goal on the Knob up there, an important work because there can be no great stride forward until the lightning has been tamed. It will undo our labor."

"I think I follow you."

"Excellent."

"And what you have drawn here is another stride?"

"Yes. When the war ends there will be a tremendous demand for electrical power, and the grid will expand to include the people living beyond the cities. Little towns like Beecher's Bridge will have streetlights. Farmers beyond the towns will have lamps to read by, to run washing machines, and tractors, and radios."

"Do you think so? I don't want a radio."

"Mrs. Truscott, believe me, everyone will want these things."

"Can they not have them?"

"They can have them, yes, but not until we fix the problems of supply and distribution."

"And that is what you have drawn? The victory over . . ."

"Supply and distribution, yes. What we see here is a piece of the puzzle."

"Why a puzzle?"

"There is this difficulty with making electricity: if we make it now we must use it now. There is no place to put it away for later."

"A battery?"

"Only for small amounts, very small, and it is expensive. The battery is not the answer."

Harriet studied Steinmetz's page, wondering what she was missing.

"Suppose you had electricity here in this house." Steinmetz dipped his pen and drew a house by the pond. "Where would the electricity come from?"

"Here." Harriet tapped the Experimental Site.

"And when would you want to use your electric lamp?"

"In the evening."

"And your neighbors?"

"They would want light in the evenings as well."

"Yes. Everyone would want the same thing at the same time. But the river, you see, is running all the time, all day and all night."

"As it should. Would you change that?"

"No, but that is a great inefficiency. In a city like New York, or Chicago, we have the streetcars that run on electricity during the day, and if we make the electricity cheaper at night, the factories will run their machinery at night, to save money. But in Beecher's Bridge you only want your light at night, perhaps very early in the morning. We cannot change that, and it is the same everywhere, in all the Beecher's Bridges of America. It is not efficient to run huge dynamos for only a few hours a day, and the grid depends on efficiency. That is its reason for being."

"This is a problem without a solution, then, if it is a problem."

"Perhaps not. My solution is here on the map. There is a battery here, a kind of battery that costs nothing. Can you find it?"

Harriet touched the tower on Lightning Knob. "Is it here?"

"No. It is not possible to store the lightning, or not yet. But that was a good guess."

"I do not see your battery, then."

"It is here." And Steinmetz put his crooked fingertip upon Dead Man's Lake. "The water in this lake will make lots of electricity any time we want it, if we let it run down the mountain. These heavy black lines are the tuyeres, pipes just like the ones that drive Mr. Peacock's wheel, but bigger, very big."

"But once you have caused that to happen, you would have to wait for the lake to fill again. A long time, I should think."

"No, we send it back up."

Now Steinmetz touched the Experimental Site and ran his finger along the line leading up to the Truscott pond. "You remember that our river flows all day and all night, yes? With the proper equipment—electrical pumps—the water in the lake could theoretically be sent back to the top of the mountain."

Harriet studied the map and chewed absently on her thumbnail. "You speak in theory, then? This has not been done before?"

"It has not, though others are thinking about it. My friend Oskar von Miller says he will do it in Austria, at the Walchensee, but it has not yet been accomplished, or even begun. This would be a great work, a model for others to follow."

"But this is Beecher's Bridge, not Chicago or Austria. It does not make sense to move a lake up and down a mountain just to light my lamp, and my neighbors'."

"Perhaps not, but you are forgetting the grid. You see by these lines, the curved ones, how we have connected Beecher's Bridge, and the Experimental Site, and our pump-storage project to the grid. The water from your lake may light the towns all around you, perhaps Hartford, even Boston. Think of that, Mrs. Truscott."

"Must it be done now? We do not even have electricity yet."

"I am an old man, and I think for the future. This will be the last great work of my life." He looked directly at her, into her eyes, and he seemed so expectant, so childlike, that she would say nothing to discourage him.

"You have spoken to my husband?"

"Of course. And to Mr. Coffin. And now to you."

"I don't know what to say. It seems so overwhelming. Of course I want to help, but . . ."

"Take your time, Mrs. Truscott, and we will speak of it again when you are ready. If you will excuse me, I think I will lie down until dinner is ready."

He bowed and left. Harriet stood over the map, looking at the pond and the dotted line around it that came very near the house. She looked out the window. Where was all that water to go?

As Harriet had wished, and very nearly prayed, New Year's Eve dawned fine, clear, and cold. It would be perfect weather for her skating party. At nine o'clock she sent Carpenter and the stable boy down to the pond with shovels and instructions to clear as much of it as possible and lay a bonfire on the ice, at a safe distance from the boathouse and dock.

Only Toma had been invited for dinner. The other guests would arrive at ten, and their way down to the lake would be lighted by the bonfire. Would there be any way, she asked Lucy, that Caroline could be put to bed early and woken at ten? Lucy objected: it was difficult enough to keep Caroline on her regular schedule. But her cousin's appeal was so emphatic—did Lucy not remember those skating parties of her early childhood? And who knew when the opportunity would come again?—that Lucy relented.

Harriet had her hands full for the rest of the day: she gave instructions in the kitchen on how the goose was to be trimmed and what was to be served just before midnight in the boathouse: cold ham, mince tarts, mulled wine, cider, and of course champagne. Then she spent an hour with her father playing checkers. After lunch—she had barely touched the food on her plate—she went back to the kitchen to make the floating island. The cook would have done it, but it never came out right unless Harriet did it herself.

At four she went down to the boathouse carrying fur lap robes and fresh candles for the hurricane lamps. The mice had made a mess of the place; she tied her handkerchief over her face and set to work with the dustpan. Evening fell quickly. When she stepped out onto the deck the pinch in her nostrils told her that the temperature had dropped below eight degrees, and there was the moon, just past full, and the evening star reflected on the ice where the snow had been cleared away. She was tired now, and famished, but she had done everything that had to be done. She looked forward to soaking in her bath.

At a few minutes before seven, she heard a stamping of feet outside, followed by the sound of the latch. Her mouth was full of pins, her hair half up and half down.

"Fowler, I think that must be Toma. Will you go down?"

"In a minute, my dear. This tie will not cooperate."

Harriet went to the banister of the stairwell and called down, "Toma, did you bring skates?"

"What did you say?" He climbed the stairs tentatively and stopped on the landing, facing her.

"There," she said, placing the last pin. "How does my hair look?"

"I am no judge of these things, but I like best the part that has come away."

She sighed and began to pull the pins. "You should know better than to come early to a party. It is your fault. Now, will you go up to the attic and find yourself a pair of skates? Take one of the candles there with you. I think they are hanging on the far wall, over to the left."

He was staring at her now, and she made an effort not to meet his gaze. "The skates, Toma." Just as she spoke, a door opened behind her and she heard the rustle of taffeta. "Lucy, you do remember Toma? Mr. Peacock? He is just going to find some skates. I forgot entirely to tell him."

"Mrs . . . ?"

"Mrs. Finsterwald. How nice to see you." Lucy's voice conveyed a different message, and she did not stop to make conversation.

THE ATTIC WAS A cavernous space made larger by the candle: beams and rafters above him shifted in its guttering light. He sat on a steamer trunk, blind to his surroundings. The line of her shoulder and neck interrupted by the clef of stray hair; the brilliance of the glancing eyes he could not hold; the thrilling cascade when she pulled the pins. For that one moment he had forgotten that they were not alone in the house.

The skates were where she said they would be, but there were many other items hanging or standing against the wall. Skis, various racquets, some curiously slender mallets, snowshoes, an artillery shell containing canes and walking sticks, and a collection of slender metal cylinders that made no more sense to him than the mallets. Fishing rods, as it turned out.

The skates were hanging from a rack of antlers. He chose a pair that seemed about the right size. When he turned around he saw his candle reflected in a row of tall glass-fronted cases. The first on his right contained dozens of eggs varying in size, color, and pattern. Then a broad cabinet of mounted specimens, from birds of prey down to a hummingbird in flight. Northeast of the Lammergeyer, *Gypaetus barbatus*, taken in Tanganyika, was a conspicuous void. The label here told him that the Roseate Spoonbill, *Ajaia ajaja*, was on permanent loan to the American Museum of Natural History. The last case held nests, from the shaggy and chaotic to the silk purse. Beyond lay a grouping of figurines in a dark polished wood, little people with exaggerated features, their limbs bent to serve as bookends and candlesticks. Along the end wall was another line of trunks. He lifted a lid and turned away from the rising fumes of naphtha. Under the layer of tissue paper a curved and sheathed sword lay upon folded silk, a garment of some sort with a brilliant blue pattern on yellow ground.

Something about this exotic clutter seemed familiar, although in his own home there had been nothing to spare and little to store: all his clothes and belongings hung on three pegs in his loft above the animals. Harwell, he thought, Harwell's home in England would look like this.

Still thinking about Harwell's collections, he opened a door—he believed it to be the same door—and found himself in a strange corridor with a narrow stairway to his right and a bedroom at the end.

"Who is that?"

Olivia came to the doorway before he could retreat. She had a hairbrush in her hand and she looked tired; her face was without expression. For months he had dreaded this moment, and now he didn't know what to say. He stood there like a stump, his mind racing, until she should speak again.

"All the places I looked for you . . . I never thought to see you in this house. But here you are. Did you get my letter?"

"Yes, thank you. All those drawings . . ."

"I didn't know what to write."

"It was the only Christmas card I had."

"Will you come in? This is where I stay now."

"No, I must go down."

"You have come for her, then." She closed the door.

THE ROAST GOOSE WAS magnificent, her floating island all it should be, but Harriet thought that the conversation was halting and measured. They rose from the table at nine-thirty, before the other guests arrived. Left to his own devices, Fowler would find an excuse not to go down to the lake. Before he could settle into a chair, she handed him a basket with a flask of brandy, silver tumblers, and his cigar case. Would he speak to Carpenter about lighting the bonfire and the candles in the boathouse? And would he see that their guests got down safely? She heard the bells of the first carriages as she went up the stairs.

It took Lucy some time to change clothes and for the nurse to wake Caroline and dress her. Harriet put on a pair of woolen drawers under her skirt and then her boots. She shook out the hooded cape of heavy black cassimere that had belonged to her mother; the perfume of camphor bark reminded her, as always, of her loss. These were solemn moments of sadness and connection, to her mother, to her father as he used to be, to herself as she used to be. She sometimes felt like a stranger in this house, a stranger or even an impostor. But tonight, wrapped in the cape and gazing down the lawn to the fire on the lake, she felt very much herself and perfectly at home.

There were many people to welcome, and some of them Harriet greeted twice: it was hard to tell one person from another when they faced away from the leaping flames. The moon was gone. A low cloud cover had come in during dinner and now returned the light of the fire in a penumbra of rose that softened the dark shore. She knew this sign; it would snow before midnight.

She was a strong, sure skater and would have given much to be off on her own. Her guests were clustered on the cleared ice and made stately circuits of the fire. But it was the parchment of perfect snow beyond that beckoned to her; there was not even an inch of accumulation, just enough to deaden the sound of the skates: it would be like flying. Perhaps there would be time for that later.

Two sounds, unexpected, occurred almost simultaneously. The first was the music of a waltz—familiar, though she could not put a name to it—played on a harmonica. Who could have brought such a thing? At first she was anxious, because Fowler was bound to disapprove. And then she thought: how perfect. She hoped it would not stop. The other sound was Caroline's unhappiness. Lucy had left her on the dock to skate arm in arm with Cecil, and for once Dr. Steinmetz's magic had failed.

"Caroline, you mustn't spoil the party with crying. What is it?"

Caroline pointed imperiously at the fire, or the figures circling the fire, and managed the word "Mama" in a strangled sob.

"Shall we find her then? Will you skate with me?" She set off with Caroline in her arms, and then, because the child was well fed, on her shoulders. Wherever Caroline pointed Harriet would go, and when they found Lucy and Cecil, Caroline crowed from her perch.

Caroline's preference was for faster and farther, and she did not want to be put down on the dock.

"Fowler, will you go into the boathouse and find me one of those hide-covered chairs? The ones with the round bottoms and no legs. And a lap robe." When the chair was on the ice she spoke to Dr. Steinmetz. "Come with me and you shall have your skating. Put Caroline in your lap, if you would."

Off they went, and the circled slats at the base of this throne clattered over the ice. Harriet's position was at Steinmetz's right shoulder as they circled the fire with the other skaters, and she had to push in as well as forward to keep the chair from escaping its orbit like a rogue planet. After ten minutes or so, with Steinmetz humming the waltz to her, Caroline slumped back into the lap robe and slept.

"It seems the expedition was a success," he whispered. "You may slow down, please. I do not need so much stimulation. There, that's better. Now tell me, have you had a chance to reflect on our conversation?"

"Heavens, Doctor, I have been so busy. I am still uncertain."

"Then I suggest that tomorrow you and I make a reconnaissance of the frozen lake on the mountain."

After supper, with just a few minutes left until the stroke of midnight, Harriet found Toma sitting on the edge of the dock. Guests clattered past on their skates, some with champagne glasses in hand, heading back to the ice and the bonfire.

"I have hardly caught a glimpse of you. Have you skated at all?"

"I tried. I went off to the side where no one could see me. I have not progressed. It seems impossible to me, not natural."

"Oh, Toma, you are as much a baby as Caroline. I'll show you how as soon as we've seen the New Year in."

She felt the first snowflakes against her cheek. The fire had subsided to embers, a richer light. "Look at that." She turned to face him. "Isn't it extraordinarily beautiful?" His face seemed different in that ruddy glow, perhaps older.

"Go now, it is almost time."

Fowler Truscott, with Dr. Steinmetz steadying his elbow, made his way out onto the ice with champagne in one hand and extra glasses in the other. He bade his guests link arms and stand in a circle around the fire to listen for the bell, which followed almost immediately but was so muted by the falling snow that many were surprised when their host launched the first note of "Auld Lang Syne."

The snow was falling faster now, and Harriet worried that she would miss her chance at the lake beyond the cleared ice. She skated up behind Toma, still standing at his place in the dissolving circle, and without a word took his arm in hers under the weightless warmth of the cape.

Toma was an apt pupil, and because her arm was always there he was soon able to match the rhythm of her glide. Around the fire they went; halfway through the third circuit she released his arm and made a turn, facing him now but floating away with her hand stretched out to him.

"That wasn't so hard, was it?"

"Can we stop before I fall down?"

"No turning back now. I will show you the rest of the pond."

Voices and sounds were lost as abruptly as if a door had shut behind them; they glided along the shore guided by Harriet's memory and the dim fluorescence of falling snow, their blades making only a whisper against the intermittent musical percussions of the expanding ice.

Beneath the cape she held his arm to her waist. The grip of his hand on her forearm was fierce. How could she not have remembered that day in Pompeii, when she had stumbled on a piece of masonry and would have fallen but for the shock of his arm, strong and so warm against hers, and his hand. That innocence was years ago and so far away that it might be a memory of two different people. She sighed.

"Are you tired?"

"No, it is nothing. But if you hold my arm so you will leave me with a bruise. Let me show you how a man and a woman skate en paire." She drew his right arm around her waist and put her hand over his, at the same time reaching out to the other hand. "Do you feel safe?"

"More than before."

"Good. And now . . ." She eased his hand away from her waist and pushed hard off her right skate. For a moment she floated in front of him, her arms spread like a black swan rising from the water, then she settled back against his left arm.

"It is like . . ."

"A dance?"

"Yes."

Again she pushed ahead, now turning under his arm, and they were face-to-face with their hands crossed.

"Now what?"

"Either I turn back under your arm, or you turn under mine, and we shall be skating backward together."

"I don't know how to turn. Or stop."

"We'll save that for the next lesson."

"When will that be?"

"Every night at midnight we shall meet here," she said, laughing, "and in no time at all . . ."

"And when the ice melts?"

"Toma, I'm sorry, I was only being silly."

"There is only tonight, then."

She said nothing, but his remark set her free. When they had skated away from the fire they entered a kind of limbo, another world, and now their isolation was perfect because time too had been stripped away. No past, no future, only this. Only tonight.

They had reached the eastern end of the pond, where a dark wall plunged down through the ice. He stopped skating, thinking they must turn around, but she towed him on until they were within arm's reach of the wall. Then the rock was on either side and they skated through this gateway into an extension of the pond no larger than a ballroom.

"What magic is this? Do the rocks open at your command?"

"I call it the Pillars of Hercules; the water is very deep there, but shallow here. Look at all the cattails, and in a minute I'll show you the beaver lodge."

"Where?"

"I'll show you."

They skated slowly now, knowing that when they had explored this last reach of ice they would have to turn back.

"Is there no further wonder to see?" She squeezed the hand at her waist by way of reply and then he fell without a word of warning, tumbling sideways and pulling her down on top of him. In the sound of the shattering reeds she heard his head hit the ice.

His body had cushioned her fall. Only her knee had grazed the ice, but Toma did not move. "Toma . . . Toma?" She found his hat in the reeds. Should she try to put it back on? Would she hurt him by lifting his head? She did not know. She settled for sliding her fingers into his collar beneath the scarf to find his pulse. Her hand was unsteady: there might be a pulse, or not. Now she bent over him, her cheek to his lips. Was he breathing? He was.

It was the cold that she feared if she had to leave him here. Her fingers fumbled with the silver clasp of her cape. It snapped in her hands and a piece flew off into the reeds. She made a cocoon around his head and shoulders, trying not to move him, put her cheek against his and spoke his name in an urgent, strangled whisper.

He made a groan that curled up at the end into a question.

"Don't move, Toma, don't move until I can tell how you are hurt. Do you hear me?" In her happiness she wept, and when she felt his hands on her shoulders she cried harder.

"What is wrong?" His words were distinct and deliberate.

"You fell, Toma, you fell and hurt yourself."

"And you are hurt also?"

"No, I am glad, just . . . so glad."

He moved as if he would get up. "Wait," she said, "wait." His arms came up around her and he held her.

"There." She sat up and wiped her face on her sleeve. "Where does it hurt?"

"My head and my ankle."

"Your skate must have stuck in a crack. Can you lift your head?" She slipped his fur hat back on and took the cape around her shoulders. "Do you think you can stand? Take my arms."

Toma's ankle was twisted, not broken. They made their way back to the fire slowly, on three skates.

"We are alone. Did no one miss us?" His question caused Harriet to think, for the first time since they had left the fire, of anyone but Toma.

"If you can find my shoes I'll be off."

"You can't go anywhere. What if you fall again? There will be a bed for you in the house, somewhere." He looked up at the house. Only the lighted windows could be seen through the snow. the dining room on the ground floor; then the landing on the staircase; above it to the right Dr. Steinmetz's bedroom. And higher still the small window that they both knew to be Olivia's.

"No. I will stay here in the cabin."

"Of course," Harriet replied quickly, wondering why she hadn't the wit to think of that in the first place.

There was still a fire in the hearth. Harriet pulled the long wicker chaise near and put the lap robes on it. Toma hobbled across the room with a bottle of champagne in one hand and two ham sandwiches in the other. He held them out to her.

"I can't. I must go."

"Of course. You must go back. But you won't get far on those." He pointed at her skates.

"It doesn't matter. My hands are too cold anyway. My gloves . . . I don't know where they went."

"Put your hands under your arms and sit down." He knelt before her. "What do you call these things?"

"Eyelets."

"I have never seen so many in one place." He had one skate off now and rubbed her foot before putting on her boot.

"My hands are better now. I can do the other."

"Warm enough to hold a sandwich? Go on."

She ate part of the sandwich and made him eat the rest. She put her hands gently on his head and felt for the bump. "Poor you."

She stood up when he was finished, and he stood as well, a bit nearer than he ought to be. She pushed him down onto the chaise. "You must not stand on that ankle, Toma, and I must go. Really I must."

"Thank you for my lesson. For everything."

How should such an evening end? She put her fingertips to his cheek, to the spot where her own had been, and wished him good night.

"HARRIET, IS THAT YOU? Thank God." Lucy spoke from the stairwell. Where was everybody?

"The others, Lucy, have they gone home?"

"Home? Well, I suppose so. They aren't here."

"And Fowler?"

"Fowler had to be helped up to bed by Cecil and Dr. Steinmetz. He'd had too much to drink. I came up just after midnight with Caroline, so I don't know any more than you do. Cecil was surprised not to find you with me, then he thought you must be in the bath. What the others thought I have no idea, but they left. Somehow I knew you were not in the house. And here you are." The tone of her voice demanded an explanation.

"I was showing Toma how to skate. I didn't think everyone would leave so soon."

"Yes. Cecil said that the last he saw of you, you were skating off into the night. I don't know how you could do it."

"Do what, for Heaven's sake?"

"Look at yourself, Harriet. Just look."

Harriet looked: at the broken clasp hanging by a thread; at the tawny down of cattail that clung everywhere to her black clothes; and, out of the corner of her eye, at a bit of reed that had stuck in her hair.

"He fell."

"It doesn't matter what he did. A woman must look after her own reputation. No one else will if she does not."

"No. No, I can see that quite clearly, thank you. But what I cannot understand is how you could speak to me this way, as if I had . . ."

"That's exactly my point. As if you had . . . finish the sentence any way you like."

"Lucy," said Harriet, seized by a chill that altered her voice, "how can you say these things? What do you think happened? We were skating and he fell, that's all. I swear to you."

"It doesn't matter what I think, or even what you did or did not do. If Cecil noticed, then I tell you it must have been pretty obvious. I don't think he really believed you were in the bath at all."

"I have told you the truth, Lucy. You cannot believe otherwise."

"Can I not? You have been so preoccupied this whole week. I knew something was different, and I said so to Cecil. I just didn't know what."

"I will not be spoken to this way, Lucy, or it is the end of a long and dear friendship. Your imagination disgusts me. I am going upstairs now, up to Fowler, and I shall pray that we both forget what we said."

EIGHTEEN

The desk in the office of the now defunct Bigelow Iron Company was almost as bare as when Amos Bigelow used it for his weekly calculation of the sun's meridian. And although the mirrors had not been cleaned or adjusted since the day of Horatio Washington's fatal accident, the one outside the window still caught the sun, casting its image on the ceiling, high or low according to the season, and for a few days a year around that sad anniversary the system worked as well as it ever had.

Toma was in a mood to be distracted. A chunk of rough rock sat in the middle of the desk, its color a clouded red. In direct sunlight it would bloom, revealing myriad faceted crystals of garnetite, but its significance was invisible, revealed only by the proximity of iron filings or a compass. Dr. Steinmetz had determined that the red rock contained the highest percentage of magnetite, and that Toma should pursue it at all costs in the excavations under Lightning Knob.

Excavating a tunnel in a straight line was a relatively simple proposition, though not without danger. But the new instructions were to follow the veins of this blood-hued rock, being careful not to disturb it, so that the linked lengths of iron could be set into it. By Steinmetz's calculation, following the magnetite would lead to a dramatic increase in the aerial's ability to attract lightning to the array of experimental protective devices.

The phone call from Stefan had come yesterday afternoon: an urgent delivery from Schenectady and new instructions. The equipment on hand—some of it newly purchased—was inadequate to the job ahead, or unnecessary. Who knew where the red rock would lead them, or how much of it there was? The task was to follow a maze through solid rock, and explosives, even heavy machinery, were out of the question. At best they might use pneumatic drills, but much of the job was bound to be handwork. Steinmetz's calculations specified three thousand feet of iron—the roots of his aerial—to be laid into the red rock and fixed by bolts. The timetable for completion was inflexible: the site must be ready by the first of June at the latest to coincide with the season of peak electrical activity. And in the meantime, starting now, or half an hour ago, there were endless costings and requisitions to sort out. Where was Harriet when he needed her?

It had been a quiet few days following the turn of the New Year. Toma knew that he could not expect to see Harriet in the office until her houseguests had departed, and the injury to his ankle confined him to Lightning Knob once he had made it up the mountain. On January 2, Dr. Steinmetz had come to inspect the excavation, as had been agreed at dinner on New Year's Eve. He seemed even more animated than usual, expressing febrile interest in every detail of the operation, running his hands over the blank walls at the bottom of the shaft where the tunnels would soon be started. Was he even then hatching the idea about the red rock? Later that day, on his way to chop ice in the stream, Toma had seen footprints in the snow on a path leading up the mountain. One set must belong to Steinmetz: he had seen the marks of that diminutive boot not three hours earlier. And whose could the other set be if not Harriet's?

It had been a week now. The fact that they had missed each other in the office several days running seemed an unlikely coincidence. He thought about the night on the ice. Could he have done differently? Had he offended her? But there was no offense: there was only knowledge. He had been a witness to something—his own feelings were no transgression—and that must be the reason for this absence that felt so like a sentence.

On the pretext of deliberating upon the instructions from Schenectady, he waited for her, drumming his fingers on the table, glaring at the rock as if he might vaporize it, startling at the sound of the noon siren, and all the while trying to fuse the sweet, dangerous knowledge of what had happened on the lake to the innocence of their afternoons in this office.

He was stoking the stove when the door opened, and it was clear at a glance that her surprise in finding him there had little pleasure in it. He stood up, dusted off his hands on his trousers, and nodded at her. Her expression softened at this display of awkward deference.

"I did not expect to see you, Toma. We must talk."

"Will you sit down?"

"No. Yes, of course I will. I don't know what's wrong with me. The last few days have been so strange. Everyone is gone and the house is a tomb."

They sat at the desk in their familiar positions, so that she was facing the wall and windows at his back rather than the center of the desk. He waited for her to speak; and when she did not, he drew her attention to the red rock and related what he had heard from Steinmetz.

She seemed to be listening, but made a tangential comment. "I wish he were here, Dr. Steinmetz. He would tell me what to do." Now it was Toma's turn to say nothing.

"Toma, I have been thinking that I must go away."

"Where?"

"Washington. I must be with Fowler, at least for a while."

"Is he unwell?"

"No, it's not that."

"Then what?"

"He is my husband, for Heaven's sake. Please don't make me explain all this."

"If you have to go. Stefan will help me here. We'll manage. But will you come back?"

"Of course I shall come back. This is my home, not Washington. My father . . ."

"But you are leaving."

"I have been thinking about this, and my mind is made up. I must do it, and that's all there is to be said." She spoke to her folded hands and would not look at him, and so he was free, as he seldom had been, to study her face in this different mood. He had never before seen the crease that now interrupted the straight dark line of her brow.

"I came to see you in Washington. Do you remember?"

"I certainly do." She smiled at the memory. "You had just come from the patent office, and you were radiant. You told me you would be rich."

"Did I? What a foolish thing to say."

"I didn't think so. I was proud of you."

"I remember that you sang, and that we sat in the front room as the sun went down."

"It will be different now, in winter, and without Papa."

"May I write to you?"

"About the lightning project?"

"Of course."

"There can't be any harm in that. It will be good to have news from home."

"Can you spare a few minutes to talk about this?"

He took the rock in his hand and the folded paper beneath it skidded a few inches, catching her eye. She opened it, thinking it was a note from Steinmetz.

"Twenty thousand dollars, Toma?"

"I keep forgetting to put it in the bank. I must do that today."

"But what is it for? This is a great deal of money." He was surprised at her reaction. The check had ceased to interest him.

"It is for the wheel. They have made a licensing arrangement."

Her eyes filled with tears, which she made no attempt to hide. She started to speak and still the tears came. She drew an uneven breath, covering her eyes, an uncharacteristic gesture that drew his attention to the size of her hand, nearly as large as his own, and its pale, elegant articulation. He asked, gently, what was wrong.

"Oh, Toma, think what this money would once have meant."

HARRIET'S IDEA OF VISITING Washington had been prompted by Lucy's letter, still propped against the silver correspondence rack on her desk when she sat down with her tea at the end of the afternoon.

Harriet had opened the letter thinking that it was late for a thank-you note, and there were too many pages. But after the pleasantries and a paragraph of doubtful sincerity apologizing for her sharp tone on

New Year's Eve, Lucy launched into her theme: the perilous state of Harriet's marriage and the steps that must be taken.

Harriet had gone to the office earlier than usual to get away from her desk and the letter she was trying to draft, and her conversation with Toma was a kind of rehearsal for what she must now write. It had all sounded reasonable enough when she spoke the words—more so than when laid out on these blue pages—and there had been an element of confession in those few minutes. How else could she ever speak to Toma about what had happened? And how could she be silent? It had been so much easier to talk to Lucy about what had *not* happened. She had done nothing wrong: there was the truth that would guide her.

She put down the pen and picked up Lucy's letter again. Lucy was more subtle on paper than she had been in person, and her observations on the difficulty of marriage were candid and therefore persuasive. She did not reproach Harriet; in fact, as Harriet realized on this new reading, she did not even make reference to New Year's Eve beyond her apology. But she did take as a given the physical coldness of the Truscott marriage, which seemed to her remarkable in light of Fowler's long absence. Cecil, she wrote, was sometimes away for a few days, shooting or playing golf, but when he returned to her bed . . . Harriet thought the point could be made, and understood, without resorting to that word.

Had the signs been so obvious? It must have been something she'd said . . . or done . . . or not done? How could Lucy know these things? How could she put her finger on the thoughts that had occurred to Harriet during her long vigil in Fowler's bed on Christmas night?

"Dear Fowler," she began again and could get no further. This was ridiculous: her first attempt had been a page and a half long; the second effort failed after two paragraphs. And now, apparently, she had nothing at all to say. Every reason she thought of sounded forced or false and the very act of writing them down seemed an admission of the failure of her marriage. What had she not done that she ought to have done? And what would she not have done? Well, the thing she could not do, as evidenced by the balls of blue paper in the wastebasket, was to announce to her husband—in either mode of confession or seduction—the intention of her visit, which Lucy rendered in the appalling phrase of seizing the bull by his horn. "It doesn't matter," wrote Lucy, "whose fault it is. But it matters very much that you take this blame on yourself, for that is the only way forward."

Perhaps it was the idea of taking the blame on herself—or even the phrase—that made it difficult to put the right words on the paper, for she was inevitably reminded of Lucy's harsh judgement the night of the skating party. That was where she drew the line. She had little pride left when it came to her marriage; every trip to his bed was a humiliation of sorts. But she would not admit that she had done anything wrong.

In the end it was a morbid reflection on what might happen to her father in her absence that saved Harriet from paralysis. She was thinking about what would be good for Amos Bigelow when she remembered the day she had promised him a surprise. She had brought him the ledger, but he had hoped it would be a child. She could do anything, even find a way to write this wretched letter, if it served the end of his happiness.

. . . And in the middle of this revelry, this Winterfest, *began the snow, as I had anticipated. I was standing on the dock with Senator Truscott, but still exhilarated after riding in the chair over the frozen depths, perhaps even a little giddy from that experience, and the sensation of the very fine snow dust on my face as I gazed blind into the heavens was the trigger to a kind of mystical vision or a trance. I do not know if that is the right word, but for several minutes I was unaware of my surroundings, because suddenly Truscott was rattling the champagne flutes in my ear and telling me it was almost midnight.*

My dear Mr. Coffin, I hope you will not be alarmed by this disclosure, but it touches on the work we have begun and on that which grows like a submarine crystal in my imagination.

In my vision I was witness to an electrical disturbance on the promontory where the tower is being built and the shaft sunk, but rather than the heat of summer, it was somehow that same night, New Year's Eve. It must have been the sensation of those featherlike flakes that set me thinking along those lines, for I had just read Göchel's discourse on the contrasting atmospheric discharge associated with the type of snow—negative for tiny flakes, positive for the largest ones—and I imagined the possibility of provoking electrical disturbances in the dead of winter, given the right circumstances and the right equipment. This premonition was confirmed by my visit to the tunnel shaft. Years of working with circuits have made me sensitive to imperceptible electrical impulses, and I recognized something when I laid my hands on the red rock 45 meters down in that shaft. It was the electromagnetic potentiality of the mountain that I sensed, as perhaps the nascent statue in the block of stone communicates itself to the artist.

I have this day sent off to Beecher's Bridge the Exner gold-leaf electroscope to measure the potential gradient above Lightning Knob. I believe we shall soon have the beginnings of a scientific explanation of the unusually high incidence of electrical activity in Beecher's Bridge.

And I have another surprise to share with you. On New Year's Day I made an expedition with Mrs. Truscott up the mountain to the high lake that we tried to find last summer without success. There was some difficulty in the ascent, but the snowfall was not great, and once we were up on the plateau we made good progress; at last we broke through the defenses of the surrounding alders onto the ice of Dead Man's Lake, which is roughly 500 meters wide and perhaps twice as long. From the thick growth around the shore one would conclude that this is a mere runoff or catchment pond of the sort commonly found in the North West Corner; but local legend describes it as dangerously deep, as the name might indicate.

With the hatchet, and Mrs. Truscott's assistance, I chopped two holes in the ice, 200 paces apart, and measured a depth of 48 meters by the plumb line in one, and 35 in the other. Rough calculations, of course, but there is certainly enough water here for the pump-storage facility.

The outing was an opportunity to speak again to Mrs. Truscott about the work that we envision, and I think I am making progress in spite of her ambivalence. She proposed the idea that man should be the steward of God's creation, and as gently as I could I pointed out that since the existence of God was in no way provable, her "idea" amounted to a sentimentality, quite powerful, but inadmissible in a scientific discussion. The admirable Mrs. Truscott, as deft in argument as she is handy with an axe, asked if I would mock her religion. Not unless you mock my agnosticism, I replied. It was a friendly and spirited exchange, and I made the point that in realizing the potential of nature, man serves both God and Science.

She took pleasure in being the one to break through the ice in the first hole and take the sounding. It was a day of luminous clarity, and with her face

*glowing from physical exertion and the stimulation of our exchange she seemed a
figure of legend. There was such a sense of satisfaction and connection in this
moment, and it occurred to me that had it been my last instant of existence, I
should have felt my life somehow complete.*

*My revised estimates on the cost of the pump-storage experiment will follow
within the week, and if it is at all persuasive to your colleagues, you may tell them
that I stand ready to contribute the last pennies in my bank account to the effort.
What am I compared to the mountain, or to this work?*

My kindest regards, etc.
Steinmetz

*p.s. It has been brought to my attention by Professor Steffens that between 1850
and 1910 the number of houses struck by lightning per year per million has
tripled. It is tempting to read a superstitious significance into this interesting
statistical aberration.*

AFTER HARRIET TRUSCOTT's departure isolation settled on the house
like a blanket of snow. For Olivia Toussaint it was a time not of peace
but of restless vigilance over things seen and unseen.

Mrs. Evans was recuperating slowly and had taken her first tentative steps only a few days before Harriet left. There were ways in which
she could be useful, even as a semi-invalid; she was the focus of Amos
Bigelow's mannerly instincts, those abiding pillars of his former self.
The cook would send up two trays at mealtimes, and in Harriet's absence the old man would keep Mrs. Evans company. He made an effort
to be tidy and helpful; if a scrap of food fell from his plate he would get
down on his hands and knees to retrieve it.

Another sight to warm the sentimental heart was the ritual
progress every afternoon from one end of the second floor to the
other. At first their goal was the door closing off the staff side of the
house. After a week Mrs. Evans felt strong enough to venture out into
the main bedroom corridor, and they would rest for a moment at the
railing of the stairwell, which was lit by the hoar-frosted dormers
above. Soon, she said, she would be ready for the stairs; she didn't intend to spend the rest of her life as a caged bird on the second floor.

One day followed the next. There were no visitors, and when the
real blanket of snow arrived early in February, they were cut off for

nearly a week, without the ordinary distractions of the mail and the milk. On the third day, the stable boy hitched Harriet's mare to the old sleigh to fetch lamp oil, milk, potatoes, cabbages, and sides of bacon from the store; but because the snowfall had smoothed the features of Beecher's Bridge, he missed the crook in the road not two hundred yards from the gate and overturned in a ditch. The mare was cut free of the harness and the house ran on short rations of eggs and black tea and a few moldy tubers from the root cellar until Barzel Treat's oxen and sledge made the road passable.

Now more than ever Olivia hated the snow, the inescapable and blinding whiteness without, the rank-smelling gloom within. She slept very lightly, with the door open and one ear cocked for sounds from Amos Bigelow's room. And as she lay in bed, aware that sooner or later she would have to go down and deal with the old man, she had a new worry: that the snow would come back in the night and swallow the house. As much as anything else she resented the way the old man could drop off to sleep like a baby, and like a baby awake at the most inconvenient time.

She did not have Harriet's affectionate patience with him, and unlike Mrs. Evans she commanded no respect other than fear. Every day the battle began anew, and the only thing that gave him peace was clanging one piece of metal against another, until she thought she would go mad. Anything, anything to stop that noise, but there was no reasoning with him, and he hid from her in the labyrinth of his deafness.

There was one thing that worked, as she found by accident. She had a pad of paper on her lap and a pencil in her hand. She was writing out a list of items that Carpenter would fetch from the store, but she knew she had forgotten one thing, and with that racket in her ears she could not think of it. The pencil, with a will of its own, wandered to the margin of the page, random lines there merging to the figure of a seated woman, facing away but turning back, as if to answer a question. Amos Bigelow rose from his bench and clutched the front of his trousers, by which she knew that he had to go to the water closet, had already done it by the smell of him. He was curious about her drawing

"Who?"

She looked up at him, then at the figure she had drawn. It could be anyone, she thought.

"It's her, isn't it?"

She drew the figure again from another angle, and while the features were still indistinct, the carriage and the tilt of the head were surely Harriet's. The old man was pleased with this bit of magic, and she gave him the page.

The trick never failed. If he caught the flash of paper out of the corner of his eye he could not ignore it, and would soon lay down his hammer. She drew from memory, sometimes Mrs. Evans, occasionally the cook or the old man himself; but his favorite subject, of course, was his daughter. One day, thinking of those crumpled letters in Harriet's wastebasket, she added an infant to the composition; Amos Bigelow responded with inarticulate approval. For the rest of the afternoon he did not touch his hammer, and made a dumb show of his concern for the sleeping baby.

There was one drawing in the middle of the pad that she never showed him, and if the Madonna exerted a soothing power over Amos Bigelow's unquiet heart, so too was Olivia sustained by an image of love.

She drew him as he had been on her bed in the silk mill when she took away the sheet and gazed at his body in a tumult of feeling, terrified desire twinned with its dark other, hope. They were born in that moment and had died together, a cruelty as stark and incomprehensible as anything Horatio had done to her.

But in her drawing none of that had yet happened. The figure there was pale and perfect, except for the wound in the foot, and at any moment he might open his eyes. When she ran her fingers over the drawing, blurring it, softening it, she felt the shock of his whiteness under her hand.

She was not surprised when Toma appeared at the kitchen door a few days after the great snowfall. He had received a telegram from Washington, he said: Mrs. Truscott was anxious about the household, particularly her father. Come in, she said, sit down. It was the first time they had sat together in five months. Did he want to take off his coat? Have a cup of tea? He did not. It has been so long, she said, and when he had no other answer than a constrained smile, she got down on her knees to unlace his boot.

"Don't," he said.

"It still hurts you in the cold weather." He nodded. She peeled off the thick, rank stocking and took his foot in her lap to massage the scar. She did not hear the cook coming until she was there towering over them, saying to him: Mister, you keep your shoes on in my kitchen; and to her: You've your own room for this sort of thing. She moved slowly in the direction of the ticking coal stove, not deigning to look at them, but permitting herself a stage whisper: The nerve of them. And in broad daylight too.

THERE WAS NO TELLING what to expect other than what she hoped, no timetable other than her urgency. The thought that he must come in the night took possession of her, and night became her day. This was also true of Amos Bigelow: he had the idea in his head that his daughter and the baby were being hidden from him somewhere in the house, and he watched for the moments when his keeper should be asleep. One day the cook called them to lunch, got no answer, and found them both dozing in their chairs.

Harriet's letter arrived on a bright morning in early March, when it was possible to hope that spring might prevail against winter. It was ten days since the spiles had been set into the maples, the thirteen colonial patriarchs along the road and the numerous smaller ones in the sugar bush under the mountain cleared by the senator's father. Every morning Carpenter and the stable boy drove the sleigh, fitted with a galvanized tank, out over the packed snow to collect the sap, and in the late afternoon they would fire the boiler in the shed behind the stable, working far into the night if the day's run had been strong. Olivia's drowsing vigils were bathed in wood smoke and maple steam, and sometimes she was jolted awake by a burst of light suggesting his presence; but it was not that glory, just the flaming heart of the boiler reflected off the snow when the doors were opened to receive the quartered lengths of oak and beech.

She was in the conservatory that morning, dazzled by the strong sun. Amos Bigelow was upstairs with Mrs. Evans. She had come in to arrange the pots that Carpenter had brought from the pit house, the gross thrusting amaryllis and the slender green fingers of narcissus that would rise too quickly to the sun unless she gave them shade. When that was done she went to the piano, as she did whenever she came in here, and found the chords of Harriet Truscott's hymns.

Lily approached nervously with the letter in hand. Lily was terrified of her, she knew, and knew also that Lily disapproved of her sitting down to Mrs. Truscott's piano. But what did Lily matter, much less what she thought?

At what point did she know what she would do? Certainly she knew what was in the letter, had been expecting it ever since the big snow. Only the urgency of Harriet's mission to Washington could keep her apart from her father for so long. She belonged in Washington, not here. Again she played the hymn, her favorite: "Abide with Me."

She gave instructions to Lily and the cook: it was, after all, a homecoming and there must be some sort of ceremony. One of those pots of narcissus was going to bloom in the next couple of days anyway; and perhaps this would be the occasion for Mrs. Evans to take her dinner downstairs, and the old man too. The letter had set these things in motion, along with airing the rooms, rinsing the mirrors with vinegar, polishing the silver brushes, setting a new pomander in the linen press. Leaving these things undone would not keep her away. Had she written to him? It was not until that afternoon when she was closeted with Amos Bigelow and his demented hammering that she realized the letter had made no mention of how long Harriet Truscott would stay in Beecher's Bridge.

She went to bed exhausted—there was nothing new in that—and with a headache too, but she dug her nails into her palms to stay awake, for the time was short and he must come tonight. The occasional illuminations from the sap house had, tonight, a sinister promise: flashes of hellfire, milestones of despair.

She slept in spite of herself, and woke to the unmistakable sound of the old man's boot on the floor. Where did he think he was going at this time of night? She went down to him, stopped at the radiator in the hall where the milk warmed, and reached into the pocket of her robe for the tincture. She heard angry mutterings. Perhaps he had seen the candle.

"That's enough, you hear? You quit that foolishness."

She watched as the drops made dark starbursts that lingered on the surface of the milk, and lost track of the number. She had doubled the dose two weeks ago, when his waking at night had taken on this new purpose. It was either that or put a bolt on the door. She made a pattern with the starbursts that reminded her of stained glass or the first and last pages of the books down in the library. How many was that now? It didn't matter as long as he slept, as long as she could sleep, for she knew it was past the time when he would come, and if not tonight, then never.

"I am coming now, Mr. Bigelow," she said, squeezing the dropper hard, and the drops blurred together.

He had one boot on and was holding the other in his hand like a weapon. Why did he hate her so?

"Put the boot down."

"I am going to find her."

"I told you: she is coming here. Now drink."

"I don't believe you."

"If you don't drink this, I'll tell her not to come."

He put down the boot and accepted the cup, but when he brought it to his lips he stopped and sniffed, looked up accusingly at her.

"Drink it, Mr. Bigelow," she said almost gently. "Drink it and you will be able to sleep." She didn't know if he had heard her, because he moved not a muscle and kept her fixed in his gaze, those pinpoint reflections of the candle.

"You," he said at last, and offered her the cup, turning it so she could take the handle.

The first sip had an odd metallic sweetness, but she didn't think it was unpleasant, and there was no odor other than the warm milk. How had he known? She would have given the cup to him, but he was smiling now, not unkindly, and as she raised the cup to her lips again she imagined that she was doing so at his bidding, that he had said, very distinctly, "Drink it and you will be able to sleep."

THE DATE OF HARRIET TRUSCOTT'S return to Beecher's Bridge was fixed in Toma's mind for another reason. On Friday, March 8, after several days of muttering and glowering and averted glances, the men, through the intermediary of the foreman, Aldren Hawley, made known that they would no longer work in the south tunnel, and that they would sooner lose their jobs than go back down there.

When Hawley came to him with a report of the tunnel workers'
complaint, Toma had made the mistake of laughing at this information.

"Music, you say? It must have been a brass band for them to hear it
over the racket down there."

"No, sir," said Hawley, twisting his cap in his hands. "Not a brass
band at all, but softer, they say, and peaceful, and I think I heard it myself."

"You think so, but . . . ?"

"I wasn't in the same part of the tunnel, not so close like, and I am
not so certain, not as certain as the men down at the face. They are
pretty damn sure of it."

"If it's peaceful music, as you say, then there's nothing to worry
about, is there?" But if he was hoping to jolly Hawley out of this bit of
nonsense, he was making no headway. Even as he spoke the words he
remembered the odd notions that bloomed in the subway tunnels of
New York: grim auguries from seepage or the phosphorescence of a
vein of rock, even its color, even the cable falling from its coil in a figure eight. And who could blame them for seeing disaster at every turn?
They were proved right often enough. The sweetness of the music was
the seal on this particular disaster: the Devil would hardly be so foolish
as to announce his work with gongs and cymbals, added Hawley with a
sniff for emphasis.

Toma had made weekly calculations and charts with the help of the
long-suffering Stefan, and he knew how thin the margin of his success
must be, especially after the influenza had so reduced his work force.
He had sent telegrams to Schenectady importuning that bureaucracy
for skilled tunnel workers or miners, so that work could proceed on all
four tunnels simultaneously. How like Steinmetz, he reflected bitterly
in the answering silence, to show up when he was not wanted or
needed, and turn a deaf ear when it most mattered. Do the best you
can under the circumstances, was Steinmetz's response.

Even if Schenectady suddenly jumped to attention, there was little
hope now of attracting labor to such a luckless site. It was easier to get
ten men to cross a picket line than one to brave this vague peril, for su-
perstition was more catching than influenza.

And so Toma made of himself a miner's canary, or an offering: he
would spend the night in the very tunnel where the devil had pitched

his tent. There was no point in such a gesture unless it were observed; he had his bedroll and a bottle of water carried down at noon with instructions to put them as far into the tunnel as the bravest man would go. He went down at four, before the shift ended, and he carried with him things that Stefan had lugged up from the office, for he had the weekly report to complete for tomorrow's mail. At the last minute Stefan slipped a half-pint bottle into his pocket and whispered to him: "I made it myself. The least you can do is offer him a drink of slivovitz."

He had been down in the excavations dozens of times, but never in such silence, a void that devoured the certainties of time and place. His father had told him of the ancient mines of Montenegro, and from that gold and silver were fashioned the treasures of the monasteries, whose beauty invited the grace of God, and gave the people of Montenegro, the true Serbs so few in number, the strength to fight off the Turks. And when the Turks were too strong, the people hid themselves in the mineshafts and in the deep, interconnecting caves in the *karst*, and no Turk dared enter these places.

Had the excavation followed the original plan presented to Steinmetz, Toma would be following a straight shaft instead of this uneven footing that twisted and dipped in pursuit of the red rock. He made two trips to carry his belongings to the end of the tunnel, where scattered tools spoke of a panicked retreat. It was on his second trip down that his mind began to map the journey, as it had in the mountains of his youth when survival depended on knowing where the north star lay behind the blackest clouds, and each turning of the mapless trail was committed to memory. So many paces south, then quartering to the southeast for another forty-five, wavering left and right as the rock ran, and down, always down. There was a pattern that he could not grasp.

He settled himself on the blankets—it was a good thirty degrees warmer down here—took a pull from Stefan's bottle, and began to work. His chamber was not only soundless but sealed against drafts and changes of temperature. He would have been grateful for the company of a mouse. When he looked at his watch it was only a few minutes before seven. He would have guessed he had been working for many hours. He ate his dish of boiled beef and cabbage and drank a little more of Stefan's brandy. Was it possible that a high wind passing over the top of the shaft could produce musical resonance? Well, there had been no such wind. Would drills and the clash of pickaxes echo in the ear or the mind? Had the tunneling released a gas that deranged the senses? The suspicion of the workmen seemed equally plausible, and perhaps if he stayed down here long enough he would look forward to a visit from the Devil.

Twice during the night he started from his sleep. He lay awake, examining the silence, wondering if he should strike a match, and eventually slipped back into his dreams. When he did at last light the lantern he saw that it was an hour past dawn. He was eating stale bread soaked in gravy when he heard a shout, probably from the mouth of the tunnel.

"Mr. Peacock! Halloo!"

"I'm here."

"Do you need help?"

"No, thank you."

Let them go on about their work in the west tunnel, he thought. The less said about this nonsense the better, and he certainly did not want to answer any questions about how he had slept.

He stooped up the tunnel with both lanterns to inspect the streaks of dull red rock. Twice he hit his head on the low jagged roof. What an awful space to work in. Could he carry out this labor alone? Certainly he could drill the holes and drive the spikes, but someone, perhaps Stefan, must help him with the segmented lengths of iron. Perhaps there had been some benefit to this night after all.

He left one lantern near the mouth and crept back down to the bottom to gather his things. And there it was: the music he had doubted and scorned, faint but audible and certainly recognizable.

THE GREAT ROOM in the Truscott mansion was not a restful space for a single occupant, especially one who had time to observe that his fingernails were not what they might have been, despite the care taken, and that his best black coat had inexplicably shed two buttons. Lily had shown him in, saying that Mrs. Truscott was upstairs with the doctor and he might wait in here. She did not say why the doctor was in the house, but cast a sidelong glance to gauge his reaction, and perhaps to judge for herself whether this was a man worth dying for.

The rumor of what had happened was all over town by the following morning, and Toma eventually heard a version of it from Stefan, who knew it from the mailman. Olivia had been unconscious for two days, but it now seemed that she would pull through. And what odd timing it was, her trying to do away with herself on the very eve of Harriet Truscott's return. Stefan glanced up at Toma after this remark, suddenly aware of its awkward content, and wished that he could take the words back. But Toma, with a very slight gesture of his hand, absolved Stefan and seemed to dismiss the idea that Olivia's fate mattered greatly to him. It would have been more accurate to say that what Olivia had done, and why, was the last subject in the world he wanted to think about.

He rose when he heard footsteps on the stair and nodded to Dr. Crowell as Harriet saw him to the door.

"Toma, please come out of Fowler's zoo. I can't think why anyone would want to sit in there, but it seems to be Lily's idea of protocol."

"She has her reasons, no doubt."

She came to him and took both his hands in hers, a mark of her own protocol. He had had no idea how they ought to greet each other.

"Let's go sit in the library. Will you have tea? Or coffee?"

"I must, uh . . ."

"Of course. You have to see poor Olivia. I have just been speaking to Dr. Crowell about what can be done. But there is no hurry, is there? Will you not have coffee with me? It has been such a long time."

"Yes, please."

He was content to let her carry the conversation, and if he paid less than rapt attention to news of the senator's consuming work on Capitol Hill, or to details of life on Q Street, that deficit was made up by his concentration on her face: those planes somehow harmonized and softened, the bloom of color as if she had just come in from a long walk, and above all the clarity of her gaze. He had imagined this reunion so vividly, so fervently, that the experience of it now resembled a memory or a dream.

"Toma."

"Yes."

"You look as if you are about to fall asleep."

"There hasn't been much time for sleep. I am sorry."

"I went to the office yesterday afternoon—thank goodness Mrs. Evans is up and about—just to look around. I thought you might come."

"No. I was working with Stefan down in the tunnel."

"Stefan can't be much help down there. And what is all this about the south tunnel anyway?"

"What do you know about that?"

"Only what was in the telegram."

"Well . . ."

"Well?"

"There has been a difficulty with the men. They do not wish to work in that particular tunnel, and so Stefan and I are finishing up."

"You haven't time for that, and Stefan is no laborer. I should never have left you two alone together, even for a week, much less six." She leaned back and closed her eyes. "It seemed like forever. But now I am back."

There was an odd exuberance in her mood that Toma could not place, and which seemed out of keeping with the unhappy circumstances of the household. She was back, and he was here: perhaps nothing and no one else mattered. Encouraged by his reading of signs, he grew bold.

"I will tell you about the tunnel, if you want to know."

"Why wouldn't I?" she asked, laughing. "Were you not afraid of what you might find down there? Even a little bit?"

"I admit to some odd dreams."

"And so you have no idea what it was that upset the men? No wonder Dr. Steinmetz is so testy in his telegram."

"I do have an idea. In fact I know with certainty what sort of monster this is."

She assumed an expression of such earnest anxiety, such disbelieving dread, that he could not help smiling.

"Are you the cat, Toma, and I the mouse?"

He whistled two bars of music. She frowned at him.

"My father used to whistle, and my mother said it was a vulgar impulse and he must not do it in the house."

More softly now he whistled the same melody.

"The 'Polonaise.' It is one of my favorite pieces of music."

"No doubt that is why you played it this morning. And last night, at about eight o'clock, you played the cradle song, the one you played in Washington."

"Can it be that you would spy on me?"

"I did nothing of the sort. I was minding my own business. It was you who intruded upon me."

She shook her head, annoyed at this riddle. "You hear the music in the south tunnel? It is not possible. What else do you hear?"

"Only that, nothing else. As to how, I would guess that we ran out of mountain, and the red rock has led us somewhere near your . . . what do you call it?"

"The music room."

"It is sitting right on the rock. There can be no other explanation."

She looked in her lap now, curiosity suddenly shrouded. "I imagine you must have waited for some time last night."

"Yes."

"And your supper?"

"I found something to eat afterward. I wasn't hungry. I . . ."

"Please don't. Don't say any more." She got up and went to the window.

"You are angry with me."

"I am not angry. I am sad."

"I think there is much else to be sad about."

She was standing close to the window, looking down over the white lawn at the still frozen lake, and when she responded to his suggestion with a sigh the pane clouded over. She rubbed the glass with her handkerchief, making no improvement.

"It would seem, dear Toma, that we cannot be apart any more than we can be together. It would be best if I did not play."

"At all?"

"It doesn't seem right."

Toma stared at her, shocked to silence by his miscalculation and this consequence. If only he had said nothing about the mystery of the tunnel.

"What is it? Are you ill?"

"Would you take this from me?"

"Take what?"

"Your music. You would give up the pleasure of playing, and take from me the pleasure of listening. Why?"

"I do not like to think of you stuck in the earth like a rat while I play. What if someone . . . ?"

"Should know? What if someone should know that I am listening in my burrow?"

"What if someone should know about us?" Now it was her turn to stare, appalled that she could have said such a thing.

"Us," he repeated, hardly daring to say the word. "What is in your mind when you think about us?" He looked at the toes of his boots when he spoke.

"I think about the great work that you have achieved, starting from nothing."

"No, us. What is it about us that must not be known?" Now he looked at her so she could not hide from the question, and was surprised when she answered so readily.

"You ask me to describe something that I dare not even acknowledge. I have no words. But it is there nonetheless, like the mountain above us the night we were skating, seen or unseen, acknowledged or not. I am the child in the nursery who will not look into the dark corner."

"Only darkness and fear? Nothing more?"

"I did not mean that at all. A thing may be both beautiful and terrible, or joy and sorrow dwell in the same moment. Suppose one could see into paradise and know one could never go there?"

"Shall I tell you what I see?"

"Please, yes." She sat down on the chair next to his.

"My paradise is furnished with little things: a glass bottle with flowers; an argument over the spacing of carrots in the row; your music in the tunnel. I do not ask for more, but I cannot accept less. The music was a gift I had not expected, like what you call a miracle. You made me so happy, without trying, without knowing."

He turned his head to look at her and saw the color rising in her face as she fidgeted with her ring.

"Oh, I knew. I was thinking about you when I played the Brahms, and my father was listening, half asleep, as he was in Washington. So you see . . . I knew."

"Well, then, you have his happiness to consider."

"Yes. That is what I shall tell myself. But really . . ."

He rose from the chair, afraid that if he let her talk on she would find new difficulties, other arguments.

"I am going up to see Olivia now. I'll be in the office on Tuesday. Will you come?"

She nodded and tried to smile at him, but then thought of what he would find on the third floor: the face without expression, the eyes that stared at nothing and never closed. Tuesday. Somehow between now and Tuesday she must find the courage to tell him her news.

Lily, bearing the coffee, rounded the corner of the doorway. "Is he gone, then?"

"Yes, Lily, he has gone up to see Olivia."

"And it's high time too, I shouldn't wonder."

"That will be all, Lily. Just put the tray down there."

Lily seemed inclined to reconsider her harshness. Had she noted the grubby nails and missing buttons and decided that Toma was in need of kindly intervention? "Shall I take something up to him, then?"

"No. I think we must leave him alone now."

General Electric men knitting for the war effort

CHAPTER

NINETEEN

Although the sun was now so bright and hot that both Toma and Stefan had stripped off their shirts, it was still early in May and the cool of the morning lingered a few paces away in the shade of young leaves, where the hobble bush bloomed white and the litter of dead leaves was punctuated by shoots of new grass and a pale scattering of spring beauties.

"Such a day," mused Stefan, resting his pry bar on the top of the wooden crate, "who would believe . . ."

"Help me with that corner, Stefan, and we're done with this one." Toma spoke without looking up at Stefan. He did not wish to be abrupt with his friend, but neither did he wish to discuss the war, not again, not now. There were several crates lying on the scarred rock of Lightning Knob, and he wanted to get the equipment inside before the rain promised by massed clouds to the west.

From the open crate he lifted a dull metal box with instrument leads sprouting from its sides and cable receptors like wounds, top and bottom.

"Which one is that?"

Toma turned it over in his hands. Something about the device, perhaps its color, reminded him of the bombs his brother had carried across the border, the bombs he had died for. "It doesn't say."

"Then I hope they had the brains to send a packing list." Stefan scrabbled in the excelsior, found a piece of paper, and drew a long breath. "Already in Schenectady they have the fighting spirit. There is maybe something dangerous in this box?"

"Stefan, just tell me what the paper says."

"'Security Alert.'" Stefan's stilted delivery, squeaky and clipped, was a Hungarian version of a German accent, perhaps a parody of Steinmetz himself. "'This device is intended for use by authorized General Electric personnel only. Tampering or unauthorized use will be punished to the fullest extent of the law.'" He let the paper drop, took the box from Toma's hands, then fumbled with the lid. "And what is this precious, secret device? What do you think? Look: a fuse box, a fucking fuse."

Toma wondered how he could reply without further upsetting Stefan. Ever since the declaration of war, now over a month ago, his friend had been preoccupied by dark consequences and ramifications that he was all too eager to elaborate. The more recent draft legislation was another link in the noose of malign circumstance that would drag him back to die in Europe. Toma had tried to reassure him that at thirty-nine he was hardly the pick of the litter, and now, with his shirt off, he was a most unlikely subject for the martial imagination: the skin like parchment, the arms not much thicker than the cotton straps of his undershirt. Toma had never seen him stand up straight.

"It's just a piece of paper they put in every box, Stefan. It doesn't mean anything. See if you can find that packing list in there. Besides, who are we if not authorized personnel?"

Stefan dumped the fuse box back into the wood shavings and began rifling the pockets of his shirt, vest, and coat, muttering as he went: "Authorized. Where is it? I'll show you authorized. Ja, here it is." He thrust the folded envelope at Toma. "This one is yours. I have already signed mine. We are authorized to unpack crates, and maybe to get killed by lightning up here."

Toma read the two pages, then began again at the top, to Stefan's impatience. "How many times you got to read?"

"I just want to make sure I didn't miss anything. It is a security clearance."

"It is an oath. See there at the bottom? 'So help me God.'"

"That part doesn't apply to me or to you."

"What matters to me is that they tell me exactly where I am allowed to go on GE property   premises, they put—and anything they don't mention is out. I can't go where I was before, down below, the desk where I do the drawings and the numbers, the shop where we make the prototype. What do they think, suddenly I'm a criminal? They don't say about the crapper. I'll ask Piccolomini about that one next time I see him."

"You should leave Piccolomini alone. You don't want to be seen as a troublemaker."

"I'm a troublemaker already, as soon as I open my mouth. 'Be careful who you talk to about your work,' it says there. 'You never know when the Enemy may be listening.' So how do we know who this Enemy is? He probably sounds a lot like me, is what I think."

"Everyone in America comes from somewhere else. Unless you're an Indian."

"It's easy for you to say, because you talk like an Englishman, and with that foot of yours you aren't going to get called up."

"People aren't so stupid as you think, Stefan."

"Probably they are more stupid. I tell you I get some funny looks, and from men I have worked with for two years. Already they are talking about the Liberty Loans down there. I'm going to have to buy double just to shut them up."

Stefan had talked himself out, and fell to the labor in surly silence. Fuses, gauges, junction boxes, cable connectors, meters, transformers, the crucial lightning arresters, and a variety of switching devices were freed from the packing material and set on benches under the canvas awning, awaiting their hierarchical connection in the nearly completed stone building. Scraps of white paper—the security reminders skittered over the rock like confetti until they caught in the branches of the low blueberry bushes.

Toma sent Stefan inside to ask if the work on the observation room would be finished in time to begin the installation this afternoon. It was not quite a make-work errand, but he could have called the foreman out. He turned again to the document in his pocket. The layout and functions of the Lightning Laboratory were described in punctilious detail, as were his responsibilities as the manager of that installation. Mention was made in passing of the offices in the old foundry. But of the works below the falls, the ever-expanding Experimental Site called into existence by the Peacock Turbine, not a word.

He could refuse to be drawn by such a bureaucratic provocation, which might be innocent enough; he would refrain from the consolation of Stefan's sympathy; but it was hard to put aside the pang of anonymity or isolation at having been so casually dismissed from history, a history to which he had, until now, paid little mind.

He thought suddenly and without exaltation of Harriet, of his boast to her that the Peacock Turbine would make him rich. The implied syllogism there—that being rich he would win her—had been hopelessly false at the time, as subsequent experience had revealed to him in cruel increments. The paper meant simply, and stupidly, that he was denied access to his own invention. But his reaction, his despair, was an acknowledgement, at last, that a larger hope lay in ruins.

Stefan saw at once the alteration in his friend's mood, and said only: "They will be finished soon. Perhaps you should go and encourage them."

Toma smiled, as if at a joke, and looked up at the bulk of the stone fortress that enclosed the excavation on three sides and braced the soaring aerial. "It will be quite something if it works."

Stefan thought, but did not say. And if it doesn't work it will kill us.

HE WAS SUDDENLY AWAKE and thought it must be the calling of the birds everywhere around him in the gray light before dawn, for it was the month of the warblers. But he had woken directly out of a vivid dream of his brother, who was climbing the rock wall to the cave where he kept the fatal devices, and he, below, could not keep pace. Through the birdsong now—the one that sounded like the working of a musical hinge—he heard again the muted clank and recognized it as a sound from his dream.

More curious than alarmed, he pulled on his boots and felt his way along the trail to the stream where it would intersect a wider footpath up the mountain. Voices ahead, low, and the brief gleam of a light. They were not coming in the direction of the Knob, but passing up toward Rachel's Leap. They did not seem accustomed to this work, whatever it was.

"Who is there?" He did not expect a reply and got none. Over the sound of the stream he heard quickened footsteps in the brush, a curse, and again the clanking as they made haste to escape down the mountain. He would not pursue them, would not provoke a fight. He walked a few paces down the familiar path, assuring himself of their retreat, and tripped headlong over a thin metal rod that had lodged in the underbrush.

SHE WAS AMAZED AT her inability to coax the flowers into an arrangement that pleased her. Columbine, Johnson's blue geranium, and the earliest peonies: these were her favorites, and she had once written in her journal that she could look at them and find affirmation of her faith, proof of His existence in the world around her. Ordinarily the flowers arranged themselves when she dropped them into the vase. Fussing could not improve upon the eccentric frailty of geranium stems, the poise of sentinel columbines, the organizing weight of peonies. And still she fussed, cutting an inch off the geraniums to curb their sprawl. At each touch the geranium shed a snow of petals until the counter was covered with those tiny, perfectly blue hearts. The familiar scents were making her feel slightly ill.

She was disgusted with her weakness. The fact, now irreparable, was that she ought to have told him when she first had the chance, before her silence progressed from delicacy to deception, before she had time to think so much on the consequences. No one else would yet know—no one did know—that she was carrying a child. The delay in disclosure would hardly matter to Fowler: What, after all, did he know about these things? More so, undoubtedly, to Lucy, who would have a greedy curiosity about the fruits of her advice. And most of all, to Toma, who could conceivably hate her for what she had not told him.

Her secret, in other moments, had this liberating effect on her: she no longer worried, as she had in the wake of her confrontation with Lucy, about what other people might think, or how they would interpret her association with Toma. Only yesterday they had met in the office and had spent almost an hour talking about birds and their songs in this season of migration and mating. Did he know the one that called out over and over the name Sam Peabody, the first syllable low, followed by three higher notes, quavering? He did not, and she must whistle it for him. He caught her hand and reprimanded her vulgarity. His hand relaxed, and now lay comfortably, but not possessively, on hers, which she did not withdraw. She told him the name of that bird— the white-throated sparrow—and how sometimes in the spring they got it wrong, the young ones she imagined, and sang the whole thing on the same note. Three birdsongs later she wondered aloud if he would come to see the indigo buntings down at the foot of the lawn: she was sure it was a nesting pair.

"Perhaps not." A look of indefinite regret, a reluctant release of the joined hands.

"She is gone, you know. Dr. Crowell himself supervised the move, made sure they got her safely down to the ambulance. She will be better cared for there." She had meant to add "at the Home" but lost her courage at the brink, and so her sentence trailed off, oddly inflected. They had talked obliquely before about Olivia's treatment, the chances of recovery from what was said to be a disabling seizure.

"For the best, I suppose," he had murmured, but she could not tell what he thought or felt about this resolution. She realized that she had used his sadness as an excuse, just as she had used happiness, their happiness, this season of discovery.

Their business transacted, the correspondence finished, the afternoon was in danger of ending on this subdued note. Let's stand outside, she said, and see if the rain has brought the veery out. And there it was, unseen as always, the song spiraling down in a minor key like the winged descent of maple seed. She whispered in his ear, I am so very sorry about Olivia, and let her lips brush his cheek, almost an accident.

"It's Mr. Peacock," said Lily from the doorway behind her.

"Here?"

"Yes, ma'am; he'd like to talk to you."

She came out to him, her hands still damp, her mind on indigo buntings, but the strange metal rod in his hand told her they had other business.

"Toma. You have saved me from making a mess of the most perfect flowers. I am almost afraid to show you."

"Have you any idea what this thing might be?"

"None."

"I found it this morning, dropped on the path by someone who did not want to meet me." He gave the rod a shake and it hummed in his hand, an angry noise.

"What is that there, the blue cloth on the end?"

"A marker, I suppose."

"The color is distinctive."

"You have seen it before?"

She did not answer him, but went out to the porch, where she took up her binoculars and scanned the shore of the lake.

"There's another one. Look where the hemlock has fallen into the shallows, in the clearing behind it. I have seen others." She handed him the binoculars.

"And the others are at the same distance from the water?"

"More or less." Her voice was soft; she gave up her information unwillingly, knowing where the inquisition must end.

"Then perhaps you know what they mean."

"I have an idea, yes."

"I thought as much. For some reason, on the way down here, I remembered seeing those footprints in the snow, yours and his, on the day of the New Year. You must tell me."

There was no way to assert her innocence in this matter, to tell him that the expedition with Dr. Steinmetz to the high lake had been an adventure, not to mention an escape from Lucy, and that every step of the way she had been thinking about him, recalling with perfect clarity the pressure of his arm about her waist. She wondered, even as she set forth the few facts of her apparent complicity, how these flags had appeared around her own pond without her knowledge. Perhaps Fowler had agreed and had forgotten to tell her? And she did not say, as she might have, that she had argued against the pump-storage project as best she could, or that Dr. Steinmetz had assured her he would tell Toma. When the time is right, he said, when I have made the calculations. She spoke only of what she had done or seen, and described the idea as Steinmetz had explained it to her, a child's version of some complicated grown-up matter. She made no excuse for herself: Would he not trust her in this?

"You think I have done wrong?"

"I think you have been foolish in your trust."

"Please, Toma, do not speak unkindly about Dr. Steinmetz."

"He has shown me no kindness, and no respect. If this scheme is to benefit mankind, why does he send his men like thieves in the night?"

"There is no excusing that." How angry he is, she thought.

"And are you content to be part of this insane experiment? There will be no water in that brook, and you will live on the edge of a very large sink—to put it politely—that is forever draining and filling. Those rocks we skated through? At high tide there will be no rocks."

"Please, I cannot bear to hear you speak this way."

"Is that why you said nothing to me?"

"It was not mine to tell. I believed that Dr. Steinmetz would—"

"You trusted him and not me?"

"Do stop finishing my thoughts, Toma!" She could feel her anger rising to meet his.

"You will say next that it is not my business. It is, after all, your property."

"I did not and would not say that." What she was thinking was that this project was too important for her to dismiss on the grounds of her imperfect understanding; much less should she recruit allies to her instinctive dislike of it. Since New Year's Day she had put the matter out of her mind. Was it too much to hope that Dr. Steinmetz, too, had forgotten about it?

She looked at Toma, wondering what part of this she could explain to him, but he would not meet her eyes. He is like a child sulking in judgement, she thought. He had come to her with an angry suspicion of her complicity and had seized on appearances to condemn her. Had he no generosity, no love? And if he had no interest in what she might say, why bother? Why not, indeed, have done with it once and for all?

"Toma." Had he not been looking at her he might not have recognized her voice. "I have something else to tell you. Perhaps we should sit down."

Portledge
June 1, 1917

Dear Senator Truscott:

Thank you for your effusive and informative letter on the plans for the July 4th celebration in Beecher's Bridge. I see no reason, now that the battle has been joined, why a patriotic holiday should not also celebrate the technical achievement of General Electric in Beecher's Bridge, and who better to address that than the distinguished statesman who has been so instrumental to our enterprise? I do indeed look forward to your remarks on patriotism and industrial progress.

But if I may introduce a note of caution: Let us guard against too much emphasis on the means of our triumph, and focus rather on the end, avoiding what might be seen in retrospect as any excess of patriotic fervor. Specifically, when it comes to the pyrotechnic display, it is all very well to invoke the blessing of God on America, but I recoil from the phrase "and destroy her enemies." He will dispose of that as He sees fit. Please find something more in the spirit of the New Testament, more congenial to our long view of peaceful prosperity.

Perhaps Independence Day will be an opportunity for you and Dr. Steinmetz to bring me fully up to date on your thinking with respect to the projected pump storage facility on Great Mountain. You mention it again in your letter, and I have had information of various kinds from Dr. Steinmetz, but the costs of all this are not yet settled, and the benefits are best described as visionary. Of course Steinmetz is a genius and we both endorse and support his research, even his far-flung enthusiasms. But it must be said that he has a great many irons in the fire just now, and that he is entirely innocent of practical politics. I would not doubt his vision of the work, but there must be serious question whether General Electric can make an immediate commitment in the context of a wartime economy, with its many emergency requirements and restrictions on business as usual.

Very truly yours,
CAC

"SO THIS IS IT . . . the big moment for the guineas?" Stefan was looking at the control panel but glancing over his shoulder every few seconds at the advance of the billowing, blackish cloud. Toma could smell his fear.

"Guinea pigs, Stefan. I'm sure the expression is guinea pigs." Toma's eyes were fixed on the display of the electroscope, whose needle indicated an intense electrical conversation between the aerial and the cloud.

"Ja, pigs, whatever. I guess part of the experiment is to see what happens to us. I should have made a will."

"You are not going to die, Stefan, unless you talk yourself into a heart attack. Every reasonable precaution has been taken. Look at us."

There was a suggestion of farce in what they wore: shaded eyeglasses, rough cotton tunics without pockets, trousers with drawstring waists, thick-soled cork clogs that creaked on the cork flooring. Around and above them, more insulating cork on walls and ceiling constructed with wooden pegs rather than nails. Their view of the aerial and the transmission lines just outside the tower was through thick slabs of isinglass with reflective coating.

Stefan was not impressed. "There are six things in this room that could kill us under the right circumstances, maybe more." He spoke with an assurance that made Toma smile.

"And here I thought you were the perfect assistant because you know nothing about electricity. Now, all of a sudden, you are an expert."

"Ja, well, I read, don't I, so I know a few things."

"Things?"

"Like those switches over there." He pointed to a row of three wooden levers in the wall. The switches themselves were positioned outside the observation room and would open the circuits on the transmission cables in case of emergency.

"There was a man in Colorado, 1908, a maintenance worker who goes to open a switch on a high-voltage line which is not in service. But you know what? Big surprise: there is seventy thousand volts of electricity in that line, static or induced, I forget which, because the cable next to this one has been struck by lightning."

"So what happened?"

"There is an arc, the electricity follows the switch away from the pole, and it kills the man, because he is now part of the circuit." Stefan sounded almost pleased with his tale, smacked his lips in grim satisfaction.

"We are nowhere near the switches, Stefan; that's the point of the levers."

Stefan rounded on him, eyes glittering in anticipation of the checkmate. "They estimate the arc in Colorado at ten feet. Ten feet, and you think we are safe with your toy switches?"

"I don't know. That was years ago, and different equipment. Maybe the guy was standing in a puddle."

"My point, boss, is that at these levels—how many volts are we talking?—everybody guesses and nobody knows. The only sure thing is that we shouldn't be so close, shouldn't be here at all."

"Aren't you curious? It is like being inside the volcano, or in the curling crest of the tidal wave. Maybe this is how the world begins, or ends. Anyway, no one has ever tried to do this."

"No one has been so stupid."

"It shouldn't be long now. You keep your eyes on the dead line and the live one in parallel, the ones farthest from the aerial. With any luck we won't have to touch the switches at all."

"Luck," repeated Stefan, making the word sound like a curse.

Walls and isinglass windows notwithstanding, the observation room commanded perfect views in every direction and inspired a sense of precedence, even possession. When Toma had first climbed the stairs he had stood on a bare windblown platform roofing the equipment room below, and he felt a tightening in his chest. It was familiar, this high vantage on everything that mattered. In Montenegro there had been a pillar of rock near his valley in the mountains, and he had sent the Englishman there to find his flowers. Harwell came back that evening and spread his drawings and specimens out on the table, but all he could talk about was the view, as if he had seen the world for the first time. Toma himself had looked down from that height, seen the pasture like a green silk handkerchief, and through the notch where the road descended to the broad plain of the Sandžak, the roof, red tiles radiant with an immanent joy, the roof of the house where she lived. He could never afterward escape from this scene, had no defense against its innocence.

And what did he see when he gazed down from the unfinished rampart of Peacock's Folly through the invisible filter of memory? The silk mill and the falls with their thundering mists, the dusty yards and shabby outbuildings of the ironworks, and the Truscott house at his feet. At his back was the mountain, as it had been in Montenegro, and, as he had then, he now constructed a story, in defiance of history and common sense, a story with a happy ending.

It was a simple thing, a machinery with but two working parts. The details and circumstances of the story might change, and had in so many ways since they first met on the docks in Naples, but that was just the shifting of scenery upon the stage. They had spoken lately of paradise because it was hard to speak directly of love, and he was sure she had seen through his words to the great unuttered fact of his paradise, which was her presence, only that, and he, if need be, might be a small figure in the corner of the scene, kneeling, transfigured.

They had passed a great crisis of the sort that must, if logic had any purchase, have shattered every connection. He had come to her in anger, literally with a rod in his hand, having judged her guilty of breaching their trust in one another; but he had been humbled by what he then learned. Perhaps she thought to end everything by telling him about the child she would bear. But it happened otherwise.

He went away from her house the way a man leaves his doctor's office after receiving a grave diagnosis. He is numb; he must not think too much on this thing or it will drive him mad; he distracts himself with the details of other matters. But the mind plays games with itself, not only when we dream; Toma, trying to put Harriet out of his thoughts, wandered to that resonant scene of his youth, became mesmerized by a distant red roof burning a hole in his heart.

He was always guarded in speaking about his home and family, the minefields of memory. He knew he had told Harriet about Aliye . . . told her what? When he had seen Harriet on the docks at Naples it seemed that by some miracle Aliye lived again. That much he must have told her: he had loved someone else and she had died. But there was more. Aliye had lived under the red roof and she died there, alone, by her own hand, and his child died with her. He remembered the night, the new moon after the rain, and the chill. How cold she must have been. He had not even spoken to her. It was Harwell who sent her away, gave his candle to light her path home. He had not even spoken to her. He saw the wavering pinpoint of light along the road, then the faint outline of her as the road turned away to the descent, then nothing. How Harwell must have hated him that night. How he hated himself, even though he was sure he had done the right thing.

His mother had said they could not marry—she is not one of us, they are not our people—and because he could not stand against her he came to accept what he had done, or not done, as a badge of strength. He was contradicted only by a certain unguarded expression of sadness on Harwell's face. They never spoke of the matter.

The question he could not answer was why did she die? What if Harriet had been brave enough to ask? And what if he had been brave enough not to send Aliye away? He did not know, but how could it have led to any greater sorrow? He would have a son; he would not have her blood on his hands.

Aliye had been taken from him, and Harriet had been set in her place. Why? So that he might love her again, more perfectly. He did not believe in divine providence but he believed this, even if he could not make sense of it. He was amazed at his own tenacity, his stupid, brute tenacity. She was married to another man, and would bear his child. But he loved her, and he knew she loved him. There was no logic here, but there was hope, which grows like a weed in waste spaces. The ending of the story would take care of itself.

He knew it was nearly time by the prickling on the nape of his neck, the hairs rising on the invisible flow of electrons from the mountain to the cloud. Any man who had worked on Lightning Knob knew this feeling, knew that he had to get under the protection of the sandbags or at least away from the aerial as fast as possible. Had he been standing out on the bare rock he would have shouted: "Cover!" Now he glanced at Stefan, who had little experience of the lightning. His friend might be staring into his own grave: the lips moved without making a sound. Perhaps he was praying, in spite of himself.

He would have spoken to Stefan but was stayed by the excruciating whiteness that penetrated everything. Of course the thunder followed before he could blink, but his impression afterward was that the lightning strike had somehow missed them. Except for the smoldering in one bank of lightning arresters and the wisps of steam trailing away from the aerial, there was little alteration in what he could see through the viewing port.

"No arc to main cable at 24 inches," he wrote. The smell of singed insulation drifted up from below, a failed connection or blown panel that he would check later. The circuits in the cables were intact; another strike would come at any time. Stefan would be better off down below where there were no windows. He made another note, and with his left hand spun the wooden wheel below his port to narrow the gap between the transmission cables and the aerial. Eighteen inches. This was an odd business, inviting disaster . . . like being a bullfighter with a cape but no sword. He closed his eyes for a moment and tried to turn the tables in his mind: What if I were the lightning?

IT IS A FACT, though Toma did not report it, that the second recorded strike at the fully operational General Electric Lightning Research Facility at Beecher's Bridge occurred in that moment when his eyes were closed. No matter: Stefan's were wide open, as wide as could be, and in his state of mortal terror he saw the sudden sword leap from the aerial to the nearest transmission line, saw the incandescent cable burst through its vaporized sheathing, the arresters showering sparks, the air around them glowing like the halo of a saint.

"Mother of God!"

Toma cranked the cable trolley away from the aerial. The arresters had failed to tame the ambient surge and now the lines were dead, which meant that the fuses had done their job. There was nothing more to be done here until the storm passed. He knew he should go downstairs and begin collecting data on the two strikes, but he yawned and thought again about what he had seen with his eyes closed.

It was early evening by the time they had everything ready for shipment to Schenectady: the readings and their observations along with the damaged equipment, which Steinmetz would want to see for himself. The storm had scoured the air, and a cool, scented draft worked its way around the half-open door. He had noticed the delicate white bloom of the bush by the steps, and wondered now if she had planted it for her father. His mind was suddenly full of her.

He sat at his desk and riffled through the envelopes there. A plain hand-written one caught his attention. There was no return address. This was the one he had been waiting for.

Dear Mr. Peacock:

I am in receipt of your letters of June 2 and June 18, in which you asked for information on the Peacock Turbine, specifically whether the Patent Office has received any correspondence touching on its design or on ancillary patents. I regret to report that I cannot help you. I have left the Patent Office and taken other employment. Remember our conversation. I can say no more.

Yours most truly,
Frederick Flaten

He turned the envelope toward the window to squint at the carelessly struck postmark. Schenectady, New York. Well, what else would a former patent inspector be doing in Schenectady? Poor, fond little Flaten with those sad eyes, he really would have been wiser to ignore the inquiry altogether; but Toma must be grateful for his foolishness, for nobody else, it seemed, wanted to tell him anything at all.

He took a card and wrote to Piccolomini a brief, formal note making an appointment for the next day to discuss security and other urgent matters at the Beecher's Bridge facilities. He signed it, then for emphasis wrote out his title, which took another two lines, and gave the envelope to Stefan, slumped and speechless in a chair by the cold stove.

"End of a long day. If you would be kind enough to deliver this to Signor Piccolomini, or to the night watchman, I'll buy you dinner at McCreedy's and all you can drink. Half an hour?"

Alone now, unsettled by the letter he had read and the letter he had written, he was in no mood to write to her. Gone were the phrases, the waterfall of tender feeling provoked by that scent just minutes ago. Tongue-tied by circumstance but clear-eyed in his anger, he had this chilling glimpse of enduring isolation: with all the time in the world he would never be able to explain to her his labyrinths. The only useful knowledge was love, bare, unadorned, unexplicated, and its price would be silence.

The letter he finally wrote was a model of compression. He put the date, then her name. He apologized for his uncouth behavior three days earlier. In another sentence he told her that he had survived the first test of the lightning. He signed it "Love, Toma," and left the unmarked envelope where she would find it when she next came to the office.

PICCOLOMINI WAS SWEATING. He was wearing the heavy black suit that served him in every weather, but the evening was not warm, and Toma's hand was dry, dangerous, chilled. Piccolomini did not meet his eye when they spoke.

They stood in the cavernous space of the old silk mill, which no amount of partitioning could domesticate. While Piccolomini waited and sweated, Toma walked an erratic circuit, trying to recall vanished landmarks on the stained concrete floor.

"What exactly is it you wish?"

"I saw on the way in that the substation, the transformers, and so on have been encased in some sort of . . ."

"Concertina wire."

"How very military."

"Yes, and the perimeter fence has been reinforced with interior bracing of heavy angle iron and an application of ten-gauge barbed wire along the top."

"And if one were to cut the wire?"

"The lights, the watchman, and the electrical circuit in the penultimate strand of barbed wire."

"So if the lights go out and the circuit fails in the same incident, you have an old chap fumbling around wondering if perhaps the enemy is jumping over his fence. A perfectly nice man, old Collins. I remember him from the forge and I had a word with him just a minute ago. But not much of an obstacle, on his own and in the dark."

Piccolomini bent over his pocket notebook, muttering as he wrote. "There will be more men. There will be a backup generator."

Toma made a show of inspecting the tall windows, now barred, and when he came to the private offices of the engineers he did not bother trying the door but hoisted himself up by the post and pegs of the side wall and peered over the top of the partition "You have a window open in there. No bars."

They came last to the new stone construction of the turbine house. The heavy oak door was locked. Toma struggled to keep his voice from rising.

"Would you open this for me, please?"

"I cannot. Only authorized personnel are allowed to enter."

"Yes. The famous security clearances. But that is my wheel, my name is on the patent, and I ask you again to open the door."

"I have no authority," said Piccolomini, as if reading from a prepared text. "This is a matter for Schenectady to decide. You must take it up with them."

"You refuse, then?" Toma dropped his eyes to Piccolomini's neck, thin and invitingly frail. "My wheel?"

"I do."

Toma turned to the door, laid his hand on the wood, first at the lock, then at the frame.

"There is someone in there now?"

"Always."

Toma struck the door with the flat of his hand and called out: "Hola! Open up in there."

"He will not open it. He has his orders, a strict protocol."

Toma patted the door as he would a dog, then drove the full force of his shoulder into its center. Nothing gave. A tool he needed, a pry bar, anything. When he turned around there was Piccolomini holding a small, bright pistol. Angry red patches in his cheeks had sucked all color from the pale, glistening face. "I am prepared to shoot."

"Don't be an ass. Just open it."

"I will not. Stand back from the door."

"Have you ever shot anyone?" Piccolomini did not answer.

"It's a messy business, and you would have to kill me." Piccolomini raised the pistol, which had been pointed more or less in Toma's direction, to aim at his chest.

"That's better. Still, you would have to make certain. A little to the left, I think, or your right." The muzzle swung in obedience to this suggestion.

"Hard to hold it steady if you haven't practiced, isn't it? I might be moving just as you pull the trigger, and then there are consequences to consider. There was a man once, an officer, who left me for dead. But I was not dead, and I found him. I killed him with a piece of broken stick no bigger than a wheel spoke. Not a fair fight, I am sorry to say, for he was already wounded; but I was angry, and it took him a long time to die."

Piccolomini did not answer; all his attention was focused on keeping his hand still.

"Put it down before somebody gets hurt." The engineer's face relaxed into an impassive, vacant stare as the aim of his weapon sank to the floor. Toma took it from his hand and put it in his own pocket.

"I shall report this."

"As you wish. Now the key."

"Where is that fool Collins?" snarled Piccolomini as he retreated crab-fashion until he was wedged into a stone angle.

"He is otherwise occupied out front. I told him to expect Stefan with a heavy package." Piccolomini looked hard at Toma's face, then his hand went to his waistcoat pocket. He held the key out as if he would put it into Toma's hand, but at the last moment he dropped it, then scuffed it with his boot into one of the covered drains carrying water from the turbine house.

"You may go fish for your key, Mr. Peacock, or go to Hell."

Toma looked upon his antagonist with bemused admiration. Suddenly he smiled, which offended Piccolomini.

"What?" He might be beaten, but he would not be mocked.

"You are no coward, I give you that, but your defense of the turbine has a flaw, and I was too angry to find it."

"The wheel is safe. You cannot open the door, and Collins will get here sooner or later. What flaw?"

"Listen."

"I hear nothing, only the sound of the wheel."

"Exactly so. The sound of the wheel. You are a fool, Piccolomini. You shouldn't play with guns, and still less should you tamper with a patent, my patent, even if it is at someone else's say-so. When this goes wrong you will take the blame."

"You are talking nonsense now. Nothing will go wrong. The patent is secure."

"I'm sure you were just following orders. Steinmetz, no doubt. A quarter inch here, another degree or so in the angle of the escape water. Isn't that how it went?"

"You know nothing, and I will tell you nothing. These are guesses, contemptible fantasies."

"I know this for certain: whatever you have locked up in there, it is not the Peacock Turbine."

Nikola Tesla in his laboratory

CHAPTER

TWENTY

"My friends, you have heard the introductory remarks from our distinguished guests Mr. Coffin and Dr. Steinmetz, and I am hard put to find the right words to thank them for coming all this way to celebrate our great national holiday here in Beecher's Bridge. But my gratitude goes deeper than that, and in my remarks, which I hope will not try your patience on this very warm afternoon, I shall endeavor to explain just how fortunate we are that the great General Electric Company has chosen Beecher's Bridge as the center of its most important research, and we thank them because we have benefited in so many ways, material and intangible, from the benevolent industry they have brought to this grand little town.

"Today we are all proud to be Americans. [Applause] And tomorrow, as soon as we have cleaned up this mess over in Europe, we will be prouder still of who we are, because we will not only have won the war, but won the peace that will follow it."

Senator Truscott paused to take a sip of water and to pat his forehead with a snowy handkerchief that fell open to magnificent proportions. He turned his head to smile at the setting sun, a noble adversary, then his appreciative gaze traversed the arc of his audience, left to right, with seeming acknowledgement of many individuals there. The red, white, and blue fans beat in rough unison, the pulse of the crowd.

"I'm a simple man, my friends," said the senator, putting the handkerchief away. "If only I could talk and fan myself at the same time, I'd sure do it today. What we need is a little cooling shower, something to break this heat and humidity that makes me feel as if I've been for a dip in the lake with all my clothes on. Now, it may sound odd for a fellow in politics to go around wishing for rain on the Fourth of July. I see you nodding your head there, Mr. Curtis. Is that what you were thinking?"

"Yes, sir, it was," barked Mr. Curtis, and a ripple of laughter ran through the crowd.

"You be quiet now, Fred," warned his wife.

"I'm afraid I put him up to it, ma'am. You all know Fred Curtis. Farmed here for thirty years at least, like his father before him. So if anyone knows what the weather here is likely to do, he'd be your man. I asked him this morning if we'd have rain before the day is out. And knowing what was planned, he said to me, 'Well, if you march quick and talk fast, you might get it all in.'"

Again the audience laughed, and the senator held up his hand. "We marched just fine, didn't we?"

"Yes."

"I can't hear you."

"*Yes!*"

"And now I want a round of applause for the Elks and the Royal Arcanum Society, who combined to provide us with such stirring martial music, and for the Volunteer Fire Department, who all but rubbed the paint off our fine new Ahrens-Fox fire engine, getting it ready to lead such a parade."

The applause was less vigorous than it might have been, as there were a good many in the audience who tried to clap and fan themselves in the same motion.

"Thank you, thank you all. Well, as Fred Curtis has pretty well promised us some rain, I want to assure you that we have taken precautions that it won't spoil our celebration, least of all the magnificent picnic supper that is waiting for us under those tents. You can see what fine big tents they are, more than enough room for everyone here on the green to get in out of the rain without being crowded. And you can see there is a kind of tent on the ground here behind us, waiting to be pulled up in just a few seconds if we get a shower, because we wouldn't want Mr. Coffin and Dr. Steinmetz to take a soaking, nor our other distinguished guests, and certainly not my wife, on whose head I will not suffer a single drop to fall."

The crowd cheered this gallantry, and the senator made a half turn to acknowledge Harriet Truscott. Seated at one end of the gentle arc of seats on the platform, Toma seemed to pay dutiful attention to the speaker, but behind the blank gaze his mind played with the puzzle of the hidden wheel, taking it apart and putting it back together over and over, an endless, fruitless exercise tainted with madness. He did not hear Truscott's gallant remark but saw him turn and bow. Now Harriet's face swam into focus—she was already in his line of sight—and he was lost in the dazzling display of expressions there: becoming pride, happiness, the momentary embarrassment yielding to affectionate gratitude. Of course these emotions were shaped to the occasion and to the public eye, but here too he sifted for evidence, for some acknowledgement, however subtle, of his rapt attention.

"I welcome the rain, my friends, and when it comes I tell you that I intend to talk straight through it. We all know what rain at this time of year might mean, and we even heard a little thunder, far off, as we were gathering for the march, so some of you might be feeling uneasy about being out here in the open during a lightning storm. But standing here today I have no fear of the lightning bolt, and neither should you, for that awful phenomenon of nature, the scourge of enterprise and domestic tranquility throughout the history of Beecher's Bridge, has been tamed by the bold genius of Dr. Steinmetz. May I draw your attention now to Lightning Knob, and to the structure there that protects us from our ancient enemy?"

The grandstand had been placed on the town green in such a position that the spectators' view embraced both the face of Great Mountain and the stark, lesser eminence of Lightning Knob. An old elm standing on the side of the green near the Congregational Church had been cut down; too hastily, some said, for though it had been attacked by the elm blight, it was still alive and might have survived. But there was no question that its removal improved this panorama.

"It looks a little like a church standing up there, doesn't it, and like the two churches we have down here in the town it protects us all, turns the wrath of the Almighty into a blessing. I'd like Mr. Peacock to stand for a moment. He is the director of the Beecher's Bridge Lightning Research Facility, and of the Experimental Site down at the falls. It was his waterwheel, the Peacock Turbine, that brought General Electric to us in the first place, and he is the fellow who took Dr. Steinmetz's ideas about lightning and put the nuts and bolts to them. Now, it's true he didn't invent the Fourth of July, but without him we'd have only half as much to celebrate here today. Mr. Peacock, will you please?"

Toma stood, blushed, and sat down before the clapping ended.

"I'll be telling you a little later about that building up there on the Knob and what it is going to mean, not just to us here in Beecher's Bridge, but to America; and not just to America, but to the whole world. What you are looking at, folks, is a very important piece in the great engine of prosperity that connects us all and will kick into high gear just as soon as we've settled the Kaiser's hash. The real business of the General Electric Company, my friends, is not electricity, but prosperity.

"But before I get into that, before I tell you how the protection of electrical lines from lightning is one of the great strides in national prosperity, I've arranged a little something to get you thinking along the right lines. Are you ready? Here we go."

Senator Truscott's hand was already poised on the nearer of two hunting-draped levers that projected from the side of the lectern, and when he thrust it down there was a moment of perfect, awed silence just long enough to entertain the thought that something had gone wrong. The familiar hiss of a fireworks fuse somewhere behind the dais was reassuring to those with good hearing, but nothing could have prepared them for the ensuing roar, not a detonation proper but a release of energy hinting at some fantastic ambition: perhaps the platform itself, guests and all, would levitate off the ground? Instead, a rocket rose through the pungent cloud of its own generation and screamed off in the direction of Great Mountain, its girth and length, so briefly glimpsed, of mythic proportions.

The launch alone would have provided a month's worth of reminiscence and debate to the adolescent males of Beecher's Bridge, but it was subsumed and obliterated by what happened next, which might be described as a dozen Fourths rolled into one. But not, mercifully, a single explosion, because after the initial report at the height of the rocket's trajectory—blinding and deafening even at such a distance and against the hazy sky—there followed a cascading series of lesser explosions and whistling effects, each announced by a metamorphosis: swarming sulphur-green bees became white phosphorus stars begat zigzagging missiles of crimson strontium, down and down until the last lilac showers, like falls of wisteria, grazed the bare rock of Great Mountain and expired there. And even this was not all, for when the pyrotechnic display had exhausted itself, another light bloomed on high, as if the mountain had caught fire, and the words "God Bless America" were spelled out boldly in alternating points of red and white.

"Them's lightbulbs now, Muriel," explained Fred Curtis to his wife. "No need to be afraid."

Toma craned his neck to see the display behind him, but it was an unwilling courtesy, for he knew in intimate detail, having supervised the preparations, the sequence of fireworks and lights to come, and he had never felt less like an American, nor so unblessed. He settled in to watch and listen, glad to have put away his barren thinking on the wheel, and diverted himself with the shallow drama of Senator Truscott's waiting game. He would talk until the lightning came, which would ignite the surprising grand finale of the celebration and co-opt the need for further speechifying. But if it did not come there must be a limit, not to his powers of expression but to the tolerance of his audience. No politician can afford to let his listeners fall asleep or go hungry. Sooner or later he would have to pull that second lever.

Toma's eyelids seemed to have weights on them; the last few days were taking their toll. Keeping up with Steinmetz's demands at this peak period of lightning activity was difficult enough. Schenectady sent racks of devices for testing, including new combinations of cable alloy and sheathing, and three variant prototypes of the new oxide film arresters. And then there were the sudden calls to battle stations, day or night, when a storm threatened. Eight days ago an urgent telegram had arrived from the office of the chairman directing him, Toma, to give precedence to the plans for the July 4 celebration, specifics to be supplied by Senator Truscott. Steinmetz was predictably furious, and since it would be imprudent to quarrel with his patrons, that fury was directed at Toma.

Under no circumstances was he to take a week's vacation from the work of the lightning research station in order to arrange public spec-

tacles. Senator Truscott's nonsense—the very word—could not be allowed to interfere, and Toma would have to see to that on his own
time. As a grudging concession and preventive measure, he sent two
cable technicians from Schenectady to help out. Truscott would have
to supply the fireworks experts.

Senator Truscott's nonsense, it turned out, was of a scale to rival
Steinmetz's own visionary schemes, and Toma was left to figure out
how the lightning might serve two masters. What Truscott wanted, if
only the weather and the lightning would cooperate, was a demonstration of the triumphant technology of peace. The bolt that struck the
aerial must be channeled away from the usual equipment, so that the
sign on the mountain opposite would not be affected by electrical failure. It was crucial, wrote Truscott, that God's blessings not be chal-
lenged by a mere thunderstorm. But the cable technicians had seen too
much to give him absolute assurance. "This stuff has a mind of its
own," said one. "If you have to be sure, then you'll need a storage battery system as a backup." The storage battery system was duly added to
Toma's list.

The immediate effect of the lightning strike would be to ignite another round of fireworks. Bombardments of rockets from the heights
of the mountain would rain down on Lightning Knob, to be answered
by fiery diagonals aimed up at God's very sign. There would be
whistling squibs that might be mistaken for the signal to attack, followed by a staccato of thousands of firecrackers to repulse the imagined onslaught of infantry. One last, tremendous starburst from the
mountain would silence the Knob, and as the first rocket of the
evening had illuminated God's Blessing on Great Mountain, so this last
stroke of the entertainment would provoke an answer, graven in light
on the Knob below the aerial and Peacock's Folly: "And Keep Her
Safe."

At two A.M. the night before there had been electrical activity over
Lightning Knob, duly recorded, and the new series of oxide film arresters had performed almost according to expectations. At ten o'clock,
just a few hours ago, Toma, Stefan, and the cable technicians had re-
configured the circuits to accommodate Truscott's extravaganza. It was
hard, hot, hurried work. Frayed tempers led to an angry exchange between the Schenectady men and the crew sent by the Giambetti fire-

works manufactory to install the display. The chief of these Neapolitans was outraged to learn that they were not permitted to light a single fuse: all must be done automatically and electrically. His injured dignity could only be expressed in the phrase: "No, no, I am the Giambetti," by which he meant, Toma discovered, that he was the nephew of the Giambetti, and no one outside the family ever touched the fuses. It was a question of honor and long tradition. Toma eventually settled the matter with difficulty and in favor of General Electric, though he got little thanks for his diplomacy. "Foolishness," was the way the taciturn fellow from Schenectady put it as he spliced and wrapped the connections with blinding dexterity. "Trying to make a million volts jump through a hoop."

Truscott forged on, stopping more often now to deploy the handkerchief or to reach for his glass of water. Also, it seemed to Toma, to catch his breath. The sun had sunk into the haze, dusk deepened without relief, and gleams of heat lightning, far away and without sound, punctuated the twilight. In this awful heat the senator's linen coat was soaked to the waist, and Toma, knowing that the second lever would set off the fireworks in the absence of a lightning strike, grew impatient with Truscott's heroic obstinacy. There was not, after all, a cloud in sight, only this malevolent haze. Chairman Coffin rested his eyes and might even have been sleeping. Harriet looked steadfastly at her husband, but the radiance of those earlier expressions was clouded with concern, for she too had noticed how he panted. Steinmetz, in his black suit, was oblivious to the heat and attentive to the speaker. He nodded approval at certain turns of phrase and applauded the patriotic references. At one point he took his pocket notebook and wrote something there. All the while he worried the stump of his dead cigar, and from time to time his eyes came to meditate upon Toma as if he were a problematic equation.

Toma returned the stare. Steinmetz was his puzzle; where else should he look? The little man's unsparing and unsettling attention made Toma think of Flaten. Poor Flaten would have no defenses against such scrutiny. *Remember our conversation* he had written in the letter. Toma had taken this as a valedictory to the friendship the fellow had offered so eagerly, too eagerly for Toma's comfort. And now Flaten sat in Schenectady, drawn like a moth to his fate, or perhaps . . . perhaps sent there? Why would he go of his own free will? And if not freely, why? Because of the patent. Toma smiled at Steinmetz. Something was tipping, obscurely, in his favor.

Remember our conversation. Not the folded paper that made a mirror of the drawing; not the anecdote of Steinmetz's cigar and the fit of asthma; not even the proffer of friendship, perhaps intimacy, from which Toma had recoiled. Flaten had warned him about Tesla's patent for the bladeless turbine, and that was the direction he must now follow, the meaning of the letter at last. Toma had thought that there was a safe distance between his device and Tesla's. The safe distance had now shrunk to insignificance, perhaps nothing. He could not doubt that this was Steinmetz's doing, history repeating itself. Had he not been hired twenty years ago by General Electric to engineer his way around the Westinghouse alternating-current patents, which were Tesla's? Had he not written a history of alternating current that barely mentioned Tesla? Stefan had lent him this book, unconscious of its irony. It was as if one should write the history of the United States and leave George Washington out of the account. Steinmetz had failed then—General Electric had to buy the patents; what if he succeeded now? Or if he failed again? He, Toma, would be remembered as the man who had tried to steal another of Tesla's patents.

This bitter thought was interrupted by an unusual sound: it seemed as if Senator Truscott had swallowed his tongue in mid-sentence. Toma looked sharply at the speaker, expecting him to clear his throat or take a sip of water. Instead, he clung to the lectern in silence while his head made jerking motions that might have punctuated the lost speech. Then the legs buckled, and in his effort to hold himself upright, Truscott tripped the second lever. The display of the Giambettis' art was most gratifying, the audience ready to be gratified; reaction to the abrupt end of the senator's remarks was confused and muted. Had he tripped? or simply lost his train of thought? It was hard to remember, afterward, the exact sequence of events, and the thrilling explosions on the heights distracted attention from Truscott's exit. The fireworks were such a success, and the picnic supper so lavish, that it all seemed to have gone, more or less, according to plan.

TOMA, ELBOWS ON HIS KNEES, sat in the deep shadow of the great room where he could watch the door of the library. Once it was determined that Truscott was still breathing, they had managed to get him off the platform. Toma took one arm over his shoulders, and the venerable Mr. Coffin, having waved Steinmetz away, took the other. It was not a perfect arrangement, as both Truscott and Toma were a good deal taller than Coffin, but the old man was strong, his footsteps sure, and they made their way through the clutter of folding chairs to the car where Harriet waited, her face the color of stone in the twilight. Truscott was dead weight, but he seemed still to have strength in his arms. They got him into the backseat: the right foot twitched every second or two and Toma noted how the lustrous shoe had been damaged in its journey across the planking. The driver could not be found, and so Harriet took the wheel. She whispered urgently to Toma, telling him to find Dr. Crowell and bring him at once.

He did not know how much time had passed, but had kept track of who came and went from the library, now the sickroom. Maids fetching water, sheets, towels, a pail. Harriet running out to the stairs and up, returning with a pair of pyjamas. Mrs. Evans hobbled down the stairs after her, and a few steps behind her, Amos Bigelow. He was not allowed in, so he walked up and down the hall, clasping and unclasping his hands.

Mrs. Evans led the old man away, and now Coffin came out of the library and dropped down into a chair not far from Toma, who was not sure he had been noticed. He cleared his throat.

"Is that you, Mr. Peacock?"

"Yes, sir."

A distant flash illuminated the room and wind ruffled the pages of a magazine or newspaper. They waited for the growl of thunder.

"Five, six miles, I should think, and the temperature dropping at last. I fear Truscott has pushed himself too far in this silly business. And Mrs. Truscott, so he told me at breakfast, is to bear a child. Very sad indeed, and one feels quite useless. Sometimes I wish I were a drinking man. Shall I have them send something to you?"

"Thank you, sir, but no. Can you tell me what the situation is?"

"Oh, I'm afraid he's for it. Doctor wants to be circumspect with

Mrs. Truscott there, but I've seen a lot in my day and often you can tell just by the look of them. I'm not a betting man either, but . . ."

Coffin stood. "Good night, then, Mr. Peacock. I'm no use to anyone here, so I shall take myself off to bed."

"Good night, sir."

There was hushed conversation from the study, and because Mr. Coffin had left the door ajar, Toma might have been able to make it out but for the gusting wind that rattled the leaves. One voice was Harriet's, another the doctor's, and the third belonged unmistakably to Steinmetz. Could they be arguing? Could Truscott be dying? He wondered if he had wished for such an outcome. Of course he had, but this was no victory; it felt more like defeat.

Lily came into the room without glancing at his dark corner, and set about shutting the windows overlooking the lake. He did not wish to startle her. She was talking to herself and seemed very upset.

"Lily."

"Oh! Is it you, sir, Mr. Peacock?"

"Yes, Lily. Would you do something for me?"

"Anything, certainly."

"I would like a glass of whiskey, if I might, but I know the liquor is kept in there, in the library."

"It's all right, sir. He keeps other bottles, and now . . . and now . . ."
He took her hand.

"I know, Lily, and I am sorry." She went away and came back with a very full glass. He thought she had helped herself as well.

"Thank you."

"What will she do now, sir?" He startled at the question, which was too close to his own. Was she too questioning his innocence? "What will become of us and of Mrs. Truscott?"

"I can't answer that, Lily, but I think she is very strong, and we must do what we can to help her, as I'm sure you will."

"Thank you, sir." He lifted the glass a few inches up and slightly away. She took it and drank. "I'd better look to the other windows now. Bless you, sir."

"And you, Lily."

There was silence in the library. The hall clock ticked off the seconds, then chimed three quarters. He didn't know what he was waiting for, and he was no longer quite sober.

He rose from his chair, and as if it had been arranged, or they were connected by a wire, Steinmetz appeared in the door of the library. He spoke to someone standing in the shadow beside him. "You have done the right thing." He closed the door behind him and stood in the hall light, blinking like a small owl.

"Ah, Mr. Peacock. Good evening. I am surprised to see you here at this hour, but it seems you are everywhere these days."

Toma refused the bait. He waited.

"You have given Piccolomini quite a turn with your dramatics. Was that necessary?"

"No. He could have opened the door when he was asked, but he was hiding something. He is anxious." Toma lowered his voice. "And you, I imagine, are ashamed. What could Tesla possibly have done to deserve this?"

Steinmetz smiled. "Deserve is a useless word in science, or in business. You do better to think of progress. Dr. Tesla is a brilliant fellow, certainly; his ideas are dazzling. But if they lead nowhere, if he cannot make them work for the general good, then there can be no progress. Do I make myself clear?"

"Yes, very clear. You will take his turbine—steal it, shall we say— and call it mine for the general good of General Electric. I think that sums it up."

Steinmetz patted his pockets until he found the matches. He relit his cigar. "You are trying to offend me, but I can tell you that no law has been broken. Of course I saw immediately the convergence between the two devices, your wheel and his, and if you are an honest man, you did too. But patents expire, and now we are in a war, which changes the way such disputes are viewed and judged. We must get on with things, and put aside squabblings, yes? Squabblings over ownership and the precedence of patent claims. The general good is not an empty phrase to me, nor is progress. There is so much to be done, and one man cannot stand in the way."

"I am sure Dr. Tesla would be moved by your patriotism, your selfless devotion to principle."

Steinmetz sighed, rubbed his forehead. When he spoke again it was in a subdued tone of voice. "Tesla may sue us. We have thought of that, of course. But I am informed by my colleagues in the legal department that he will not win, and so he would be well advised not to try."

"You can do it, and so you will. A very German point of view."

"You forget yourself, Mr. Peacock. I am an American and a patriot. You . . ."

The door of the library opened and Harriet passed between them without a glance. She walked with Dr. Crowell to the front door, where she listened with her head bowed. When she came back to them she seemed too tired to smile or to make small talk.

"You were arguing just now."

"Do not trouble yourself, my dear Mrs. Truscott; we were just discussing a difference of philosophy. I was recommending to Mr. Peacock that he follow the example of your husband, who has devoted himself to progress. But I see that you are tired and Mr. Peacock has come to pay his respects. I bid you both good night. If anything is needed you must call me. I am a light sleeper."

"Thank you. Good night." Toma nodded but did not speak.

A dazed and distant smile, the eyes silently filling with tears, the invisible mantle of her impending widowhood: never had she belonged so completely to Fowler Truscott, and Toma was borne away from her on the deep current of her sorrow. What was left to him? Words of comfort, if only he could find them.

"Is there anything to be done? Anything I can do?"

She shook her head.

"What did he say to you?"

"He said there had been great damage to the heart, and it is perhaps only a matter of time. I must prepare myself."

"No, I meant Steinmetz. He thanked you."

She looked down.

"Please, I must know."

"It was a piece of paper about the project up on the mountain, something they discussed last night at dinner with Mr. Coffin, and afterward in the library. It was still there on his desk just now."

"And you signed it for him?"

She nodded.

"Do you know what it was? A deed? A contract?"

"A lease of some sort, I think, but I did not read it." Now she looked up at him, defiant and perhaps angry. "I knew only that it was what Fowler wanted, the one thing that I could do for him. Now the work will go forward."

"Progress."

"Yes, I suppose, but I did not think of it that way. It was not for Dr. Steinmetz, and certainly not for myself. It was for him. Can you not understand that?"

"Only too well." Angry or not, at least she was looking at him. Her anger was a lifeline, a connection, an acknowledgement of binding complicity.

He understood now that there was, after all, something he could do, something he must do. The risk and uncertainty of it were obvious, but the great obstacle was time.

"Shouldn't you try to get some sleep? You look exhausted."

"Funny"—she was almost smiling—"but I was just going to say the same thing."

"What if I were to sleep here for a couple of hours? Then I could sit with him while you rest."

"Are you sure? I could always call Lily, or Mrs. Evans."

"I might as well. It is a bad time to go up the mountain."

"Oh, the storm. I forgot. Yes, of course you must stay. But there is only her room."

"It does not matter. I can find my way."

"There are candles in the pantry, and matches. Shall I call you?"

"There is no need. I am used to rising at strange hours."

"Good night, then, Toma, and thank you for everything."

HE LAY ON THE BED, naked except for the silk cross around his neck, and listened. Lily muttered in her sleep next door. Someone, probably the cook, turned over in bed. Thunder might wake them, but the rain would put them sound asleep. He would have to wait for the rain. After a carelessly loud trip up the back stairs he had undressed and folded his clothes neatly on the chair. He wouldn't need them until later, but he had to think about the boots. Would it slow him down to go barefoot? Might he reinjure his foot? Yes and yes. But then what would he do with the soaked and filthy things when he got back? A trace of mud on the carpet would betray him. It must seem as if he had never left his bed, this bed which, because of the heat and the closeness of the room, gave up the odor of Olivia's hair. Wires. That's what she had said in disgust as she brushed her hair, hating the copper color in it and the texture. Everything depended now on wires.

Any moment, he told himself. But the moments passed and he wondered if he should go back to reason with her, beg her to tear up the paper, explain what Steinmetz had done to his wheel. A waste of time. She would not be able to listen or think clearly or believe such things of Steinmetz, and in the end he would be no better than Steinmetz, cajoling her over the dying man.

Lightning flashed in the near distance, and there was Tesla sitting in the chair by the window, his head wreathed in jagged light exactly as it had been in the famous photograph. But didn't everyone know the photograph was a fake, a double exposure? Tesla had not been in the laboratory when the generator discharged its spectacular display. Why was he here now? He lit a match. There was a lazy roll of thunder. Tesla was gone.

He had no religion, but signs and apparitions were different; they always meant something. When he had spoken with Steinmetz, trying to pierce that maddening forbearance—the victor's magnanimity, as it would turn out—his only thought had been: This must be punished. Only minutes later he was looking at her, and she at him, and in that moment vengeance took a specific shape—this plan—and was in the same instant reframed, transformed. He would do it for her. He loved her more than he detested Steinmetz. Now Tesla had visited him and the ground shifted again, taking away all his doubt. He would do this for himself, and he alone would know. *I will take it back. It is mine.* His body went rigid with anticipation of the deed, and the danger. And the rain came.

There was a portion of the roof just below his window ledge and he worked his way around the corner until he found the drainpipe. If he felt it starting to give way, he would drop into the bed of shrubbery below so that it wouldn't fall. How he would scale the wall again in that case he had no idea, but he was no longer concerned with what might go wrong.

The path was muddy and of course steep, but he knew every rock and root of it. He went as fast as he dared, and faster when he had the help of the lightning. In the tangle of wires laid this morning there was only one that he needed. It had been strung through the scrub oaks to reach a battery of rockets around the shoulder of the Knob. Too much slack in that wire, he had said to the cable technician, who shrugged and replied: All this comes down tomorrow. Somebody would remember that exchange.

He was out now on the bare top of the Knob, with the aerial and the tower at his back. The storm had come across the valley of the Buttermilk and was so close that there was almost no delay between the lightning and its thunder. He could even smell flint, which made him think that there had already been a strike here. He walked out to where he thought the wire should be and waited for another flash.

He saw the wire and remembered Stefan's story. If lightning had already struck here there might be a residual charge in this wire, and he would be the ground when he touched it. There was no time and no choice: the next bolt might kill him as surely as the last one. He took it in his hand and knew that tonight he was immortal. The lightning would do his bidding.

He had worried about the arresters and the fuses, but with this fire in his mind he did not have to think any more. He took a branch, heavier than the wire, lighter than the wind, and wedged them both against the stout conduit below the fuse box. There was now nothing but a few thousand feet of cable between him and the silk mill, between the lightning and the wheel. He followed the wire back toward the aerial in the open embrasure of the tower, pulling a bit of slack from the far end as he went, leaving his anchor undisturbed. The lightning would jump from the aerial to a cable, but he must leave nothing to chance. He ran his hand down the aerial to the collar at its base and looped his wire once around a bolt. One hand on the wire, the other on the aerial, he felt the sodden hair rising on the back of his neck. He would walk, not run, for he had nothing to fear. *I am the lightning.*

70,000-volt choke coil for use with lightning arrester

Pile of 2,000 old flat irons taken in exchange for electric irons

High-head hydroelectric plant in Chile, 1923

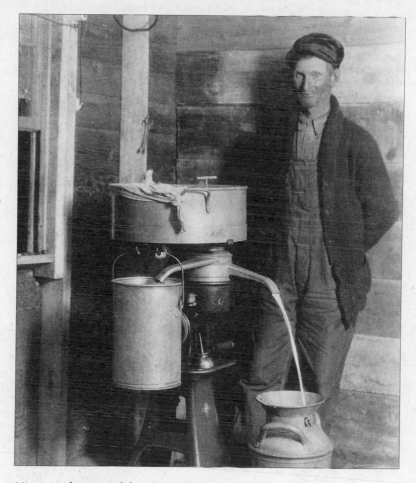

Minnesota farmer with his electrically driven cream separator, 1924

It is a mystery why this man has such hatred for me, and why he should go to such lengths to punish the firm that has raised him from obscurity. Of course I regret my remarks, and I have already offered my profound apology in a personal letter. But I insist that the publication of those characterizations of him was a complete misunderstanding; it was something written in the heat of the moment and appended as a postscript to my account of the catastrophic events in Beecher's Bridge. The article itself was typed, as all my contributions to the Journal of Advanced Engineering *have been, and the remarks, which you see for yourself are handwritten, were a personal and private communication from myself to the editor. I meant merely to suggest a possibility, a theory without proof, concerning the circumstances that led to the fire in the Experimental Site and the destruction of the Peacock Turbine.*

—from the deposition of C. P. Steinmetz in the
action *Peacock v. General Electric et al.*

EPILOGUE

Much has been written and still more said concerning the fire that destroyed the Experimental Site and effectively ended General Electric's salutary endeavors in our town, and in the desired event that my own history should one day be published, I will not enter into any dangerous speculations as to the causes of that conflagration. It seemed, and this is still the opinion of most folk in Beecher's Bridge, to be an act of God.

The Experimental Site might have been rebuilt, given time and goodwill, and absent the distraction of the war. But the publication of Dr. Steinmetz's allegedly defamatory remarks cast a pall over relations between the principals, and the libel action pursued by Mr. Peacock was not resolved until after the war had ended. The case never came to trial, but was settled out of court for an undisclosed amount of money. Also, and perhaps more significantly, the rights to the Peacock Turbine were reverted to the inventor. The work that Dr. Steinmetz envisioned was never resumed or pursued, but in 1922 he perfected the artificial generation of lightning in the GE laboratories in Schenectady.

The tower still stands on Lightning Knob, and it is still known as Peacock's Folly. The water of Dead Man's Lake follows its natural course down the mountain through Rachel's Leap to the placid, unaltered pond below the Truscott house. It might seem, taking the long view, as if nothing ever changes in Beecher's Bridge, as if the words of the Congregational minister—uttered in bitter dissent to the decision of the railroad commissioners—are an inescapable prophecy: the history of Beecher's Bridge is the history of failed enterprise.

But there is a nearer perspective in which everything changes: Senator Truscott dies, and after a suitable period of mourning, his widow—the mother of his child—takes as her husband that same Thomas Peacock who had lately been her chauffeur, then laborer in the ironworks, then, by some obscure stroke of fate, inventor. We do not have very rigid social distinctions in Beecher's Bridge, and yet this match is certainly the object of much curiosity and gossip. It would be one thing if she had simply been Harriet Bigelow, but her status as the widow of a United States senator altered how people, some people, looked upon the match, and they say it can come to no good.

I take a more charitable, or relaxed, view of the matter. People will find their own happiness, or the opposite, and how such things turn out often defies expectation or common wisdom. Indeed the chronicle of recent events in Beecher's Bridge, from what I term the nearer or human perspective, is nothing if not a series of astonishing, unforeseeable reversals and cataclysms. Which is why, perhaps, I take refuge in the longer and more peaceful perspective of history, and leave such unknowable things as the workings of the heart to the imagination of novelists.

ACKNOWLEDGEMENTS

I am very grateful indeed to the following people and organizations, whose collective efforts, enthusiasm, and generosity have sustained me in the researching and writing of this book:

For research on facts and photographs: Patricia Chui, John Crowley, Chris Hunter, Michaela Murphy, and Barry Webber.

For editorial guidance: Tim Duggan, Jonathan Galassi, and Earl Shorris.

For reading, sound advice, and other courtesies: Catherine Brown, Sarah Chalfant, Richard S. Childs, Starling W. Childs, Linda Corrente, Susan Corrente, Michael Hudnall, Nelle Harper Lee, Michael Lewis, Allison Lorentzen, James Mairs, Robert Morgan, Howard Norman, Jay Pittman, Jenny Preston, Allen Wheelis, John Williams, and Andrew Wylie.

For their erudition, which opened so many doors: Margaret Cheney (*Tesla*); Theron Wilmot Crissey (*A History of Norfolk, 1744-1900*); David Freeman Hawke (*Nuts and Bolts of the Past*); Thomas P. Hughes (*Networks of Power*); Ed Kirby (*Echoes of Iron*); Ronald R. Kline (*Steinmetz*); J. Lawrence Pool (*America's Valley Forges and Valley Furnaces*); Matthew Roth, Bruce Clouette, and Victor Darnell (*Connecticut: An Inventory of Historic Engineering and Industrial Sites*; Thomas J. Schlereth (*Victorian America*).

Special thanks to the Corporation of Yaddo for allowing me two residencies, during which much of the writing was accomplished; to the

Norfolk Historical Society for making available its photographic collection documenting local Connecticut history; and to the Schenectady Museum for access to the extraordinary General Electric archive of documents and photographs pertaining to the history of the electric power industry.

ILLUSTRATION CREDITS

About the author

About the book

Insights,
Interviews
& More ...

Read on

Meet Starling Lawrence

Dan Deitch

I WAS BORN IN 1943 when my father was off at war, and so I did not have any memory of the gentleman who showed up in late 1945 and was introduced as Daddy. No, I insisted, Daddy was the fellow in the photograph on the piano. It was a rocky beginning, and perhaps it explains something about my life-long skepticism of any claims to Higher Authority.

Ours was a large family—many siblings and first cousins—and with two older sisters and an older brother, I already had more Higher Authority than I could handle. My brother was a splendid fellow—still is— but much too attractive and athletic for his own good, so I had to find my own path. I read a lot (but not as much as my younger brother), grew fat, and cultivated Attitude. My first literary effort, now lost, was a poem concerning a shrimp who went up in a blimp.

Boarding school—I will do everyone a favor by not naming the institution—was undoubtedly a godsend for my parents, but

❝ I read a lot, grew fat, and cultivated Attitude. My first literary effort, now lost, was a poem concerning a shrimp who went up in a blimp. ❞

2

I was a fish out of water. My caustic wit won me few friends and I was not very interested in anything beyond the academic work.

Three years flew by like a life sentence, and those summers in Connecticut were a paradise lost over and over. When I graduated, I was months younger than my classmates, and so my father suggested that although I had managed to get into Princeton, I might do something else for a year. Like what? Go to school in another country; see something of the world. It was the best advice I ever had.

I chose a boarding school in England, Malvern College, and thanks to the forbearance of my housemaster, with whom I still correspond, I had a wonderful year. I was no longer fat, but certainly large, and I found I could be useful at rugby football if I simply fell on people. The coursework in English and history was interesting, but it was what I read under the table that made the year for me: J. R. R. Tolkien's recently completed trilogy, *The Lord of the Rings*.

My years at Princeton did indeed fly by. I spent my time reading more English and tuning my skills as a drag queen in musical comedy. When it came time to choose a thesis topic, I opted for Tolkien and *Beowulf*, the latter because JRRT was the foremost *Beowulf* scholar of his day. I still remember the expression of shallow pique on my adviser's face when he asked, "Let me get this straight: you mean you are going to write about . . . fairies?" Another failure with respect to Authority.

In the summer after my junior year I followed my father's advice again and went off to Africa on a student work program run by Crossroads Africa, an old-fashioned organization that believed in kids, ▶

> " My years at Princeton did indeed fly by. I spent my time reading more English and tuning my skills as a drag queen in musical comedy. "

About the author

❝ I had, and still have, the pleasure and honor of editing such authors as Michael Ondaatje, Vincent Bugliosi, Martin Katahn, Michael Lewis, A. N. Wilson, Earl Shorris, Allen Wheelis, Alistair MacLeod, Sebastian Junger, Mary Lee Settle, and Patrick O'Brian. ❞

American and African, getting their hands very dirty.

After Princeton I went to Pembroke College, Cambridge, for a couple of years—in the late '60s you didn't want to be a young man with nothing to do. There I read *Beowulf* in the original, rowed, played more rugby, and was a member of Footlights, the musical comedy club that had produced *Beyond the Fringe* a few years earlier.

Then it was back to Africa—Cameroon—in the Peace Corps, the perfect experience for a young man with interests but no particular skills. I taught English to kids who spoke French, among other languages, and had the time of my life. I had just got married, the people were wonderful, the volcanic landscape surprising and thrilling, and all things seemed possible. It wasn't an answer, or a calling, but a corrective to many of the assumptions and conventionalities of American life.

Back home, and now beyond draft age, I was hired by the publishing company that still employs me . . . another inexplicable stroke of luck. I thought I might edit books during the day and write them at night, but having children—triplets, if you please—put paid to that, and it was not until they were all out of the house that I set pen to paper in earnest. In the meantime, I had, and still have, the pleasure and honor of editing such authors as Michael Ondaatje, Vincent Bugliosi, Martin Katahn, Michael Lewis, A. N. Wilson, Earl Shorris, Allen Wheelis, Alistair MacLeod, Sebastian Junger, Mary Lee Settle, and Patrick O'Brian. ⌇

Writing
The Lightning Keeper

THE LIGHTNING KEEPER was always supposed to be my first novel, but by a curious circumstance it became my second.

I had been fascinated, from childhood on, with the story of an immigrant Serb scientist/inventor who had made a great success of his career. His name was Michael Idvorsky Pupin, and he built an extravagant stone castle in the same town in northwestern Connecticut where my family spent the summers. He had a very colorful private life—scandalously romantic according to local legend— and in the 1920s he wrote his autobiography, a splendid book that won a Pulitzer Prize.

What a character, I thought, what a life. Using Pupin and his story as a very loose model, I hoped I might be able to write a resonant love story that would get at the psychological and social complexities of the immigrant experience and take the reader inside the excitement of science in the early twentieth century.

Pupin's story was compelling, but I was going to write a novel, not a biography. I began to do some reading on the Balkans, hoping to find enough story material to create an interestingly plausible background from which my character, Toma Pekocevic, might have emigrated to the United States. I read history and literature, everything from Rebecca West's wonderful *Black Lamb and Grey Falcon* to Ivo Andric's haunting novel *The Bridge on the Drina*, with stops in between for slightly cracked English travelers who wrote such works as *With Gun and Camera through the Balkans*. ▶

" I had been fascinated, from childhood on, with the story of an immigrant Serb scientist/ inventor. [He] built an extravagant stone castle in the same town in northwestern Connecticut where my family spent the summers. "

5

I had a wonderful time doing this research, but I had never written a novel before. There was more story material than I knew what to do with, and when it came to the writing, I bogged down in this embarrassment of riches. Instead of a prologue about where Toma had grown up, or a first chapter, or even a Part One, I realized that this was a whole book in itself. The novel was called *Montenegro*, and although the reader knows that Toma is headed for the New World, the story ends when he boards his ship.

What was it that I found so compelling about scientific activity in the years before and during World War One? First, the characters, defined by their Promethean ambitions, seemed larger than life: Thomas Edison, John Hammond, George Westinghouse, Charles Steinmetz, Nikola Tesla, to name just a few. The latter two figures were, like Toma, Central European immigrants; they would come to play a part in my story. And the stakes of scientific enterprise in those times were enormous. On the horizon loomed the universal electrification of America—homes, factories, cities, transportation systems, even the most isolated farms. In today's terms, you could take Silicon Valley and biotech, roll all that up into a ball, and you still wouldn't approach the changes wrought in individual lives and society at large by electrification. I was fascinated not only by what these scientists and others like them achieved, but by how they thought about what they did, and by what they dreamed.

There was another element to my interest. My maternal grandfather, Charles Albert Coffin, was the first president of General Electric. He was not a technical man, having started out as a shoe manufacturer in Lynn, Massachusetts; but he saw how electricity was going to change the world and he shifted gears. He became the chief financial officer of an electrical manufacturing firm, Thomson Houston, and when Edison and Westinghouse had exhausted themselves fighting over patents, J. P. Morgan arranged a merger of Edison's firm and Coffin's much smaller rival operation. Morgan, to Edison's surprise and outrage, chose Coffin to lead the new enterprise.

Since General Electric, by the time World War One rolled around, was the most important player in this field, why not have my character, Toma, invent something of particular interest to GE? I was curious to see what happens when a man of individual genius gets caught up in a world where he is no longer master of his own fate, or at least the fate of his creation.

The burden of research was even greater this time around than for *Montenegro*; my orientation is so non-scientific that I usually manage to avoid reading the science section of *The New York Times*. Also, there is a limit to how much technical detail readers of fiction will tolerate. But the potential for embarrassment was great: suppose I had Toma invent the ball-bearing seventy-five years after it had in fact been done? Once I started reading, I was relieved to find that the story material in the history of science was no less thrilling than the stories embedded in Balkan history. I hope that excitement comes through in the book.

But *The Lightning Keeper* is not just about science, and when asked to describe it, the first thing I say is that it is a love story, and even more specifically, a Romeo and Juliet story. The prologue to the book takes place in Naples, Italy, where Toma meets an American girl, Harriet Bigelow, who is on holiday with her family. He is sixteen, she fourteen, and although they are divided by nationality, class, and to some extent language, their attraction is immediate and overwhelming. Their time together is brief, and Harriet returns to America; but she will haunt Toma's dreams and his waking hours until he can find her again. As in the story of Romeo and Juliet, their love seems both impossible and inevitable. This is the tension, the energy, that sustains the entire novel. ➤

Author's Picks
Further Reading

MANY OF THE BOOKS I read as background to *The Lightning Keeper* were a kind of penance for not having paid closer attention during those high school science classes, and they might be forbidding to the general reader. But there are a couple of books of gentle scholarship that I can wholeheartedly recommend, ones that encouraged me to understand my own story in a broad rather than a narrow way. One thing I realized early on is that you can't write about science during a certain period if you don't know what discoveries or achievements paved the way. And the same applies to history in general. How can you understand a situation of any sort, past or present, without having some inkling of its antecedents? The first two books on my list explain the background of the science and of the social setting in which the story takes place

NUTS AND BOLTS OF THE PAST,
by David Freeman Hawke

There are many books about invention, some about the exploits of individuals, some of a more general, abstract nature. In this book David Hawke writes about those largely anonymous individuals who were responsible for the industrial advances of America in the nineteenth century, men whose genius resided at least as much in their hands as in their heads. They were the practical fellows on the shop floor who knew how to bend the metal and could come up with design improvements when something didn't work as well as it should.

> 66 One thing I realized early on is that you can't write about science during a certain period if you don't know what discoveries or achievements paved the way. 99

He calls them "mechanicians," which is not at all a synonym for "mechanics." They were the workers and shop foremen who built Fulton's steam engines or who carried out the effort to standardize parts in the Springfield Armory or the Colt factory. From this book I got the idea that the history of American industrial progress is the history of tolerances, a word that needs some explanation. In the shops where steam engines were built in the 1820s and '30s, the standard measuring device was a rule marked off in tenths of an inch. By 1900 or so, automobile engines in the Leyland works were being milled to tolerances of one ten thousandth of an inch. In that difference resides efficiency, economy, mechanical advantage, and untold riches.

VICTORIAN AMERICA, by Thomas Schlereth

It is hard to separate my admiration for this book from how useful it was to me, but it is one I will read again with pleasure. It is about the changes in American domestic life between the Philadelphia Centennial Exposition in 1876 and the Panama-Pacific Exposition in 1914. Schlereth tells us what people ate and read; how they shopped and traveled; how the mail came to be delivered to our doorsteps; and how Standard Time and the four time zones came to replace— over considerable local opposition—the chaos of every city and town in the country having its own distinct noon.

THE RINGS OF SATURN, by W. G. Sebald

This book is so dazzling that readers (and prize committees) are uncertain whether to call it fiction or non-fiction. The chapters start out as essays on the odd landscape ▶

> " It is hard to separate my admiration for [*Victorian America*] from how useful it was to me, but it is [a book] I will read again with pleasure. "

and history of East Anglia, once the richest part of England, thanks to the wool trade and the fisheries, now in steep decline and dotted with crumbling reminders of its former glory. So far this may sound like pretty standard non-fiction. But in the middle of a chapter on Joseph Conrad's experiences as a ship master in the coastal coal trade between Newcastle and London, Sebald's imagination bolts to the Congo, where Conrad served briefly as a steamer captain, later writing *Heart of Darkness* about the horrors he witnessed. A chapter on an abandoned railway crossing the marshes opens out into a hallucinatory evocation of life in the court of the last emperor of China. The train that ran along those tracks in East Anglia had originally been commissioned by the Dowager Empress for her son. The order was cancelled rather late in the day, and local residents told Sebald that beneath the black paint one could see the faint outline of the imperial dragon.

Sebald's book is unique, and I wouldn't dare imitate his style or imaginative leaps. But his use of photographs in the text, usually without captions, seemed an interesting way to get readers to think about period and place without having to spell everything out on the page. Collecting the photographs for *The Lightning Keeper* was a great satisfaction, and I think that they add a resonance to the story. ∾

66 Collecting the photographs for *The Lightning Keeper* was a great satisfaction, and I think that they add a resonance to the story. 99

Montenegro
An Excerpt

*In this epic, richly imagined novel, a young
English traveler named Auberon Harwell
enters the valley of Montenegro. It's 1908,
and World War One is a dark prophecy on the
horizon. Posing as a botanist, Harwell lives
among the Serbs and studies the area's native
flowers. His real mission is to serve as a
confidential agent for a powerful English peer,
who hopes to assess the possible advantages
and threats in the region. One of Harwell's
new neighbors is Toma, only son of the valley's
warrior patriarch, Danilo Pekocevic. Toma
loves a girl he cannot marry, the daughter of
a neighboring Muslim landowner. Harwell,
against all reason and hope, falls in love
with Toma's mother. Bound by obligations of
honor and duty, Harwell is eventually forced
from a position of careful neutrality into a
confrontation that will forever change the
world he thought he knew.*

"Starling Lawrence has created a stirring
account of turn-of-the-century political
intrigue—and an intriguing romance."
          —*New York Times Book Review*

Excerpt: From Chapter Six

 Stephan led Harwell away then, around the
side of the church to a spot where several
sheep fretted in a pen of wattles and stakes.
Down the valley, at the point where the
steep descent of the gorge began, Harwell
saw the arches of an old bridge across the
Morača, a Roman bridge, he guessed. It was
peaceful here after the din of the courtyard,
and at least he could hear himself think.
He counted five sheep in the pen. ▶

Montenegro: An Excerpt *(continued)*

Stefan unwound his sash and laid the knife and the pistol upon it, then pulled his cassock over his head. Underneath he was wearing plain breeches and a homespun woolen shirt that reached only to his elbows. From the shoulders and the thick, veined forearms on this fellow, thought Harwell, he has done many things in his life besides praying.

"If we would eat meat," said Stefan, lifting a sheep effortlessly over the wattles by the scruff and the tail, "then we must kill it first." He held the animal down under his knee and bound its feet with a length of rope. The animal, once bound, did not struggle further, and Stefan reached into the pen to catch another.

"All of them?" asked Harwell.

"All," replied Stefan. "And even then I am afraid we may not have enough. You have seen how many have come to honor the saint, and if we do not feed them well, they will drink all the more, and then God knows what might happen. Listen, it has started."

Harwell listened to the singing, in which he caught the oft-repeated words *"Tamo je Serbija,"* and when the song ended there was a rolling volley of pistol shots and much cheering. "I do not understand," he said, "why they are singing about Serbia: 'Yonder is my Serbia' indeed, but we are in Montenegro, no?"

Stefan looked up at him from his work. "Wherever Serbs live, that is Serbia, according to our way of thinking. Where you wish to go is very near the Sandžak of Novi Pazar, which is but a finger of land between Montenegro and the kingdom of Serbia, where the other free Serbs live, and the Sandžak is Serbia. Also there"—he pointed north—"is Bosnia, and there to the west and north is Herzegovina, where the princely family of Njegoš comes from, and behind us are Peć and Kosovo and Prizren, the heart of Stefan Dusan's kingdom of old."

Harwell had never slaughtered a sheep, but he had certainly dipped his hundreds, and shorn them too, and so he caught one now and handed it, kicking and bleating, to the monk. "But is Montenegro, then, Serbia as well? It is tiny compared to those lands you have named."

"We are all one, and Montenegro is the heart of Serbia, for there the sultan has never had his way, even after the defeat at Kosovo, and Serbs everywhere know this is true. Look," and he knelt to scratch a map in a patch bare of grass. "Here is Montenegro, and Serbia, and the Sandžak lying between them. And what we call the Idea, the Idea of Great Serbia, is that the lands I have named should all come together, along with Dalmatia and Bulgaria, and be one nation again, as they were before Kosovo, in the time of King Stefan Dusan. Who then could stand in our way?"

This famous Kosovo, reflected Harwell, though he did not dare voice his thought, *was a good five hundred years ago, and then some.* "An ambitious plan," was what he said aloud, "and who would lead such a coalition, or empire?"

"Some say our Prince Nikola should be given pride of place, some say the king of free Serbia. It does not matter to me as long as Serbs, wherever they are found, are allowed to have their schools, in their ▶

> " Harwell had never slaughtered a sheep, but he had certainly dipped his hundreds, and shorn them too, and so he caught one now and handed it, kicking and bleating, to the monk. "

own language, and follow their God, as they cannot do now."

"And would you fight for this Idea of Great Serbia?"

Stefan did not answer at once, for he was crossing himself and then closed his eyes briefly in prayer before taking the bound sheep, one by one, and slitting their throats with his great curved knife. Harwell looked at the heavy blade, the whorls of Damascus steel bright beneath the blood. Such a weapon, if swung rather than drawn across the neck, might sever a man's head in one stroke. When the sheep were finished thrashing, he cut the thongs and hung them by the back feet to a rack against the wall of the church to bleed. The final sheep, having struggled free of the knot, got to its knees, spraying blood in every direction.

"Knock him down!" cried Stefan. "He is past hurting now." Harwell kicked the legs out from under the ram and held it down with his boot until it stopped moving altogether. When he looked down at his shirt he saw that he wore a badge of blood on his left sleeve, near the shoulder.

Stefan grunted as he worked the knife under the skin of a ram, flaying it from head to tail and leaving the naked, gleaming corpse. Harwell would have helped, but it was a messy business, and his offer was acknowledged, and refused.

"I do not like this work," said Stefan when he had finished gutting the last one, "and I do not think I would be much good at killing men. But my friends there who have not taken holy vows, they will fight for Great Serbia, and kill gladly for her."

"And when will that be?"

"No one can say. Our prince tells us it will be when all is in readiness, but we have been waiting for that moment for thirty years, since the rising in Herzegovina, or even since he came to the throne. We must have the blessing of the Great Powers, he tells us, and he works ever towards that end. But it seems to me that the Great Powers showed themselves to be fools when they drew lines on a map and told us where we must live. The Devil himself could not have made a worse job of it, and if you ask the Vasojević where the border runs they say that it floats on blood. And so there are those who say that the Great Powers will never see the truth of this matter, and we must act on our own. They say our prince has waited too long."

"The Turkish Empire," began Harwell, with no clear idea of how he would finish his thought, "is still . . ."

"The Turkish Empire cannot stop the Serbs. It is as dead as that sheep whose head you were standing on, or would be, without Austria to patrol the Sandžak, and without the guns and money and even great ships that your queen sends to the sultan."

"The queen is dead, has been for seven years now."

"It is true, she is dead, but what has changed? It is said among us that in order to buy an English rifle you must kill a Turk."

"I cannot explain this to you. I do not understand it myself, and can only hope that such policies will change." Harwell thought then of Sir Percy Foote, and knew that his words were empty.

"The young men will not wait for this change, or until Nikola tells them the ▶

> 66 It is said among us that in order to buy an English rifle you must kill a Turk. 99

15

time is right. Some of them, indeed, say that our prince is paid by Austria, and Russia, and will never act. They say he is now the enemy and cannot be trusted."

Seeing Harwell's look of polite disbelief, the monk squatted where the sheep's blood had pooled and dipped his hand into it. Then he crushed a dark clod of dirt in his fist and spread his fingers before Harwell's face. "Do you know what this is?"

"A hand," said Harwell, then thought: *No, it is a black hand.* "I know what it is."

Stefan pressed his palm to the flayed hide of the last ram, leaving a distinct mark on the fleece which he then smudged away. "I did not say it, and you did not say it. The words are never spoken, but this is the sign of a brotherhood united in desperation and sacrifice. Above all, this thing must never be mentioned where you are going, for it is the woe of the Vasojević, and in particular of Danilo, who had three sons, and now has but one." He wiped his hands on the grass and stood to put on his cassock. "I must clean my hands now, and you should put some water on your shirt. Will you carry my sash for me, and my pistol?" ∿